THE FINAL REMNANT

THE FINAL REMNANT
BOOK 1

TERRY JAMES

HEATHER RENAE

The Final Remnant
Paperback Edition
Copyright © 2022 Terry James and Heather Renae

CKN Christian Publishing
An Imprint of Wolfpack Publishing
9850 S. Maryland Parkway, STE A-5, #323
Las Vegas, NV 89183

cknchristianpublishing.com

Paperback ISBN 978-1-63977-696-2
eBook ISBN 978-1-63977-110-3
LCCN 2022944111

THE FINAL REMNANT

ONE
DON'T DISAPPEAR

CADEN INHALED, instantly wide awake. He could hear movement outside. Was it the wind or someone's footsteps moving through the grass? They sounded too similar at the worst times. Actually, all times were the worst times. He craned his neck and stared out the broken window. Caden squinted and sat up quietly in his bed, not wanting to disturb his younger brother, still fast asleep. He saw nothing. How could he? Nights were so much darker now that streetlamps, or any light for that matter, had been dead for years.

Probably nothing, he told himself. *But that's what I thought last time.* He didn't move back into bed, his brow furrowing. With a sigh, Caden grabbed the baseball bat beside his pillow and stood.

As he passed his brother, he couldn't help but notice that Trace still slept with a blanket tucked against his chest, even at fourteen. *Or is he fifteen now?* Caden shook his head and stepped out of their room and down a black hallway.

He stopped, suddenly forgetting the layout of the house. He briefly considered waking Harrison and making him come outside too, but thought better. The last time he woke the brute, they hadn't found a threat, and Caden nearly got a black eye. He let Harrison have his beauty sleep, as Caden risked his very life for the gang, like a real man would. He found the front door, undid the locks, but didn't open the door.

I hate this. Caden took in a slow breath and adjusted his grip on the bat. He stepped out, and the night's chill pricked his skin.

Standing on the front porch, Caden realized it was a half-moon, and the faint, ghostly light scarcely illuminated his surroundings. Rows and rows of near-identical houses lined the street in front of him. A car had crashed into one, the bottom half of the car buried under debris. Once manicured lawns were now overgrown, and some trees lay sprawled on their sides. Half the houses across the street were burned down to ashen rubble. A telephone line had fallen into a house, and Caden suspected the hot lines had sparked the fire.

Must've been a while ago, he thought. He looked down at the yard and listened. He could hear crickets and the wind moving through the few trees. There wasn't the buzz of electricity or the murmur of any other life. He and his gang were alone. *We should be,* he thought, glancing to where he had heard the grass stir.

It may have been the wind, but what if it was a wolf? Maybe another gang was in the area. They might be armed. And full-blown adults instead of Caden's few nineteen years. They might want Caden and Trace's things. Or their lives. Everyone seemed to be psychopaths these days.

Caden gritted his teeth and stepped off the front porch, his heartbeat thudding in his ears. His legs felt like jello, but he made them keep walking forward. *I am big. I am strong. I am mean!* He lengthened his strides and raised his bat, drawing closer to the broken window of his bedroom. He gritted his teeth, about to yell, but stopped, hearing the noise again. It was further away, around the back of the house.

Caden cursed and pulled his shirt over his nose before walking forward. He knew he should've demanded that Harrison pile the bodies further from the house. Their stink attracted all the bad things.

Probably a Freak, he thought. *Or a looter.* It was surprising how much stuff the dead had on them sometimes.

Caden rounded the side of the house, and the smell of death lingered in the air. It wasn't too bad, just unpleasant. The bodies had been dead for a year and looked like a family. They had been huddled in one room together. Trace had said it was kind of cute, a family's last group hug. Harrison and Soph had demanded to get rid of them before settling into the house. The bodies weren't that gross to move and were pretty much clothes and some bones, with a little meat on them. That was enough to attract some though.

Caden crept quietly, his bat raised, as his eyes darted all around. His heart steadily quickened as he squinted, hardly able to see a thing. Something darted from the pile. Caden rounded, his body tensing for action. He breathed out a sigh and realized it was a squirrel, its fluffy tail bouncing behind it. It raced to an overgrown tree and chirped.

Caden ran a hand over his face and lowered the bat. "Stupid squirrel-"

The animal turned and stared at him. In the moon's light, eight eyes glowed from the little creature's face. Another set of arms sprouted from its stomach. From its mouth stuck two long fangs. Caden cursed and recoiled, nearly tripping over the leftovers of someone's leg.

"Get out of here!" he cried. "Shoo!" He waved his

arms and brought his bat up, unsure of what this Freak of Nature could do.

Hate Freaks, he thought, his heart pounding in his ears. *Why do they have to be so creepy!* The spider-squirrel crawled up the tree, its several limbs making it climb faster than a normal squirrel. Caden panted as he watched it go but knew it would be back. He shivered and stepped away. Though the Freak was chilling, it couldn't kill them. *Unless it's got poison spider venom now,* Caden thought. *Can it make webs too? It could store all its nuts in web sacks. Or us. Maybe it liquidizes victims, then stores them underground to save for the winter. Or maybe-*

Caden shook his head and forced himself around the house again. *Idiot! All that for a squirrel-thingy,* he thought, knowing he couldn't sleep now. *Well, at least try to sleep. We've got things to do tomorrow.*

Caden headed back inside, now shivering from the chill and the adrenalin quickening his heart. He stumbled down the hall, trying to be quiet for the others who slept in different rooms, but slowed as he came to his room. He heard quick movements and frantic breathing. He raced forward, finding Trace throwing Caden's blankets off his bed.

"No, no, no," Trace whimpered, backing against the wall, his face in his hands. "You can't-"

"What're you doing?" Trace startled and raced to Caden, grabbing him. Caden stumbled back and stared down at his brother.

"I thought you were gone," Trace gasped, his head buried in Caden's chest. "I thought you left! Like-like everyone else!"

Caden wrapped his arms around Trace and drew him close. "I heard something outside. I wanted to make sure-"

"You can't go. You can't just disappear!"

"I didn't."

"Not like everyone else."

"I'm still here."

"Not another Day of Vanishing."

"Trace, Trace." Caden gave him a gentle shake. "Dude, I'm right here. Did you see my clothes still in the bed?" Trace sniffed and shook his head. "Then I didn't disappear."

"But, but it could be different this time. They might want you to have your clothes and-"

"Trace-"

"I'd be all alone-"

"Calm down, just calm down! It's going to be okay!"

"That's what Mom said!"

Caden fell silent, his chest tightening with emotion. He swallowed the hard lump in his throat. He stepped back, leaning against the wall, and slid to the floor with Trace in his arms. His shirt was damp from Trace's tears. The two brothers quietly sat on the floor in the dark, unable to speak.

———

CADEN TOOK a long smell of coffee grounds in a tin. How long had it been since he went to Starbucks? He always got a mocha with lots of whipped cream and an extra shot of espresso. What a beautiful way to wake up in the morning.

"Don't even bother," a woman said, walking into the kitchen to join him. "It's decaf."

"I know."

She flicked her long, black dreadlocks and got to work getting breakfast out. Caden still couldn't decide if she had made her hair into dreadlocks, or if her kinky hair had done it naturally. If only he had darker skin too, he could ask her. She started removing cans from a backpack and setting them on a bar. Caden watched her remove two cans of black beans, canned pears, and one can of peppers.

"Yummy," he muttered and ran fingers through his hair. He sat back, looking at his fingertips. They were covered in a grimy film. He shifted in his seat and smelled the coffee again. "Soph, can't we have some of that canned cheese we found yesterday?"

"If you're going to complain-"

"I'm not complaining-"

"Then look through the burned-down houses for your breakfast."

Caden fell silent and tried to not think of eggs, bacon, gravy, and biscuits. *With a side of coffee,* he thought, smelling it again.

"Trying to get high or something?" a man asked, walking in. Caden ignored him and set down the tin.

The person who had lived here before obviously loved chickens. Caden glanced around the dusty room, confused again why anyone would want a stinking, clucking, brainless animal as a kitchen decoration. All the cabinets were chicken decorated, the table had a chicken centerpiece, and even the kitchen sink's spout had a chicken for a head. Sophia tried the sink handle, but as expected, nothing came.

The man chuckled. "Think you'll get something?"

"Shut up."

A kid, maybe thirteen, shuffled in, rubbing the sleep from his eyes. "There's coffee?" He asked, pointing.

"Decaf," Caden answered. The kid, Simon, shoulders sagged with a sigh.

"Where's Trace," Sophia asked.

"He went scavenging," Caden said. "Plundering, as he calls it."

"You mean he's wandered off."

"No," Caden frowned. "He's looking for supplies."

Sophia sighed heavily. "He's always wandering!" The gang went to the table as Sophia finished pouring their daily rations of slop into bowls.

Caden sat and saw movement out of the corner of his eye. A bearded, skinny guy was across the room. He was sitting down and staring at everything with dark eyes. Caden made a fist, his heart skipping a beat, but relaxed suddenly. His mouth dropped open. A cracked mirror hung across the room and showed how pretty he looked now. His chocolate brown hair hung to his shoulders and fell over his eyes. He knew he had a beard but didn't realize how patchy it was. He turned his head, frowning at the little bald spot by his ear that never wanted to grow.

At least it covers how sickly I am. Kind of, he thought. He started at his hallowed, dark brown eyes and felt the obvious curve of his cheek bones. It looked like he hadn't bathed in months. Dad always said Caden would be living his fullest at nineteen.

"You'll be fit, just like I was. That gets all the ladies, let me tell you!" Caden looked away, wishing the mirror wasn't there.

"What?" Simon asked. Caden shook his head and waited for his slop. Simon didn't look as bad. His face was dirty and his brown hair a mess, but there still was some meat on those bones. Trace had a bit more meat on him too. Caden hoped he hadn't figured out that Sophia always gave him a few scoops of Caden's share. Caden still hadn't believed he told her to do that. His little brother would probably never notice. *It's my job,* Caden thought. *I've got to protect him.*

The man across the table coughed suddenly, sniffed forcefully, and spat on the floor. Sophia groaned. "Harrison! I told you to stop doing that!"

"Who cares?"

"*I* do! Just because civilization's dead doesn't mean we

can't at least try to be civilized." Harrison only grinned and slid a clawed knife from a small pocket within his sleeve. He started scraping the table, as though it had done something wrong.

Caden stared at him, his back stiffening with unease. *But how can I protect anything against you?*

Harrison was the largest of the gang, the second oldest after Sophia, and built like a tank. He still wore his gauge plugs for some weird reason, and managed to always have a toothpick, a bit of grass, or wheat in his mouth. Trace had said Harrison's blond hair reminded him of barbie dolls, but Caden didn't see the resemblance.

"Here," Sophia said, placing their rations before them with a mismatched assortment of utensils. Caden got a butter knife. "Say thank you!"

"Thank you, Soph."

"Thanks." Harrison stabbed a pepper with his knife and ate it without a word. They ate in silence.

"So," Sophia said after a while. "What's the plan today?" She looked across the boys and her eyes fell on Harrison.

"Scavenge. Find a water source. Keep heading north." Sophia glared as Simon snorted.

"That's what we do every day."

"You got a better plan, shrimpy?" Simon looked away. The gang fell quiet as everyone pretended to enjoy their meal. "And remember," Harrison said all of a sudden. "Whenever I do things three times in a row, attack."

Caden's eyes narrowed as Sophia sighed. "That's the vaguest defensive strategy I've ever heard," she said. Harrison shrugged. "Three of what?"

"Anything. Three sneezes. Three claps. Three coughs. Stuff like that."

Her brow arched as she grunted. "Very unsuspicious."

"Just move when I do it. Can you handle that?" Sophia glared at him but didn't answer.

Caden shifted in his seat and raised his chin. "Why bring that up now?" Harrison faced him and Caden tried hard not to turn away. "Do you know something we don't?" They all quieted and stared at Harrison.

"I saw Giant footprints," Harrison mumbled. Everyone stopped eating. "We've gotta move."

Sophia leaned toward Harrison. "Are you sure it was them?"

"It was Giants. Three of them."

"When did you see them?"

"Yesterday."

"And you didn't tell us?"

Harrison smiled again and Sophia sat back. "I say what needs telling."

"Well! We- we've got to move! Like, in an hour!"

"Don't get your panties in a bunch-"

"No! You don't understand what I've seen! Those things aren't heroes like everyone says they are!"

Caden tried to swallow his beans without coughing. Panic had a nasty habit of constricting his throat though. "We can't leave without Trace."

"We most certainly can!" Caden glanced at Soph. She fell quiet and rubbed a palm against her forehead. She stood suddenly, her chair bouncing across the floor. "I'm going to start packing. Unbelievable! You didn't even tell us! How typical!" She stormed from the kitchen, her breakfast half-eaten. Harrison quietly grabbed her bowl and poured the leftovers into his own.

Caden and Simon said nothing. Caden licked the odd combination of pepper, pear, and black bean juice from his bowl and sat back. He felt full and half-heartedly wondered how small his stomach had shrunken down to through the years. He glanced at the stranger in the mirror. Mom would've told him to shave. And take a bath. And eat something other than canned foods.

Quiet footsteps padded behind him, and a short, curly-haired teen glided into the room. Trace served himself his portion and sat next to Simon without a word. Caden noticed he was more dirty than usual and stank. That part was usual. The kid started inhaling his food, and he never seemed to notice when they ate the same meal over and over. Caden saw him as a kid even though he was only three years older. Still. When someone acted like a kid, they were a kid.

"Find anything?" Caden asked.

Trace jerked his head in a quick nod, his long curls bobbing back and forth. "Morning bro! One house's toilets aren't drained. Four of 'em, enough to fill our canteens. There's a garden next to that. Mostly weeds. Some grandma must've grown it; it's set up so nice, kind of like Mama Lo-"

"Focus," Caden calmly said. "The garden?"

"Tomatoes, small but red, and some peas-or maybe they're green beans, and other stuff we could eat. Dandelions too. That's eatable. Did you know that? Don't taste too bad. Well, not the leaves. Oh, and a radio tower to the west... south." Trace paused and stared at his fingers. "Yeah, the west."

Caden blinked slowly and nodded. "Great."

"And someone said there's a nice guy giving out meat a few streets down." The table stared at the quickly eating kid.

Caden's eyes narrowed. *No one is giving out meat. Not ever. And who are you talking to?*

"And who said that?" he asked.

"Toby."

"Who's Toby?" Harrison piped up.

"Oh, he's really nice. We sat and talked. He lives a

block over, three houses down. That big, big house with a birdhouse thing out front. Nice Toby; a real good boy."

Caden had seen the house. He had also seen that no one lived there. *Not again,* he thought as he reached for his brother.

"Trace," Harrison said, leaning across the table. Simon sat back, but Trace didn't notice. "What've I told you?"

"Lots of stuff. You boss me all the time."

Caden grimaced. *He's excited. He's always more spazzy when he's excited.* Harrison's toothpick went from one corner of his mouth to the other as his smile grew. Simon got up and walked behind Caden. Harrison made a fist, and Caden could clearly see the lined scars and indents in his huge knuckles. *Dang it, Trace!*

"Hay!" Caden blurted, grabbing Trace's shoulder. The mass of curls bounced as Trace looked up. "Trace, um, look. I know you like talking to dogs, but you need to stop."

"I like dogs."

"Me too, but you can't listen to what they say. Especially dogs that haven't accepted things are different."

"But Toby is nice! He wasn't lying."

"Trace, any dog that still thinks people are feeding them don't really see what's happened. Just stay away from them, okay?"

"I like dogs better now that they talk. All the other animals too! Cats say mean things though. And birds just repeat themselves-"

"Trace," Caden said, squeezing his shoulder. He could see Harrison's big fist getting ready to beat the kid's words back into his face. "Just do it, okay?" Trace stared at Caden and, for once, held still and stopped talking. Finally, he noticed Harrison ready to pounce. "Sure thing. Bro. Yeah, I'll stop talking. All done with that."

Caden nodded and pointed to Trace's breakfast. "Eat

up. We've gotta get going." Trace nodded and kept eating like a ravenous animal.

Caden watched as Harrison sat back, his iron fist loosening. Harrison's creepy smile still stretched his face as he glanced at Caden. "You better pray to that God of yours we find Adderall."

"He's not my God," Caden snapped. Harrison didn't answer as he returned to scraping the table with his knife. Caden glanced behind his shoulder to check on Simon and rubbed his eyes with a finger and thumb. He didn't want a cup of coffee anymore. He *needed* it.

TWO
MORE FREAKS

IT DIDN'T TAKE LONG to pack up, but it did take a while to convince Trace not to bring Toby. He kept whining and saying how lonely he'll be here and that they needed a watchdog. "You said he's a pug," Simon had muttered.

"Dude, I don't judge you by your looks." Simon had socked him in the shoulder. That helped shut him up.

They loaded up their two trucks and, at Sophia's very loud demands, were ready to go. "Giants are so bad, you have no idea!"

"Have you talked with one?" Trace asked.

"They can't be talked to! Can't be reasoned with!"

"Have you tried?"

Sophia also looked ready to punch Trace, which was impressive; three people wanting to beat the spazzy kid up before lunchtime. It was a new record. Caden talked her down. Sophia's patience had run out, her voice getting a little higher and squeakier as she told everyone to shut it. Caden had grit his teeth and grabbed his bugout bag as he nudged Trace into Harrison's truck. Trace insisted he could drive Harrison's truck. After all, he got his driving permit before the World's Crash.

"That was two years ago."

"So?" Trace said with a grin.

"No."

"Come on-"

Caden elbowed Trace in the ribs. "Shut up!"

"Fine," Trace grumbled as they piled in the truck. "But I can hope and pray!"

Caden shot him a look. *I don't do that.* He decided to keep quiet and tried to ignore his younger brother's dumb ideas of God. He needed to hold onto something. Even if it was a lie. A big, watching, grinning bundle of lies. Kind of like Harrison's creepy smile. Caden knew better.

He grabbed Trace's elbow and drew him close. "Don't talk."

"I'm not."

"For the entire drive."

Trace's eyes widened. "That could be hours!"

"Can it! You almost got it this morning."

"Nah, Harrison was just playing-"

Caden yanked on Trace's arm, his eyes becoming dark. "Be quiet." Trace ducked his head and nodded.

They drove in silence, Caden wedged between Harrison and Trace, as Harrison led them from the suburbs. Caden hadn't caught the name of this place. It was hard when every town or suburb looked like the set of a horror movie.

"Tell me about your uncle?" Harrison said suddenly. Caden shifted uncomfortably and fixed his eyes on the road ahead. They had to steer around two cars lying on their sides and another wrapped around a telephone pole.

"Unk Spence is fine," Caden said. "Don't worry about it." Harrison didn't answer, but his toothpick slid from one side of his mouth to another. Caden glanced down. "He's a hard worker. Has fifty or so acres. Lots of space for us. There are cows and-"

"Who is he?"

Caden's fingers rapped on his knee. "He's a felon. Drugs, I think."

"You think?"

"We didn't talk a lot, alright? He was the bad uncle Mom always said not to turn out like." *That was the wrong thing to say,* Caden thought, quickly shutting his mouth. Harrison smiled. *Maybe not.*

"You sure he needs help?"

Caden nodded. "And he has cabins. Hunting cabins. He likes to hunt deer."

Harrison didn't answer, his toothpick bobbing as he gnawed on it.

Caden's stomach twisted and he kept staring out the window.

He saw his uncle years before the World Crash, so that was a long, long time. He didn't know a thing about his Uncle Spencer. He remembered Aunt May was nice, kind of a tomgirl, always smelling like animals and tracking horse poop wherever she went. He loved visiting her; it was the only good thing about living with Dad. She made the best coca-cola cake. They would eat it with lemonade under the huge trees in her front yard.

I hope they're still alive, Caden thought, pain tightening his chest. He looked down and shifted his weight, not wanting to bury another relative.

"You heard from them?"

"Last year," Caden lied. It was actually three and a half years ago, over the phone, when phones were still around. "They found our radio channel and we talked. They offered to take us in."

Just Trace and me, Caden thought, but didn't want to elaborate.

"Well," Harrison said with a sigh. "You better be right, kid. Or you and I will take a long, long walk." The large man's grip on the steering wheel tightened, and the leather groaned with protest. Caden's throat bobbed; it was as though Harrison was already practicing squeezing the life out of something.

What is wrong with you, man? He faced the window again, seeing more burned-down houses and a gathering of crows beside another turned-over car. He closed his eyes before he saw what they were eating. *We're surviving,* he concluded wearily. *That's it.*

The squawk of the radio broke Caden's thoughts as Harrison started flipping through the channels. The grating sound of static tickled the back of Caden's throat and he rubbed his ears. Static and the sound of frocks against teeth had always bothered him. He noticed Trace also shielded his ears. Finally, from the random buzzing, the fuzzy sounds became fuzzy notes. Harrison froze and nearly drove off the road. He swerved back and everyone listened, too focused to be bothered by his driving. It was a song, instrumental, and kind of whiny. Caden's eyes narrowed. He had heard that instrument before, so long ago. What was it?

A violin.

He inhaled a painful breath, remembering Ellie had tried to play the violin. She would've sounded better with a pot and a wooden spoon. Caden and Trace had discussed burning the poor instrument; it obviously needed to be put out of its misery. He remembered Ellie clumsily tucking the violin's chin-part between her shoulder and chin and trying to hold the stick-thing right. She made them all pretend they were at a jig way-back-when and they had to dance. It was horrible.

Caden looked down, knowing he would dance until he dropped if that meant his little sister would be with them again. The music carried on, reminding him more and more of her, making him sick. His finger drummed his leg, wishing they had ridden with Sophia.

———

THE MILES PASSED at a painfully slow rate. Like watching thick syrup make its way down an upturned bottle when you only want one little drop.

Pancakes, Caden thought, his stomach growling. Sometimes, he wondered if his stomach had morphed into a forever angry monster.

He fixed his eyes on the road and tried to ignore the tight pinch of hunger. It was late afternoon, and the gang hadn't stopped to eat. There weren't enough rations. Sophia had announced they were done with lunches, and possibly dinners. Caden rubbed his eyes and sighed. They needed to find more food. They couldn't last like this. He didn't want to see Trace waste away to nothing. He shook his head, knowing he couldn't suffer through that again. He swallowed the hard lump in his throat and narrowed his eyes. He motioned for the glove box and Trace quickly retrieved the map.

Harrison's brow arched. "Know where I'm going."

Caden didn't answer as he unfolded the faded, flimsy map. *What's this road? S-something. S… Star Ln! Yep, we made that turn, and there's the house with the silo.* His finger ran along the road, outlining where they were going. They needed a town. Something where lots of people had lived, yet was dangerous enough they all left in a hurry. Though they were heading further into the country, there were more loony preppers who, irony would have it, were right all along. Their stockpiles were pure gold. Caden had only seen one once, two gangs ago. It was the first time he felt safe after the World's Crash.

"Here," Caden said. "We turn left ten miles up."

Harrison didn't respond. Caden glanced at him. "There's a town twelve miles that way. Nockville." Again, Harrison didn't answer. Caden sighed and dropped the map in his lap. "We need to restock. Siphon gas. Rest." Harrison's toothpick danced from one side of his mouth to the other. Caden shut his mouth and looked ahead. With a clenched jaw and a shake of the head, Caden folded up the map, not too gently, and shoved it back into the glove box. They sat in silence again.

You'll get us killed, Caden concluded. It wasn't until they reached the turn, and took it, did Caden realize Harrison had been listening.

Nockville seemed like the name of a lively place in the middle of overrun farm fields and rusting tractors. It turned out to be a small, dusty town, filled with overrun farm fields and rusting, well… everything. Everything was left as though everyone instantly decided to leave.

"The Day of Vanishing," Trace whispered, shrinking further into the seat. Caden stared at the cars stopped in the middle of the street, unlocked store doors swung open by the wind, and an abandoned baby buggy that had rolled its way against a tree.

"No bodies," Caden said. His eyes narrowed further. "No bodies anywhere."

It was very much like the Day of Vanishing. Too much. Caden felt the hair on the back of his neck stand on end as the silent, ghost-like town closed in around them. He rubbed his eyes, not wanting to think of that horrible day two years ago when over half the entire earth's population suddenly disappeared without a trace. All that remained had been their clothes and the terrified screams and tears of those who had been left behind.

Did it happen again? Caden feared. It was unlikely. The Day of Vanishing heightened the world's standard level of chaos for a while. Things were still crazy, just not *that* crazy.

"There," Harrison said, lifting his chin. "That's why they left."

Next to the road was a teetering sign saying "Welcome to Nockville". Beside that, held in place by fresh cement, was another sign. The words were printed instead of painted. The paper was sealed and nailed down in place. It read:

"The people of Nockville thank his Majesty and his civilized citizens for rescuing us. Now we have three square meals *every* day, protection, baths, beds, and a civilized community to raise our children and start over. The king is just and merciful, slow to anger and tender hearted. All hail the king! May his kingdom come to all lands! May his will be done! If you want to join as allies, the King's United Society was here June 6th, 2145 and continued traveling northwest. Long live the king! May his Sovereign Lion watch over you."

"What's today's date?" Harrison asked. No one answered. How should they know? Harrison's fists gripped the steering wheel again as he stared intently at the sign.

Long live the king, Caden thought. It was strange to hear about kings and allies and a society after so long of surviving and scavenging. It would be nice to sleep in a bed that was his. To stop constantly moving. To stop needing Harrison's supposed protection. *He wouldn't protect us,* Caden thought, a muscle in his jaw flexing.

He had heard of the KUS before from the last gang Trace and he traveled with. One of the guys said they were good, kind people who healed his wounds and gave him food. He swore they only asked for information and gave him some chores, but, over all, just wanted to help him. *We should find the KUS,* Caden thought. *They might help us too.*

As they stared at the sign, a bird landed on it and opened its beak to sing. Instead, it barked. Caden could barely make out the small, jagged fangs inside its mouth. His stomach clenched and he looked away as Trace flinched.

"Let's park and find tracks," Harrison said, ignoring the Freak. "Maybe we just missed the KUS."

They drove to the middle of town, two roads away, and parked, Sophia right behind them. Caden grabbed his baseball bat and a near-empty backpack. His chest tightened with unease as he glanced in the bag, seeing a can of cat food and a half-filled water bottle.

We've got to find food here, he thought. *We can't start skipping breakfast too.*

"The KUS!" Trace cried, leaping from the truck. "Why're we stopping? Let's go! They can't be far! I want some bread! With butter. Do you think they have jelly too?"

Harrison threw a backpack at Trace. "Split up," he said. "We've got to find supplies."

"Then we'll go? Please! Please!" Caden raced forward, grabbing Trace's shoulder and dragging him toward a dark restaurant, forcing him to obey Harrison. Simon trailed close behind.

"Stay within earshot, boys!" Sophia called as Harrison and she headed into a convenience store. Her steps slowed as a fawn strolled out from between two buildings. The baby dear had paws, like a cat, and one eye was missing. She cursed and avoided it.

"This is exciting!" Trace said. Caden inwardly groaned as he kept an eye on the fawn. "I've heard the KUS let anyone join. Without first doing favors or trading or nothing! So nice! So nice!"

"Uhum," Caden grunted. "Let's go to the kitchen." The three trailed through the dust-covered, yet orderly room. Most chairs were scooted from the tables, and plates of green, moldy food collected flies.

Good, Caden thought. *They left maybe a week ago.*

None of the lights worked, and Caden figured the restaurant had been a meeting place instead of a business. The kitchen hadn't been used in years. They made the mistake of opening the freezer. The overwhelming smell of rot nearly made them fall over. Pots and pans still hung around the cooking stations and there was a nice collection of knives worth commandeering.

"I'm gonna check the front," Caden said as the two boys looked through the cupboards.

He went to the register and opened it with a loud ding. Inside, the various faces of long-ago precedence stared back at him. Their eyes were hollow and frowns more set than he remembered. Maybe they knew money was as useful as toilet paper now. Except for tams.

After the World's Crash, it hadn't taken long for the little green pieces of paper that used to mean so much to become a fire starter. Thanks to the king, money had resurrected, but this time everyone had the same currency. Caden had seen a tam once, a little metal square with the king's symbol stamped onto the front and the words *His Kingdom Come* on the back.

Caden slammed shut the register door and headed toward a wood stove against the wall, hoping to find a fire poker or matches. Trace walked behind him, his soft footsteps barely heard.

"There might be an attic," Caden said as he turned. "I saw some stairs over-"

He stopped short and stared. Trace was still in the kitchen, something else walked behind Caden. In the shadows of a hall across the room stalked a wolf. It looked like a skeleton wearing a fur coat. Caden's heart stopped as a thrill washed over him. He set down his backpack and held out the bat, his movements slow and controlled.

That's *why everyone left*, he realized. *They got too many Freaks.*

The wolf's eyes bore into Caden. They were hungry and wild, all four of them. One of the wolf's heads lowered while the other head pulled back its lips in a snarl. *I could get onto the counter*, Caden thought. *Can wolves jump that high? I could run through the kitchen, leave out the back... Trace.* He couldn't leave his brother. Caden blinked and rolled a shoulder as he stepped closer. *Be big. Be tough. Be mean.*

The wolf's tail swooshed as its hackles raised along its back. It stalked forward, a low, deep growl rumbling from its duo throats. Caden forced himself not to step back. *It's just a ball*, he told himself, remembering his years of baseball practice and the proper form to hit a home run. *Just a very hairy, angry ball. That could eat me.* His eyes darted between the two growling heads, seeing rows of yellow fangs. He cursed under his breath, wishing the King's United Society was still there.

THREE
NOT A FUR COAT

NO ONE really knew where the Freaks of Nature came from. The poor animals had mutated somehow, and now weird monsters roamed around, struggling like everyone else. Caden had seen a five legged horse and a six eyed cat. That was creepy. He'd heard talk of coyote packs, each with two heads, or extra limbs, or two entire dogs stuck together. He heard somewhere Freaks didn't live long, and they couldn't reproduce, like Ligers. Someone said humans were becoming Freaks too, but that was nonsense. Giants made sense, but a person with an extra eye here or a hand there was too far-fetched. Had to be.

Focus! Caden told himself, watching the wolf creep closer. He tightened both hands on the bat, his feet firmly planted, as he stared at his target. *They're just baseballs,* he told himself, knowing if he managed to hit one, he'd have to wash his jacket somehow. He'd learned blood was a messy business.

The crash and clang of metal pots filled the room. Caden and the wolf turned with alarm, the animal snarling and Caden raising his bat higher. Trace and Simon burst from the kitchen, each banging pots and pans as loud as they could. With shouts that made no sense, the two teens advanced on the duo-headed dog. Trace had a baking sheet taped to his torso and Simon wore a pot on his head. The wolf recoiled, seeing it was greatly outnumbered, and fled out the cracked door. The boys stopped their clambering and Caden lowered the bat, his head dropping against his chest.

Check that off my list for today, he thought, running a shaken hand over his sweaty brow. A sudden noise caught him off guard. He turned and glared at Trace. His brother was laughing, his mouth gaping.

"You should've seen the look on your face!"

"Shut up."

"You weren't going to die!"

"You don't know that!"

"We're here."

"Oh! Yes! What was I thinking? The Tin Man and Captain Pot-Head here to save the day!"

Simon scowled. "You mean thank you?" Caden ran fingers through his hair and gradually nodded.

They found the attic stairs, which led to a few useful supplies. Nothing edible though. "Let's go check on Harrison and Soph," Caden said, trying not to sneeze in the cloud of dust they kicked up.

They strolled outside, the quiet, abandoned town twisting Caden's stomach. *They just abandoned the town, that's all,* he thought. *They're all together in a new place, safe and sound. No one vanished or disappeared. It's not another Day of Vanishing.*

Caden shook his head and ran fingers through his hair. He chose not to think about that horrible day, the day that changed everything. He had just been accepted into OSU. School was canceled, of course. Everything was canceled after the Day of Vanishing. And he almost died that day too. Or was that the next day? At least one good thing happened; his dad had died.

Guilt struck Caden's chest and he sucked in a breath. What would Mom say if she could hear his thoughts? Caden shook his head and lifted his chin. He took a deep breath, feeling his heart gradually return to its constant rhythm as he forced himself to calm.

"They went in there," Simon said, pointing to a convenience store. *Nockville's Market* read a sign over the door. The *open* sign was still hanging in the window.

Caden glanced around. "Keep a look out for other Freaks."

"I saw a bird," Trace said. "It had a long tail, like a cow or lion. Kind of a cool one."

"I mean threatening ones, doofus."

"Then say that!" Caden was about to shove his brother when gunshots echoed in the stillness. The three boys lurched back, crouching low.

We don't have guns, he thought, panic heightening his senses. It could only mean one thing: Strangers.

The three boys started sprinting to the nearest buildings as two wide-eyed adults crashed from the store. One was an arm-waving black lady and the other a huge, barrel-chested man, his gun pointed wildly behind him. Caden's retreat hiccupped as he recognized Sophia and Harrison. *What is going on? Where's the bad guys? Why do you have a gun!* He caught Trace's arm and dragged him behind the nearest building, Simon trailing close. Sophia's curses and Harrison's heavy pants followed.

"What's happening?" Caden cried, but no one answered. The gang ran one street over, then another. Caden dared to look over his shoulder. No one was hunting them. The gang finally stopped and leaned against a rundown house whose yard was littered with toys.

When Caden at last caught his breath, he faced

Harrison and Sophia. "What's going on? No one's chasing us!"

"You weren't there, kid!" Sophia cried, her eyes filling with tears. "And even if they were chasing us, we couldn't see them anyways!"

Caden lifted his chin and blinked slowly, understanding. He glanced at Harrison. The boulder-of-a-man clutched his gun as his eyes darted to everything that moved. His face was pale.

"What'd it look like?" Caden asked more calmly.

Sophia scoffed as she swiped tears away. "What do you care? You and your brother apparently don't taste good; they always leave you alone!"

"They could always snap and turn crazy, kind of like how you're acting right now."

"I swear, Caden Johnson! You sometimes act like nothing's wrong!"

"Well, I almost died just now too-"

"Everything's wrong! You hear me? *Everything!* If it's not Giants, it's the Freaks. If it's not the Freaks, it's strangers who don't play nice with others. If it's not strangers, it's starvation. Not starvation, it's war. If it's not war it's-" she waved her hand in the direction of the convenience store, "it's *those* things. What happened? Did death up its quota? All Hell has broken loose and you're asking what it looked like?"

Caden stared at Sophia as the tears streamed down her face. She shook her head and stepped closer, a finger pointed at his chest. At the last second, she shut her mouth. Caden let out a breath and turned away.

"Well," Trace muttered, kicking a toy truck in the dirt. "All Hell has broken loose. Didn't you go to church before the Crash?"

Sophia spun, her dreadlocks lashing like Medusa's slithering hair. "Shut up! Just shut up!"

The gang fell silent as Caden quietly watched Harrison out of the corner of his eye. The large man had lost his toothpick; things must've been real serious. *The small ones aren't too bad,* Caden thought, feeling the steadily growing emptiness in his stomach. They needed supplies. Desperately. The nearest town was hours away, and who knew what they would find. *Maybe I could go in, get the things we need.*

"A bigger one," Sophia quietly said with a sniff. "It was a bigger one."

Nope, I'm out, Caden thought, turning away. Sophia sighed heavily and put her head in her hands.

"They have canned goods," she whispered. "A full shelf. I could see them. That thing knew what we wanted. How do they always know?"

Caden saw Harrison straighten. The large man stood from the house and tucked his gun in the front of his pants. Color had returned to his face and he was staring right at Caden. Caden looked up at Harrison, and his hair stood on end.

"You're going in," Harrison said.

No, I'm not. Caden didn't answer.

Harrison slid his backpack off and held it out to Caden. "Back hallway. Third door on the left." Caden didn't move. Harrison dropped the backpack and stepped closer. "We need the food."

"There's another town not far-"

"No." Harrison's large hand grabbed the gun. A shiver ran up Caden's spine. "Fetch it up. Now."

Caden swallowed and lifted his chin, his feet planted firmly. *Do I look like a dog?*

"I'll go," Trace piped up, raising a hand. "They, um, they don't really like me either. They'll leave me alone. Dude, I'll tell you what it looks like."

Caden's stomach managed to knot itself again. No

wonder he couldn't eat much. He cursed and turned away from Harrison. "I'll go."

Trace's brows pinched as he shook his head. "No, I just said that I'll-"

"Don't be stupid." Caden stooped and snatched Harrison's backpack off the ground. The gang quieted and Caden realized no one was going to object further. Caden gave Harrison one last glare before shouldering on the backpack and handing his bat to Trace. Without a word, he started out to Nockville's Market.

"Shouldn't he take his bat?" he heard Simon ask.

"For what?" Sophia retorted.

"Oh yeah. I forgot."

"Don't worry!" Trace called. "They don't like to eat us!"

Caden shook his head, a muscle in his jaw flexing as he held back a cutting word. *And today's the day my luck runs out,* he thought, the store coming in sight. He gripped the backpack straps and forced himself to keep walking. With every step, his stomach tightened further and his hands became cold. *This is stupid!* Half his mind screamed. *You know they'll mess with you! They mess with everyone. And it's a bigger one!*

The other half of his mind kept thinking of Trace. His brother was *not* going to be around those things if Caden could stop it. Trace's thoughts already spun out of control on their own, he didn't need an extra nudge into insanity. Caden told himself to walk up the store's steps and walk straight through the door. If he stopped, he wasn't sure he could keep going. As he decided this, he realized he was standing still a pace away from the steps. He couldn't feel his legs. Was he sweating? He wished he had taken his bat, but he knew it would slow him down. He ran a hand over his face and sucked in a breath.

Let's go, you wussie! You're big and bad and mean. He swallowed hard, knowing they were bigger. Badder. Forget mean. It was debatable if they even had a soul. They weren't human after all, not even close. Caden would face a Freak any day. Freaks were startling and threatening at times, but they couldn't talk inside someone's head, twist reality with lies, and turn good people into psychos.

Move it! His legs felt a million miles away as they dragged him up the steps. *I'll come in nice and slow,* he told himself. *Maybe I can sneak in. They won't see me.* He grabbed the door and gently swung it open. *I'll be fine-*

Over the door, a bell clanged. Caden stiffened as though dumped in a bucket of ice water. The bell's noise steadily hummed to silence, but it was already too late. Caden searched the store, he wasn't sure if he was breathing. There was a cash register against the far wall, some posters of race cars and cows, and empty aisles. A stuffed deer head mounted on the wall stared at Caden, its glassy, hollow eyes black in the shadows.

Caden looked down and shouldered the backpack. *This is for Trace,* he thought, suspecting Harrison would make his brother scavenge here if Caden kept refusing. He walked in, his steps suddenly loud and terrifying.

The front half of the store had been picked over. Wrappers littered the floor beside several sets of footprints. As Caden walked deeper in, he could see further into the store. Nothing had been touched. He pressed on, his heart trying to beat its way out of his chest and run away. *They're in the back,* Caden thought. The back. Down a hallway and passed some doors. You know, right where Harrison told him to go. *Great.*

He ran a hand over his face again and quietly stepped forward. That creepy feeling of eyes burning a hole in his back made his hair stand on end. His legs kept moving. They seemed even further away now, and on autopilot, like they had no clue what was happening. His steps slowed as he entered the hallway. The only footprints here had huge strides, like someone running. Lots of them were scuffed and smeared.

Panic, he thought, his heartbeat loud in his ears. *I'm so stupid.* He walked on and realized, with little surprise, the natural light didn't reach the hallway too well. It was darker. It was like a throat he was willingly walking down. *Just get in and out,* he told himself. *They'll creep you out, but they don't like you, remember? You don't smell right or something. Good thing Trace isn't here. Hope he's okay.* Caden's brows furrowed as he glanced over his shoulder. He couldn't see the gang through the window. *Harrison better not do anything. Where did he get a gun? He didn't tell us! What else is he hiding from us?*

Caden's eyes narrowed as he shook his head. *Should've known. That lumbering ogre can't be trusted with anything!* A thought struck Caden like a smack to the face. *Then, why'd I leave Trace alone with him?* He swallowed the hard lump in his throat and fought the urge to turn back. *He wouldn't hurt Trace, would he? I mean, we've only known each other for three months, and Trace had always annoyed him. And I'm not there. I can't stop him from...*

Caden stopped walking and stared at a corkboard filled with fliers. A homemade poster hung with a photo of a smiling lady, her makeup overly done and clownish, glued to the center. She wore the store's uniform and, arching over her head, read *"Jessie: Employee of the month"* in glittering words.

I can't bury another brother, Caden thought, his chest tightening with emotions he fought to ignore. *I can't do that again. I can't-*

He forced himself to keep walking but quickly found he had stopped again. He remembered how cold Nate had felt. Caden hadn't touched someone that cold before. It startled him. It made sense, and he'd heard dead bodies cooled off, but this was his brother. Nate had always been warm, smiling, telling jokes, stealing his boots or baseball gloves, calling him Cade. He wasn't cold. He wasn't supposed to be cold.

I should've shared that can of cat food, Caden thought. *I should've- But I didn't, and now he's dead.* Caden's head dropped against his chest. His legs refused to move. *And Trace will die too.* He put his head in his hands. *Dad was right. I'm a failure-*

"and incapable."

Caden shook his head. *I'm sorry, Nate-*

"He can't hear you. He's dead."

I know. I wish I could've said goodbye.

"If you'd stayed with him instead of running off, doing your own thing, you would have."

I was trying to find food-

"You were running from responsibilities. Again. And now Nate is dead."

Caden's breath shuttered through him. *I tried my best-*

"Was it adequate? Ellie's dead too."

You don't know that!

"My knowledge vastly outweighs your own." Caden's chin trembled. "Your limited perspective is staggeringly pathetic. Believe me when I say Ellie is in an unmarked grave, covered in sand and scorpions." Caden choked, his eyes closing. "Curious as to how she met her end?"

Something touched Caden's hair. He lurched away and spun with a gasp. The corkboard's posters fluttered, and Jessie, the employee of the month, slowly drifted to the ground. Caden frantically searched, his chest heaving and eyes glossy with tears. He saw nothing.

They found me, he thought, his throat constricting. He glanced down at the clown-woman's smile. It was a tight smile, fake and painful. With a groan, Caden wiped his face again and turned around. *Down the hall, three doors down,* he thought, moving forward. *Three doors… or did he say two? Is this the correct hallway? Why didn't I repeat Harrison's orders? My incapabilities are insurmountable and numerous. I'm just an impotent human-child-*

Caden shook his head and swatted at the air. "Get away!"

He ran to the third door. He threw it open and rushed in, seeing he had reached storage. The little light beyond the door showed rows of cans and boxes, tools, and cleaning supplies. Caden ripped off the backpack and opened it. He swept his arm across a shelf, toppling everything and hopping something of value fell into the bag. He didn't care. He was losing his mind again and couldn't stop feeling his brother's cold skin on his fingertips.

Something creaked behind him. The light faded. The door shut with an ear-clapping slam. Caden was plunged into blackness. He didn't move. All he could hear was his breathing. He slowly turned and found a thin strip of light squeezing beneath the door. Someone walked by, their feet casting shadows. Caden backed against the shelf. The feet stopped and turned toward the door. Somehow, he knew it was staring at him.

It was the second time that day Caden was convinced it was the end. His world hyper-focused, his senses strained to feel everything, and all he thought, all he knew, was that moment. He was trapped. Alone. With one of *them.*

He stumbled further back into the room and bumped against a long, fur coat hanging from a shelf. Had a coat been there before? It was warm too. Caden froze, his mouth opening to scream, but fear constricted his throat. The coat was taking deep, quiet breaths.

Operating on pure animal instincts, Caden leapt away from the furry creature, crashing into boxes and nearly falling over. He scrambled to his feet and sprinted to the door. He didn't stop to consider the second one standing in the hallway; all he knew was to run. He burst through the door and sprinted down the hall. He was nearly out the store's front door when he realized he was holding the backpack. He shoved his arms through the straps and ran without stopping, eyes wide with terror and lungs burning.

The sun blinded him as he ran, and he stumbled, nearly running into a car. He managed to stay upright and kept going. He finally reached the lawn scattered with children's toys and rounded the house, panting. Caden doubled over and coughed as he leaned against the house, his eyes shut tight.

"There!" He cried, letting the backpack fall to the ground. "Got it. Happy?" Exhaustion nearly pressed him to the ground right then and there.

"Hi-yah, kiddo."

Caden's head jolted up and he stared. The gang was gone. There was no sign of them. Caden's mouth slackened as he tried to breathe and figure out what was going on. It took far too long for him to realize someone was standing in front of him.

"Let's get a move on," the stranger said with a chipper smile. Caden straightened, regarding the stranger. It was a man. Not a just-became-a-man, like Caden was, but a real, all-the-way grown-up. He was big. He wore a ballcap and trench coat, and was holding his hand in a funny way.

Why's he pointing at me? Caden thought. Slowly, he recognized what was in the man's hand. It was Harrison's gun. "Are you kidding me?" He sighed, slumping against the house.

The man cocked a brow at him. "Um... no? Grab the backpack."

Caden stared at his feet, his breathing finally slowing. His heart still beating a thousand miles an hour. His side hurt. And his knee was bleeding. What had happened? Did he slam it against something in the store? Yeah, that sounded right-

"Kid." The stranger cocked the gun with a click. "Move it. I can't do warning shots anymore. Not enough ammo."

Caden moved from the house and grabbed the backpack again. It was heavier than he remembered. He shouldered it on and gave a glance to the stranger before stepping forward. He didn't bother asking where they were going, he knew he wouldn't get an answer.

Trace, he thought, his breath quickening again. *If you're watching, God, this is a sick joke You're playing!* That was the extent of Caden's prayer for help.

FOUR

ON THE COUNT OF THREE

CADEN FELT like he was stuck in the store again with those monsters. His thoughts kept whirling out of control. Were they following him, getting into his thoughts again, and dragging him closer to becoming a psycho? *They don't follow me,* he reminded himself. *They never do. But they could. And I could be bringing them to Trace. If he's still alive. Where's my bat? Did I grab any weapons in the store?* His stomach knotted with each step until it felt like he was going to puke.

He had felt this dread the time his teacher caught him with weed. The same fear of the unknown and gnawing terror had heightened his senses as he saw his father coming. That look in his eyes had been so dark. So hateful.

I am big. I am bad. I am mean, he thought.

His dad's words whispered through his soul, words spoken far too often: *"You are puny and weak and too caring, GJ"*

He's right, Caden thought, a corner of his mouth twitching. Caden shook his head and ran a hand over his face.

Buck walked a pace behind him, watching with

narrowed eyes. That's what the stranger said to call him, Buck. Caden hadn't given him his name, and Buck hadn't asked. Caden decided to start counting his steps; he had to focus on something.

The stranger took Caden a few blocks down until the houses thinned and the road out of town was in sight. As they drew nearer to a barn surrounded by a corral, Caden heard dogs barking. And voices. Stranger voices. A muscle in his jaw flexed as his face became impassive. Steel entered his eyes. He took a deep breath, knowing he could die... again. There should be a limit to how often someone could die in a day.

He instantly started looking for Trace. Inside the corral, Caden blinked as he recognized Sophia and Simon, both hunched over and sorting a large spread of belongings. It took a moment for Caden to realize it was *their* belongings. He found Harrison tied against the fence, his bleeding forehead didn't stop him from glaring at the guards. There were four guards who paced around the corral. One held a sawed-off shotgun, one had two pistols, and the last two had rifles. Chained to the corral were two German shepherds, who kept pulling on their chains and barking at the prisoners. Their fur was bristled and, even at a distance, Caden could see their bared fangs.

Outside the corral, and seated around a picnic table, were four men, each in rugged, rancid clothes. Another German shepherd lay at their feet, this one was not chained, and began barking upon seeing Caden. As they turned, he saw they were decked out in weapons of every kind. Knives. Pistols. More sawed-off shotguns. Belts of ammo.

Where's Trace? Caden thought, hope giving his wound-up body some relief. *Did he get away? He might've run off. He's such a spaz, maybe they couldn't catch him.* Caden blinked, his thoughts spiraling again. *Or he opened his mouth and annoyed them instantly. He could be dead behind a house we just passed.*

His thoughts cleared as he was brought before the seated men. He was always caught off guard by the lack of humanity in most strangers' eyes. It was as though the Day of Vanishing had taken more than random people. It took everyone else's souls, making them hollow shells, doing what needed doing to survive, whatever the cost. Caden stiffly stood before them, his heart slamming in his ear drum again.

"He's right," Buck said, jerking his chin toward Harrison. "The kid did come out of the store."

Traitor, Caden thought darkly, but with little surprise.

"Na," one of the men muttered. "He got those supplies before going in."

"Didn't see," Buck muttered.

"Nobody gets into that store. It's haunted," another said.

"Maybe he's a Puppet," a third muttered. A shiver ran up Caden's spine as he made a fist.

Buck shook his head. "Don't think so."

"And how should you know, man?" One of them stood, a spindly guy, a head taller than Caden. His thick beard, which had two beads in it, was nearly as black as his teeth. "I've seen a Puppet look so normal it was like a choir boy," he said, drawing closer to Caden. "It wasn't until later, after all the hysteria and scream'en, we found he killed five people."

Caden forced himself not to step back as his entire body tensed to run.

"When asked why he did it, he just shrugged and smiled like a crazy person. He just wanted to; something like that."

"Does he look the same, Seth?"

Seth leaned forward, his eyes narrowed sharply as he looked Caden over. "Hum… he could be a Puppet."

"I'm not a Puppet," Caden retorted. He was surprised his voice didn't shake.

Seth's brows rose as his arms crossed. "Is that so? Well, slap me silly, what was I thinking? Let's believe the kid and give him a break! Want some water or food?"

Caden turned away as the men laughed. As he turned, he glanced at Harrison. The large man sat at an angle, as though protecting a wound. *Or cutting the ropes with that creepy little knife,* Caden thought. He remembered Harrison's secret pocket in his sleeve. Did these bad guys miss it when they searched him? One look at Sophia and Caden knew she was ready to fight. A lumpy sock lay next to her. He wouldn't be surprised if that lump was a can of beans, turning the sock into a homeschool version of a medieval morning star.

"We should tie him with the big one," a seated man said.

Seth frowned as his fingers rapped his arm. He shook his head slowly. "No."

Caden tried to stand tall as his insides coiled. He'd heard that tone of voice before. It was low and unfeeling from someone who totally forgot Caden was a real person. The tone his dad used all the time. "We need to get rid of him."

Caden blinked. *I'm not a Puppet,* his mind screamed. *They messed with me, but they're not still here. I swear!*

"Wait," a seated man said. It was the first time he had said anything. The others turned and looked at him and Seth, with an annoyed frown, stepped back. Caden glanced at the stranger, seeing him lean forward and study him. The others fell silent and waited for him to speak.

You're the leader. Caden realized. He was a bigger guy, his dark hair cut short, and some pistols were tucked into his belt. His studded earring and sunglasses propped on his brow seemed out of place. Especially the sunglasses, they were blue-rimmed, and the lenses were smokey with a greenish sheen.

"We can't just let him live, Grant," Seth blurted. "Puppets are way too-"

Grant held up a hand and Seth's words grumbled to silence.

"Where'd you get the supplies, kid?"

"I'm not a kid."

Why did I just say that? Caden found himself staring at the stranger too. *Look away! They're totally going to kill you!* He didn't. He'd faced too much today to stop fighting now.

Grant actually smiled. "What's your name?"

"Max."

Where's my brother, was on the tip of his tongue, but Caden caught it just in time.

"Okay, Max, how'd you get the supplies?"

"There's a storage shed out back."

"Is there?"

They know I'm lying.

"There were loose floorboards," Caden said. "Somebody had a stash there."

"Uhum." The silence that followed made Caden's skin crawl. Grant cocked his head to one side with a sigh. "There's no shed-"

"Go look for yourself."

"We did. Picked the store over too. Nearly lost two men going into that place. But you." Grant grunted, his smile still there. Caden lifted his chin as he stared into those dark, hooded eyes. "You waltz right out, free as a jaybird."

"I ran," Caden said. "For my life. Like everyone else."

"Why are we talking to him?" Seth snapped. "He's a Puppet! That's the only reason they'd let him go!"

Caden glared at the shrunken guy and slowly grabbed the strap of the backpack. "I'm not a Puppet."

"Prove it." Caden didn't answer, his grip of the backpack becoming slick. "Hey, Billy," Seth nodded to one of the men. "Go get those chains from the barn. We'll make him break loose."

Caden grimaced. "I can't do that! I'm not a Puppet!"

"Chain him, and I'll make him try," Seth continued, pulling a pistol from his side. "Don't need your kneecaps, do yah, kid?" Caden stepped back and felt Buck's beefy hand land on his shoulder.

"Stop, stop," Grant said quietly. "Put that away, Seth." With more grumbles, Seth obeyed. Grant stood and Caden felt Buck's fingers dig into his shoulder.

What does he want? Caden thought, watching Grant approach.

"Listen, kid," Grant said calmly, as though they were discussing the score of a ballgame. "We all know you got those supplies from the *back* of the store. It's been picked clean, we all saw, except a room in the far back. A storage room. Yes?" Caden looked away. He felt sick. "So, what I want to know is, why don't the Haunts kill you?"

Caden stared at the German shepherd quietly listening, the dog's tail wagging. He slowly shook his head. Caden's stomach twisted as his guts told him not to talk. Something was up. This Grant character had something in mind, something Caden wouldn't like.

Now Buck's fingers were trying to poke a hole right through Caden's shoulder. "Get off," Caden muttered, trying to pull away. He couldn't budge, and he could've sworn Grant smiled in amusement.

Grant lifted his chin and stepped forward, but stopped

as a gray truck drove up. Two men jumped out, both staring at the ground with shoulders hunched. The passenger quickly walked to the back of the truck and dropped the tailgate. Grant regarded them quietly as Seth swore.

"Why'er you two back?" Seth demanded.

One, his face poked by scars, gave him a quick glance. "Found him."

Caden's heart leapt into his throat as his blood turned to ice. *Did Trace try to run?*

The one at the tailgate started heaving something out the back of the truck. It flopped onto the ground in a limp heap. It took Caden far too long to recognize a body. A very bloody body. Seth cursed again as others of the group moaned. Caden's throat bobbed as he craned his neck to see the face.

The hair was dirty blond, and it was a boy older than Trace, more around Caden's age. His body was bent, his clothes torn, and huge gashes ripped along his side and face. Caden turned away and closed his eyes tight. He had seen plenty of bodies, but most were two years old, from the Day of Vanishing, and didn't look like humans anymore. Fresh, still-bleeding bodies were a different matter.

"Don!" Seth cried. The poked-faced man stopped approaching and crossed his arms. "What happened? We needed that boy! *Alive!*"

"He ran! He kept running and hiding through town! We didn't see him go into that store until we heard all the screaming."

"What store?"

Grant scratched his jaw as he regarded the shredded body. "Nockville Market."

"Yeah," Don said, nodding to Grant.

A chill crept up Caden's spine. *That could've been me,* he

thought. *What's wrong with me? Why don't Haunts harm me or Trace?*

"I thought this kid would have any sense and not go in there. Ghost signs were everywhere! He just," Don shook his head, "he just ran in to hide, I guess."

Seth raked a hand over his face and kicked at a rock on the ground. "Great work! Now everything's ruined!"

"No it ain't!"

"No ransom money now for a dead kid!"

"We could lie! Tell them-"

"What? Hum? What!" Seth muttered and paced as Grant motioned to the man still standing beside the body. He pointed to a house across the street, and the man started dragging the body toward it, leaving a trail of blood. Caden stared at the ground and tried to look as small as possible. He was grateful Grant's attention was elsewhere.

Seth shouted suddenly, forcing Caden to flinch back. "You owe me now, Don! Fifty-eight tams! That was my share." Caden's brows rose, the sum definitely worth yelling about. "*You* destroyed my share," Seth said, steel entering his voice. "Now it's your job to give it back." Don stared at the spindly man, and his face became a shade paler.

"How'd you get the body?" Grant asked as he removed the blue sunglasses and began cleaning the lenses on his shirt.

"Ah," Don muttered, glancing between Grant and Seth. "He dragged himself to the front of the store. Died a few minutes later, I guess."

Grant nodded slowly as Seth stared expectantly at him.

"Well?" Seth demanded. Grant sniffed and turned to Seth. "Well, I want my money!"

"We could use him!" Don yelled. With a jolt, Caden

realized Don was pointing at him. "He looks just like him! His uncle won't know the difference!" Goosebumps dotted Caden's arms as a hard lump formed in his throat.

Grant held up a hand and nodded gently. He slid his hands into his pockets and sauntered toward Don. "Donald," he said. "Take off your coat. Please."

"My what?"

"Your coat." Don stared at his leader a moment longer before obeying. "Thank you," Grant said. "Just set it on the ground there. Right there, that's fine."

Caden watched out of the corner of his eye. He felt Buck's hold of him loosen as the huge man sighed heavily. Buck whispered a curse and shuffled his feet.

What's happening? Caden thought, his pulse quickening.

"And your shirt," Grant said. Don stared at him, his pale face turning whiter. "Donald. Your shirt."

Don took half a step back and wiped his brow. "Why?" he mumbled as he lifted the shirt up over his head.

"Don't want it messy," Grant said as he stepped forward, jabbing his hand into Don's middle. Don doubled over with a scream. Caden recoiled and would've ran, if not for Buck holding him in place.

Don, his shirt still pulled over his head, collapsed and gripped his stomach. Grant grabbed Don's coat and slowly stepped back. Without a word, Grant gave a high, sharp whistle.

All three German shepherds charged. They leapt on Don, each sinking their teeth into an arm or leg. His scream became shrill. Caden stared in panic as the dogs ripped and tore. His chest heaved with gasps as he shook his head. Grant sniffed, slowly turned from Don, and strolled toward Caden. Caden's eyes fell on what was in Grant's hand; a long hunting knife. Blood dripped off the sharp tip.

"Wait," Caden whispered, all color leaving his face. "Wait!" Buck grabbed his wrist and twisted, securing his arm behind him as he tightened the grip on his shoulder. Caden gritted his teeth as he tried to fight back, but he was helpless. Grant walked to Caden and grabbed his shirt collar.

"No, stop! Please!" Caden's gasps became ragged as Grant drew the knife closer to his neck. Grant meticulously started cleaning the messy knife on Caden's collar. Caden couldn't stop himself from shaking as Don's screams still filled the air.

"So," Grant said. "Are you going to answer my question?"

Caden's eyes fluttered, desperately trying to remember what was asked. "Um," he stammered, "yes. But- what was it again?"

Grant finally let go of Caden's collar and inspected the knife, turning the blade over and over inches from Caden's face. "Why do Haunts let you live?"

"I don't know." Grant looked directly at Caden, the knife angled toward him. Caden shook his head. "I swear! I don't know! How could I know?"

Grant slowly lifted his chin. "Do Haunts always let you escape?"

Don't tell them. Don't tell them. Caden thought as he stared at the knife. Don's cries heightened with desperation. Caden closed his eyes tight and pushed against Buck.

"Kid," Grant whispered.

"They don't like me. I don't get it. I'm nothing special! That's all I know! I swear, I swear." Caden lowered his head, waiting for a blow. "What else do you want to know?"

Grant chuckled. "Good boy." Caden suddenly wanted to be a Puppet. He could easily throw Buck off and, with one punch, knock off Grant's head and that horrible smile with it. "Do Haunts always let you escape?"

Caden sniffed. "Yeah."

"What?"

"I said yes."

Grant leaned closer, still unable to hear him, and growled. He turned suddenly and waved at Seth. "Shut him up!" Seth drew a pistol and the gunshot cracked, echoing off the vacant houses. Caden shivered as Don's screams were finally quiet. He let out a shaky breath, not daring to look at the dogs and what was left of Don.

"Have you ever been a Puppet?" Grant asked, returning to Caden. He held up Don's old coat before removing his own.

"No. I swear, and they're not controlling me now either."

"What do they do when they see you?"

What's he getting at? Caden thought, his eyes narrowing. *And what did he do with my brother!*

"How should I know, man?" Grant didn't answer, and Caden cursed under his breath. "Look, all they ever do is follow me around, say a bunch of messed-up stuff-"

"You hear them?" Grant asked as he slipped into Don's coat. "They don't just sound like your thoughts?"

"Most of the time they do, but," Caden looked away. A yank from Buck sharply reminded him to keep talking. "I hear them. Outside my mind. Like I hear you. And they get close, but don't touch me. Most times."

Seth whistles. "He's crazy."

"Do you see them?" Grant asked. He adjusted Don's coat here and there and stuck his arms straight forward. His wrists extended beyond the sleeves by several inches. He frowned.

Caden's eyes narrowed. "Everyone sees Haunts sometimes."

Grant stared at him with wide eyes and stayed quiet. "See any this time?"

"I backed into one. Didn't see it though."

Some men at the table barked laughs, and Grant's brows arched sharply. "You- you just backed into one?"

"It's the truth."

There was more laughter. The men at the table shook their heads. "He's a Puppet!" The others muttered their agreement. It was like a table of wolves readying for the kill.

Grant gave them a sideways glance, and they quieted again. With a sigh, he pulled off Don's coat and tossed it to one of the men. He grunted and put on his trench coat again.

"Didn't fit?" Seth asked.

"Na."

Animals, Caden thought. *Pure animals.*

Grant took a step closer to Caden. He seemed to be rolling something over in his mind. "Well, Max, or whatever your name is, it's nice to meet you. You and I will get to know one another." Caden faced Grant and realized he was closer. And that smile. That horrible smile was still there. "You're far more valuable than all the loot we've found today."

What does that mean? Caden thought, his hair standing on end. "You... you want me as part of your gang?"

Grant chuckled. "No, kid. Think of yourself as an employee, but you don't get paid. And you don't have a say. Nor are you ever off the clock."

Caden blinked. It was suddenly difficult to breathe. He gritted his teeth and forced himself not to slump to his knees like he wanted to. "That's a slave," he muttered.

"There!" Grant clapped his shoulder. "Now you're getting it." Harrison coughed. Three times.

The signal! Caden thought, making himself not look at him. *The signal for what? What's going on? Someone save me!*

"He's not valuable," Seth hissed. "He's a-"

"If he's a Puppet," Grant interrupted. "Then I'll have fun sorting him. I know how to handle Puppets."

"Like those poor frogs you play with?"

Grant didn't answer as he continued to stare at Caden, as though already planning which limb to dismember first. Caden tried to pull back, but Buck was so strong. It was like trying to push a tree over. "Think of it, boys," Grant continued. "All the loot we'll get now that this untouchable kid's on our leash." Caden saw Sophia discreetly grab the lumpy sock and wind it around her fist. "Not even Haunts will get in our way now."

Caden secured his hold on the backpack straps and hopped there was a bowling ball inside. He looked down, trying to act defeated, afraid, something to make them lower their guard. *I have five around me,* he thought vaguely. *Harrison and the others have four.* He felt every muscle tensing, readying to move, to fight, to run. To survive. Grant opened his mouth to speak again, but Caden never heard. Out of the corner of his eye, he saw Harrison stand, his little knife slashing at one of the guards.

FIVE

ONE LAWNMOWER BATTERY

BEFORE A FIGHT, Caden always panicked. At the beginning of the World's Crash, the panic felt like a black monster curling him into a little tight ball. Now, after so much garbage had happened, the panic was more like a hiccup. It was still there, that sudden idea to throw in the towel and just close his eyes, accepting defeat. Letting death come. Sometimes it felt like the right idea.

But what about Trace? He always thought. *Or Ellie? She's still alive. She has to be.* Usually, the panic left once he decided to fight. Usually.

That hiccup of panic grabbed his throat as Harrison's little knife gleamed in the sunlight. The panic stopped his breath for a moment and weakened his knees. *I can't die,* he thought, a muscle in his jaw flexing. *I won't die.*

The next moment, he realized the backpack was off his shoulder and swinging at Grant's head. Thanks to Harrison's distraction, Caden easily made impact. The backpack's sudden stop against the side of Grant's skull sent a shockwave up Caden's arm. *It's just a ball,* he thought, pretending he was in a grassy baseball field. *Hit a home run, but if you don't win, the other team will kill you.* He didn't wait to see what happened to Grant.

He spun, grabbing the pack's straps with both hands, and windmilled it into Buck. Finally, the huge man moved back with a grunt. It was only a step, but that's all Caden needed. He flung himself through that beautiful empty space and ran. *Cover. Where's cover!* They had guns. He had a backpack. Not good odds. Behind him, someone was screaming. When did that start? Was that Sophia or one of the men?

"Don't shoot!" shrilled a high-pitched voice. Was that Grant? "Alive! I want him alive!"

Please be talking about me! Caden thought. A two-lane road and houses' yards lay before him. Flat, open ground. No cover. Not even a tree or truck to shield him. *Maybe I can reach one of the houses,* he thought. *Go around back. Or a front door-*

Something snagged the back of his clothes. His legs kept moving, but his body didn't. He cursed under his breath, stumbling. The snag shoved, sending him rolling across the middle of the road. He didn't feel his elbow scrape on the asphalt or hear his pants rip. He rolled, the world a cruel carousel, and stopped with a gasp. Something slammed his guts, forcing him into a ball. He couldn't breathe. All he thought was pain.

"Come here, Puppet boy," someone seethed. Caden looked up and saw Seth standing over him. He held a gun but wasn't pointing it at him. He wanted to, Caden could see it in his eyes. Seth sent his boot into Caden's guts again, kicking him back a step. Caden tried to suck in air, but it felt like breathing jello. He coughed and tried not to puke.

"Shouldn't take you with us," Seth muttered. "Puppet's are psychos."

"I-" Caden rasped, "am not," gasp, "a Puppet!"

"Do Haunts die when their Puppets do?"

Caden licked his lips. Why could he taste blood? Wait, what did he just say? Caden focused and realized Seth didn't have as much self-control as he had hoped. The gun's dark barrel stared down at Caden. He met eyes with Seth, his mouth moving to shout a plea. No words came, for he saw, in that one look, it would be wasted breath.

God! His mind screamed. *Help! Oh, God, save-*

A roar shook the ground. Dust and little rocks flung through the air, stinging Caden. He lurched back, seeing something massive sprint past. There was a metallic thud. Caden gasped, crawling back, and looked at Seth. He wasn't there anymore. *What in the-?*

He turned and saw a truck slamming its brakes a few paces away. As the truck stopped, something rolled off its hood and fell in a heap. Caden blinked, realizing it was Seth. He didn't move, and his arm was bent funny. A curly head popped out the driver's window.

"Get in!"

Caden's heart leapt at the sound of Trace's voice. He scrambled to his feet and threw the backpack in the truck's back. Gunshots clapped his ears. Oh yeah, Sophia and the others. How long had that been going on? Caden pulled himself into the truck but snagged on something. Again. Strong arms wrapped around his middle. He felt lifted from the truck.

I'm done! Caden's mind screamed. *No more dying today!*

An enraged cry lifted from him as he threw back an elbow. It hit something hard. The arms loosened but didn't let go.

"Come here!" It was Grant. His grip tightened again, and he heaved Caden from the truck.

Caden's throat felt weird. He realized he was screaming nonsense. He raised his elbow again but found Grant's arm wrapping around his neck. His screaming was cut off. And his air. Caden kicked and bucked. Grant turned him around, trying to walk him away from the truck. Above the frantic pounds of Caden's heart, he heard the squeal of tires. Grant suddenly flew forward, crashing into Caden, and they both fell. With a desperate gulp of air, Caden's thoughts cleared. He kicked Grant, who had landed on him, and forced himself free. Grant was doing something weird. His face was twisted in horrible pain, and his mouth gaped, but he wasn't making a sound. He was sucking in air and lots of it.

What was over them? Caden vaguely identified the opened truck's tailgate. It was a Dodge. The little picture of a ram stared down at him. He crawled, for what felt like an eternity, and heaved himself into the truck's bed. He dragged himself close to the cab and tried to knock on the back window to let Trace know he made it. He more or less punched it. Before Trace hit the gas, an inhuman scream made Caden drop. His heart raced, the cry like a dying animal, as the truck raced forward and nearly sent Caden on his face.

Caden looked back and saw Grant. The man withered in pain as his entire body shook. He held his leg. It was bent completely backwards. *He won't last,* Caden thought, knowing a broken bone could be fatal. Grant rolled onto his side and screamed at the fleeing truck. Half Grant's face was covered in blood, and Caden knew in a distant, unfeeling sort of way, that his backpack had caused that. *He* had done that. He saw the look in Grant's eyes, and panic threatened to grab his throat again.

I hope you don't last, he thought.

Caden lurched back in the truck bed as Trace accelerated. They surged forward, the engine roaring. Caden glanced over his shoulder, and his eyes widened. He ducked, bracing for impact. The corral didn't stand a chance against the truck's grille guard. With a clash of metal, the brothers burst through. Caden tried to hold on, but Trace drove like a maniac. He whiplashed back and forth, nearly sending Caden rolling out onto the ground.

Dust choked the air. The sharp smell of gunpowder stung Caden's nose. There was more shouting. Something landed in the truck bed. Another backpack. A wild-looking woman leapt in beside Caden, Sophia's eyes were wide as she held a gun. Where'd she get that? She fired, the sound deafening, and Caden shrunk back with his hands pressed over his ears. She was nearly thrown down as Trace sped the truck in another direction.

They slammed into something smaller than the corral, and Caden saw a body ping-ponging off the truck. Something kept zipping through the air. It was like bees, but louder and faster.

"Get down!" Sophia cried, grabbing the back of Caden's head and shoving him.

Bullets, he thought, staring at the dirty bed floor. *Right.* A thought struck him, sending all breath from his lungs. They were shooting at the crazy driver running their guys over. *No,* Caden thought, starting to look up, *I've got to-*

The truck reversed without warning. Someone shouted orders. Someone huge threw himself into the truck, slamming into Caden. Harrison panted, his bloodied face dripping sweat. He held his shoulder. Caden heard someone yell to hang on. It sounded so far away. So unreal. The truck's tires peeled out, spewing dust into a huge cloud, and the truck roared as it raced away.

Caden felt when they hit the road, the truck took off, nearly sending Sophia to the quickly passing asphalt. The three in the back clung to the side of the truck bed, keeping low as the peals of gunfire crackled through the air. By the corral, Caden could see the men getting into the other trucks parked along the barn. His stomach lurched.

We can't get away, he thought. *They'll catch up. They'll kill us all.* A lump formed in his throat, remembering they wanted him alive. So, he'd just have to watch as everyone else died. As Trace died. *Not another dead brother,* he thought, looking around for a weapon. All he found was his backpack. He grabbed it, his breath quickening, knowing that wouldn't save Trace. *Maybe I can refuse to work for Grant,* Caden said. *Maybe I could barter.* He knew that wouldn't work. Men like Grant didn't change their minds.

Caden faced the enemy again, readying for the worst, but his thoughts slowed. Why weren't they coming? The distant trucks were still parked by the barn. As the neighborhoods turned to farm fields, Caden saw the men get out of the trucks, their arms waving. He heard Sophia laugh.

"Smart kid," she muttered. "Wasn't Trace wanting to be a mechanic or something?"

Caden nodded as his hold of the backpack loosened. He watched until the enemy gang faded from view. He sank against the truck and drew his knees against his chest. It was cold, and he was hungry. When did he last eat? He glanced into the sky and saw they had a few more hours of sunlight. He hoped they'd get far enough away before darkness covered them.

He hung his head and took a deep breath, assessing his body. Was he wounded? His knee throbbed. That's right, he had hit it on something when running from the Haunts. His elbow stung too, and he found a sore on his tongue. He probably bit his tongue when Seth had thrown him. His stomach and ribs were tender, also compliments of Seth. All in all, he wasn't banged up too bad.

Then why am I covered in blood? Caden blinked and lifted his head, seeing it was on his shirt and pants. It wasn't his. *I didn't... Had I?* No, no, he couldn't have killed anyone. So who was bleeding? Harrison moaned and rolled on his side, still holding his shoulder.

Caden leaned closer, squinting in the fading light. "You're shot," he said.

"You think?" Caden didn't move, his eyes darkening. "Well?" Harrison snapped between gritted teeth. "Patch me up!"

Caden stared at him. "You told Grant and his crew about me." Harrison didn't answer as he held Caden's stare. "You almost got me killed!"

"Couldn't let you miss out on all the fun." Caden cursed and sat back, debating on whether or not to kick Harrison out of the back of the truck.

Sophia sighed and opened a backpack. She removed a length of rope and tied it around Harrison's arm like a tourniquet. Sophia held one end of the rope to Caden. "Here." He didn't move. "Oh, get over yourself and take it!" With a shake of his head, Caden grabbed the rope and helped secure it in place. He looked down the road again, half expecting Grant and his gang to be gaining on them.

They can't come, Trace took care of it. He kept finding himself glancing down the road as the miles flew by. He couldn't stop thinking of the look Grant gave him. A promise to avenge was in those eyes. *He'll die,* Caden thought. *He can't survive a break like that.* Caden swallowed hard and checked the road again, uncertainty gnawing at him.

———

THEY DROVE until the sun was a glowing arch on the horizon and the sky was gold and orange against gray. They found an abandoned gas station that was completely gutted. The gang parked behind the station, not wanting to draw attention by parking close to the road, and went through the back door. Everything important, from the stuffing in the bar seats to most of the cardboard-looking ceiling tiles, had been taken. Most windows were shattered, bullet holes pelted most. Lots of bullet casings littered the floor, and two shriveled corpses stank up the place. Most gas stations showed some type of violence. Everyone, at least at the beginning of the Crash, wanted two things: toilet paper and gas.

The breakroom, however, didn't smell too bad and was big enough for everyone to fit in. Someone had made a firepit right in the center of the room. The floorboards were ripped up, and a black, ashen rim outlined the circle. The ceiling was blackened with smoke, and a few small holes acted as chimneys.

Sophia dumped out their even fewer belongings as Caden and Simon helped Harrison into the room. How Caden got stuck with *that* job, he didn't know. They set Harrison on the floor, and he slumped against the wall, eyes half-closed and breath shallow. Caden stared at him and, even in the fading light, could see he was pale.

He's losing a lot of blood, he thought, glancing at the trail they left through the building.

Simon found some of the floorboards in the bathroom were loose and quickly got enough for a fire. Sophia actually started it. She kept track of the matches and wouldn't let anyone else touch them. Caden watched her from across the room as she got the little box out. As she opened it, her lips pressed together and her eyes fluttered.

We're out, he thought, even more tired than before. *Or almost out.* He hung his head, wondering how this horrible day could get any worse. *At least Trace is alive.*

His eyes narrowed and he looked around. "Anybody seen Trace?" No one answered. He cursed under his breath and quickly walked from the room. If Trace died, Caden was going to kill him.

How many times do I have to tell him, Caden thought. *Don't wander off! This is ridiculous-*

"My nest! My nest!" Caden reeled, the sudden voice shaking him. His eyes darted around as he raised defensive hands. Black wings fluttered as a raven landed on an endcap. Caden sighed and ran a hand over his face. "My nest!" the bird cried again, its face cocked at an angle as it glared at him.

"Shut up," he muttered. "It's ours now."

"My nest! Got the nest! My nest!" Caden glared at the bird, thinking of Kentucky Fried Chicken and suddenly wanting a net. Instead, he picked up an empty beer bottle and hurled it at the bird. "No! No!" the raven cried as it flew away. "My nest! Shut up! My nest!"

"Shut up!" Caden cried and fell still as footsteps raced behind him.

"Dude! I got a cat!" Caden turned and found Trace running down empty aisles with a huge grin on his face. "A cat! It's trapped in some barbed wire. Can't get out. Seems like it's been there a bit, but it's still breathing."

"We can't have pets."

"My nest!" Trace ducked and Caden pointed at the raven. "Bad cat. Bad."

"Creepy," Trace muttered. "Um, but cat steaks! We can finally eat some meat!"

Caden stared at his brother, not sure if he should be proud of his find or sad about his excitement. *I didn't want this for you,* he thought, *Mama Lo always talked about something better not... not this.*

"Looks like Sammy's old cat. Remember?" Trace asked. The one with the broken tail and two different eye colors. I really like the ones with lots of toes. This one's real sassy though!"

The raven fluffed its wings. "Sammy cat!"

"Shut up!" The brothers cried.

"Shut up!" the bird answered.

Caden cursed under his breath and faced Trace again. "Okay," he sighed. "Did you grab it?"

Trace's smile faded and he looked down. "Ah... no, I thought you'd want to, you know... take care of it."

"Why would I want to take care of it?"

"I don't know, dude! Just- just come on. Please? Go do it. Please?"

Caden stared at his brother and gently placed a hand on his shoulder. "You okay?"

"Sure," Trace said, shrugging him off. "It's out there." He jerked his head out the front door and went to join the others. Caden watched him go, his brows knitted together. With a sigh, Caden walked to the door and found a crowbar covered with dust and a dead mouse.

"Bad cat," the raven called. "Eat the cat. Eat. Eat. Eat!"

Cat steaks weren't so bad. They made it a feast with the can of olives and easy cheese found in the backpacks. Sophia and Simon had managed to grab a few essential items before they made their escape from Grant's crew, but not much. It wasn't anything, actually.

We won't last five days, Caden realized, looking over their few supplies.

The backpack Caden had brought from the Nockville Market wasn't much better. Turns out he hadn't grabbed a bowling ball like he'd hoped. It was a lawnmower battery. A dead one. Caden turned it over a few times and chucked it against the wall, sending it bouncing and denting the drywall. He'd grabbed several pens, rubber bands, some window cleaner, and two rolls of shop paper towels.

"If only we worked in an office," Simon muttered as he grabbed a rubber band and a few pens. He started sling-shotting the pens toward the wall. A few stuck.

"How much further to your aunt's place?" Sophia asked as she gnawed on a cat leg.

Caden stared at the fire as it cast everyone in bright orange light and deep shadows. "A day or so, by car."

"Oh yeah," Trace piped up. "We're almost out of gas. I used a lot going fast."

"Awesome," Sophia sighed, smoothing back a stray dreadlock. "So by foot, that's-"

"Find the KUS." Everyone turned as Harrison managed to open his eyes.

"Sheesh!" Trace laughed. "I thought you were asleep! Or dead."

"We've got to find them," Harrison rasped. "They'll give us food. Water. Medicine."

"But," Caden said, "We're almost to my aunt and uncle-"

"They alive?"

Caden's stomach twisted with uncertainty. "Yes."

"They'll take us in?"

"Yes!"

"You bet your life on it?" Caden stared at Harrison; he didn't know what to say. "Because I'll be betting *my* life by going," Harrison shifted and yelled through gritted teeth as his wounded arm moved maybe an inch. No one helped him and Caden looked away. "The KUS will help."

Simon shook his head. "You don't know that-"

"Then don't come!" The room fell silent as Harrison closed his eyes and looked near-dead again.

Caden noticed the steadily growing dark pool beneath Harrison's arm. *Better you than me,* he thought and suddenly felt guilty. He looked down and picked at the scraps of meat on the little cat bone. *Pretend it's turkey. This is after Thanksgiving dinner. And you're just topping off the meal with cat.* He stared down at the bone and found himself smiling. How insane life had become. He turned to Trace and found his brother staring into the fire. He wasn't moving and hardly blinked.

"Dude." Trace didn't stir. "Hey, Trace?"

He flinched and looked up. "What?"

"Did you eat?"

"Yeah, sure."

Caden frowned. "Did you eat?" Trace leaned back and glanced away. "Trace."

"Not hungry." Caden stared at him and opened his mouth to continue. "Just leave me alone, alright? You're always mothering me like some hen or something. Just back off!"

Caden lifted his chin and returned to his food. *He's had a bad day too,* he remembered. The crackling fire hissed as Simon placed more bathroom floor boards onto it, the embers dancing up in the dark room. *Hope the ceiling doesn't catch on fire,* Caden thought. He checked his elbow and knee, both scuffed during the day's activities. He had cleaned them the best he could but wasn't sure if it was enough.

They could get infected, he thought. *How does gangrene happen again? Infections first, then everything starts to rot?* He sighed heavily and ran fingers through his hair.

Ellie wouldn't let him think that way. She always knew when he was overwhelmed. She'd give him a gentle nudge and tell him to stop freaking out like a girl. He'd deny it all, but value her company. She had a talent for finding the positive in the horrible. *I could use some of that right now,* he thought, watching the fire again. *I hope you're alright, Lil El.*

His chest tightened with emotion and he cleared his throat, turning away. Ellie was going to be fine. She was resourceful and smart. She knew how to surround herself with the right people. Even on the other side of the world, she'd keep herself out of trouble. A corner of Caden's mouth twitched. He hated liars, especially when he lied to himself. He briefly thought of all he had done in the name of survival. He was older and stronger than Ellie. He wasn't alone. He had at least one family member at his side. What did she have?

An unmarked grave covered in sand and scorpions, Caden thought, remembering what the Haunt had said. *I can't think like this-*

Something was moving outside. A car. Is that what he heard? Two blinding headlights streamed through the window, washing the breakroom white. Sophia cursed and grabbed the gun. Caden scrambled up, crowbar in hand.

Come on, he thought, forcing himself to forget how tired he was. *I have to sleep sometime!*

"They could be friendly," Simon muttered.

"And I'm the queen of England," Sophia grumbled, cocking the gun.

From another room, the raspy voice of the raven crowed, "Bad! Bad! Bad!"

Caden felt the weight of the bar. It was like a bat. He liked bats. He knew bats. This wouldn't be so bad. *Stop lying, you idiot,* he told himself.

SIX

THE OFFICER

THE CAR DOORS SLAMMED. There were several doors. Several people getting out. The headlights flickered as people walked in front of the blinding stream of light. Caden's breath quickened. *There's too many,* he thought.

"Hide!" he hissed and grabbed Trace's shirt, dragging him from the room. They raced to the bathroom, threw open the doors and Caden shoved Trace in. "Get down."

"Down where?"

"The ground!" They knelt and grabbed the loose floorboards, tearing at them like madmen.

We'll get under them, Caden thought, jamming the crowbar between two boards. *There's got to be enough room for us to crawl out. What if there's no opening to the outside? We'll make one.* He blinked, easily seeing the strangers, who he assumed were armed with the worst automatic guns he'd seen, firing into the floor. *Under a gas station,* he thought, his throat constricting. *That's my tombstone-*

"Hello in there!" A voice called in the night. Trace slowed but Caden nudged him, nearly knocking him over. "My name is Officer Nathaniel Mason. We mean you no harm!"

Right. Caden thought, flinging a board out of place and seizing another one.

"We are allies in the King's United Society."

Caden stopped. He gleaned out the door, his crowbar ready to pry up more wood. It didn't move. *The KUS! We're saved!* He heard the crowbar clatter to the floor.

"Thank God," Trace whispered.

"God's got nothing to do with it," Caden snapped.

"They've got beds!" Caden nodded as he stood. "And food. I hear some camps have showers too."

Nathaniel's voice quieted them. "Does anyone need our help?" A sudden, scratchy cry lifted from the room behind the boys. Caden flinched and realized Harrison was shouting as if his life depended on it.

Well, he thought. *I guess it does.*

"Sir?" Nathaniel's voice sounded closer. "May we enter, sir?"

"Come here!" Harrison bellowed, followed by several curses.

Caden heard the front door open. Footsteps beat the floor. In that moment, he wasn't too sure. *They could be lying,* he thought. *Anyone could say they're the KUS. Get people to lower their guard. Come in. Take everything. Kill.*

He blinked, realizing someone stood in the doorway. Caden snatched up the crowbar without thinking and held it back, ready to swing as Trace stood behind him. The stranger looked unnatural. His face was round and had a reddish color, and a thick, full beard covered his jaw. His brown eyes were bright, even in the dark hall, and his arms and chest seemed bigger. He wasn't fat, he was just filled out and, well...

Healthy, Caden realized.

The stranger wasn't dirty either. Even his leather boots weren't caked in mud and nearly falling apart. They looked brand new. He was dressed in a white uniform, brass buttons dotted down either side of his chest, and he wore a warm-looking trench coat that was smokey gray. A holstered gun was on his hip. He was smiling.

"Hello, sirs," he said as he touched the rim of his white service cap. "Be at peace. I am Officer Nathaniel Mason. What's your name?"

Caden Johnson, Caden thought, but all he did was move away like a frightened dog. He didn't lower the crowbar either. He knew it was a useless weapon against a gun, but if a backpack and lawnmower battery could save him, maybe a crowbar could too.

Nathaniel stepped back and turned away. "You may come out if you wish. If not, may the king's Sovereign Lion watch over you. Sirs." He tipped his hat again and continued down the hall. Caden counted two men following him, each armed with automatic guns. They were also in the strange, white uniform. Caden didn't move. He didn't know what to do.

"Dude," Trace whispered. "What's your problem? Here's our way to keep going!"

"We've got to think this through-"

"You think too much!"

"And you think too little!"

"Do you want to die out here, eating cats? Or look like them?" Trace nodded to the doorway. "They haven't skipped a meal in weeks!" Caden looked down. "You can drop the crowbar." He did, realizing his arm was starting to hurt. Trace sighed. "Do you wanna go?"

"Let me think-"

"No! Stop that! Do you wanna go? Do! You-!"

"Yes! Yes, alright! I just," Caden groaned and ran a hand over his face. "I don't want them to find out about us."

"About what?"

"How Haunts or Ghosts or whatever they're called leave us alone. They can't find out."

Trace shrugged. "Don't think they'll care."

"Grant sure did."

"He's a creep."

"Just don't tell anyone."

"Sure. Who cares?"

"I do!"

"Harrison'll talk again! Our gang knows our secret. They'll talk. So will the Haunts." Caden turned away. He could hear Nathaniel's calm voice as he spoke with Harrison. The wounded bear-of-a-man was demanding help between gasps and coughs. More men came in carrying a stretcher.

The raven flew through the room. "My nest! Bad! Bad!"

"Maybe they know how the world's doing," Trace said.

And if El's still alive, Caden thought, nodding slowly.

Trace started for the door, but Caden grabbed his arm. "Don't tell them."

"I won't."

"And stick with me."

"Then walk cuz I'm getting out of here!"

For a moment, neither brother moved. Caden could hear Harrison's cries as the strangers laid him on the stretcher. A woman was talking. Sophia. *Maybe it really is safe,* Caden thought and lifted his chin. He led the way out and the two stood in the storefront, waiting for the others.

Simon came out of a closet against the wall and got behind Caden. "They're from the KUS?"

Trace nodded. "We're going to be alright. They'll feed us! Give us a bed!"

Simon's eyes widened. "Why would they do that?"

"Because the king is just and merciful, slow to anger and

tender hearted." Caden arched a brow at Trace. "What? That's what the sign in Nockville said."

The trio stilled as heavy footfalls thudded down the dark hallway. Harrison was grunting and groaning as four men hauled his huge bulk out of the building. Behind them walked Sophia and Nathaniel. She was talking his ear clean off. Caden hadn't seen her talk that fast before. Nathaniel nodded as he listened, his hands behind his back as though he were strolling in a park. He politely held up a hand and glanced at the quiet group of boys.

"I'm glad you could join us, sirs," he said, looking at each in turn. "If you wish, you may join us in camp. Supper is over, but I'm sure the cook can rustle us up a meal." Caden's body answered for him by growling like a wild animal. Nathaniel chuckled and held out his arm to Sophia. "It's settled then."

Caden stared at the man's gun. *This could be a trap.* He frowned, his eyes narrowing. *Look at them! They're the real thing! Anyone can wear a costume and lie, but no one can lie about looking that healthy.*

"How far is camp?" he asked, finally stepping forward.

"Not far," Nathaniel said. "Less than an hour's drive east. Come. It will be very late when we arrive. Do you have all your belongings?"

Sophia scoffed. "I'm not interested in packing our cat dinner."

Nathaniel smiled as he led them to the door. "There's no need for that. There's plenty of food in camp." Trace moved from Caden, his eyes wide.

Get back here, Caden thought as the three boys followed Nathaniel out.

"Is there bread?" Trace asked. "I love bread. I haven't seen any for a long, long time. Well, I saw one bag, but it was all green and moldy. Made me sick later."

"Yes, we have bread." Caden's brows rose. He was

listening so hard he didn't notice the chill of night as they walked around the store to the KUS' car. "And meat and a few fruits," Nathaniel continued.

"Fruit?" Trace nearly grabbed Nathaniel's other arm with excitement. "Blueberries? Bananas? Strawberries? What kinds?"

"Well," Nathaniel cocked his head to think. "I believe there's-"

"I love strawberries. Mama Lo had some growing out back. Always made strawberry cake. Angel cake? So good. Do you have Angel cake?"

"Angel food cake," Nathaniel said. "And no, sorry. Maybe in one of the king's great cities."

Trace gasped. "There are cities? I thought all the cities blew up or were abandoned!"

"Many did. There are new ones now."

"Are there buildings people live in again, or are they in tents? Did someone find wires and fix the electricity?"

"Most are still in the dark, but I've heard there are a few with power in select buildings. And yes, most cities have buildings instead of tents-"

"And police? And food for everyone? And stores? Oh, and school?"

"Some cities, yes, yes, and the king is working on schools as we speak."

"I miss school! I miss English class. All the stories. Always had an 'A' in that class. And the teacher, Mrs. Wilson-"

Caden grabbed Trace's shoulder, pulling him back. "Shut up! You're annoying, dude. He'll kick us out!"

Nathaniel actually laughed. "Nonsense! Well, he's just a touch annoying, but questions are how we learn and grow."

Caden stared at him and realized he meant it. Trace shrugged Caden off and kept asking questions and chattering excitedly. All the while, Nathaniel answered patiently, nodding now and then, and listening. The gang loaded up into the KUS car. Turns out it was a military hummer. Harrison was loaded in the back, taking up all the room. Simon, Sophia, Caden, and Trace had to ride in their truck.

"We're out of gas," Trace announced. "Do you have any?" Caden stared at his brother, baffled at how casually he asked such unreasonable questions. It was like asking a random stranger for a thousand dollars or someone in the desert for a gallon of water. Who'd just hand that over? Someone like Nathaniel. As the officer got the gas can, Caden opened the truck's gas tank.

"Thank you," Caden mumbled as the priceless liquid poured into the truck.

"Thank you for trusting me," Nathaniel said. Caden frowned and didn't answer. Nathaniel chuckled. "You don't, do you?" Caden moved back and crossed his arms. Nathaniel stared at him and nodded. "Good. Trust is precious."

Caden met his eyes and squared his shoulders, unsure of what to do. *What's he getting at?*

"Ever play baseball?" Caden's eyes narrowed. "You held that crowbar in perfect form to swing a home run. Just in the nick of time too; my team's been trying to recruit another player for some time."

Caden scoffed. "What?"

"Every Saturday, when we are able, there's a ball game. We could use someone like you."

Really? A ball game? Are the bats wooden or metal? Is the ball broken in? And there are teams? People who just want to play and not fight to survive? To play. To just run around and finally win something.

He refused to voice his thoughts as Nathaniel secured the gas cap. "Think about it," he said and walked to the hummer. Nathaniel ordered one of his men to ride in the back of their truck and keep a lookout.

"There's a free seat in their awesome army truck," Trace muttered, stepping toward Nathaniel.

Caden grabbed his arm. "Stick with me."

"You're so annoying!"

Caden's hold tightened. Trace sighed and pushed him off but stayed. Sophia rode with Nathaniel instead and Caden drove the truck. Everyone ignored Trace insisting he could drive. As Caden followed Nathaniel's hummer, his hands felt empty. Shouldn't he be carrying something? A bat? A stick? Something to protect himself?

Relax, he told himself. *You're not with bad guys anymore.* He sighed and his shoulders loosened. He didn't realize how tense they had been. *We're going to make it.* He faced his brother, still talking away, a huge smile on his face. Caden found himself smiling too.

———

CAMP LITTLE ROCK was closer than Caden imagined. That was comforting; if it was further than Nathaniel had said, Caden would've deemed him a liar and sped the truck in the opposite direction. "Not everyone likes to kill people," Trace had reminded him. "Just the psychos and the Puppets."

Caden could see the cluster of tents long before they reached them. The dotted glow of torches flickering in the night's stillness between the tent's dark outlines. There were so many tents. *How many people are here?* He didn't mean to, but the truck began to slow.

Trace nudged him. "Keep up."

"Am I driving, or you?" Caden grumbled and caught up to the hummer.

Dogs barked their greetings at the camp's entrance.

Caden could see a guard, armed with automatic weapons and in a white uniform, talk with Nathaniel before waving them on. He gripped the steering wheel tighter as he eyed the guns. How many shots could it fire in a second? Five? Ten?

They protect the camp from people like Grant, Caden reminded himself as he drove in. The guard actually nodded as he sped past.

The boys in the truck fell silent as they entered Camp Little Rock, eyes widening. There were tents everywhere, some small for individual use, others huge. Though it was night, people were still out and about, freely walking between the tents, talking, or attending to their duties. Caden gaped as a young man and woman sat on a bench between tents. They were holding hands and she was laughing.

This isn't normal, Caden thought. *People don't sit around. They don't laugh. They used to.* He blinked, following Nathaniel's hummer around a corner. *Maybe the World's Crash didn't break everything. This is the New Kingdom after all.* They stopped before a large tent filled with tables and benches. Someone had even gone out of their way and put little flowers on the tables. Caden stared at the ornamental plant as he got out of the truck. Mom used to do that. Everyone used to. Trace gasped suddenly, his mouth wide open.

Caden stared at him. "What's with you?"

"What's that?"

Caden's brow raised. Trace shoved Caden out of the way and raced into the tent. "Hay- Trace!"

Nathaniel laughed as he got out of the hummer. "He found the mess tent, I see. Caden, help him pick a table, will you?"

"Mess tent?" Simon muttered.

"That means-"

"Food," Caden said, following Trace.

They grabbed a table close to a torch outside. At Nathaniel's instruction, they all sat and waited as he got some food. Trace couldn't sit. He walked between the tables, circling one, and nearly got on top of another. Caden didn't blame him; he had heard of the food in the KUS camps. Hot. Fresh. Fulfilling. Homemade, not some half-rusted can to eat with a spork. Caden wiped his mouth, realizing he was salivating. He glanced around, hoping no one noticed, and realized they all were equally as ravenous.

Nathaniel returned with a tray of steaming bowls of soup and bread. He said he was sorry for something ridiculous, something about the bread being a day old, but no one heard him. All Caden remembered was the soup was hot. It might have had carrots or meat in it. He wasn't sure. The bread was like eating cake for the first time.

"Don't eat too much now," Nathaniel cautioned. "It'll make you sick and you'll vomit all this good food up." Again, no one heard him as they ate as fast as they could. Caden sat back, rubbing his belly, and fought the urge to lay his head on the table.

"Want more?" Nathaniel asked.

Caden shook his head. "I'll blow up."

Nathaniel smiled. "I was right about the shower bladders. There are still some left over from today. They sat out in the sun, so they are a touch warm."

"Are you kidding?" Sophia said around a bulging mouthful of bread. "I'd shower in ice water at this point!"

Caden glanced at Nathaniel and shifted in his seat. "What do you want?"

Nathaniel took off his hat and ran fingers through his beard. "What do you think I want?"

Slaves, Caden thought, feeling his tender shoulder where Buck had held him. *Our stuff. Our lives.* He didn't answer as he stared intently at Nathaniel. *People aren't this nice,* he thought. *Even before the Crash, nobody did things like this.*

"You are guarded," Nathaniel said calmly. "That's good. In time, you will see the allies in the King's United Society don't require anything of you. Freely we have been blessed by the king, so freely we give to others. It is our joy, and it brings joy to our king."

Caden's eyes narrowed. *Who is this king of yours?*

"Well," Trace piped up, holding out his hand. "Can you feel more joy and give me more bread? Do you have any butter? Do you need all this eaten tonight?"

Nathaniel smiled and handed Trace another slice. "There will be more bread tomorrow, young sir. Do not make yourself sick." Trace nodded, but his hungry stare was intent on the bread. Caden watched this stranger with narrowed eyes. Nathaniel faced him again and nodded. "You will see, young sir."

Caden turned away and grabbed another piece of bread. He stuffed it in his pocket, in case Nathaniel's generosity remembered the world was over and survival of the fittest ruled. Apparently, Nathaniel still wasn't remembering, because he took them to the bath tent next.

Caden hadn't remembered the last time he cleaned his entire body. Maybe last summer? There was a cleanish river Trace and he found that was nice. This was unlike anything he'd seen in a very long time. The shower bladders were hung overhead, each had a small hose and shower head attached at the ends. Wooden pallets had been laid to permit the water to fall on the ground without dirtying people's feet.

A thick curtain separated the boys and girls sides and, to Caden's astonishment, there were little gray bars of soap. He was hesitant to remove all his clothes but was startled to see Trace all set to wash, bare buns and all.

With a sigh, Caden peeled his clothes off and wondered why they hadn't fallen apart yet.

Simon came in last of all, shoulders hunched and glancing all around. "Think we'll be okay?"

"This is amazing!" Trace yelled, spraying himself in the face. "I'm dead! Tell me this is Heaven!"

"Yeah," Caden said to Simon. "I think we're safe."

The water was warm. It pitter-pattered over Caden's face and through his hair, as though washing away the filth of the world he now lived in. He closed his eyes, letting himself only feel the water.

He imagined he was home at Mama Lo's house. It could be right after a baseball game, and Mama Lo was making that chip dip dinner he always loved. Mom was in the kitchen with her, chatting away, and Caden imagined the thump-thump of drums as Nate practiced in the basement. Trace was out somewhere, running with the dogs or fixing Papa's tractor. And Ellie was home. She was on the red sofa, hugging a pillow as she read another book about ancient Egypt.

They were all together. All a family. No one was dead. Dad was long gone. They were all safe. The world never crashed, the Day of Vanishing never happened, and so many people didn't die. Caden took in a slow breath, never wanting the waking dream to end.

Maybe this world can be fixed, he thought. *Maybe this king knows how. But nothing can fix my dead brother. And Mom's gone too.* His eyes opened slowly as he stared at the drops falling at his feet. *Would Officer Nathaniel have news from the Middle East? Ellie might still be alive. He could know how to find her. Maybe I can send a message to her.* He lifted his head, his shoulders squaring. He was determined to find out.

SEVEN

THE LION

EVEN WITH A FULL BELLY, a cot all to himself, and
several warm blankets, Caden couldn't sleep. They were in
a new camp, filled with strangers. Strangers who could be
just like Grant and the many others who had tried to take
from Caden and his brother. They shared a tent with five
others, who were already asleep, yet the sounds of those
outside and the movements and snores of the others kept
him awake. *They just want to give,* he told himself as he
stared at the sloped tent ceiling. *They don't want anything.*

The other half of his brain laughed at him. Caden had
tossed and turned as Trace slept like a baby. Caden
couldn't find his crowbar. He would've felt better sleeping
with it close by. He fell asleep at some point because he
opened his eyes to find that the night had faded and the
light of dawn made half the tent look orange. Caden's eyes
widened as his entire body tensed; there were voices. Lots
of voices. They were everywhere. He reached under the
cot but remembered his bat was gone too.

We're surrounded- No. He closed his eyes and took a
deep breath, willing his body to relax. *This is the KUS. The
closest thing to the old world. Back when people could afford to care*

for others. His strained nerves unwound a little bit. He would've relaxed a lot more with his bat in his hand. At least they were alone, their tent mates had already begun their day.

Trace groaned as he stretched, his bedding slipping off onto the rugged floor. "Ah! So good to sleep! Oh! Now we get to eat. Again!" He smacked his lips and sat up, his hair even more wild than usual. He patted his head, the curls bouncing, and laughed. "I look like Einstein!"

Caden scoffed and sat up. "Just like him, dude."

"At least I've got his IQ."

Caden shook his head. "Right."

"Hey, look." Trace stood and walked to the tent's wall close to the door. Several pairs of clothes sat beside newish-looking boots. "Wow! New clothes!" Trace snatched them instantly and scrambled out of his old ones.

Caden stared at the generosity of the KUS. *We can't pay them back at all,* he thought, unwilling to claim his own clothes. *But… maybe they really don't need anything.*

"Here," Trace said, grabbing a white shirt and throwing it at Caden. "Stop staring and get dressed. Weirdo."

Caden glared at him but put on the new shirt. It felt thicker than he was used to. It was stiffer too, like it had been washed. "This smells funny," he muttered.

"Yeah," Trace said, sniffing his shoulder. "They don't stink. Haha! Think of that! What's not stinky is weird now." He shook his head. "So messed up."

"I feel funny too," Caden muttered.

"Yeah?"

"Like, my skin."

"Same! I found so much dirt in my hair last night. A bug too. It was a little crawly guy. Kind of cute. Do you know of any bugs that live in hair?"

"Um… lice?"

Trace shook his head, handing Caden a pair of jeans. "No. I could see it."

"You can see lice."

"It was bigger. Like a... " Trace fell quiet, for once, and struggled to find the right word.

Caden straightened his clothes. "Shut your mouth when you're thinking, Einstein. You'll look smarter-"

"Like a bigger bug. Whatever. Did you have bugs in your hair?"

"No, Trace. No bugs in my hair."

"Anywhere else?"

"That's disgusting."

"Maybe one could live in your armpit. You don't look in your armpit very much."

"I wouldn't tell you even if I did find bugs somewhere."

"Or maybe inside your ear. Hum... but you'd hear it moving around."

Caden put on some white socks and wiggled his toes. When was the last time he saw white socks? White anything? The guards and allies were dressed in such clean, pure white. It was like they were calmly defiant against a filthy world.

Trace, still deep in thought with his mouth wide open, scratched his head. "What about bugs up your-"

"How'd you sleep, Trace!" Caden glared down at him, crossing his arms.

Trace grinned. "You don't want to talk about your secret pet?"

"Man, there is something wrong with you." Trace laughed and Caden smiled.

Caden grabbed his boots that were a bit big, but too big was better than too small. He stood, feeling his clean clothes and clean boots against his clean skin. He wondered if newborn babies ever felt like this.

"Hay, um… " Caden faced Trace and watched his brother button up his shirt. He was quiet for once and stared intently at the floor. Caden straightened and drew closer. "Have, um, have you ever seen a Spirit, Ghost-thingy with lots and lots of eyes?"

Caden brows furrowed as he crossed his arms. "Don't talk about them here," he whispered.

Trace scratched his head again. "I know. I know. But, have you?"

Caden glanced around to see if they were alone. "I've seen one like a spider. You were there too." Trace nodded. "And then there's the little ones that look all shrunken that disguise themselves as other people."

"Withers, right?"

Caden nodded. "And then there's the snake ones that make people pets and trick them into doing nasty things. I call them Vipers."

"Is that what was wrong with that one guy? The dude who kept beating people up for no reason?"

Caden nodded. "And the bigger, furry ones-"

"Don't talk about Shades." Trace visibly shivered and Caden fell silent.

He was grateful Trace had never stumbled across a Shade. Those white, furry beasts made Caden's heart stop at the mere sight of them. They had too many fangs and claws. They also had a nasty habit of talking inside some-one's head.

They're probably the ones in the Nockville Market, Caden thought. He scratched the back of his neck, feeling his skin tingling, and forced himself to stand tall. "Why'd you ask?"

"I don't know. I," Trace sighed and stopped moving.

He's not even fidgeting, Caden thought and became very quiet as he waited for Trace to speak.

"I just saw something last night," Trace whispered. "It was just… lots and lots of eyes."

Cold washed over Caden. "Were they looking at you?"

Trace nodded. "Yeah, well, they looked at everything all at once. There were a lot of them."

"Where?"

"They were bunched here," Trace said, motioning between Caden and Trace's cot. "And it's arms were weird like… like really big, with lots and lots of fingers. Its arms were spread out like, over us."

Caden lifted his chin, his mouth opening. "It was going to grab us?"

"Ah, no. It just stood there. Looking at everything. Not moving." Trace shifted his weight and scratched his head again. "I don't know, dude. I couldn't see it after a while. Can't see it now. Can you?"

Caden looked between the cots. His insides twisted in knots. *Haunts. Here. In the KUS? They don't come to places like this. Right?*

"So have you?" Trace whispered. "Seen one like that before?"

Caden shook his head. "Was it big?"

Trace nodded. "Taller than you. Than Harrison."

Caden didn't speak, his crossed arms ridged and his shoulders bunching. His hands were cold. *They will get us someday,* he thought. *But why haven't they already?*

"We should tell Nathaniel-"

"No." Caden shook his head.

"I can't act like it didn't happen-"

Caden grabbed Trace's shoulder and stepped closer. "You can and you will. If you say you saw it standing over us, and everyone will clearly see we didn't die, they'll know Haunts or Spirits or whatever they are, leave us alone. It's not safe. No one can know." Trace nodded and Caden clapped him on the back. "Come on," he said, clearing his throat. "Let's see if they'll give us breakfast too."

Caden forced himself to step toward the tent's flap, suddenly uncomfortable to walk between the two cots. He turned, seeing Trace wasn't following him. "Dude. Come on."

Trace rubbed his head and stepped forward but stopped again. "They were so crunchy," he whispered.

Caden frowned. "What?"

"When I drove over them." Trace put a hand over his eyes. "They sounded like kindling when Papa would make a fire."

Caden's chest tightened as he watched his brother's shoulders hunch. He went to his side and wrapped his arms around him. Trace was shaking. "You saved us," he whispered.

"That's why I couldn't kill that cat," Trace mumbled. "I'd killed enough that day-"

"Better them than us."

Trace shook his head. "I kept hearing it last night. Even when I dreamed."

Caden squeezed his brother, wishing he could trade places with him. *I'm sorry I couldn't protect you,* he thought, anger rising in his chest.

He sniffed gruffly and clapped Trace on the back as he stepped away. "It happened. It sucks, but it happened. I'm just glad you never got your driver's permit." Trace snorted a laugh and wiped his nose. "Let's go eat." Caden grabbed Trace's arm and led him to the door. "We can cry about stuff later."

"I'm not crying," Trace grumbled with a sniff.

They stopped talking, but Caden watched his brother out of the corner of his eye. *He's too soft for this.* He could see with each conflict and messy death, a distant, shadowed stare overtook Trace. The shadow got darker and darker each time. *I've got to work harder,* Caden thought, a muscle in his jaw flexing. *I've got to protect him better-*

All thoughts stilled as they went outside. There were people everywhere. They were all dressed in the same white uniform as Caden and Trace. Some had lines on their shoulders and a few on their chests. Some had brass buttons, others didn't. Everyone walked about with intention, but it wasn't hurried or frantic. They walked with ease, chatting to each other with smiles and laughter.

No one's armed, Caden realized with surprise. He looked at the strangers' faces, seeing they had full, round cheeks, bright with healthy coloring, their hair silky and smooth, and, so far, no one stank. They were healthy. They were clean. And they were happy. *Could this be real?* Caden thought.

"Look!" Trace nearly shouted, pointing. "Look! Look!"

On the other side of the dirt road was a little girl walking a dog. Caden and Trace gaped at her as she skipped along, the dog happily keeping pace. Caden tried to remember the last time he had seen a kid, one that was alive. Maybe last year?

She's alone too, he thought, glancing around the crowd for anyone guarding her. *Her parents trust everyone here. Or maybe she's orphaned.* Somehow, he doubted that. The boys hesitantly joined the crowd of people, which thrilled Trace and made Caden jumpy. Strangers. Strangers everywhere. *Unarmed, happy strangers who've given you food, clothes, and a place to stay.* He ran fingers through his hair, trying to relax.

The mess tent was also crowded. People sat in little groups, eating and talking as though the World's Crash hadn't happened. Trace excitedly found Simon and sat. "Hey, Simon! Caden has a bug up his butt!"

Simon frowned. "A bug? Up... what?" Caden groaned and slugged his brother's arm.

A flushed-faced woman rushed up to the brothers and smiled down at them. Her white uniform was covered in a stained apron and a metal pitcher was in her hand. "Blessed morning to you, boys," she said. "Wanna eat some eggs or pancakes?"

"Yes!" Trace answered.

The woman smiled. "You're the new ones, aren't you?"

Caden didn't answer and glanced at the pitcher. *What did you put in there?*

"I'm Ally Julian. And you are?"

"I'm Trace. This quiet guy's Caden."

Ally is a funny first name, Caden thought.

"Pleasure to meet you boys," the woman said. "I'll be right back with your grub."

No, Caden thought, *Julian's her name. Ally is, is... Why did she say that?*

He listened while Trace and Simon talked and surveyed the huge tent. There were no guards. No dogs on chains, keeping everyone in line. No guns, knives, or any weapons at all. *Relax,* Caden told himself. The food helped him forget his worries for a bit. Again, while eating the warm pancakes, soaked in melted butter with fluffy scrambled eggs, he felt reborn. He had to tell Trace several times to slow down and not choke himself. He had to remind himself too.

"Good morning." Caden looked up, finding Officer Nathaniel standing behind him.

"Morning!" Trace said around a mouthful of food.

"I hope you slept."

Don't say anything about the Haunts, Trace!

"Sure did!" Trace said with a nod. Caden shrugged and returned to his food. He knew the officer was watching him, but Nathaniel didn't seem to be bothered that he didn't answer the question.

"Good," Nathaniel said. "Eat up. I'd like to show you around camp."

Caden's eyes narrowed. "Why?"

"In case you require something, you'll know where to go. And, if you feel inclined, I'd like to have Doc take a look at all of you. We like to do that for every newcomer; some ailments that enter should be kept separate until treated."

"Sure," Trace said as Caden kept eating.

And how are those ailments treated? Caden thought darkly.

"Alright," Nathaniel said with a smile. "I'll be back in a few minutes and we'll be off." Caden watched him go. The officer stopped at several benches, talking with people, shaking hands, even hugging a gal.

"He's a nice guy," Trace said.

Caden raised a brow. "They usually seem that way at first."

Simon glanced at him. "Really, Caden? After all they've given us?"

Caden looked down and stabbed his last bite of eggs. "Nothing is given for free. Not before the World's Crash, and definitely not after."

Simon shrugged. "You could be wrong."

I hope I am, Caden thought as he took the bite.

———

THE CAMP WAS beyond anything Caden had seen before. There was a section for the sick where other people actually took care of them. There was a form of police that helped keep the craziness of the world outside of camp. They were called Sentinels, and their white uniforms had two black lines running from one shoulder, across the chest, and to the other shoulder in an arc... They were armed, but each gun was holstered. There was the shower tent Nathaniel said they could use once every three days and even gave them their own soap. A recreational tent, with board games, cards, and a dry version of beer pong, was right next to an opening in the center of the camp.

Doc Hampton, a stooped, bug-eyed-looking guy, confirmed Caden didn't have any bugs in his hair. Caden gave Trace a piercing glare, promising pain and suffering if he mentioned his 'secret pet'. Trace, thankfully, took the hint. Besides being malnourished, dehydrated, and needing strong toothpaste, they were healthy enough to stay out of the sick tents.

"You need to sleep, son," Doc said, staring up at Caden. "You'll give yourself an ulcer if you keep carrying that around."

"Carrying what?"

"That worry. Guilt. You're not superman." Caden hadn't answered.

Trace asked how Harrison was doing and Caden realized he had completely forgotten about him. *Serves him right,* he thought. Turns out, Harrison was recovering. He didn't even have to lose his arm like Caden suspected. He was still very weak and needed rest, but Doc figured he'd be up and moving within a month.

Will we stay that long? Caden wondered. He blinked hard and turned away from the stooped doctor, trying to hide his fears. *They're helping us,* he reminded himself. *Remember what that is? Good people doing good things?* He sniffed and rubbed his nose, still wrestling with his bitter experiences and the sincere sounding promises the KUS could provide.

In the absolute center of the camp was a flagpole with a large flag fluttering in the wind. It was the flag of the United States of America, but there were twenty-seven stars instead of fifty. In the flag's center was a lion's face, a crown resting on its head. Caden watched the flag bounce around in the breeze. He felt the lion staring down at him, that firm, yet calm gaze unwavering.

"Hey," Trace said, finally looking up. "Why'd you change the flag?"

Nathaniel shrugged. "Why keep the same what's obviously different? The key elements of the American flag the king kept the same. There are still thirteen stripes to remember our origins of the thirteen colonies. The red still represents valor and hardiness, the blue for vigilance and justice, and white for purity and innocence."

Innocence, Caden thought. *It should be gray now, not white.*

"But the states are all fractured," Nathaniel continued. "The lines are blurred and, in most instances, nonexistent. Now, there are twenty-seven zones within the King's United Society."

"What zone are we in?" Trace asked.

"Zone Nineteen. Zone Kaiti."

"Kai-what?"

"Key-ate-tee," Nathaniel said slowly. "Each zone is named after the gods or goddesses which once ruled the people. Kaiti was the Native American god of bears. Instead of a god, we now have a king we can see and touch and hear. He protects all who enter his New Kingdom. It is safe within the camp, but the forests and mountains beyond are definitely not. Freaks roam freely as well as ruffians and gorilla gangs. Stay in the camp if you wish to be safe." He seemed to notice Caden's growing unease and added, " No one will stop you if you wish to leave. However, it is not advised."

"What about Haunts?" Trace asked. Caden nearly murdered his brother with his glare. "Or Ghosts. Whatever you call them."

"Herald," Nathaniel said. "And yes, they are in the forest too, though they do not harm us."

Caden glanced at the officer as Trace's face scrunched into a frown. "Ah, they harm everyone," Trace said.

"We of the King's United Society are protected under his rule. The Heralds know they are beneath the king and his allies are to be respected."

"Wait," Trace muttered. "How is the king over them? Ghosts can respect people? And why call them Heralds?"

"The king is over all. He had all authority and power over heaven and earth, the seeing world and even the unseen. Though some are evil, the Heralds are his invisible warriors and, often, his messengers. They appear to us in visions and dreams, helping us, being our advocate, and reminding us of the king's supreme rule. With the Heralds, we can have peace that goes beyond our mortal understanding. There is joy in the knowledge of the king that gives us strength to face another day. There is a still, small voice whispering deep within, telling us this is the way, walk in it. Haven't you ever heard that small voice?"

Yeah, when they were trying to make me feel insane, Caden thought, remembering the market in Nockville, but shut his mouth.

"I have," Nathaniel continued.

"They're freaky!" Trace blurted. "They're not good! They are creepy monsters that only know to attack." Caden tried his best not to slug his brother right then and there.

"Do you follow the king with all your heart, soul, and mind?"

Caden's eyes narrowed as he glanced at Nathaniel. *Isn't that a Bible verse somewhere?*

"If one doesn't choose to follow the king," Nathaniel said, "then they are against him and his Heralds. All are welcome, yet few enter and find rest and peace. The

Heralds know not to harm those of the New Kingdom. And, I know they appear creepy and freaky, but I would assume a helicopter or a tank would be creepy and freaky to an ignorant mouse. It is the same. We fear what we do not know."

Caden nodded slowly and looked up to the lion, trying to hide his quickening heart. *Don't say anything else, Trace!* Caden thought. *We shouldn't be talking about this! We'll slip up, say something wrong! He'll learn their Heralds leave us alone!*

"Yes," the Officer said, running fingers through his thick beard as he also faced the lion. "I find myself locking eyes with the king's symbol. The Sovereign Lion is so... "

"Alive," Caden muttered, grateful the conversation was turning. Nathaniel nodded, and the two looked up and stared quietly. "Why'd he pick a lion?"

"What other creature best represents kingship?"

"Tigers are bigger than lions."

"Yet, they are solitary creatures. The allies and I belong to the New Kingdom. A united union of law and order. Something this world needs desperately."

"You keep saying that. Allies."

"Those who serve the king are called allies. It is a constant reminder that we are not just allies to our lord and king, but to one another. We all share a brotherly love, just as our king loves us." Caden glanced at Nathaniel, who didn't acknowledge Caden's skeptical glare. "Your full bellies, clothed bodies, and constant safety while in the king's camp should be a taste of his love," he finally said. Caden turned away. "And once you have a taste," Nathaniel continued. "You will see that he is good. That his love is given to any."

That sounds totally weird, Caden thought, reminded of Mama Lo dragging them off to church to sit on hard pews and listen to an old guy talk about an even older book.

Glad you like your king, Caden thought. *But you can keep his so-called love to yourself.*

"I've tasted his goodness!" Trace blurted. "It is super, super good! I love bread!"

Nathaniel smiled and clapped him on the back. "And that is only one side of his generosity. In time, you will see more. Such as tomorrow. There's a baseball game this weekend. When you are rested and have regained your health, please join our team. We need more players." Caden's head snapped up as he looked at Nathaniel. A thrill washed over him and he fought hard to not show his excitement.

"Oh, baseball!" Trace grinned ear to ear. "That would be so much fun! Do you wanna win?"

"Um… " Nathaniel frowned. "Yes?"

"Dang it. Okay. Well, I'll just watch and cheer you all on then."

"You could try to play."

"Nah. I can't hit the ball. Ever. Even if it was rolled, I think I'd miss. Can't catch either. Don't throw too well too."

"So," Nathaniel said slowly. "What I'm hearing is-"

"He sucks," Caden cut in. "If baseball was about sucking, then we'd want him to play."

"Hey!" Trace tried to sock Caden's arm, but Caden batted him away.

Nathaniel smiled. "It sounds like you want to join, then?" He turned and stared at Caden, the smile still on his face. It was a kind smile, inviting and peaceful.

Nothing like Harrison, Caden thought. *Or Grant. Or Dad.* How many kind smiles had he seen this year? He ran fingers through his hair and turned away. He shoved his hands in his pockets so he could make fists. He wanted to feel a bat so bad! And to be thrown the ball by someone who actually knew how to play! Trace could keep his bread if Caden had his baseball. *As long as they don't call me GJ. No one knows that nickname, but… I can't give them a reason to call me that.*

"Sure," he finally mumbled. "I'll play."

"Good!" Nathaniel beamed. "We'll win for sure now!" Caden actually found himself smiling. "We'll have to practice a bit first. Let me know when you feel better."

I feel fine now, Caden nearly said, but bit his tongue. He knew he was weak and unable to play anything for a while. He nodded.

"We'll have fun," Nathaniel said. "But for now, let me introduce you to a few key people in case you need anything." They walked into another part of the camp, Trace talking Nathaniel's ear off again, and Caden trailed behind.

He glanced over his shoulder at the flag. The Sovereign Lion was still looking at him. *Maybe it's not so bad here,* Caden thought.

EIGHT
GOLDEN INK PEN

THAT NIGHT, Caden had slept a little better. The sounds of life around his tent still woke him now and then, and he still wanted his crowbar, but not as much as before. Each day, Caden kept expecting Nathaniel or one of the Sentinels to demand payment of some kind. Forced labor was the only thing Caden could come up with. Instead, the allies of the KUS kept letting him rest, offering him non-hostile conversations, and consistent food. Caden still didn't sleep through the night, but each morning he felt more rested than the day before.

After a week of regaining strength, Nathaniel brought up baseball again. "Let's practice tomorrow afternoon," he had said. The next morning, Caden was up a bit earlier than usual, annoyed it wasn't noon yet.

"You're better this morning," Trace said as they got dressed. "Still thinking they'll kill us off one by one?" Caden only smiled. "Bro. Please tell me you don't think that. These are good people! Let's stay here forever!"

"I don't think that," Caden admitted. "I just-"

Trace threw his pillow at him, socking him in the guts. "You'll ruin breakfast!"

"Thought you couldn't throw."

"I was aiming for your ugly face."

"Looser."

Breakfast was quiche with spinach, mozzarella cheese, and buttery crust. Mama Lo made something like this for them once in a while. Caden remembered it had ham in it and something green. Broccoli? She always insisted they prayed before meals. It never made sense.

"God gives us all we have, Cade," she'd say. "We must be thankful. Now, bow your head." It was stupid. God didn't give Caden quiche, Mama Lo had taken the money Papa earned, bought the fixings, and made the darn thing. Not God. Last Caden checked, God rarely rolled up His holy, white sleeves and cracked an egg for anyone's breakfast, let alone some puny human kids.

He called us worms, Caden thought, remembering a verse he had found once. How comforting. Caden shook his head, trying not to think of Mama Lo's invisible 'Friend'. He loved his grandma dearly, but she could keep her God all to herself. Besides, it's not like God wanted Caden either.

So we understand one another, Caden thought, pretending God was listening. Caden knew He wasn't. No one that powerful would let a Caden-worm think the thoughts he thought. Mama Lo had a word for it. Was it blasphemy? That sounded right. She always turned red and flustered when he'd voice how he viewed God. He only wished he could watch God squirm as much as Mama Lo had.

Caden sighed; he missed Mama Lo so much. Almost as much as Mom. *But God had to steal them both,* Caden thought as he stabbed his quiche with more force than necessary. *And now he's trying to take Ellie-*

"Hey, Caden?" He looked up, finding Simon staring at him from across the table. "You okay?" Caden nodded and returned to his food, ridding his mind of the cosmic bully and His games.

"Anybody seen Soph?" Trace asked.

Simon pointed to the back of the tent. "She's in the kitchen. She likes to cook."

"She likes food," Caden said.

"She said something about needing to be around women and talk women-talk. Whatever that is."

Trace's brows rose. "What does that mean?"

Simon shrugged. "So, how long are we staying?"

"Forever," Trace mumbled with a grin. The two fell silent as they waited for Caden to answer.

I didn't ask to be their leader, Caden thought as he scooped up more food. He didn't taste it and his stomach twisted again. *I don't want this. I could decide something horrible and we're all dead. Or worse.* He couldn't shake that animal-like smile on Grant's face as he watched the dogs rip that poor guy apart. What was he going to do to Caden if he ever caught him again? Caden shifted in his seat, feeling the weight of Simon and Trace's stares.

"We'll see," was all he could manage. The conversion turned, something about how many pretty girls were in the camp, but Caden wasn't listening. He kept eating his tasteless quiche, wishing Mom was there, or Papa. Someone who could be the boss, the 'adult' to keep them all alive.

Doc's right, Caden thought. *I can't keep going like this.* No wonder people died so young in the dark ages.

It took forever, but the afternoon finally arrived. Caden kept looking for Nathaniel behind every tent, expecting to see him with bat and ball in hand. *He's busy,* Caden thought with a sigh. *I'm stupid. Why'd I think he'd come-*

"Caden!"

He turned and caught a white ball just in time. He

looked down at it, feeling the ball's smooth curves and rough, red stitches. Well, they weren't red anymore, more like a rusty, muddy brown, but Caden could imagine they were still red. He looked up, finding Nathaniel strolling toward him with a pair of catcher mitts.

"We can practice behind the mess tent. There's a road that's rarely used."

The two walked in silence, Nathaniel smiling and nodding to people they passed and Caden wondering what Trace was up to. He had left him with Simon in their tent, but he knew better. They had heard the mechanic needed a hand and Trace nearly sprinted to the maintenance tent on the spot. Caden met the mechanics the other day, Spencer, Thadeus, and Mac, and they seemed okay.

Just like everyone else around here, Caden thought, eyeing two women chatting as they carried laundry baskets. They waved to Nathaniel, who asked how one of their daughters was doing.

"You know, Caden," Nathaniel said as they kept walking. "There's a theory that people can still wave at each other, even after the Crash."

"Hum?"

"They were waving at you too."

"Oh." Caden glanced behind him at the women; he hadn't noticed. *No one waves anymore.*

"I was an outfielder," Nathaniel said. "There was so much satisfaction in catching a ball that could've been a home run. To hear the crowd cheer was just," he grinned, "Heaven. What position do you play?"

Caden glanced at Nathaniel, a bit irritated he wanted to talk. "Second base mostly."

Nathaniel nodded. "How long did you play?" Caden shrugged and was grateful Nathaniel fell silent.

They reached the mess tent and, as they went around to the back, Caden could smell the grease fires and hear the cooks busily working. "Harrison's recovering well," Nathaniel said. Caden didn't answer. "You're uninterested in his well-being?"

He betrayed me to Grant, Caden thought. *And he'd trade me for a hot meal if it was offered to him.* "He's not a friend."

"Ah." They fell silent again and Caden walked a few paces from Nathaniel. "Let's start closer and work our way out," Nathaniel said.

Caden frowned and continued walking away from him. He turned and hurled the baseball at Nathaniel. He felt his body step into the proper position as though he had been practicing all along. The ball flew from his fingers, arching between them, and nearly hitting Nathaniel in the head. The officer ducked, his mitt rising, and caught the ball with a loud whack. Caden found himself smiling.

"Alrighty then," Nathaniel said and lunged, sending the ball right at Caden. Caden cursed under his breath and caught it, the impact stinging his hand despite the mitt. He glared at Nathaniel, who had his turn to smile.

Is that what you want? Caden thought, stepping forward, his arm raising, preparing to launch the baseball like a catapult launches a boulder.

The two rocketed the ball back and forth, nearly hitting the other in the face. Their smiles kept growing and their arms became sore. The sharp smack of a ball impacting leather lifted into the air. Caden noticed some people had stopped in their work to watch. He wanted to study them, see who they were and anticipate their intent, but he couldn't look away from the ball.

I'll get a broken nose for sure, he thought, watching the ball rush at him. He could almost hear it whistling through the air. It was wonderful. He never wanted to stop, even when his body ached and his catches kept getting slower and slower. Nathaniel finally held up his mitt and waved his hand.

"Done already?" Caden asked with a grin.

Nathaniel chuckled as he rolled his shoulder and walked closer. "You can throw."

Caden tossed the ball up and caught it. "Were you a pitcher?" Nathaniel stared at him, a twinkle in his eyes. "I knew it!"

"Now, why would I give away all my secrets?"

"Outfielders don't throw like that."

Nathaniel shrugged and removed the mitt. "I was from a small town. We had to operate in several positions."

"Sure you did."

"Let's get some water," Nathaniel said as the two started for the tent's entrance. "There should be a barrel in the mess tent."

"Then we'll throw more."

"What? No. Look at you. Your arm's shaking!"

Caden, fully aware his body was completely done and ready to revolt and collapse at any moment, just smiled. "Afraid I'll take your place on the team?"

"You? Replace me? This scrawny, boney kid? I'm surprised you can lift the ball at all."

"I'm surprised you didn't have a heart attack, old man. AARP isn't here to save you anymore."

"I was being gentle with you. I can throw nearly one hundred miles an hour."

"Keep telling yourself that."

The two ladled water from a barrel in the back of the mess tent. Caden took his turn and found it was difficult to bring the full ladle to his lips. *Why's the water shaking?* He thought, staring at the water in the ladle. Nathaniel started laughing. "Shut up!"

"You're pathetic."

Caden didn't answer, he was focusing too hard on getting his arm to do what he said. He spilled half of it, luckily back into the barrel, and let the weight fall from his hands in the end. "Whatever!" He declared, rolling his shoulder.

"My grandpops taught me to play," Nathaniel said. "He used to do it in college and missed it. We would go to the park and pretend trees and rocks were the bases."

"How did you play a game with two people?"

"We'd pretend there were ghost runners." Caden's brow pinched together. "You know." Nathaniel smiled then lifted his hands and weaved back and forth whispering, "Booooo".

"Now that's pathetic."

"Who taught you?"

Caden's smile fell as he glanced out the tent's entrance. He watched people walking by and a truck carefully pass. "My Dad."

"Hum," Nathaniel grunted. "Never had one of those."

Caden didn't answer, his eyes narrowing. "You didn't miss anything."

He felt Nathaniel face him, but he didn't acknowledge him. "That bad, hum?"

Caden swallowed, emotion tightening his chest, making it difficult to breathe. "He liked it in college too and saw I could throw. He'd show me the ropes. It was fun. Until I realized I couldn't make a mistake. Ever."

Caden didn't want to remember his stomach trying to empty before every game. He knew Dad was watching like a predator ready to pounce. If Caden ever slipped up, his form wasn't just so, or he didn't win the entire game, Dad would say something. He always had something to say. Caden remembered his words felt like knives in the back. If Caden's team miraculously won, Dad would boast Caden inherited his skill from his father. It made Caden sick, and he wanted to punch him all at the same time.

"He'd call me GJ," Caden said, tossing the ladle back into the barrel with a bit too much force.

"Kind of a tongue twister," Nathaniel mumbled.

"Means Gochnaur Junior," Caden said. "John Gochnaur played in the MLB in the early nineteen hundreds, was a shortstop, and the worst baseball player in all of history." Nathaniel fell silent as Caden shook his head and crossed his arms. He couldn't ignore the hot emotion tightening his chest, or the quickened beats of his heart. He had punched Nate for calling him GJ once. *No one* called him that. No one but Dad.

"Where is your dad?" Nathaniel asked, breaking Caden's distant thoughts.

"Car accident. He was on the highway on the Day of Vanishing."

"I'm sorry."

Caden snorted. "You're the only one." He rolled his sore shoulder and lifted his chin, done thinking about his dad. "Hey, um... how's Cairo doing these days?"

Nathaniel arched a brow and stared at Caden. "I couldn't say." Caden nodded and turned away, unwilling to acknowledge Nathaniel's questioning stare. "But," Nathaniel muttered, "I can have someone look into it."

"Sure," Caden said and sniffed. *Is he really going to do that? How would he find that out?*

"Is there any other information you're interested in?"

"Well, um... I have some family in northern Idaho. Can you see how that place is doing?"

Nathaniel shrugged. "I'll see what I can do."

No, Caden thought. *He wouldn't waste time or resources on me. I don't owe him anything. Just forget about it. He won't do it.*

"Thanks," Caden said. "Come on." He tossed the ball in the air and stepped toward the door. "I'll make you tired again."

"No, we're done."

"But-"

"We'll do it again. You still need time to rest and heal. You're getting some meat on those bones. You'll be back and playing in no time."

"I'm playing this weekend." Nathaniel cocked his head at an angle and started to say something. "I'm fine! I've been resting. Eating good. I'm not missing a game!" Caden stared at Nathaniel, waiting. *For what? He's not my dad or something.* He kept waiting, hoping Nathaniel would agree.

"Let's try it," he said at last. "If I see you starting to shake again, you'll need to sit out."

"I don't shake."

"You're still shaking."

"I'm excited."

Nathaniel stared at him with a raised brow. "Right. Let's do this tomorrow." Caden frowned. He frowned further when Nathaniel held out his hand for the catcher's mitt. "They're special."

"Yeah, yeah," Caden muttered, handing it over. He shoved his hands in his pockets, suddenly not sure what to do with them.

"Go back to your tent," Nathaniel said as they left the mess tent. "Get some rest."

"Yes, mom."

Nathaniel lay a hand on Caden's shoulder as Caden smiled. "I mean it."

"Yes, mom."

"Little punk!"

Caden laughed as he shrugged Nathaniel off and turned down another road, headed to his tent. "Tomorrow?"

"Tomorrow."

Caden waved and kept walking, realizing how exhausted he really was. He started analyzing his moves, his form, his execution, finding any weakness or mistake. *Should've done that better,* he thought, frowning. *I will next time.* He glanced over his shoulder and realized, with surprise, that he hadn't flinched back when Nathaniel grabbed his shoulder. *I'm trusting him.* He blinked thoughtfully, unsure if that was good or bad.

He went back to his tent and found it blessedly empty. He zipped the entrance flap up tight and kicked off his shoes. With a sigh, Caden collapsed into bed and stared at the sloped ceiling. It moved gently as the wind touched it. He closed his eyes and smiled. *This could be a good place to stay,* he thought. *I wonder how long they'll let us be here. Maybe we could start working with the others. Earn our way. The king sounds like he lets anyone join his kingdom, or whatever it's called. I'll have to ask Nathaniel-*

The doorknob turned.

Tents don't have doorknobs.

Caden's eyes flew open. He jolted upright and stared at the far wall. It was moving. Caden blinked several times, unsure of what he was seeing. It wasn't real, it couldn't be! The far wall was folding toward him, but only a small section, like an upright rectangle. Warm, yellow light streamed into the tent from behind the folding shape. He could hear birds chirping. Voices talking in a different language.

The rectangle unfolded, more like swung, out of the way. Caden scrambled back, falling off his cot, and shielded his eyes from the bright light. He stared from between his fingers, his mouth gaping.

Through the open rectangle, he could see fruit trees and miles and miles of rolling hills of the greenest grass he had ever seen. The sky was a vivid, pure blue and birds flew among the clouds. The silhouette of a person blocked most of the view. Caden blinked, squinting his eyes to see. It was a kid, maybe thirteen, and he was strolling through the opening. He finally noticed Caden, sprawled on the floor with bed sheets tangled in his legs. He stopped and stared. He held something that could've been an ink pen, but the tip emitted a soft, golden light. Caden stared up at him, unsure of what to do.

The boy dipped his head, a peaceful smile on his face. "*Shalom.*"

Caden didn't answer, completely distracted by another sensation. *What is that?* He thought, feeling the warmth of the sunshine from beyond. The warmth touched his skin, but did something more, something he'd never felt before. Somehow, he *felt* that warmness inside him. It filled his body, ridding any trace of exhaustion, and his eyes filled with tears. He felt home. He felt safe in Mama Lo's house, with Mom close by and all his brothers and sister within sight. But it was more than that. Deeper.

What is *that!* Caden gasped, tears trickling down his face. He had never felt such intimate, intense security. It was something unearthly, unnatural. *Peace,* he realized with a start. *I feel peace.* It was pure, unhindered, and reckless. He never wanted it to end. It took a moment for Caden to realize the stranger was speaking to him. He blinked, refocusing on the boy. He couldn't understand a word the kid was saying. What language was that?

"I," he stammered, wiping tears. "I don't speak that."

The boy stopped, his head tilting to one side. "*Saba?*"

"I… I'm sorry. I don't…" Caden sat up and stared beyond the stranger, still in awe.

I'm going there, he thought, slowly standing. *I want to be there-*

"Gideon!" The boy turned and a woman stepped through the rectangle, grabbing the boy's arm. She began speaking to him in the foreign language, her eyes narrowed and tone stern. Gideon turned away and

glanced at Caden apologetically. The woman faced Caden
and her eyes widened with a gasp.

She looked old, her light brown hair turning silver and
her pale skin wrinkled. But her eyes, such a dark brown,
were sharp with clarity and life. She stood tall, strong, like
a young woman, but Caden knew, looking into those eyes,
the wisdom only years could give was in their depths. The
woman stared at him, slack-jawed, and slowly shook her
head.

"Oh, Cade," she whispered. He blinked, unable to
speak. "You look terrible." She had an accent. Was that
German? Maybe Russian?

With a lift of her chin, the woman nodded to him and
pulled Gideon back. She muttered something to him in
their foreign language, and the boy gave a quick wave.
The woman gave Caden one last long look before leaning
forward and grabbing the folded open rectangle. She
closed it, as one closes a door, without a sound. The light
went with them.

The warmth, security, and peace Caden felt flooding
into him abruptly ended. He was left, staggering, gasping,
as though the very air he needed to survive had been
denied him. He stared at the wall, waiting for them to
come back; for the peace to return. He didn't know how
long he waited. The tears continued falling, but they
turned from awe-filled bliss to bitter despair.

He had grieved over his mother's tombstone, literally
dug his brother's grave, and his father was mangled in a
heap of crushed cars on a highway somewhere. There was
nothing to bury of Mama Lo. His Lil El was probably
dead. His entire world was broken, destroyed after the
Day of Vanishing.

Yet, after such a personal acquaintance with grief,
Caden had never felt loss as he did at that moment. The
cold emptiness of the world he knew surrounded him,

squeezing the life out of everything and everyone. There was no pure, warm peace here. There was blackness. There were Haunt-Spirit monsters. There was death. With a gasp, Caden collapsed to his knees and sobbed. He sobbed until there were no more tears to cry. He laid there, staring at the far wall, thinking of the raw peace he desired with everything he had.

NINE
MURKY ICE

CADEN DIDN'T SLEEP much after seeing that other place. Actually, he didn't do much of anything. The joy and excitement of finding rest in Camp Little Rock seemed useless next to the total security and warmth of... whatever Caden had seen. Another place? Another time? He didn't know. All he knew was that he wanted it back.

He hardly slept, and forced himself to eat as everything seemed cold, gray, and useless compared to the life he had seen for a moment. Those people, Gideon and the older woman, seemed completely at ease, as though there were no worries or reasons to fear. He missed them and wanted to get to know them. The woman obviously knew him. And what had Gideon called him? *Saba*, whatever that meant. Why hadn't he flung himself through that open rectangle?

Doors are rectangles, Caden realized. *Maybe that was just a door. It swung open like one.*

It took several days for Caden to pull himself out of his depressed stupor. Trace helped, nudging him now and then asking where his brother went. Nathaniel had sat down next to Caden and randomly said it was normal to feel sadness or grief once in a safe environment. Caden hadn't answered. He guessed he was grieving; grieving the loss of a place he longed for. The Door and its feeling of security, love, and peace.

Caden suspected Nathaniel was trying to help one day when the officer came to Trace and Caden and told them to follow him. "I have answers for you, young sirs."

Caden didn't know what he meant but followed him to a tent in the center of the camp. He wasn't sure what was weirder: being surrounded by armed strangers or the piles of wires and squawking radios. He rubbed his ears, hating the staticky sound. He stood in a tent filled with tables covered with books, maps, and papers, like a reckless version of an office. A huge board was suspended between two tent poles, which was filled with data collected over time. Nathaniel explained whenever newcomers came, any information was gleaned and written on the board.

"Why didn't you ask us?" Trace asked as he played with his fingers.

Caden glanced at him and Trace shoved his hands in his pockets, though his fingers still kept wiggling. *Spazzy excited,* Caden thought.

"We asked Sophia," Nathaniel said. "She detailed your travels and what you saw."

Caden frowned. "I'm our navigator."

Nathaniel smiled at him and nodded gently. "She said you thought you were." Caden glared and turned away.

"Ah," Trace whined. "He's pouting."

"Shut up."

The radio in the far corner chirped and a man seated before it sat upright. He adjusted knobs and dials on various instruments Caden couldn't name and listened. Another man joined, stooping low to listen.

"All the king's camps communicate through radio,"

Nathaniel said. "We have to make sure we camp a specific distance apart not to deplete all the resources at once."

"What resources?" Caden asked. "There's hardly anything worth finding in towns."

"Natural resources. There are deer, rabbits, places to plant gardens and grow a little harvest. Not much, however, we're always on the move."

"That's dumb," Trace muttered. "Why keep moving when you find a good place?"

"Dude!" Caden hissed, seeing one of the armed strangers glance their way.

"It's alright," Nathaniel said. "Valid question. It is the king's wish we find others who want to follow under his Sovereign Lion and join his New Kingdom. All may enter and find rest and a home."

I know, I know, Caden thought, turning away. *Man, he really wants us to join this kingdom thing.* He stared at the board of information, not looking at anything in particular. *Would joining be so bad though?*

"Officer Nathaniel," a spindly man called from a desk of books and maps. "Ah, sir, if I may," the man stood and walked over, giving Caden and Trace nods. "There's news of the king's neural implants."

Nathaniel straightened with a small smile as Caden's head tilted to one side. *I must've heard that wrong.*

"Go on," Nathaniel said eagerly.

"We've received word that the trial runs are successful and, currently, Zone Apollo is offering it to the public."

Nathaniel laughed as Trace scoffed and glanced at Caden. "I heard that from a sci-fi show once!"

"This is wonderful," Nathaniel said. "The king's New Kingdom will draw more allies closer and closer together, as one, huge family! Thank you, Mr. Matthews." The spindly man nodded. "Do keep me updated. And let me know whenever neural implants come overseas. I must have one too."

Matthews' brows lowered to shadow his eyes and he shoved up his glasses. "Yes, sir, well... that may take many more years. We are considered a Dark Land now."

"What's that mean?" Caden asked.

"Electricity," Nathaniel said. "We have limited resources here, yet in Europe and the Middle East, we hear light switches turn on again, and cars are back up and running. Oh, this is wonderful! Maybe in three years, maybe five, we can be a closer world again. Hum, I may not be able to wait."

"What, sir?" Matthews asked. "Go to Europe yourself?"

"Or the Middle East."

"Um," Caden muttered. "What's the king doing to people's brains?"

"He's connecting us. After the World's Crash, we all lost more than we can bare. The lives of loved ones, land, and, for some, our sanity. The king's implants, ah, what are they called, Matthews?"

"Neurologically Integrated Interdependent System. Or NIIS."

Trace grinned. "Maybe it's pronounced like 'nice'."

"Possibly," Nathaniel said. "This new implant will help us communicate efficiently, giving us access to call for help when lost, harmed, or in danger. Unlike now."

"Now we just die," Trace muttered.

Caden's eyes narrowed. "Sounds like Big Brother to me."

"You are a big brother," Nathaniel said. "I see you looking out for Trace, checking on him, securing his safety. That is all the king wishes, the safety of those in his kingdom." Caden fell silent as he slowly shook his head.

"Also," Matthews said. "There's chatter that there will

be another implant, but in the hand. With it, we can carry digital tams, our identification, who our children are, and, some say, even means to regulate the body's health."

"Incredible," Nathaniel said.

Caden glanced between the two and scratched the back of his neck. "Sounds dangerous."

"The procedure is quite simple, I'm told," Matthews said. "Not very invasive. Two surgeons utilize the nasal passage to reach the brain to implant the NIIC on the frontal lobe. It takes a month to recover, which is staggering because, even before the Crash, neural implants took three months of recovery."

"Wait," Trace muttered. "These implants happened before the Crash?"

"They aren't new."

"Cool!"

Caden shoved his hands in his pockets and glanced at Nathaniel. "Didn't you bring us here for some reason?"

"Oh, yes. I apologize. I get very excited about the king's successes," Nathaniel said. "You said you needed information about Idaho?"

"Yeah."

Nathaniel frowned and fell quiet. Caden's stomach coiled as Trace cursed and shook his head. "Northern Idaho?"

Caden nodded as a weight pressed on his chest. *They're all dead. Why is everyone always dead?* With a start, he realized he wasn't surprised.

"Idaho was hit rather hard when the famine came."

"Which one?"

"The Great White North Famine. Most people migrated. The ones that survived banded together under new leadership. All they grow or find must be donated to the community. And the leaders who protect them." Caden and Trace stared at Nathaniel.

"Giants," Caden said at last, steel entering his voice.

Nathaniel tilted his head to one side. "They are good people. They came when the people were dying left and right. They brought seeds, food, water, and a new way of life."

"They *aren't* people."

"I cannot speak for your aunt or uncle, but if they decided to accept the Giant's protection and stewardship, they survived."

"But not their so-called ranch?"

Caden turned, finding a large person quietly sitting in a chair in a shadowed corner. His stomach tightened further as he saw Harrison slowly rise and walk toward them. "You said you talked to them not long ago." Caden's pulse quickened. His jaw flexed as he faced Harrison. Those in the tent stopped their work and watched.

Harrison, his arm in a sling and looking a few pounds lighter, shook his head as he drew nearer. "And the Great White Famine was two years ago. They're dead. We've been traveling this whole way, for what?" He stopped a step from Caden, his dark eyes narrowed. Trace scurried behind Nathaniel and out of reach. Caden's hands felt cold as they became fists at his side. He stared up at Harrison, refusing to look away.

"Stop this," Nathaniel said. "I'm sure Caden didn't know-"

"I suspected they were dead," Caden said. Harrison shook his head, drawing closer still. Caden tried not to step back, but he couldn't help it. He could smell Harrison's breath, he had been eating some form of meat and onions.

"You lied, boy. To me." He leaned down, coming eye to eye with Caden. "To me."

And you betrayed me to Grant! He was going to make me a slave! Probably kill Trace!

"I needed someone big and dumb who'd keep us alive," Caden whispered, lifting his chin.

Harrison's free hand seized Caden's shirt and slammed him against a tent pole. The wind knocked out of Caden and he gasped, trapped beneath Harrison's hand. "I can still beat you, boy," Harrison muttered.

Caden looked up and realized he was smiling. *Why didn't you die in the sick tent?*

A hand grabbed Harrison's wrist and twisted, manipulating Harrison's nerves so that his fingers weakened and curled. Caden slipped from his grasp and stepped back finding Nathaniel calmly walking Harrison backward. "Gentleman," the officer said. "This is not how things are done here."

"Let go!" Harrison barked, ripping his arm free. "You stand up for this kid? He's a liar! And cursed!"

Caden stiffened, a shiver washing over him. *Don't tell them,* Caden's mind suddenly begged. *Don't tell them about the Spirits ignoring us!*

"Every group these two join die off!"

Caden's brows furrowed. *How'd he know that?* He glanced at Trace and saw him staring at his feet. *Thanks, bro,* Caden thought, anger rising in him.

"They'll get us killed," Harrison continued. "They're cursed."

"Sir, they are not cursed," Nathaniel said. "I think you require rest."

"I require my foot up that kid's-"

"Not here!" The tent stilled and heavy silence followed. Nathaniel lifted his chin, his calm, controlled voice returning. "Go back to your tent, sir. Now." Harrison stared down at Nathaniel a moment longer before turning his piercing gaze onto Caden.

I'm dead, Caden thought, his heart skipping a beat. *If he ever gets me alone, I'm so dead.* Without another word,

Harrison turned and marched away, cursing and muttering as he went. Caden glanced at Nathaniel, suddenly concerned if he thought less of him. *Why does it matter? I barely know the guy.* He looked away, realizing it mattered very much what Nathaniel Mason thought of him. With a sigh, Nathaniel went to his side.

"Thanks," Caden finally said.

"Don't lie. The king detests lying lips." Caden nodded and wiped his nose. "Stick with me a while, lad," Nathaniel said, clapping him on the back. "The both of you. I dare say that man, though wounded, can sort you both at the same time. Wouldn't want that."

Caden shifted weight from foot to foot, uncomfortable with someone else sincerely caring for him and his brother. *He's not faking it though,* Caden thought. *He really means it.* They made eye contact and nodded. "I'll stop lying."

"Good. You can start by telling me why Harrison believes you two are cursed."

I gotta teach Trace to shut up! Caden thought as he crossed his arms.

"We join gangs or groups of travelers and, well... things happen. It's not our fault. Things just happen!"

"Such as?"

Caden sighed and silently thought. "We left the last group when they all got sick. We didn't get sick, but, you know... we left before we did. The one before that got into a firefight with some thugs. Freaks hunted us too a bit, but nothing we could control. It wasn't our fault!"

"I believe you," Nathaniel said, laying a hand on Caden's shoulder. "Life is far more fatal now."

Caden nodded. "Yeah, yeah, we don't want to hurt anyone." Caden's heartbeats finally slowed as Nathaniel grunted and stepped back. *Don't kick us out,* Caden wanted to beg, which surprised him. He wanted to stay. He felt safer here than anywhere else. The three stood in silence for some time, watching the work around them.

"Hum," Nathaniel grunted suddenly. "Caden, you had questions about the Middle East?"

Trace glanced at Caden and scoffed. "Waste of time," he muttered and walked to one of the maps.

What's his deal? Caden thought, giving his brother an icy stare. He sighed and looked away. *He doesn't want to hear more family's dead.* He didn't blame him, but he couldn't just guess if Ellie was dead or alive. He had to know.

"Yeah, Cairo."

Nathaniel clapped his hand. "Right! Yes. Mr. Matthews, did we gather that intel?"

He tasked someone to find that out? Caden's mouth dropped open as Matthews straightened.

"Officer Nathaniel!" Matthews said. "Yes, sir, we, um…" He opened a worn notebook and leafed through the pages. Before finding the page, he stopped and gave Caden a long hard stare. "I must ask, are you Alex?"

Caden frowned. "No. I'm Caden."

Matthews also frowned, his eyes scrunching behind his glasses. "Are you positive?" Caden opened his mouth to speak but wasn't sure how to respond. "You see, you match the description of an Alex Whitney. A young man whose uncle has an overwhelming amount of tams for anyone who finds him. Hum. Very curious. You do really match the description."

"Well," Caden said. "Let me check." He patted his chest and looked down, as though searching for something. "Yep. Still just Caden."

"Mr. Matthews," Nathaniel said. "If you please."

"Right, right, sir," Matthews muttered, returning to his notebook. "Cairo. Here we go."

Caden stood in rigid attention. Could he really find out

if Ellie was alive or not? *She's dead*, he thought. *No girl could survive over there. It's impossible-*

"It took some time to gather this intel, yet, with our allies in Zone Apollo and Zone Thor, we uncovered a few things. Cairo fell under extreme difficulties three years past. The Day of Vanishing eliminated roughly twenty percent of the population. The government nearly collapsed, yet seventy-three percent of Egypt is within Zone Ra, which is Zone Three."

"How encouraging," Nathaniel said.

Caden shrugged. "What?"

"Egypt is in Zone Three. Each zone was numbered in numeric order meaning Egypt is literally the third zone to sign an allegiance with the king." Nathaniel smiled and grabbed Caden's shoulder. "Though peace is not yet a reality, odds are, most people are still alive. The order and rule the king brings has been established in Egypt for at least two years. That long of a time would solidify his sovereignty and law. This is good news! The king treats all equally, he longs to save all, protect all, and love all!"

Caden faced Matthews. The man shoved up his slipping glasses and grinned. "Officer Nathaniel is correct. The population, though depleted after the Day of Vanishing, has nearly returned to its former numbers. Immigrants are flocking there, finding refuge." Caden looked down. His eyes misted over and he sniffed roughly.

"She's alive?" Trace asked. "She's alive! Yes! I knew it!" He raced over and grabbed Caden in a huge hug. "Sis is okay! She's alright!"

"Your sister is in Cairo?" Nathaniel asked. Caden nodded.

"Well," Matthews said hesitantly. "There's no guarantee-"

"Maybe she'll come back! They'll open up the sky

someday, won't they? She could fly over. There's room in our tent. Oh, she's alive!"

"The skies are already open," Nathaniel said. "Portland, Seattle, LA. Mostly through one airline, Whitney Wings, so not as many available seats as before the Vanishing."

Caden felt his brother hug and bounce around at the same time. He wrapped his arms around him and smiled, feeling warm tears fall. *You're alive, Lil El,* he thought. *Hang in there. Maybe you'll come home.* Then, a thought occurred to him, one he had never dreamed of before. Caden stiffened, knowing the simple thought was crazy. Suicide. There was no way at all he could do it.

But maybe I could, somehow, he thought. *Maybe I could get to Egypt. I could find her.* Caden shook his head as Trace kept jumping and hugging and talking unendingly. *That's insane,* he told himself. *That'll never happen.* Deep down, he knew the dream had already turned into an ambition.

———

AFTER SO MUCH WAITING, Caden was finally going to play baseball. He met the team the other day. They had practiced a bit, but not all of them could join because of work. Caden didn't care. He didn't care if they won or lost either. He just wanted to play!

Another lie, he thought, restlessly moving the baseball from hand to hand. *I win. That's what I do.*

He surveyed the wide field before him that was alive with activity. It wasn't really a field, more like a flattish spot of grass with four flat pieces of wood painted white where the bases should go. The dugouts were at either end of the field with buckets of water nearby, instead of water bottles. The bleachers were the benches from the mess tent, tents for shade from the communications tent, and blankets to sit on when they ran out of room. Instead of concessions, there were honey sticks, jerky, and caramel apples.

Everyone had come out to join in the fun. Kids ran around, dogs barked while women talked and laughed, and the men speculated who'd win. Caden stiffly stared out across the field and glanced at the sun. It would set in a few hours. Everyone knew they'd have a late dinner. No one cared.

Caden sighed heavily, the joy of baseball dimmed by The Door. *That's what I want,* he thought. *That peace. Those people. A little, dumb ball can't give me that.* He had thought it could, but that was before The Door. Caden couldn't stop thinking about it. Did they play baseball there?

A hand fell on Caden's shoulder, and he found Nathaniel standing next to him. "Ready?" Caden shrugged. "You'll do great." Nathaniel squeezed his shoulder and stepped back, already eating a caramel apple.

"You playing?"

"You bet I am."

Caden nodded as he looked over the steadily growing crowd. *There's so many of them,* he thought. *This is going to be embarrassing.* He looked down and moved the ball from hand to hand again. He saw Nathaniel watching him out of the corner of his eye.

"Stop it," Nathaniel finally said. "You're making me nervous."

Caden grinned and held the ball. "You never get nervous."

"Me? I'm nervous all the time."

"Whatever."

"I was nervous the day I met you. You could've struck me with that crowbar. Shattered some ribs, my collar bone."

"Well, when you barge in like some crazy looters, who knows what'll happen?"

"Glad you didn't."

Caden nodded and glanced at Nathaniel. "Yeah. Me too." They stood in silence for a time.

"Play for yourself," Nathaniel said at last. "Don't worry about all of them." He jutted his chin at the crowd. "And play for the king."

"He's not my king."

"He could be," Nathaniel said as he brushed a white, long hair off his shoulder.

Caden's eyes narrowed, and he watched the hair drift to the ground. "Yeah. He could be."

Nathaniel shook his head and licked the caramel off his fingers. "And it is in the name of the king I try to protect you. Like tonight." Caden glanced at him. Nathaniel discreetly motioned to behind the row of benches and smiling faces. One face, set in a large head with shadowed eyes, stared intently at Caden.

Brooding monster, Caden thought as he looked away from Harrison. He felt his heartbeat quicken again. He hadn't known Harrison long, but he didn't strike Caden as the forgiving type. *What am I going to do?* Caden swallowed hard.

"I'll talk with him," Nathaniel said quietly, and he gave Caden a small smile. "You stay here."

"What? No. He'll hurt you!"

Nathaniel looked Caden square in the eyes. "You're worth it." Caden blinked. "You remind me of my brother. He died in a raid before the king brought peace to our zone. He could throw a fast one too." Caden turned away and stared at the baseball in his hand. He sniffed and shuffled his feet. Nathaniel clapped him on the back again and headed toward Harrison.

Caden watched him go, suddenly wanting him to be

standing beside him again. *We'll stay here,* he thought. *As long as they'll let us, we'll stay. If they don't see me as a failure after today.* With a heaved sigh, Caden returned his attention to the field. *They'll all be watching,* he thought. *I didn't practice enough. I can't just wing it!* His eyes narrowed as he moved the ball from one hand to another. *But I can't miss this. I have to win-*

"Where'd they get caramel?" Trace bumped into Caden's shoulder. "Who knows how to make that? Mama Lo said it was really, really hard to make. I bet they raided a candy store or some little kid's stash." Caden didn't answer. Trace glanced at him and smiled. "Oh, yes, Baby Ruth. Get all mentally prepped. Go through the moves. And again. Now one more time."

"For the love of God, shut up." Trace gasped, grabbing Caden's shirt. "Get off me!"

"You said God!"

"So?"

"You never talk about Him!"

"I wasn't, you dimwit!"

"I see nothing's changed." Both brothers stopped their jostling and found Sophia staring down at them with an arched brow.

"Hey!" Trace smiled brightly. "There's Soph! Haven't seen you in forever."

"You two don't look like walking carcasses anymore."

Caden frowned. "Thanks."

Trace stepped way too close to her and narrowed his eyes. "You look different."

She scowled down at him. "You can't tell?"

"Are you wearing makeup or something?"

"Does it look like I am?"

"No."

Caden rolled his eyes and scratched behind his head.

"She unbraided her dreadlocks, dude. Back up! I bet your breath is rank."

"Dreadlocks aren't braided," Trace corrected as he stepped back. "They're a bunch of knots. Unknotted."

Sophia ran fingers through her much bigger hair, nearly an afro. It bounced even more than Trace's curls. "Like it?"

Trace opened his mouth, but Caden elbowed him. "Sure," Caden said quickly.

Sophia glared at them and held out a tray she had been holding. A delightful display of caramel apple slices suddenly made Caden forget the game. "Want some?" Sophia asked. "And when I mean some, I mean two. That's one, two. Not three. Got it?" The boys said no more as they selected the largest slices they could find. Steps fell behind them as Simon raced to the tray.

"Didn't you have some already?" Sophia asked.

"Nope," he said, snatching two. "Nice hair. Really pretty like that. Matches your personality."

Trace snorted a laugh. "What? Wild, bouncy, and huge?" Caden fought down his own laughter as the younger two broke out in hysterics. Sophia lifted her chin and took one apple slice from each of them.

"Oh, man," Simon groaned as he stared at his final slice. Sophia smiled and stormed away, her hair swaying with each step. Trace hadn't stopped laughing. Caden watched him, Trace's cheeks turning red, his mouth open, and his eyes squeezed tight. He smiled. "That's just wrong," Simon wined.

"That's so great," Trace gasped, holding his side. "Did you see her face- hey! Where'd my apple go?" Trace looked down and followed a trail of smeared caramel down his shirt, pants, and onto his shoe.

"Way to go," Simon muttered. "Go get changed, toddler."

"It's not too messy," Trace said, licking his shirt.

"Dude!" Caden grabbed his arm. "Stop that! We're actually around decent people now so just... go change."

"It's not bad-"

"Trace."

His little brother's shoulders sagged and he swatted his hand. "Yes mom."

"Shut up."

"Mom never said that to me!"

"I bet she wanted to!"

Simon laughed as Trace headed for his tent. "What a weirdo."

"Tell me about it."

Simon turned and looked through the sea of faces, his eyes narrowing. "Where's Soph? She was just right here." Caden shrugged and smelled his apple. The caramel smelled so good. Maybe he should wait until after the game, like a prize for winning. "I can't find her," Simon said.

"She's here dude."

"I'm going to go look."

"She won't give you anymore."

"She's already given me five. She can't keep track of everything."

Caden chuckled as Simon headed off in the crowd. He sighed and glanced down at the apple slice. *It's making my fingers sticky. I should just eat it now.* He raised the delicacy, opened his mouth, and froze.

Across the field, behind a seated family, something caught his eye. It stood taller than a man and its fur, pale as a ghost's, gently waved in the breeze. Its legs were bold and bird-like, the long gray talons curling from spindly fingers. Its cat-like tail twitched as its tiny pointed ears flicked. The red mouth was crowded with teeth, most sticking from the wide opening. Those eyes, gray as murky ice, were looking directly at him.

Caden forgot to breathe. He forgot to think. All he saw were those dead eyes and that wide, red mouth. The mouth twitched, and its lips stretched, showing even more teeth.

It's smiling, Caden thought, his eyes burning from not blinking. *That Spirit is smiling at me.*

Beneath the Spirit, the family kept talking and eating happily. Caden felt like he was going to puke. The father stood, his head rising to the Spirit's shoulders, and waved a large blanket to spread out on the ground. As the fabric moved, it blocked the Spirit from Caden's site for a moment, and the Spirit was gone. Caden blinked over and over and dragged in a lungful of air. He staggered back, his eyes darting everywhere. Where did it go? Was it still there? Coming toward him? Why was it here?

That was a Shade, Caden thought. *Nathaniel said Spirits were safe. Here's one! What's it want?* Caden ran fingers through his hair, smearing caramel unknowingly. *This isn't good. Whenever Spirits smile, people die. What is going on?*

Caden looked back at the family, but there was no sign of the Shade. He licked his lips and shook his head. *Something's happening or going to happen. I have to tell Nathaniel! I have to- no. I can't tell him a thing. They'll lock Trace and me up, or think we really are cursed like Harrison said.* Caden kept looking through the crowd, expecting to see that monster any second. *If there's one, there's more. If there's more, there's death.* He gritted his teeth until it hurt. With a growl, he set off to find Nathaniel. Caden was going to tell him everything, even if it terrified him.

TEN

THE LAST THING YOU WILL EVER SEE

CADEN RUBBED his sweaty palms on his shirt as he raced through the camp. *Where'd he go?* He left the crowd of the ballgame spectators behind and plunged into the camp. His hair stood on end and he kept looking over his shoulder, half expecting the Shade to follow in the shadows. He had seen one run once. Though they could stand on their back legs, they ran on all fours, like a huge, white monster. He hated them.

At least it didn't try to eat you or anyone else, he thought. *Yet.*

He gritted his teeth and kept searching. Half of him doubted Nathaniel could do a thing. What could a mortal human do against an invisible, flesh-eating terror? Some people thought they were aliens who invaded Earth. The day they invaded was said to be the Day of Vanishing, and everyone who vanished had actually been stolen by the aliens. The hundreds of thousands of loved ones suddenly gone were all locked away in spaceships, hovering outside Earth's atmosphere.

Others believed their loved ones hadn't gone anywhere

and instead were the invisible monsters themselves. Evolution, something like that.

Regards, Caden thought. *They're Spirits and Ghosts that mess with reality now for some reason. Had the Day of Vanishing made them able to get to us?*

He had been there when Mama Lo said her last words on the Day of Vanishing. Before her clothes flattened to her bed and she was just... Gone. Caden dragged fingers through his hair, growling despite himself. *Focus! Don't think of that! Where would Harrison and Nathaniel go to talk?*

He zig-zagged through camp, his anxiety heightening. What was the Shade doing right now? Were there more? *We could be surrounded. They could be planning an attack. I've heard they can do that. The ones they don't eat or kill they'll turn into Puppets-*

Caden's rambling thoughts stopped as he saw Nathaniel step from a distant tent around the corner. The officer whipped a handkerchief from his pocket and was cleaning his hands. Caden opened his mouth to yell for him, but someone beat him to it.

"Hey! Officer Nathaniel!"

Nathaniel stopped, his wiping motion freezing, and he coolly turned as Simon raced up to him. "Hello, young sir." Nathaniel smiled. "Why aren't you joining the others in festivities?"

"I was, but um... have you seen Soph? I've been looking for her." Nathaniel lifted his chin and kept wiping his hands clean.

He looks so tired, Caden thought. He stepped to join them but stopped. *What's he wiping off his hands?* The white handkerchief was turning red.

"Miss Sophia is in the mess tent. Helping the other women prepare food."

Simon frowned. "No. I just came from there." Simon

blinked and leaned closer, his eyes narrowing. "Something's all over your face. Looks like-"

Simon's eyes widened. His face went white. Caden's stomach twisted into a solid knot. Nathaniel seized Simon, turning him around with a hand clamped over his mouth. Simon struggled until his back arched, his body shaking, and his muffled cry abruptly cut off.

Caden flinched back, knowing a stabbing when he saw one. Simon's body shook as Nathaniel drove the blade into his back again. Caden sucked in a breath through gritted teeth. He nearly tripped over himself as he sprinted to his tent. *That was blood!* His mind screamed. *He was wiping blood off his hands!*

Was it Sophia's or Harrison's? Caden's ragged breathing burned his lungs as he neared his tent. *Be alive, Trace!* Caden prepared himself for a bloodied mess, another brother dead, but this time one he couldn't bury-

He ripped back the tent's flap and leapt in, nearly slamming into Trace.

"Woah! Watch it!" Trace stumbled back, arms raised.

Caden was so relieved he nearly hugged him. *No time.*

"What's your problem-"

"They're all dead!"

Trace frowned. "Are you okay?"

"They're all dead! We've gotta go!"

"Who-"

"Run!" Caden grabbed Trace's shirt collar and dragged him outside. The two raced around their tent and skirted low to the ground.

"What's going on?" Trace hissed, but Caden didn't answer.

Why did I trust them! How could he be so foolish?

Caden heard movement. He stopped suddenly, Trace running into him, and the two waited crouched behind a barrel. A woman walked by, humming softly to herself as she looked through her picnic basket. Caden tried not to move, not to breathe, and wondered if she could also hear his loud heartbeat. She passed, oblivious.

Caden motioned for them to continue. *We can't just sneak past the guards,* he thought as they were nearing the camp's edge. *They'll see us. They have guns.* The panic before a fight consumed him, demanding he raise his hands and receive whatever Nathaniel had for him. Maybe he'd let them live. He liked Caden, they were pals. *He killed my friends!* His eyes narrowed with firm resolve and he stood. Trace followed, and the two stood catching their breath.

Trace grabbed his arm and leaned close. "What's happening? I'm serious!"

"Follow my lead."

"I mean it! Tell me!"

"Follow me, or we're dead!" Trace's mouth snapped shut as he studied his brother's eyes. Without another word, Trace gave a curt nod and followed Caden into the open. The two strolled toward the guards at the front entrance. "Good afternoon, allies!" Caden called, forcing himself to smile. He saw Trace wave beside him.

The Sentinels turned and nodded. "Not watching the game, allies?"

"Officer Nathaniel sent us," Caden said. "We're one baseball short, and he thinks one of the players hit it way into the outfield. Like really far."

"How far?"

"Into the woods there," Caden said, pointing deep into the thick barrier of trees.

The Sentinel's brow arched as he stared down at Caden. "And he sent you two? Those aren't safe woods."

"He said it's not that far in."

"And how could he know?"

"He wanted all the balls accounted for before the game started. May we go do our job? I don't wanna keep everyone waiting. Caramel apples are good, but they only go so far."

Come on! Come on!

With a sigh, the Sentinel stepped back. "Be quick."

"Yeah, we don't wanna go," Trace said. "But he said he's counting on us. Thank you, ally!"

Ally, Caden thought with a flash of sudden hatred.

"Let's be quick," Trace said with a nudge, and the two took off running down the dirt road that turned into the woods.

Caden glanced at the sky and remembered the sun would set in a few hours. *We don't have any food or water. Or blankets. Am I even wearing a jacket?* He cursed under his breath and signaled for Trace to run faster. They fell into a dead sprint, the forest closing in around them. On either side of the road, the thick forest passed, casting them in deep shadows. *They said there are Freaks in here,* Caden remembered. Freaks weren't as dangerous as killer 'friends' and grinning Shades.

"I," Trace gasped, "I've gotta stop!"

"No!"

"Can't breathe!"

"Try!"

"No, man!" Trace slowed.

"Trace! I mean it!"

"My side!" Trace grimaced as he gripped his ribs, his chest heaving. They both stopped, panting desperately. "Ah! This hurts so bad!"

"A bullet hurts worse!"

Trace glared at him. "You sure you're not being paranoid?"

"No!"

"Because that one time those good people came around, you said they were Puppets."

"Trace, I saw-"

"They were just board theater students-"

"Nathaniel stabbed Simon!" Trace stared at Caden, his face void of emotion. "I saw it." Caden coughed, realizing how much his side hurt too. *Anything to distract me,* he thought, the surprised look on Simon's face replaying in his mind. "He stabbed him. And he was wiping blood off his hands, so I think..."

"Where's Soph?" Caden shook his head. "Harrison!"

Caden shrugged. "We're it."

Trace sputtered, wiping his hand across his face. "But, I mean... What the heck! Why would Nathaniel do that?"

"I don't know-"

"That makes no sense! He took care of us and then, then... you sure?"

"Do you think I'm making this up?"

"No! It just was so, so perfect there. You know?"

"Too perfect." Caden kicked a rock and looked into the forest. "Let's get off the road. They won't be able to track us as good."

"They'll hunt us?"

"Plan for the worst."

"But what if we go talk to Nathaniel. I mean, what if there was something the other guys did and we didn't. What if we could stay just one more night. He wouldn't mind-"

Caden grabbed his brother's shoulders and shook him. "Do you hear yourself! You'll die if you go back! We've got to go. Now!" Caden blinked, realizing Trace was trying to pull out of his grasp. He released his brother and then took two steps back. They were pale. Caden felt his hands shaking.

"I'm scared," Trace whispered.

"Me too." Caden said, laying a gentle hand on the back of Trace's neck. "But we've got to be scared while we run-"

"I can't live in this."

"In what?"

"This!" Trace waved his arms around. "I can't live in this world anymore-!"

Dogs barked in the distance. Both turned with sharp gasps. "Go," Caden hissed. "Go now!"

They crashed through the underbrush, not knowing where they were going. Caden weaved between trees and ripped his shirt free from a brier. *I trusted you,* Caden thought, remembering his time with Nathaniel. They were going to play baseball. Caden was going to learn so much from Nathaniel. *I trusted you.* He was made a fool. Again. And they were going to pay for it with their lives.

The ground began to get steeper and steeper as the mountain rose. Caden cursed as he tried to run uphill. *They'll see us for sure,* he thought. *Can't hide uphill!* Trace was falling behind again. Caden gritted his teeth, willing himself to slow and stay with his brother. "Move it!" he hissed. Those two words took so much strength. He panted, his mouth gaping. His side ached as though his muscles were ripping in two. He pressed on.

"I can't-" Trace gasped. More dogs barked. They could hear voices shouting through the trees.

Caden cursed and grabbed Trace's shirt. *I'll carry him,* he thought, but knew that was impossible. He looked up the hill, seeing it continue on and on as though trying to touch the sky. Trees gave way to rocky ground high above, some jutting out over a great drop. There was no time to plan or think, just act.

"There," Caden said, pointing, and then took off running, Trace stumbling to keep up. The sun had begun to sink into the west, stretching the shadows and turning the light sharp yellow. The two ran, Caden's full focus intent on reaching the rocks.

We'll hide in those. There's got to be a cave. A crack. Something to squeeze into. Dogs howled below them. Caden's insides tensed. He couldn't help but think of Grant casually watching as his dogs ripped Don to shreds. He could still hear the screams sometimes. Dogs also meant they could be sniffed out. He couldn't change his course; there was nowhere else to go.

"Up there!" a distant voice shouted behind them.

Caden suddenly felt nothing as all energy, everything he had, was focused on propelling himself faster up the hill. A sharp, cracking sound split the air. A tree's side exploded, the bits of bark showering the brothers. Caden ducked, shielding his eyes.

They're shooting at us, he thought with factuality, as though telling someone else's story. This wasn't his story. This type of thing didn't happen to him. Not in real life.

Behind a tree in front of them, stood a man in a white, furry coat. The fading light made him difficult to see, but Caden made out long knives held between the man's long, slender fingers. He was smiling too, a red smile. And his teeth! There were so many of them-

A Shade. Caden stared at the grinning monster, unconsciously swerving away from it.

"Cade!" Trace grabbed his arm as Caden felt his foot slip, falling into nothing. He shouted, seized his brother, and looked down. He nearly ran off the rocky face of a drop-off. A hundred feet below, the tops of trees pointed up at him. Caden lurched into Trace's arms, and the two nearly fell to the ground. They fought for balance and continued running.

Electrifying pain shot up Caden's shin with each stride, but he hardly felt it. The Shade was here. Of course, it was here. Another peel of gunfire sounded, crashing into a tree close to Trace's head. He yelled, nearly dropping into a ball. Caden reached to grab him, but dirt flew in his face as another bullet rocketed into the ground at his feet.

Caden's ears rang as more shots fired through the air. Coughing through the dust, Caden seized Trace and dragged him behind a tree. He sat him against it, seeing that Trace clutched his arm awkwardly. The ping of stray bullets forced Caden back because Trace's tree wasn't big enough for both of them. Caden scrambled away and pressed his back against another tree, his chest heaving and body drenched in sweat.

I'm big and bad and mean! He thought, closing his eyes as bullets cut into the trunk. He flinched with each crack of gunfire. His mini motivational speech was a joke. He was going to die. After, of course, watching Trace get filled with lead. He'd see the life fade from his brother's eyes, just like he saw Simon's.

Remember how Simon looked? That strangled scream as he tried to cry for salvation or plea for mercy? There is no mercy within the King's United Society. What else did you expect, human fool?

Caden grabbed his head as his eyes flew open. The Shade, undisturbed by the chaos around it, crouched at an arm's length from Caden. Its tail tip flicked like a cat playing with a cornered mouse. Caden's entire body shook as he saw his terrified expression reflected in the Shade's pale gray eyes.

Get out of my head!

The Shade's smile grew, stretching its face until it looked ready to rip in half. Caden stared at it, waiting for those knife-like claws to sink in or the teeth to find his throat. The Shade didn't move. The trunk's side exploded in a spray of wood and bark. Caden lurched back, grabbing his arm with a cry. He felt blood between his fingers. Had he been shot? There wasn't time to see. Caden flung himself behind the tree again and turned back to Trace.

"Let's move! They're closing in!" Caden shielded his eyes from the dust and more frequent sting of flying bark and wood. "Come here!" Caden squinted, holding out a hand to his brother. He barely made out Trace's details in the falling dusk. Trace sat against the tree, staring at him.

Why isn't he blinking? Caden thought.

Trace leaned back and fell to the ground. Smeared on the tree behind him was blood. Lots of blood. Caden stared as he sucked in one shallow breath after another. The leaves beneath Trace turned red as blood pooled beneath him. Time slowed, and Caden couldn't hear the gunfire anymore. His outstretched hand didn't move, as though still waiting for his brother to rise.

Get up, he wanted to scream. *We've got to move! We can make it. Trace!*

Trace didn't move. He kept staring at Caden, his face noticeably paler than before. He still wasn't blinking. Caden felt nothing. It was as though all his internal screams of terror had turned into a shrill. The shrill rose higher and higher until it became one blurred-together sound. A constant, unchanging white noise. A sound that could be ignored and, heard long enough, forgotten. Caden sat in that illusion of stillness, his nerves too raw to feel a thing. He was empty. A shell that only knew to breathe, and breathe again, and again.

There is nothing left. The thought echoed in his inner emptiness. His reaching hand felt heavy and weak. He let it drop. Caden forced himself back and he sat against the tree. He didn't move. He didn't want to. He looked ahead, trying to find his bearings, but found himself staring at the Shade again. Had it moved closer? He swallowed hard, suddenly not as afraid of the creature as he was before.

"You murdered your brother." the Shade whispered.

Caden groaned and looked away. *Someone, save me,* he thought, not sure who he was talking to. *If anyone cares about me anymore… save me. Please. Please, help me.* His head lowered, recognizing the peals of gunfire again, knowing no help would come. No one heard. He was of no consequence to anyone or anything. Wolves would feast on his body just like Grant's mongrels who disemboweled Don *before* his death-

"Shut up!" Caden spat at the Shade, who flicked its tail with amusement.

"See him?" The distant question reached Caden's ears as a final shot echoed off the mountain. His head turned, listening.

"Think he's over there."

They've lost me.

"Set the dogs on him?"

"Send them in." Nathaniel. That was Nathaniel's voice. Fierce anger heated Caden's blood as his teeth bared. There was the traitor; Judas himself. Caden took in a breath and stood. He couldn't live for Trace anymore. He didn't want to live for himself; he was too much of a failure. No, he was going to live to spite Officer Nathaniel Mason.

"Feast for wolves," the Shade muttered as Caden squinted in the gloom, looking to the rocks.

I can't see a thing-

Swiftly moving paws thudded from behind on both sides.

"Wolves," the Shade said calmly. "They favor the flesh of prey still breathing."

Caden sprinted towards the rocks, knowing he'd stop off into nothingness at any moment. He slammed his foot into a boulder, fought back a cry, and surged on. *What am I doing? I can't fly!* He half ran, half felt forward. He could see outlines of things, a rock here, a fallen tree there. Beyond was the blackness of the drop-off.

Caden felt the ground angle down sharply. He

crouched, feeling forward. Racing paws approached. His heart leapt into his chest. A dog's snarl caught his breath. A solid, furry body slammed into him, flinging him forward. He cried out, hearing snapping jaws and feeling hot breath. He slid down and, without warning, the ground was gone.

Caden gasped, his mind completely blank. His body crashed into sharp sticks and slapping leaves. His feet slammed into a rock and his legs buckled beneath him, hitting the rock hard. He gasped as pain consumed him.

My legs are broken! I'm so dead now! A yip sounded above, and a black thing fell with a crashing thud at his feet. He lurched back and the fallen dog disappeared again, its baying wail quickly fading. It ended abruptly with a solid thud far below. *I didn't fall all the way down,* Caden realized, reaching out and feeling the edge of a rocky ledge.

He dragged himself back. Branches and sticks grabbed at his hair and neck. He ducked until he sat against the sheer rock face, panting. He looked up, unable to see a thing in the heavy darkness, but he could hear. Dogs sniffed back and forth above him. Their movements rustled the grass and sent little pebbles bouncing down.

Don't move, he told himself. *Don't breathe. Don't do anything.* He heard voices approaching. How far away was the top of the drop-off?

"Ricky! Bring that light over here!" Caden's stomach lurched. He huddled in a tight ball, too terrified to notice he could move his unbroken legs. He waited, sealing his mouth with a shaking hand, hoping to muffle his breathing. He shut his eyes, as though that would hide him better.

Above, footsteps stopped on the rocky edge. There were so many people after him. What had he done? Caden gritted his teeth, fighting back a groan.

"Let me see."

Caden's brows drew together at the sound of Nathaniel's voice. He heard the squeak of a moving lantern and another squeak as the mirror behind it was adjusted. A circle of reflected light shot down like an arrow in black waters. Caden pressed himself against the rocks, feeling the rough edges pricking his skin. The lit circle trailed back and forth, drawing closer with each passing. Caden's breath quivered and he fought to contain himself.

They're going to find me, he thought. *I can't escape. There's no use. Prepare for an inevitable demise. After such lust for survival, such a wretched way to end. Isn't fair. Isn't right. It's God's final laugh at your countless failures, GJ.*

Caden's eyes opened. He found himself face to face with the Shade. It lay beside him at eye level, watching his every move. Caden got the sickening feeling that the monster was ready to catch every detail, every twitch, every gasp as the bullets ripped him apart.

The Shade's furry head tilted to one side as its small ears flicked. It nodded once and kept watching, those haunting eyes scarcely blinking. *"I will be the last thing you will ever see,"* Caden heard it say within his mind. He couldn't move as horror gripped him.

ELEVEN

LIKE A FREIGHT TRAIN

CADEN WAS LOSING HIS MIND. He was sure of it. If he wasn't, he would soon. No one could put up with everyone trying to kill everybody else. Two-headed wolves and other crazy Freaks of Nature, not to mention Spirits that could talk inside his head. Why didn't anyone else see them so much?

Caden gritted his teeth, his eyes squeezed shut again, but he could feel the Shade's hot breath on his cheeks. He knew Nathaniel's light would find him at any moment. His arched back tingled with the anticipated blow of bullets. What did it feel like to get shot? Like getting punched? But the punch went through you?

"You will discover within time," the Shade whispered. Caden wanted to plug his ears. *Your defenses are futile against our arsenal,* the Shade said within his mind. Caden's entire body shook. He just wanted it to be over. Was there anything good anymore?

That Door, he thought weakly. *That Door was good. Whatever place that was... that was good.* He fought to focus on the memory of the unnatural Door. He remembered that warmth that had washed over him, filling him with comfort and security. Peace. Pure peace.

But it was all a lie. Another cruel game from a cruel God. It had been a hallucination. He hadn't been feeling well and what he saw and felt was nothing more than-

Get out! Caden's mind screamed. *Get out of my head! Get out!* The Shade gave a low, gravelly chuckle. *It was real,* Caden told himself. *Whatever it was, it was real.* He willed himself to focus on The Door's light, the vivid green grass, the peaceful smiles of the strangers he wanted to know. The acceptance. The boy who waved at him and the woman who knew him.

"It was all a dream-" the Shade whispered in his mind.

I felt it.

"Are feelings truth?"

It was real-

"Such purity doesn't exist."

I want it.

"Your touch with reality is slipping."

A tear slid from Caden's closed eyes. *Come back,* he thought, as though pleading for that place to hear him. *I want to live there-*

"The light approaches." Caden's breath quickened. *"Ready yourself to join your brothers. Your mother. Your father. Your sister."*

She's alive!

"It is of no consequence, for you shall die."

Caden ducked his head and waited. *Remember the light,* he told himself. *Remember how warm it was?* He mentally saw The Door opening again. There was peace in those hills.

Nathaniel's light fell across him. Caden dared to open his eyes and saw the piercing shaft splotching the rocks around him. Something was between him and the light, blocking a clear path of sight. Caden blinked, recognizing the dark shadow of leaves. He remembered falling through sticks and leaves and he felt the little scrapes marking his body. *Am I under a bush or something?* He didn't dare move. The light stayed a moment longer, then was gone. Caden blinked in the sudden darkness, his heart beating loud in his ears.

"Caden!" The cry echoed off the rocks around him. "Caden Johnson!" It was Nathaniel again. Caden could hear him take in a deep breath to shout again. "I know your secret!" A shiver ran up Caden's spine. "Mr. Harrison informed me you see Heralds *and* survive the experience. Repeatedly. Only those deep within the KUS survive such encounters." Caden blinked rapidly as he tried to stay as still as he could. "But you... you are not one of us." Others grumbled their agreement overhead.

"All who oppose the king will perish!" Nathaniel shouted. "We could not suffer you and your friends any longer."

We didn't do anything! Caden internally screamed. *You killed my brother!*

"Only those of the King's United Society can enter and find rest in the New Kingdom. All else will be cast out with weeping and gnashing of teeth. The Heralds have declared the king's bidding. Long live the king!"

"Long live the king!" shouted the men beside Nathaniel. Caden shivered, their voices echoing again and again.

"We hand you to the Heralds," Nathaniel said, his voice lowering. "May they bring justice by whatever means necessary." Caden shook as something far below caught his eye. It was moving fast, running on all fours. It was white. His stomach dropped as the internal screaming became white noise again. The nothingness consumed him as another Shade was racing to join the fun.

"And may it be swift," Nathaniel muttered. Did he sound sad?

Caden couldn't hold back a whimper as the Shade before him watched his every move. It still smiled that wide, unnatural grin. Without another word, Nathaniel and his men turned and walked back to camp. Their shuffling footsteps faded quickly, sending little pebbles rattling down the drop-off to bounce against Caden. He lay there, curled in a ball, waiting.

No one's going to save me, he told himself. *What am I waiting for?*

He closed his eyes and lay his head on the rock. It was cold on his cheek, but he ignored it. His entire body ached. Blood oozed from his wounded arm and several scrapes along his back and legs. His uniform was ripped in several places and the night's cold touched his skin. He had no food, no water, and no way to stay warm. There was no one else to fight for. Trace had been his fuel, his reason for life, but now...

Now there was nothing. Nothing but the internal screaming that seemed to have always been there. Caden hadn't noticed until now. It wouldn't stop. It filled him, echoing in the emptiness inside him, reminding him now abandoned and alone he truly was. Who would've noticed if he died tonight? Who would morn?

No one, Caden thought. Even if people did find his body, it would be another casualty in this game called life. This game he was losing. Why play any longer?

Caden opened his eyes and glanced at the rock's edge. He didn't know how far the drop was. It wouldn't be hard to roll over and find freedom in the weightlessness of air rushing all around him. He'd have a moment of no restraints, no questions, no worries. He could take control and decide when his end would come instead of continually running. He could decide for himself and-

"No," Caden said hoarsely, raising his arms to defend himself. "No, no, no." He scooted away from the Shade

and his foot brushed against fur. He gasped and curled into a ball again, realizing the second Shade had joined. The two Spirits lay on either side. In the darkness of night, their white fur looked gray and hauntingly luminescent. Somehow, he could still make out their piercing, dead eyes.

"Go away," he moaned. "You can't make me jump off the cliff." They didn't answer.

What are they going to do? Caden gasped and held back a sob. He didn't know what was worse, being filled with lead or left alone with Shades. *I'm not going to make it,* he thought. *They'll make sure of that. Maybe I should just end it all. It wouldn't be difficult. A simple stride would be sufficient. I'd feel no more pain. You'll be free. It's your choice-*

Caden let out a cry as he jammed his fingers in his ears. They wouldn't get out of his head! He really *was* going mad.

The Door, he thought.

"Enough with fantasies!"

Think of The Door. It was so warm. So beautiful.

"All a lie." The Shade's voice shook Caden to the core.

It was real. That peace was real!

"Failures do not deserve peace."

"Have you earned admiration, GJ?" the other Shade asked.

It was warm and-

"Fantasies of a deluded mind."

-given to me. For a moment-

"And retracted just as quickly."

"Rightly so."

"Even those pure, loving strangers rejected you."

"Who can love you?"

That was real.

"No, Caden. *This* is real."

Caden gritted his teeth. "That peace was real," he whispered.

"If so, it is gone-"

"It was real."

"-never to return."

"Like how peace is supposed to be. Nothing held back. All the way."

"No one does that."

"Raw Peace," Caden said. "Raw Peace."

"You cannot obtain an illusion," one Shade said.

"Only a depraved mind would stoop so low," the other said. "A mind that should cease its blabber."

"One that should end," the other continued. "To rid the world of its failures-"

"Raw Peace," Caden whispered forcefully, digging his fingers deeper into his ears until it hurt. It didn't help. He could still hear them. "Raw Peace," he repeated, determined to focus on that vision or hallucination or whatever it was.

The Shades kept talking, sometimes verbally, sometimes directly in his thoughts. Caden kept repeating those two words over and over. He didn't know what that Door was. All he knew was the warm, pure sense of security it brought. In that moment, it was keeping him alive. He hoped.

———

IT DIDN'T TAKE LONG for the shock and weariness of his escape to hit Caden square in the chest like a freight train. He slumped to the rocky ground and closed his eyes. Rest was far from him. His arm throbbed with fury as dried blood stuck his clothes to the wound. He still didn't know if he was shot or not. His legs weren't broken, but they were bruised and battered. Scratches from the bush he fell through lined his body, and several rips exposed him to the night's cold. He kept shaking, but with cold instead of terror. He wanted to sleep. To escape it all. The Shades wouldn't let him.

Once sleep swallowed him, they were in his dreams, replaying Trace's dead stare and the smell of gunfire. Caden would awake with a gasp, his stiff and bleeding body aching at the sudden movement. The Shades would laugh.

How many were there? There were two, but maybe more now? He didn't know anymore. There were too many red, smiling mouths, too many pale, ghostly eyes, and too many voices talking. Inside his head, and then audibly, making him feel more and more crazy.

Caden didn't think he'd last the night, but when the morning's light split through the darkness, he stared in shock. *I can make it,* his exhausted mind thought. *Here's another day. Another chance to fail and watch other people I love die around me. Pity. Maybe you should plea to that God of yours. Isn't He benevolent? Full of compassion and tender mercies? Here is His mercy, boy. Do you feel blessed?*

The Shades laughed as Caden closed his eyes, no longer able to yell at them when they entered his thoughts. *Raw Peace,* he thought. *Raw Peace.* He tried to imagine The Door again, the warm light crashing across the shadows of this world. Had Shades been there too? No, no, they were putting themselves in his memories. *Can they really do that?*

"Why assume our abilities are limited?"

I've got to get out of here.

"Where can you flee?"

I've got to do something!

A Shade laughed as another shook its head. "Foolish human child."

In the growing light, Caden dared to crawl closer to the rocky drop-off. He looked down, the wind buffeting his face. He stared, seeing he was not as far up as he had thought. Below, two dogs lay twisted. He stared a long time, scanning the rockface and looking for a way down.

"You will slip," a Shade muttered.

"You are already wounded," another pointed out. "Do you find pleasure in pain?"

"If the descent doesn't fracture your skull, you shall be reduced to a cripple."

"Certainly."

"And then what? Scream for salvation?"

"Crawl to what? Another cliff to plunge off of?"

"Raw Peace," Caden whispered.

"Is he blabbing about that again?"

"Apparently."

The Shade scoffed. "Ravings, I say."

I'm not going mad, Caden thought, his eyes narrowing.

"It has been my experience," a Shade said, its tail flicking as the wind washed over it, waving its fur. "All madmen claim sanity. Thus is their twisted beauty." The other Shade nodded.

Caden leaned forward, grabbing the edge of the rock. He realized his fingers were numb. His simple movements sent shocks of pain from his arm and back. He gritted his teeth and closed his eyes. *I can make it down-*

"Why keep fighting for survival?"

-then I can get away.

A Shade barked a snarled laugh. "Yes! The simplicity of standing on solid ground will repel us!"

And then I can get to Ellie.

Both Shades' tales lashed as one rolled on its back. "She is dead," it said. "The scorpions have made a nest in her skull."

Caden's eyes clenched tight and his teeth bared. *I will find her!* For once, neither of the Shades answered. Fear grabbed Caden's throat and made it hard to breathe. *What are they doing?* They hadn't touched him, let alone killed him. *What are they waiting for?*

He glanced at them and found both staring straight into the sky. Their smiles had vanished. The napes of their necks were bristled, making them look twice as big. Their tails flicked restlessly. He looked up too but saw nothing but the yellow underbellies of clouds before a gray sky. In the distance, dark clouds billowed high overhead.

He could hear the cold wind, the rustle of plants clinging to life on the rocks, and wings. His eyes narrowed as he glanced around. It sounded like a flock of birds was flying very close, but nothing was in the sky. How hadn't he heard it before? A low, chilling growl rose from one of the Shades. Caden cowered back, his hair standing on end.

Both Shades had drawn back their lips, exposing rows and rows of jutting fangs. His breath quickened and he scooted away from them, only to find the drop-off. With a yowling snarl, one of the Shades turned on him, claws scraping across the rock as it moved. Caden shrunk back and screamed. *I'm dead-*

"Jump!" the Shade barked. "Jump! Now!" It snapped its jaws with crushing force and saliva splattered Caden's face. He shielded his eyes and realized he was still screaming. "Jump! Join your family! You have nothing left!"

Caden sucked in a gasp and tried to move back but felt his leg slip over the rocky edge. "No, no!" He heard himself cry. He made a fist and tried to send it into the monster's face. His hand passed right through the Shade, as though it wasn't there.

As he withdrew his hand, the Shade swatted at him, long claws slashing. One caught the side of his hand, tearing through the skin with flaming pain. Caden screamed and drew into a ball. He was going to die. They would get what they wanted. Wolves would have their feast-

The wind struck with fury. The sound of wings roared in Caden's ears. He heard a dog-like snarl and several whining yips. Rocks shifted with movement. Caden dared to look and saw the Shade who touched him was gone. The moment his mind registered this odd fact, something hooked his dangling foot. It pulled.

Caden's world lurched down. He scrambled for a hold, but it was no use. He was falling. Spinning. The trees weren't so far away anymore. The ground struck him, just like the freight train. Caden's head bounced, his eyes rolling back as bright sparks blurred his vision.

Before he could see again, a shockwave of pain shot up his leg. Caden moaned, eyes clenched tight, and rolled onto his side. He grabbed the ground beneath him as his painful leg began to shake. *I'm alive,* he thought. *And hurt. Oh, that hurts!*

The wind struck him again, with it the sound of dozens of wings. He shielded himself from the sudden gust, dust and leaves filling the air. Something moved over him and stomped the ground; he could feel it.

What was that sound? Above the wind and wings, the agony gripping his leg, and his spinning head, something was caterwauling. Loudly. Painfully. Like a cat being shredded. Caden covered his ears, gasping, trying to make sense of it all. With a shrill, the wings beat again, hurling the wind all around him. Within a blink, the wind and wings were gone.

Caden clung to the ground, still in a ball, shaking with pain and terror. He dared to open his eyes and stared in total shock. The Shade who had sliced his hand lay beside him. Its ragged breathing grated Caden's ears, and its ghostly white coat was stained red. Smoke curled from blackened fur on the Shade's side as raw, seared flesh sizzled beneath.

Caden blinked, struggling to understand. *What just happened? How did my fist just go right through him, but the fall wounded him? Or... did something else-*

"You cannot overcome us!" the Shade rasped. It looked to Caden, and its gaze was filled with hatred. Murderous rage.

Caden flinched back, realizing one of its ears had been ripped off. From its cheek to its mouth was a huge, bloody wound. Caden suddenly thought of the racoon who had tried to steal his dog's bone. Rover had nearly bit the thief's face right off. The Shade's wound looked the same. Caden had the sinking feeling something very important had just happened. Something he didn't understand in the slightest.

The Shade coughed, its bald, clawed hand cupping its bitten face. "You will survive," the Shade whispered. Its hate-filled gaze pierced through Caden. "Strangers will discover you." Caden blinked, his insides tightening with each breath. "They will drag you through the mud. They will claim your boots. Steal your clothes." Caden forgot to breathe. "And they will tie you down. For days. And days. And days." Caden couldn't hold back a groan as he began to shake. "No one will acknowledge your pleas."

"Stop-"

"And no one will save you."

"Please-"

"And you will curse yourself for not leaping from the rocks." The Shade grunted as it lifted itself to its bald feet, holding its burned side. It stared down at him for a moment longer, and Caden braced himself for the claws to end him. With a forced grin, the Shade turned and started limping away.

"Do it," Caden heard himself call. What was he

saying? "Do it!" He gasped and held still, every movement excruciating.

"No," the Shade said over its shoulder. "We're not done playing with you."

Caden choked a sob and lay in the dirt, unable to move. As he lay, a drop of rain splattered his back.

The Shade's remaining ear cocked, and it looked to the rising mountain and deeper into the forest. "Fortify your soul, boy. The strangers approach."

Caden shook his head, unable to speak, and the rain began to fall. *Can't be seen,* he thought. *I've got to move. I've got to hide!* He tried, but every ounce of strength had left him. He cursed under his breath and glanced around. The Shade was gone. He couldn't turn to look, but he suspected the one still on the ledge had vanished too.

Come on! He thought bitterly. *Move! Do something!* Footfalls crunched the forest floor. *Please!* Caden begged himself. *Please! Don't just lay there! You've got to... got to...*

He closed his eyes and slumped as the rain drenched him. He felt the dirt turn to mud and coat his clothes. *Should've jumped,* he thought, realizing there were several footsteps. *Shouldn't have trusted Nathaniel. Shouldn't have led the gang to Nockville. I want to go home. Mama Lo, please...*

Someone shouted suddenly. The footsteps stopped and began again, heading straight toward him. Caden set his jaw, holding his bleeding arm and drawing his wounded leg beneath him. *I am big,* he thought. *I am bad, I am mean.* Lies. All filthy lies. With a shaking exhale, Caden's thoughts returned to The Door. He knew what he saw was real. A real hallucination perhaps, but it was the only good thing he had seen in, well... his entire life. *Raw Peace,* he thought. *Raw Peace.* He repeated the thought again and again, even as the strangers surrounded him, and their hands grabbed and pulled.

TWELVE

A GRANDMA'S PRAYER

"YOU HAVE to let me go. I haven't done anything! Stop it. Stop!"

That's what Caden wanted to say. He tried, but his mouth wouldn't work. His eyes weren't seeing things right either. He'd see the forest, the stranger's boots, and then blackness. He'd stop hearing things too, for a moment.

I'm blacking out, he realized. When he could see again, he had moved, though still laid down. *That doesn't make sense,* he thought weakly. *I move by walking. I can't walk and lay down.* His arms were stuck over his head, and they were caught on something. Something was rubbing him from his back down to his legs. It was wet and rough. It kept catching his clothes and scratching him.

It's the ground, he finally concluded. *I'm moving on the ground. I'm... they're dragging me.*

Caden squeezed his eyes shut tight as the rain kept falling. Mud cacked him. He could smell it. Hands held his arms and kept pulling. Someone grabbed his legs. Without thinking, Caden kicked, his back arching as pain overwhelmed his senses. His boot collided with something solid. Voices lifted around him, but he couldn't understand. Was he passing out again? No, they weren't speaking English. Caden gulped for air as they kept pulling, dragging him over the forest floor and through the mud.

Through the mud, Caden thought, panic tightening his chest. *Next, my boots will be taken. And then my clothes. And then...*

He blacked out again. When he blinked awake, he lay in the mud with dark figures standing over him. They huddled against a tree, the tallest one stretched a blanket over the shorter ones. *I'm taller than all of them,* Caden thought. *I can take them! They won't tie me up!*

He told his arms to move and his legs to draw beneath him. Nothing happened. He huffed a desperate breath and tried again. Nothing. The stranger started talking again. Some moved away. Caden blinked hard, trying to stay awake. *Can't black out. Can't do that. Must see. Must know what's happening-*

Firm, huge arms hooked under him. Caden gasped as he was lifted up off the ground. He grabbed his wounded arm and tried to protect his leg. It didn't work. Any movement sent pain through his body. He moaned, suddenly finding the huge arms moving away. The ground was cold now and very bumpy. It rumbled too, vibrating with a loud hum.

I'm in a car, he realized, feeling the world lurch forward. *A truck bed.* Things pressed around him in the back of the truck and he slowly understood those things were people. He didn't know how long they drove. Something was laid on him. It shielded him from the rain. He shivered.

God's last laugh, Caden thought, remembering what the Shade had said. *This is it. But that Shade said I wouldn't die.* He swallowed hard, feeling his heart pounding. He wasn't sure what was the better option, to be in the hands of strangers or end it all.

He blacked out sometime along the way, but the next thing he knew, he was being carried. The rain wasn't falling any more, and the trees were gone. The sun somehow had become orange. Oh, wait, no. They were inside. Caden could hear the roar of a fireplace. Long shapes, that Caden finally realized were people, were huddled about him. Their words were buzzing white noise. He fought to keep his eyes open.

Tell them my name, he thought. *Psychos forget their prey is a person. I've got to remind them!* He opened his mouth to speak, but nothing came out.

The arms that carried him moved away and he realized he was lying down on something hard and flat. The floor? A table? He didn't know. A hand grabbed his hurt leg. Caden kicked with his free leg, hitting someone again. Orders were barked and hands grabbed his arms and legs, pinning him. Caden sucked air through gritted teeth, his heart trying to beat from his chest.

Get off! He wanted to scream, but he couldn't speak. *Get-*

They yanked his wounded leg. Caden's world descended into pain again. Someone was screaming. He was screaming, it took him too long to realize that. He dragged in a lungful of air and tried to wiggle free. He could hardly move.

"Please," he finally whispered. "Please-"

"Hold leg still." A woman. A woman was talking to him. Was that the dark shape over his head? Yes, there were her eyes. She was smiling.

All the evil things smile, Caden thought. He didn't stop moving. He had to keep fighting. He couldn't let Nathaniel win.

"Hold leg still," the woman repeated. "The little bone broke."

He gritted his teeth and closed his eyes tight. He didn't notice the tears falling. They were touching his wounded leg, moving something over it again and again. Caden's head swam with pain as his chest heaved with each breath. He opened his eyes and saw darkness closing in around the edges of his vision.

His arms and chest were cold suddenly. He heard something wet fall to the floor. He glanced down and, very slowly, registered the muddy, bloody ball of cloth was his shirt. Panic constricted his throat as the darkness closed in and he knew he was about to black out again. *Raw Peace,* he thought, grasping at something good to set his mind on. *I will feel that again.* He tried to imagine The Door opening, the overwhelming flood of security and belonging, but the darkness overtook him. He blacked out.

———

THE LAST TIME he had seen Mama Lo, Caden thought he had lost his mind. Turns out, he wasn't the only one. The day after he got his driver's license, Caden forged a sick note to his high school teachers, told Dad he had an away baseball game, and ordered his siblings to cover for him. They would. They always covered for each other.

He had driven the two and a half hours to Mama Lo's retirement home, trying not to think of the Hell that would be let loose if Dad learned the truth. Dad despised Caden and the other kids being around Mom's family. After the kids moved from Mama Lo's house into Dad's, he had done his best to isolate them. It didn't work.

Caden was surprised to find out Mama Lo was a very sweet, but very sneaky lady. Well, he could be sneaky right back. He remembered driving into the parking lot, so excited to tell Mama Lo he got a baseball scholarship to OSU. Not even Lil El knew about that yet. He raced through the retirement center, eager to find her.

He still felt the same jolt of surprise as her weak, thin arms wrapped around his neck. She kissed his cheek, her eyes watery and voice shaky. It was the first time she actually looked old. Sure, she'd always had gray hair, but now she was worn down. Shriveled had come to mind. Her letters and whispered phone calls had seemed to change once Papa died.

Caden had sat down, setting the flowers he got for her on the end table, and pretended he didn't notice anything different with her. Grief stabbed his chest, for he knew, sooner than he wanted, she would pass too.

"How's my kiddos?" she had asked as she held his hand. He felt her bones and veins through her paper-thin skin. He told her all the good, happy things he and the other kids were up to. He avoided the stuff about Dad's rage and how he wouldn't let Ellie date the nice guy on Caden's team. Trace's medication was late again because Dad forgot to order it, and Nate's drum set was destroyed, thanks to Dad stepping through the bass drum. Oh, and the fact that Caden was a few steps away from punching Dad.

No, he kept it light. Happy. She didn't need to hear more sorrow. But he knew she knew. He saw it in her eyes. He sat with a hunched back, his shoulders dropped as though the weight of the world rested on his shoulders. He wanted to tell her he felt all alone, like it was his job to protect and provide, but without authority. He felt stuck and ready to explode. Her weathered hand squeezed his suddenly, and he fought back tears.

"Let's pray," she had said.

"No." Caden didn't mean to snap at her, it just came out like that.

Her eyes filled with tears and she sighed. "Caden, you can't do this all on your own." He had lifted his chin, his gaze dark. "Life's too hard-"

"I won't use religion as a crutch."

"I don't. I use it as a stretcher." He had scoffed and turned away. "I can't do anything without God holding my hand, cheering me on, and, more often than not, cleaning up after me. He's a friend, Caden. An all-knowing, all-powerful friend who wants to help you. If someone who loves you knew the future and what's best, wouldn't you want to be their friend too?"

"God's not my friend."

"He's given you so much."

Caden couldn't withhold the piercing glare he had given her. "He killed Mom. He killed Papa. He's letting Dad slowly kill us." Regret crushed Caden as he saw her turn away. The pain in her eyes hurt him too. He sighed and looked at his feet. "He'll steal you too-"

"He doesn't steal."

"You said he was like a thief."

"A thief in the night, young man. Don't twist my words and, *most certainly,* don't twist scripture." Caden hadn't answered. "When he comes, we won't see it coming."

"Great. Just what I need. Someone else to rip the carpet out from under me."

"He's not like that."

"Maybe He's nice to you. He hates me."

Mama Lo shook her head and took his hand in both of hers. "He loves you, Caden. He *died* for you. When's the last time someone's done that?" Caden's jaw flexed as he shook his head. "He wants to be your helper. I pray that he does. I pray every single day for you kiddos. I pray that no darkness can touch you. That God sends His angels to protect you with their swords and His Consuming Fire. I know He hears my pleas. I know He will honor it."

Mama Lo paused and Caden glanced at her. He could tell she was waiting for a response. What could he say? That God lied all the time and only found enjoyment in people's suffering? *Just like Dad,* Caden thought. *They're the same.*

"Whatever you say, Mama Lo," he finally managed. She hadn't answered after that. He knew he was hurting her, but he couldn't fake trusting God. Not even if he tried.

Without another word, Mama Lo closed her eyes and started praying. "Dear Lord, thank you for my dear boy, Caden." Caden sighed and rolled his eyes, knowing her prayers were bouncing off the ceiling and splatting on the floor. "May You draw him closer to You every day. Keep wooing his heart, Father. Use His love of baseball for Your glory." Caden arched a brow but held his tongue. "May You protect him and not give him more than he can handle. Thank You for his life. Thank You for all You've done and all You will do."

He'd done nothing, Caden thought. *Just killed people I love.*

"And may he follow You someday. In Your holy Son's name, my blessed Jesus-"

She stopped praying and let go of his hand. Caden waited for the 'amen', but it never came. He looked up and stared, dumbfounded. Mama Lo was gone. In her place was the thin nightgown she had worn. The pillow was still indented where her head rested. Her hearing aids had tumbled onto the bedsheets, and, if he had looked, the screws implanted during a knee surgery years ago were tucked under the covers.

Caden stared wide-eyed, his breath quickening. He didn't move, blinking rapidly, knowing he was seeing things. Something clattered to the floor. He looked down and found the bracelet she had been wearing. *What just happened?* Screams had shaken him into motion. They came from everywhere. It had been the last day of the Old World.

The Day of Vanishing had driven everyone a bit insane and the world, very quickly, crashed. Planes fell from the sky. Massive car crashes made highways unusable. Hysteric mothers raced through the streets, demanding their babies or little children back. The government tried to regain order, but who could contain a worldwide panic?

The economy tanked. Trade stopped. Food became scarce. People became animals. Then the Giants popped up out of nowhere. Freaks too. Caden felt the Spirits had always been here, just unable to mess with the physical world. Now, their restraints were obviously gone. People talked of wars. Famine struck the land. Those who were left died right and left. The World Crashed.

He always steals, Caden had thought. *God takes what he wants. I hope He never wants me.*

Caden blinked his eyes as he lay in a bed, the memories of the last time he saw Mama Lo fading as he awoke. Had he been dreaming of her? He missed her.

Once Mom had been diagnosed with cancer, Caden and his siblings moved in with Mama Lo and Papa. Mom needed rest and knew she wouldn't be a good mom while she died at the same time. Mama Lo filled that role. That was the golden year. The year Caden finally had a chance to breathe. But it was only one year. Mom had died, and the family tried not to fall apart. Things didn't go so well. Mama Lo and Papa's health declined. The weight of the grief of losing their daughter and raising four young teens, not to mention dealing with their narcissistic father, had taken a toll. Caden tried not to blame himself.

Papa's first heart attack had occurred while driving Ellie home from a seminar about ancient Egypt. They nearly died in the crash. That had been enough for Dad to swoop in and trick the courts into giving him the kids back. Caden never understood why. It wasn't like Dad enjoyed having them around, or even liked them. *He liked controlling things,* he thought. *He didn't call us peons for nothing.*

Caden closed his eyes and gritted his teeth, hatred for his father burning in his chest. *Enough about the past,* he thought. *I have enough to worry about right now.*

His body ached and he felt his leg secured in some type of wrapping. He felt his chest and found clothing again, but it was fresh and new. He glanced around and saw he was in a small room with one window overhead. He could see roofs and chimneys with a star-speckled sky beyond. He was too tired to care where he was or who had him. He slumped back into his pillow.

Why did you take Mama Lo? He thought, glaring at the ceiling, hoping God could hear the loathing fury in his thoughts. *She was all I had left!*

"Nah, you've still got me."

Caden blinked and looked beside him. Trace lay in the bed with him. His brother smiled gently, his curly hair a wild mess across the pillow. " You look terrible. Like when Dad got mad at you for not coming home on time. But, you know, worse." Caden stared at him, trying to decide if he was crazy.

Trace smiled. "No. I'm alive. I got away. Nathaniel thought I died, that's why he left me. I tried getting to you, but you were already gone."

"I…" Caden stammered. "I would've come back."

"You didn't though."

"I didn't want to leave you."

"Why did you?" Caden didn't answer. "This sucks, man," Trace said. "I thought you got my back. I always had yours. Remember Grant? He was going to make you a slave and stuff. I got you out of that!"

"I'm sorry-"

"Sorry doesn't cut it." Caden closed his eyes and turned away. "You messed up, man," Trace said and grunted. "That's why Dad always called you GJ. I should start calling you that too. GJ."

Caden's eyes squeezed tight and he gritted his teeth. Another tear slid from his eye. "You're dead," he growled.

"I'm right here, idiot."

"I saw you. You're dead." Caden faced his brother again, his eyes dark. "Trace would never call me GJ."

"I just did-"

"And I didn't tell anyone Grant wanted to make me a slave."

Trace stared at him in silence. He sighed heavily and glared right back. "Fine."

Trace's cheeks shrank, and his bones could easily be seen beneath thin skin. His eyes seemed to bug from his head as they turned a dirty yellow color. His curly hair thinned to sparse tufts, and his body shrank down. His clothes seemed to swallow him, and when he lifted his hand, he looked like a skeleton with skin stretched over it. It was as though he withered to nearly nothing. Caden's stomach turned and he tried to move back. The pain and exhaustion kept him where he was.

"There," the shriveled creature said, its voice weak and rasping as though ready to collapse at any moment. "Happy?"

"Get out," Caden whispered. "I hate Withers-"

"I hate you-"

"Get out!"

"Want me to be Mama Lo?"

Caden's skin grew cold. "I said-"

"You have no authority over me. Over any of us."

"Get out!" Caden reached out to shove the Spirit, but his hand passed right through it.

The Wither coughed a horse laugh. "Or maybe Dad. You'll listen when I've got his skin on."

A lump formed in Caden's throat and he tried to drag himself away. *Why won't these Spirits leave me alone? Please! I can't keep doing this!*

"Caden!"

He froze, the voice and tone sending a wave of panic over him. He looked and saw his father lying in the bed. His eyes were dark, uncaring. Caden knew that look well; Dad had never been good at seeing people as well... people.

"Why did you kill your brothers?"

Caden flinched back, the words stinging like a blow. *Get away, please-*

Dad reached for him. Caden yelled. He shielded himself and punched at the disguised Spirit. Half his mind knew he was fighting a Spirit and couldn't hurt it, but the other half wasn't thinking. It was reacting, like a trapped animal.

Caden couldn't stop shouting. He didn't stop when someone burst into the room. He wouldn't calm down after a lantern was lit and the strangers surrounded his bed. The Wither was gone, but were they ever really gone? Caden heard someone talking, but, again, he wasn't listening. All he knew was God had killed his family, and he was surrounded by dangerous strangers and tormenting Spirits.

I've got to teach them not to mess with me! He thought, making a fist. He sent it into the closest stranger he saw. He hardly felt his knuckles impact and struck again. The strangers started shouting. He tried kicking, but his wounded leg reminded him to hold still. He yelled at the strangers, cursing them, threatening them. He didn't know what he was saying or who he struck.

Big, strong hands grabbed his shirt collar and threw

him onto the bed. He struggled, but couldn't free himself. "Quiet!" It was a man's voice, shouting inches from his face.

Caden yelled back and tried to hit him. The man grabbed his arms and pinned them to the bed frame. Something wrapped around his wrists. Caden thrashed, realizing they were tying him down. Just like the Shade said. He pulled on his bonds, but nothing worked. He was stuck. Trapped. Again.

"You don't hit anyone," the man ordered. "Or I hit you."

Caden sucked in painful breaths and finally faced the stranger. He was a big guy. His dark beard and hair nearly melted into the darkness around him. His dark brown eyes stabbed into Caden, and his hands were already balled into fists. *He's going to kill me,* Caden realized, seeing the danger in the man's gaze.

He forced himself to hold still and stop yelling. His body shook. His throat was raw. The man stared at him a moment longer and drew back. He turned to the others and spoke in their foreign language.

Who are they? Caden stared up at the dark figures, the lantern barely illuminating their features. Everyone listened as the man spoke. Someone else piped up, waving his arms about the room, and everyone glanced around, looking concerned. The big guy nodded and said something else. Everyone mumbled and left the room, all but the second man to speak.

Caden stared at the one who stayed as he grabbed a chair that had been leaning against the wall and set it beside Caden. He lifted his lantern and Caden got a look at his face. He was an old guy, his skin tan, and his graying hair brown and slightly curly. *Am I still in America?* Caden wondered as the stranger glanced at him.

"My name Hakeem." Caden just stared at him.

Hakeem smiled gently and, with his free hand, opened a little book he pulled from his pocket. He cleared his throat and began to read. His accent made it difficult to understand, but after a page or two, Caden could follow enough to understand.

"-guides me along the right path for His name. Even though I walk through the dark valley, I fear no evil." Caden's eyes narrowed. He had heard this before. It was something Mama Lo read when they lived with her. "Your rod and staff comfort me."

The Bible, Caden thought. *Why is he reading that?* He wanted to hit the book from Hakeem's hand, but remembered he was tied down. He stared at the ceiling, mad that he couldn't even plug his ears. He closed his eyes, trying to not listen to the lies in that old book.

THIRTEEN

GREEN LIKE POISON

CADEN DIDN'T KNOW how long he had been lying there. A few days? He had no idea. Whenever he was awake, which was rare, he felt his body shaking and his new clothes sticky with sweat. He always expected to find someone standing over him, an evil grin on their faces and a knife in hand. He thought he saw that one night, but the Wither shed the terrifying skin and disappeared as a woman entered.

She came into Caden's room often, usually humming a soft tune. Her face was bruised, tape and bandages covered her nose, but, in no time at all, she healed. It felt like no time to Caden, but he suspected it was far longer than he knew. *Who hit her?* He wondered, worry gripping his stomach. If they beat their own, what would they do to him?

She spoke to him, but he could never understand. He shook his head at her one day. "What are you saying? I don't speak that. English. Do you know English? Where am I? What do you want?"

She only smiled at him and continued inspecting his leg. He cursed under his breath and glared at her. She gave a quick look out the door and came to his side. "Where's your cow?"

Caden blinked, his heart leaping. "You do know English!"

"We like more milk."

"Where am I?"

"Where's your cow?"

"Does it look like I have a cow?"

She nodded. "Did. It walked all around you, am, in mud. Footprints all over when I found you."

"Why aren't you telling me where I am? What do you want with me?"

She held up a hand and sighed. "Peace. You need rest."

"I don't need rest! I need answers!" The woman smiled gently and returned to his leg. "Hay, come on," Caden said. "Please, just talk to me!"

"You are safe."

"That doesn't tell me anything!"

"Rest-"

"Talk to me!"

"Doctor's orders, young man. Rest." Caden growled through gritted teeth and lay still, knowing he couldn't make her do a thing.

He used to flinch whenever she drew close to his broken leg or wounded forearm. He knew now she was helping him. She had stitched his sliced hand, and his broken leg was sealed in a cast made of mud and clay. His forearm was wound in bandages and smelled like herbs. A man came in once when he first arrived. He didn't look like the rest. He was tall, blond, and seemed happy with what he saw. It tightened Caden's insides with unease. What did they want? Whatever it was, they needed him healthy.

Why? Caden glared at the ceiling as the woman

hummed and looked at his arm. The sunshine shone through his window at an angle. *What time is it? Have they been feeding me?* He didn't feel hungry. He felt weak, but it was more like he was tired, not starving. In fact, he wasn't starving at all. *They're taking care of me. I don't get it.*

He glanced up at the woman and wished she could answer all his questions. Her smiling face was wrinkled, and a few strands of silver hair disrupted her flowing black locks. Her broken nose was healing, and her black and blue cheek had turned a faded green. Her eyes were dark and skin tan, as with nearly everyone he saw in this place.

I can't be in America anymore. I'm in, like... the Middle East? His heart skipped a beat, realizing Egypt was in the Middle East. *Lil El,* he thought. *I could find her. I've just got to get away and-*

He gritted his teeth and looked away, anger tightening his chest. *You're still in America, you idiot! You can't get away from these people! What's wrong with you?*

The door creaked open and someone new entered. He was a bit older than Caden, and his dark eyes darted from Caden, the woman, and back to Caden. They stared at one another and Caden's heart quickened. *He hates me,* he realized and turned away.

The stranger ran fingers through his short beard and turned to the woman. They spoke, the language sounded random to Caden, but their tones surprised him. The guy seemed pissed at something. At her? She spoke back, waving her arms and pointing to Caden's leg. The guy didn't agree. He stepped from the door and she shook her head.

"Do you see her face?"

Caden turned with a start, staring at the stranger. His accent was there, but his English was good. "I... I do"

The stranger's eyes narrowed. "You did that."

Caden's brows furrowed as he glanced at the woman. "I didn't-"

"You kicked her. Right in the face."

Caden turned away and made fists, his quickened heart beating even faster. *That's why he's pissed. Great. Now what?* He was surprised, and a bit sad, to realize he didn't care what happened next. The woman sighed and gave Caden an apologetic look. She said something to the stranger, and he frowned.

Grumbling, he stepped closer to Caden and faked a smile. "Pretend I'm saying I'm sorry," he whispered.

"What?"

"Pretend I'm saying sorry."

The woman glared at them. "I hear you."

Caden glanced between the two strangers and snorted. "Is that your mommy or something?"

"Yes."

"Oh." A lump formed in Caden's throat.

"And you kicked her. In the face."

"Yeah, um-"

"So I should not apologize to you. You're the one that should be sorry." Caden didn't answer. "At least, you will be." Caden's fists tightened as his hands became cold. His throat bobbed, and he waited. Okay, he was a bit concerned about what happened to him.

"Asher," the woman said, drawing the stranger's dark glare off Caden. She shook her head, speaking softly, and Asher's frown darkened further. Muttering under his breath, Asher stepped closer to Caden and grabbed his wrists.

I am big, Caden thought, his heart beating faster, but he suddenly felt the ropes fall from his wrists.

"Get up," Asher said.

Caden rubbed his freed wrists and looked at his forearm. Light bandages wound about it, movement was stiff, with little pain. Caden told himself to sit up, but his abs didn't respond and his back refused to budge. "I said get up."

"I'm trying!" Caden grit his teeth and forced himself to move. He slowly sat up, his head spinning as he groaned. The woman came closer and reached out to support him, but Asher held out a hand and she stopped. They spoke and she frowned before turning and walking out the door.

Don't go, Caden thought weakly. *This guy doesn't like-*

Caden's head flew back as pain electrified his face. He crashed onto his pillow and held his bleeding nose with a moan. He wanted to just curl up on the bed and sleep some more.

Asher had other plans. The stranger chuckled and rubbed his now reddened knuckles. "I said," he whispered, "get up."

Caden lightly touched his nose and was surprised to find it wasn't broken. Feeling blood drip nearly every second, he slowly sat up again with an arm raised, waiting for another blow. Asher grunted and tilted his head to one side. "They're waiting." He walked to the door and swung it wide. "And take the pillowcase to clean your nose."

Caden obeyed, numbly removing the case and pressing it under his nose. His shirt was ruined. Probably the sheets too. He wanted to ask where they were going, or who was waiting for him. He didn't waste his breath, knowing he'll just have to wait to get the answers.

Will these other people punch me too? he thought. *Or worse. But why would they heal me?*

He gritted his teeth and tried to focus on his feet. How long had he been in this bed? His feet slowly slid to the floor. More like dropped. It was terrible. He forced his muscles to move and his legs to straighten, fully expecting to fall flat on his face and break his nose for sure. He teetered for a moment and took a shuffling step. The improvised clay and mud cast would've made anyone a clumsy walker.

Don't I get a crutch? He glanced at Asher and saw the amusement in his dark eyes. *Guess not.*

Caden shuffled one foot forward and dragged the casted foot, expecting any moment to find his face on the ground. His leg felt like it belonged to some stranger and he needed to convince that stranger to swing it forward on time to catch his body. He was surprised it didn't hurt much. Yet. He realized that, with each step, it was beginning to throb.

To distract himself, Caden looked around. He realized he was in a cabin and, once stepping outside, he was in the midst of the mountainous forest. The crisp mountain air tickled his nose as the rustle of wind through trees surrounded him. He was at a campsite with mini cabins bunched together. It looked like an old resort that had been converted into a village.

People walked about in the midst of their daily tasks. Their clothes were worn, and thick coats covered most. Some wore deerskins, and most looked like they needed a bath months ago. Two men carried a dead deer whose legs were tied to a pole held between the men. A dog padded through the houses. The very muddy road wasn't marked by tire tracks but by horse hooves. Caden felt he had gone back in time.

Not everyone was from the Middle East as Caden had thought. Most were Americans, but a few looked like they were from overseas. He didn't have much time to study, his leg was really starting to hurt, and they were nearing a large building. It had been the dining hall for the camp, but now had been converted into the meeting room for those in charge.

Once entering, Caden felt raw, hot warmth from a huge fireplace at the center of the room. The stone chimney rose up to the high ceiling. Before, it was a long table with a random collection of chairs, couches, and stools gathered around it. Only two seats were taken. When Caden entered, the conversation hushed.

They're looking at me, Caden thought, trying not to show the pain he felt. Asher not-to-gently showed Caden to a padded chair. Caden grabbed his knee as the pain from his leg throbbed up into his thigh. He felt the eyes of the strangers on him; it reminded him of Grant and his pack of wolves. *I won't be a slave,* he thought. *I won't!*

"Shalom."

Caden glanced up at the speaker, surprised. *That's what the kid Gideon said, the one that walked through The Door. Shalom. It's a real word?*

The speaker was a middle-aged man who looked like Asher. He had the same dark hair and beard, the same dark, near black eyes, and the same tanned skin. He was a big guy, and Caden had seen him before. *He's the one that pinned me down,* he realized. *The one who had me tied up.* Caden turned away. *That better not be Asher's dad. If he is... I kicked his wife in the face-*

"Call me Elijah Mizrahi."

Caden didn't answer. *If he says the same words as Gideon, maybe they know where The Door is. Or what it is.*

"What is your name?"

I could get information from them. They might actually be useful.

Caden glanced up. "Caden Johnson."

Elijah nodded. "Welcome. Umm... feel better? You were sick, very, very sick."

Caden frowned. "What about my leg?"

"Broken. Little bone, umm..."

"Fibula," a blond American said with a nod. "If I remember Dr. Ophir correctly."

Dr. Ophir, Caden thought. *Is that her name?* He thought

of the woman always attending to him. The same woman he kicked in the face. *Please don't tell me that's Asher's mom.*

"And your arm," the American continued. "It was grazed by a bullet. You're a very lucky young man."

Caden finally faced the stranger and froze. Wrapped around his neck was a Viper. Its scales looked like little flakes of bronze, catching the light as it moved, and it's triangular head was studded with little horns. A black forked tongue leapt from its mouth, and two pale eyes, green like poison, slowly turned and regarded Caden. Its four stubby legs shifted as its curled claws dug into the American's neck and shoulders, though he didn't seem to notice. Caden's pulse quickened as he turned away. He knew no one else saw the Spirit, and he hoped the Spirit didn't realize Caden's abilities. Out of the corner of his eye, Caden could see that the Viper kept staring at him, its pale eyes unfeeling and unreadable.

This is bad, he thought. *These people are bad! Why is one a Spirit's pet? Is he a Puppet too?*

"Your fever broke a few days ago," the American said, oblivious to Caden's uneasiness and the Spirit looped around his throat. "We nearly lost you. Thank God you're still kick'en!"

Caden blinked, realizing he knew the American. He'd seen him once before too. *He came to my room once. He said I'll fit the bill.* Caden's stomach turned as his jaw clenched.

"James West," the man said with a smile. His teeth were still white and, by seeing them, Caden realized no one else had such a luxury. "You've been here for four weeks."

Inside, Caden's heart skipped a beat. *That's so long! What've they been doing? I hardly remember a thing for this entire time!* Externally, though, he maintained his impassive stare and didn't flinch.

"Hi," Caden said. They sat in silence and Caden

sniffed, the pain in his leg turning his growing worry into irritation. "So... what do you all want?"

"Mr. Johnson," James said, "were you ever in an acting class? Part of a drama club?"

Caden lifted his chin and crossed his arms. *Don't trust a word from this guy,* he thought. *I bet the Viper's prompting everything he's saying!* "What do you want?"

James smiled. "We need you Mr. Johnson."

"Caden. Stop trying to butter me up."

"Fine, fine, Caden. Have you heard of Alex Whitney?"

Caden cursed. "Just spit it out!"

Elijah held up a hand and James sat back. "You look like Alex Whitney." Caden's frown deepened; he didn't like where this was going. Hadn't someone else said that too? "His uncle is looking for him. He's giving reward money to whoever finds him."

Caden cursed again and sat back in his chair. "You're kidding me."

"Three thousand tams," James said. "That's enough for anyone to begin a new life, even after the World's Crash."

Caden shook his head. "This is crazy," he muttered.

"You're telling me." Asher scoffed.

"Caden," James said, leaning forward again. "Can I call you Cade?"

"No."

"Fine, fine. Caden, this truly is a simple way to earn a fortune. All we need from you is to look like, well, yourself, and to play a little game." Caden's eyes narrowed. "I'll work with you, help you get into character per say, and-"

"No," Caden said. "I'm not doing any of this." *Especially with someone who's a Viper's pet!*

"But think of the fortune-"

"I don't need money."

"You could get all your heart's desires."

"Everything I desire is dead!" The room fell silent.

Caden shook his head and looked down. He didn't know if what he was going to say was foolish or not. He didn't care anymore. "Look, thanks for helping me with my leg and all, but I didn't sign up for this. I'm not going to help you con one of the most powerful and richest men in this part of the world. Dumb idea. Really dumb." Caden scoffed as he shifted in his seat. "You all must be desperate."

Asher pointed at Caden. "I told you this was a bad idea." He turned to Elijah and started talking in their language.

"Please, please, gentleman," James said, raising a hand. "Please don't speak Hebrew now. We want to hear your thoughts."

"Just give him to me," Asher said. "I need to pay him back for what he did to Ima." Caden's blood chilled, but he didn't move. Elijah arched a brow and motioned to Caden's nose and bloodied shirt. It had luckily stopped bleeding, but his nose ached and his shirt was ruined. "He fell," Asher said with a shrug. James huffed a short laugh.

I'm not a slave or something to toy with, Caden thought.

"Well, I believe Caden's *fall* has been retribution enough, Asher," James said. "Let's continue talking, like civilized people. We can come to an understanding."

"We have three weeks."

"I understand your deadline, however not all of us are under such pressures-"

"He won't listen." Asher shook his head and glared at Caden. "What could we expect from someone who jumps off cliffs."

Caden glared back. "What? That's not how I fell."

"Oh yeah? Tell us then."

Shades, Caden thought and bit his tongue. "Ah... I just... fell."

Asher's brows rose. "Do you see this, Aba?"

"Elijah, a heavy hand doesn't help anyone," James said quickly.

Elijah, who hadn't moved or shown concern the entire time, glanced between them and continued to stare at Caden. Caden watched him, realizing his fate rested on the stranger's decision. He looked down at his still throbbing leg, irritated at the suspense. They all knew Asher would get his way; everyone seemed to want to hurt or use Caden somehow. Everyone but his family.

And they're all dead, he thought, not wanting to lie to himself about Lil El anymore.

"Caden."

He looked up and stared at Elijah. *He's like Dad,* Caden thought, recognizing the willpower in Elijah's eyes. They were like Dad's, but a little different. Elijah was calm. Peaceful. It made Caden uneasy.

"What is something you want?"

Caden shook his head. "Nothing."

Elijah's head tilted to one side. "We all want something."

"Can you bring back the dead?" Elijah didn't answer as Caden forced a laugh and rubbed the back of his neck. "What do you want?" He faced Elijah again, a mocking smile curving his mouth. "You're so desperate for the money. What's it for?"

"Answer his question!" Asher snapped. "Or you'll *fall* again-"

"Asher, peace," Elijah whispered, and the young man fell silent. "A flight leaves in three weeks. It will take us home."

"Home, hum." Caden sniffed. "And where's that?"

"Israel."

Caden fell silent. An idea crashed through his impassive state and collided with his heart, sending it beating faster and faster. He lifted his chin, the idea stirring fear within him. A fear that was easily crushed. "Um…" he stammered, feeling excitement tingling his fingertips. "How, um… how far is Cairo from Israel?"

Elijah shrugged. "Six hundred, forty, maybe fifty kilometers."

"And that's, what?" Caden asked. "Like a thousand miles or something?" Asher chuckled.

"Not that far," Elijah said. "You could drive to Cairo in, am…"

This isn't worth it. I'll never get to Lil El-

"In nine and a half, ten hours.."

Caden blinked, his heart beating faster and the excitement tingled from his arms to his chest. "That's close," he muttered, his thoughts spinning. He ran a hand over his face as he questioned this new, brash idea. With a lift of his chin, Caden leaned forward and chose to ignore the Viper. He squarely faced Elijah and knew he had nothing to lose. Besides, he decided weeks ago he was going to save Ellie.

"I can be Alex Whitney for you," Caden said. "I will do whatever you want."

James beamed. "Marvelous-"

"Only!" Caden snapped, holding up a finger. "Only if you take me with you to Israel."

Asher laughed, then frowned sharply. "Wait, he's serious?" Caden didn't answer as he held Elijah's gaze.

"It not safe there," Elijah said calmly.

"I don't care."

"Evil will come to Israel."

Caden lifted his chin with a smirk. "You know the future?" Elijah, his face as serious as before, nodded. Caden fell silent. "I'm still going."

"Very dangerous."

"There's dangers here."

"No. Not like here. Worse."

"Oh yeah? Will there be massacres? Genocide? Freaks ruling over people and Giants seen like gods?" Again, Elijah nodded. A cold chill dampened Caden's excitement. He looked down a moment and shifted in his seat. "I am going with you." He turned back to Elijah, his jaw set and shoulders square. "Whether you like it or not."

Elijah stared at him a moment longer before making a small smile. "Very well."

Caden wiped his hands on his pants; they were sweaty. "Three weeks?" Elijah nodded.

"That's not enough time," James muttered. "There are other flights. Bide your time and-"

"No," Caden said, steel entering his voice. "We'll make three weeks work." He turned to James and settled into his chair. "You said you knew Alex. Tell me about him. I want to know everything."

James' brows rose as he regarded Caden. "Well, well, maybe you are the right fit after all. There is one more thing, however."

Caden raised his chin, readying himself. *And here's the catch-*

"We, unfortunately, must pull one of your molars."

Caden blinked. "Come again?"

"Alex Whitney had a golden molar, far left. It was a frivolous, flashy accessory to gain attention. I assume you don't have a gold tooth?" Caden didn't bother answering the ridiculous question. "Therefore, we must remove the evidence against you."

Caden stared at James, making sure he wasn't pulling his leg. *More like pulling my tooth,* he thought darkly. He glanced at the Mizrahis, who were watching his every move. He straightened with a gruff sniff. "Anything else?" James thought for a moment and shook his head. "Alright. Pull it. Start telling me about Alex."

Caden tried to focus as his leg continued to throb.

Shortly, his jaw would too. It was hard to listen because the Viper kept staring him down. Also, he kept thinking of Ellie, across an ocean, in a land he'd never seen. *But I might see it soon. I'm coming Lil El,* Caden thought. *Hang in here. I'm coming!*

FOURTEEN

BLOND

DOCTOR OPHIR WAS NOT AT ALL pleased by Asher's treatment of Caden's face. Caden didn't know what she was saying, but her waving arms and pointing fingers had made Asher frown. Caden tried to hold back a smile, but it was difficult. He couldn't smile after that because, later that day, James had called him over, holding a pair of pliers and a bottle of whisky.

Caden hadn't been one for a drink, but happily indulged as he wished his left molar goodbye. He offered some whisky to James, who looked nervous, but he quickly refused. "Alcohol and I are not compatible," he had said. "It can change a man."

Caden smiled, his face flushed with the liquor, and scoffed. "Makes you something nasty?"

"No," James said. "It loosens my tongue, and secrets are no longer safe with me."

"Have lots of secrets or something?" James had smiled, but the Viper around his neck turned its angular head and stared at Caden. He stopped asking questions after that. He honestly didn't remember his tooth getting ripped out, but the soggy gauze and constant bloody taste in his mouth were ingrained into his memory.

It was worth it. Everything had changed after learning Caden could actually have a chance to find Ellie. He had something to live for, someone to fight for. Something to distract him from the agonizing loneliness he felt whenever alone.

He should be hearing Trace talking incessantly about a bug or weird thing he found. He should be looking for his little brother, hoping a Freak hadn't found him or a talking animal tricked him into doing something stupid. Caden rubbed his head with a knuckled fist, hating himself whenever those thoughts haunted him.

He could still be out there. People survive bullet wounds. He might be starving. Paralyzed. I've got to go back-

His knuckles dug into his temple and he gritted his teeth. With a gasp, he stopped his shuffling steps and stared at the floor. Ophir's footfalls padded behind him. "Keep going," she whispered. "You are doing so well." He dragged in a breath and coughed, trying to ignore the crushing weight of despair. He looked ahead and kept walking.

He was in a hall between the kitchen and the dining room. It was the only flat floor inside no one really traveled through. Over the past few days, Caden had come to the hall to practice walking.

It had gotten easier when his cast had come off. Talk about a heart attack, watching Elijah take a hammer and chisel to the hardened clay and mud had been terrible. Asher had offered many times to hold Caden down, though Caden wasn't moving. The two young men avoided each other like the plague. Whenever they did make eye contact, Asher had a talent for making Caden feel squishable. "Don't touch my mom," Asher said loud and clear through those narrowed eyes.

Elijah hadn't said anything, but he had a killer glare too. It only happened once, over dinner on the first night that Caden wasn't bedridden. Over venison, some flatbread, and dandelion, leek salad, Caden had caught him staring. Caden had quickly turned away and ducked his head, his heart pounding. Asher would hurt him, but Elijah...

He'd kill him and not lose sleep.

Caden kept those thoughts in his mind as Ophir checked on his wounds and helped him regain his strength. When Caden wasn't pushing himself to heal faster, he and James would sit down and Caden listened.

Apparently, James knew Alex very well and wanted to make sure Caden knew everything about him. He had been given a notebook and a pen and it was half filled after their first session. "That's a good start," James had said. Caden felt like he was in school again. A school where students don't flunk a grade but get a bullet between the eyes.

"What would happen if we get caught?" Caden asked one day as he limped after James through the filled dining hall.

"If we are caught," James said slowly. "We will be given to Mr. Whitney's security detail. They are the best in Seattle."

"We're going to Seattle?"

James nodded as he set down his tray and ripped off a bite of flatbread. "The KUS runs the city, but they need Mr. Whitney to transport whatever they need wherever they need it. With this necessity, he is given freedom. More so than a common civilian."

"What are you saying?"

"I'm saying he has a prison under his mansion." Caden's insides coiled in on themselves. "And no one would blink an eye if we walked in and never walked out."

Caden stared at James in silence, his heart thudding in his ears. *Do it for Lil El,* he thought, realizing he no longer wanted to eat dinner.

"Great," he said dryly. "What if we bring in guns?"

James' eyes narrowed. "Might as well come in waving huge, red flags, singing *We, the Guilty Three.*"

"Haven't heard that song before."

"No guns. Nothing suspicious. Honestly, how have you lasted this long?" Caden shrugged. "Enough questions. Let's begin discussing Alex and his relationship with his uncle. Do you have an uncle?"

Caden shrugged. "I did."

"He passed? Hum, such is life now. Were you two close?"

"I didn't see him much."

"I see, I see. What about your father?" Caden could almost hear the grind of stone as the internal wall erected itself between himself and James. It was all he could do to shake his head. "Did you have a good-"

"He's dead."

"But did you-"

"Why does this matter?"

James smiled and scratched his scruffy chin. "I just want to make a relatable connection between Alex and his uncle and you and your father. I see you both had an estranged relationship." Caden didn't answer and James nodded. "Very good. That will benefit us."

"Why does my Dad matter?"

"Alex's father, Anthony, died when he was young. Sleeping pill overdose. His mother, Cynthia, was lost overseas after the Day of Vanishing. Growing up, Alex's only male, living relative is Thomas Whitney. Thomas could have been a father figure, but, alas, there appears to be something between them. Though Thomas and his wife Amanda sent Alex gifts, trips, tuitions, all a young child and man could want, they never invested in his life. Honestly, I believe the gifts were from Amanda, not Thomas. That is why this little game of ours will work; the Whitney's knew their nephew from afar. They never truly visited him one on one. They don't really know him. Therefore, your efforts will have a chance."

Caden's brows rose. "A chance, huh?"

James swatted a hand and huffed. "More than that, by the time we're through. But, you must see Thomas Whitney as a potential father figure who fell short. Very short. Now, Caden. Think of your father."

No, thank you-

"Now, pretend he's never liked you,"

Check.

"And never knew how to handle you."

Check.

"Now, pretend the KUS adores him." A hard lump formed in Caden's throat. "Pretend they'll stop at nothing to keep your father and his assets well and alive. All that he cared for. But this excludes you."

Thomas Whitney is loved by the KUS? Caden thought, panic slowly rising inside him. He knew James had mentioned that already, but it didn't click until now. *What if I see someone from Camp Little Rock? Would Nathaniel get on the radio and warn other camps about me?*

"Are you listening, young man?"

Caden blinked and masked his chilling idea with a smile. "Yeah. Keep going."

These guys won't take me if they know the KUS is looking for me. I may get them all killed. Or worse. Caden stared at James as he kept talking, but Caden didn't hear a word. *But I've got to get to Cairo. I can't just sit here anymore. And if I make it there, maybe the KUS communications won't travel so good. Maybe no one there will be looking for me.*

Caden blinked, firm resolve narrowing his eyes. He leaned closer to James, focusing on the complicated life of Alex Whitney, doubting he was going to live through this.

———

CADEN HESITANTLY STARED at the huge, smelly beast in front of him. It was just too tall and strong. He could see its muscles rippling as it moved. No animal that size could be called a pet. Asher, who had been loading supplies, stopped and glanced at Caden.

"It's called a horse," he said. "Hhhooorrrssseeee."

Caden glared at him and tried not to show his fear. He continued tying a sleeping bag, but he couldn't help but stare at the horses. There were five of them, one for Elijah, Ophir, Asher, James, and Caden. They didn't seem so big on TV, and they didn't stink so much either. He stared at their eyes, and they seemed wrong.

Octopuses have those eyes, he thought. *Not something with hooves. You shouldn't have eyes like that.* It was creepy.

Caden sighed and continued packing, knowing there was no other way off the mountain. James explained there were trucks hidden a few miles from the mountain that would take them to Seattle. Caden had breathed a sigh of relief when he learned that they would be traveling in the opposite direction from Camp Little Rock.

Trace is that way, though, he thought. *I can't just abandon my brother.* Caden yanked a little too hard on the bag's straps before he turned to the next bag. *I'm finding El,* he told himself. *Trace is… Trace'll be fine.* His vision blurred and he grit his teeth, fiercely rubbing the tears from his eyes. He limped to a satchel and held it out to Asher.

Asher grinned and walked by. "They don't bite," he said. "Too hard."

Caden cursed under his breath and stepped a little closer to the horse. It turned its head and regarded him with that creepy octopus eye. Caden lurched back with a gasp and dropped the satchel.

"You will be sitting on one soon," Asher said, smiling too eagerly. "Just touch it."

"Back off," Caden snapped.

"Weak?"

"Hey!" The two faced one another, Caden's heart pounding. *Who does this guy think he is?*

A deep, baritone voice shouted from behind and Caden flinched, glancing over his shoulder. Elijah stormed to the boys and set down his huge load of supplies. Caden stepped back, knowing it would've taken him two or three trips at least to pack all Elijah did at once. Elijah stepped between them and faced Asher. Caden looked away, hating when they spoke Hebrew when he was around. He told himself they weren't talking about him, but he was never too sure.

Asher motioned at Caden, his response loud and voice fluctuating with irritation. Elijah gave a quick, stern response and Asher shut his mouth. With a final glare at Caden, Asher sauntered over to Ophir, who was struggling with her horse's saddle.

Elijah watched his son for a moment and turned. Caden thought he was going to leave. His throat constricted when he realized the huge man was staring down at him. "Stay away from Asher." Caden suddenly found his feet very fascinating. He nodded without a word. "He picks fights. He will beat you."

"I'm not weak." Caden found himself returning Elijah's stern gaze. Half his brain ordered him to turn away and shut up. He didn't listen.

"Stay away."

Caden didn't answer until Elijah lifted his chin. Caden

stepped back and stared at the horses. "Sure thing, boss." Elijah grunted and started organizing the provisions he'd brought out. Caden cursed under his breath and helped Elijah.

"Everybody ready?" A cheery voice called. James laughed as he descended the stairs and joined the others, carrying a small pack under his arm. Caden rolled his eyes and didn't answer. James took a deep breath and smiled. "What a glorious morning to begin an adventure. With fortune as the prize!" James clapped Elijah on the back as he passed, who didn't acknowledge him one way or the other and went to his horse.

Yep, Caden thought darkly. *Great way to start an adventure.* His hair stood on end and he glanced over his shoulder.

Leaning against a cabin in the shadows was Dad. Caden's heart leapt into his throat. He forgot to breathe. He readied his legs to run. Dad grinned and melted into himself, condensing down to a small, ragged half-life. Caden sucked in air, regarding the Wither with wide eyes. A large hand lay on his shoulder. Caden groaned and lurched away, raising fists he didn't know how to swing. Elijah withdrew his hand, his brow pinched with concern. Caden turned away and ran a hand over his face.

I see nothing, he thought frantically. *I see nothing. I'm not cursed. I don't kill my crews! I, I'm fine!* He coughed and returned to his work, forcing himself not to look for the Wither. *I see nothing. I see nothing.* He cursed again, his heart thudding in his ears. *Raw Peace,* he thought. *Raw Peace. I'll find that again.* He didn't see the Wither again, but, for the rest of the day, he felt as though they were following.

———

CADEN LEANED back in the minivan, feeling like his legs were about to drop off his body. It was as though Asher had already beat him up, every muscle ached. He never wanted to see another horse again for the rest of his life. They had come down from the mountain and it had nearly taken all day. It might have taken a million years and Caden would've felt the same.

James nudged Caden as he buckled into his seat. "Ready for a pop quiz?"

Caden groaned as the van started up with a grind and rumble, Elijah at the wheel. The poor van was stuffed to the brim with supplies and passengers. Asher, luckily, sat in the front seat with Elijah, and Ophir in the seat behind. James and Caden took the back. They drove over the several branches that had draped the car, hiding it from view, and onto a dirt road.

"I hate tests," Caden muttered, rubbing his eyes before forcing himself to sit upright.

"Remember Cairo and your long lost love waiting for you."

"Shut up." James smiled. "Let's get this over with."

"That's the spirit. Now, who are you?"

"Alex Raven Whitney."

"And why are you named Alex?"

"After Alexander the Great, because my ol' man wants me to be awesome."

James arched a brow and nodded. "Ah… a down-played answer, but yes. Are you great?"

Caden closed his eyes, trying not to sleep, and shook his head. "Nope. I'm a straight up jerk."

"Mr. Johnson, please take this seriously."

"What? He is. Taking the thousands he got for his birthday to buy a plane, telling his uncle he'll learn to fly, only to purposefully crash it." Caden shook his head. "And just to see what it feels like to free fall? What a whack job."

"Yes, well… Good. You're remembering. Tell me about Alex."

"He's a crazy jerk. Doesn't care about anyone. Loves to watch people squirm or pee their pants. Can act nice just to get something out of you. Can't spell worth a darn. Likes pet birds and money most of all."

"Who was his last girlfriend?"

"The official one?" James grinned. "Trick question, hum."

"You've got a sound memory, kid."

Caden glanced out the window as the forested land-scape rolled by. *Not always the best thing,* he thought. *Some things are meant to be forgotten.*

"Lisa," he said. "Lisa was his last official girlfriend."

"And who was Alex's childhood valet?"

"You know, I don't think we need to dive that deep into Alex," Caden said. "Really, who's going to grill me on the old staff at Mr. Whitney's house?"

James shrugged. "You never know. Gunner O-"

"O'Brian, yah I know."

"Good. Any questions for me?"

"Can you stop talking now?"

James smiled. "What do you think of blond hair?"

"Blondes? They're hot. If they're tall with a little chunk to them. I like curves."

James laughed and shook his head. "What do you think of your own hair dyed blond?"

Caden's eyes narrowed and he regarded James with a dark frown. "Great," he grumbled and slumped back into the chair with his eyes closed.

"Don't worry, kid," James said. "It'll wash out in a few months. We'll do that at our next stop. Rest up now. When we arrive at the Four Seasons Hotel, that'll truly be your first test. You'll meet with the head of Whitney's security, Mr. Bobby Rut."

"So you've said," Caden muttered as he focused on finding something to rest his head on. He needed a distraction, his heart was beginning to pound faster than necessary, and his hands started to tingle with anxious anticipation.

James lay a firm hand on his shoulder and Caden glanced at him. "This is serious."

"I know-"

"If you mess this up and we're caught, it's all over. Mr. Bobby Rut knows the Whitney family, he has for years. He even worked a bit for Anthony Whitney when Alex was in his teens. He will know you are a farce if you fail to pull this off. We won't see a single tam, and you won't get to Cairo. You know why? Because we'll all be dead."

Caden shrugged off James' hand and set his jaw before leaning closer to him. "I understand." He blinked, the wheels of his mind turning. "If we do get caught, call me Oliver Deker." James' eyes narrowed. "I have family. I wouldn't want the Whitneys coming after them."

"I thought everything you wanted is dead."

"I have an aunt and uncle," Caden said firmly. "They're still alive." *Unlikely, but he doesn't need to know that.*

James studied Caden a moment longer before sitting back. "Very well, Oliver Deker."

Should've introduced myself by that name, Caden thought, wishing he wasn't always exhausted or wounded so he could have good ideas for once. *Nathaniel knows my real name. He won't be looking for an Oliver.* James didn't ask any more questions and Caden lay back, making a note to tell everyone else his pseudonym. He closed his eyes, he desperately needed sleep. He needed some escape from this crazy world.

He dreamt of a blond kid crashing all the airplanes in

the world with a snap of his fingers. He was laughing hysterically, his eyes bloodshot and wild. But it wasn't Alex. It was Caden. There was a bullet wound between his eyes, the blood trickling down and dripping off the tip of his nose. Caden woke up drenched in sweat.

FIFTEEN

ONE MASSIVE CHAIR

THAT EVENING, as everyone rested around a campfire and tried to stay warm, Caden kept cycling through everything he knew about Alex. He had to get this right. He had to be perfect. Beyond perfect, he had to be Alex. *I can do it,* he thought, then sarcastic words spoken far too often shook his heart:

"Yeah, sure you will, GJ." His dad never knew when to shut up.

Caden touched the tufts of his still wet hair and knew the dark color was now a dirty blond. James had done his best, bleaching his hair first, which burned his scalp. Nobody warned him. How did girls do that all the time? He had been blond as a kid, but it felt weird now. Ophir had a small pocket mirror, and Caden tried to catch his reflection by firelight.

James sat on the van's floor, the door wide open as he whittled a stick. The Mizrahi family huddled together and softly spoke in Hebrew. Elijah was pouring over a small book, after a while, Caden realized it was the pocket Bible. It looked like the one Hakeem had read to him. *Where did he go?* Caden thought, realizing he had only seen the elderly guy once. *What does it matter?* He thought with a sniff. He huddled deeper into his blankets, glad for once he couldn't speak Hebrew; the Bible was the last thing he wanted to hear.

Dinner had been boiled eggs and jerky with a side of water. Yummy. *Better than canned cat food*, Caden reminded himself. *It could always be worse.*

He glanced up and stared at the vast collection of stars scattered overhead. It always surprised him how many stars there were. Before the World's Crash, he'd never seen so many stars. Now that electricity was reserved for the wealthy, the stars' glow were no longer challenged. The fire crackled and Caden sighed. His insides were, for once, not twisted into knots. His pulled molar wasn't throbbing as much, and the gape in his gums had stopped bleeding. At that moment, he wasn't afraid for his life or worrying about anybody else. Sure, they could be all dead by the end of the week, but that was days away. For now, he just wanted to sit and rest.

Maybe this is what it's like on the other side of The Door, he thought. *But I don't think their peace ends like it does here-*

"Hay, James," Asher piped up. "I've been thinking."

"Hum?" James grunted.

"How close does this kid's face match Alex's?"

Caden's eyes narrowed as he glared at Asher. "I'm sitting right here."

"Very close," James said. "He has the right build. Skin tone is accurate. He's adapting to Alex's walk well after those lessons."

"That's not what I asked."

Caden lifted his chin, his hair slowly standing on end. *So much for peace.*

"His face," Asher repeated. "How close is his face?"

James set down his whittling stick and turned to Caden. He shrugged. "Close."

"But not perfect."

"Well, no one is perfect-"

"He's going to see Alex's family."

"They haven't seen him since he was six-"

"But they've seen pictures."

Caden tilted his head to one side as anger tightened his chest. "What are you getting at?"

"His face," Asher said, still talking to James. "We'd be idiots to think they'll just, umm, glance over wrong details."

James frowned and sat up straighter. "What do you suggest?" The Viper wound about his neck lay its scaly head on his shoulder. As it moved, its pale green eyes caught the firelight.

Caden turned away, his heart quickening. *What's that Spirit up to?*

Elijah shut the little Bible and shifted. "Bandages."

"But, once removed, our lie will be exposed even more blatantly."

"Umm..." Ophir stammered. "What about sunglasses?"

"They can also be removed," James said.

He does have a good point, Caden thought, glancing at Asher. He stared at him for a long moment before setting his jaw and lifting his chin. "Asher." The young man grunted. "You still haven't paid me back for breaking your mom's nose." Asher set down his jerky and faced Caden. His shadowed eyes seemed to sparkle. Caden cursed under his breath but didn't move.

"No," James said, raising a hand. "There is another way-"

"I remember kicking her," Caden said, forcing himself to smile. "It was fun."

Asher needed no more encouragement. Caden took in a

breath and closed his eyes. He'd been punched before, but not like this. The world spun as Asher's fists came down. Caden found himself flat on his back, his head jerking right then left.

He raised his hands defensively without even thinking. It was a flimsy defense against Asher's obvious training. Someone started shouting. Caden couldn't see, and something had filled his mouth. Asher finally stepped away. Caden rolled on his side, gasping and coughing. He couldn't see right. What was wrong with the firelight? It was flashy and bright and made his head spin. No, wait, that was just his head spinning. He opened his mouth and something flowed out into a little puddle. Caden stared at it with one eye, the other already swelling shut. It was blood.

That better be good enough. He tried to sit up but couldn't. It took some time to realize Elijah was kneeling beside him, his hand on his shoulder.

"Ho's satt?" Caden slurred.

Elijah's large hand grabbed his shirt and dragged him upright. Caden's head felt like a bucket of sludge getting sloshed back and forth. He panted, feeling blood dripping from his face. Was it his nose? Or more from his mouth? He glanced at Elijah just in time to see his fist increasingly getting bigger.

Then he was on the ground again, his head on a pillow, with a warm blanket thrown over him. A woman was talking. Ophir. She was angry. Caden tried to open his eyes, but one was sealed shut. It was hard to move. He was glad he already ate dinner, he didn't think he could chew. Or open his mouth. Or swallow. He tried to roll over, but Ophir snapped at him, grabbing his shoulder and gently laying him down.

Asher chuckled. "She said you almost got a concussion." Caden had a lot of fun, crude remarks to fire back at

Asher. A pity his mouth was out of commission for the moment.

"Well," James sighed. "No one will recognize him now. By the time we reach Seattle, he'll be a swollen, black and blue mess."

"Nice," Asher said.

Caden heard the smile in his voice. Ophir shook her head and spoke softly to Caden. She dabbed at his cut cheek and split lip. He hardly felt it. *I better get to sleep before the adrenalin wears off,* he thought. He relaxed the best he could, hoping his dreams didn't haunt him again.

"Mr. West," Elijah said, his deep voice so different from the others. It drew Caden from his rest. It wasn't that Elijah's voice was threatening or hostile, it simply commanded attention. "How much longer to Seattle?"

"Two days," James said. "We're making good time."

"Money supply?"

"Oh, could be better. I must save a great deal for Seattle. There are bribes to pass around, especially if we want this boy to get out alive."

They're talking about me, Caden thought wearily. *If. James said if they want me to live.* Caden's throat bobbed, knowing the Viper wound around James' neck was having far too much fun. There was silence for a while as the fire popped and an owl hooted overhead.

"I have to give it to you, kid," James muttered. "You are very dedicated. Whoever is in Cairo must be very special."

Caden didn't answer as he tried very hard not to think of what the Shade had said. His Lil El, buried under sand and scorpions in an unmarked grave. No, he wouldn't think about it. He just dreamt of it.

———

A FEW DAYS LATER, Caden slowly awoke and stared at the white ceiling. The maple fan overhead spun lazily, giving a soft humming sound. Caden groaned and started to rub his eyes, but he stopped for two reasons. First, his face had become a swollen black and blue mess, like James said. One eye still couldn't be opened, it was hard to speak because of his swollen and split lip, and he got dizzy way too much.

The second reason he stopped was because there was a fan. And it was spinning. Not with a string or someone manning it. It was like... magic. He opened his one good eye and watched it in dumbstruck awe. The fan kept spinning, as though oblivious to the World's Crash, limited supply of electricity, and, well, everything.

We made it, Caden remembered. *We're in the hotel.*

The last two days had been a blur. He had slept through most of them, trying to regain his strength from Asher's contribution to his disguise. Caden knew he would punch his lights out too, if they survived and he learned how to punch like that. He vaguely remembered the honk of other cars, blinding lights from lightbulbs, not warm firelight, and the soft oblivion he now knew was the bed.

This is Heaven, Caden thought as he tried to stretch out. He bumped into something and found James laying inches away from him, his mouth slack and drool dampening his pillow. Caden just ignored him. He had seen worse. He ignored Elijah when he came into the room and Asher when he opened the drapes.

"Get up!" Asher snapped. Elijah muttered in Hebrew and Asher smiled. "What? We've got to go!"

Caden moaned and closed his good eye. "Go away."

"Wow," Asher sighed. "You're looking worse every day." Caden remembered his fingers were functioning well and showed Asher his middle one.

"Stop this," Elijah said. "Breakfast does not last all day."

That got Caden moving. He still felt dizzy whenever he moved too quickly, but after stumbling into the wall a few times and ignoring Asher's comments about drunk sailors, Caden managed to shove himself into clothes. Asher went on ahead to get them a table, and to Caden's surprise, Elijah stayed. He sat down at a desk and withdrew stationary and a pen from a drawer. Caden arched a skeptical brow as Elijah began to quietly pen a letter.

It didn't take long for the two to be ready to go. Ophir joined them as they walked down the hotel's hall. Caden couldn't help but watch Elijah kiss Ophir's cheek and call her *neshama*. He learned later that it was Hebrew for sweetheart. Elijah and Ophir linked arms and continued walking, talking softly to one another. Caden glanced at Ophir and saw that her nose wasn't black and blue anymore.

"Hay, um… Mr. Mizrahi?" Elijah glanced at him. "Can I say something to Mrs. Mizrahi?" For the second time since meeting Elijah, Caden saw him smile. Sort of. It was more like a small lip-twitch, but it counted for something. He nodded once and Caden glanced at the expectant woman. "Um, how's your nose?" She smiled and nodded, touching her nose gently. She always had the best, real smiles out of everyone.

"Much better, thank you. How are you? Umm, your face? Still looks very bad."

He scoffed, which hurt his split lip. "Still hurts," he muttered, trying to relax his face, and Ophir gave him a saddened frown. *She acts like she really cares about me,* Caden thought. *It's not normal.*

The couple continued speaking Hebrew and Caden listened. Only one word made sense to Caden: *shalom. The people who live behind The Door said that word too. What does it mean?* Caden gave Elijah a sideways glance and took in a breath.

"Um, I-I was wondering what *shalom* is. I heard it before. I-" He stopped short. Was he really going to tell them about The Door? "What's it mean?" he asked quickly.

"It's said to greet and bid farewell," Ophir said. "It means harmony, prosperity, and peace."

Peace, Caden thought, not surprised.

"Okay," he said. "Ah... what about *saba*? Do you know that one?"

Ophir giggled. "Why do you know these words?"

"They're just, um, I just heard them once. Never mind."

"In Hebrew, *saba* is grandfather."

Caden blinked, remembering Gideon calling him that. *Grandfather? But... that doesn't make any sense! I'm not even old!* Caden nodded as he fell silent, remembering Gideon and the older woman staring at him through The Door. She knew him obviously; she said his name. But the kid called him grandpa? Caden rubbed his temples and took in a sharp breath as he faced ahead. *So,* he thought. *They speak Hebrew behind The Door. Maybe I should learn it too. If I ever see those two again, we could talk.*

Breakfast was wonderful. Apples, bagels, jam, scrambled eggs, and, coveted most of all, coffee. They could only smell the heavenly brew because a cup was fifteen tams a pop. Once James joined, much later than the others, he announced that Caden needed to be properly outfitted with clothing. He knew where they needed to go, which brands to buy, and the style Alex had worn.

"We're not getting too much," Caden cut in.

"Whatever do you mean?"

"Because you said you need to save some money for,

you know… getting me safely on that plane with the Mizrahis."

"Ah… that, yes, well. There will be enough." Caden's brows rose. "I assure you." Caden crossed his arms. "Have I let you down thus far?"

"You've not had a chance to," Caden said. "And the fact that the first chance you could let me down could cause my death, I'm going to be a bit pessimistic."

James sighed. "Then we'll get half of what I intended."

"I will," Elijah said. "I and Caden."

James glanced at him. "You and-Mr. Mizrahi, you and your family can prepare for your trip back home-"

"You go to House Whitney. Make bribes. Talk to your people. Get things ready. I can't do that. You can. Don't waste time. Plane leaves in five days."

"Mr. Mizrahi-"

"Why do you do that?" Caden asked. "You always use people's last names when you want them to do something for you." James shot Caden a glare that wasn't just an irritated glance. It suddenly reminded Caden of Grant. Still lounging across James' shoulders was the Viper. Its black tongue suddenly lashed and two sickly green eyes opened and regarded Caden. There was poison in those eyes.

"Fine," James said. His voice was calm and heightened the ice in his glare. "But follow my directions exactly."

Caden didn't answer. *What did I just see? Was that the real James?* He blinked, watching the man he met a few weeks ago continue eating. *Is his name really James?* He was suddenly glad Elijah was coming with him. *Elijah could be lying too. They might be terrorists. They could be bringing bombs onto the plane and will take us down over the Atlantic.*

Even as he thought those things, he knew the Mizrahi family was anything but authentic. There was something about them, something different. He couldn't put his finger on it. They nursed him back to health, and yes,

Asher did beat his face and Elijah had a killer jab, but he had it coming. They were letting him join them to Israel. They were being honest with him.

Why are they like that?

He was going to muster up the courage to ask Elijah while out, but the shock of seeing a sort-of functioning city distracted him. Because electricity was reserved for the high and mighty, bikes were everywhere. There were some two-seater and even three-seater bikes. Some horses trotted here and there and, on occasion, a car sputtered by. The rules of the road seemed to default back to one hundred years ago. Everyone went where they wanted, how they wanted, but was sure to move aside if something bigger and faster was traveling down the road.

Most stores had changed from luxury, impractical, or frivolous items to more essential retail stores. Several stores were converted entirely into greenhouses, the space consumed with plants that were heavily guarded. Instead of advertisement boards, teens stood on street corners and shouted their employers' latest sale or deal. Between all, bicycle messengers with red helmets peddled swiftly between people, from the road, onto the sidewalk, and back again, always going somewhere way too fast.

In the distance, Caden could see a plane had crashed into a skyscraper, probably on the Day of Vanishing, but no one had dealt with it. The Space Needle was gone. Caden heard one of the advertising teens shouting about an art exhibit at the New Needle. The kid held up a painted poster of the Space Needle flat on its face, apparently still open for business.

Above all the noise and activity was the stench. The jobs that removed waste seemed to not exist at all anymore. Everyone walked around with bandanas close to their faces, ladies carried flowers to smell instead of the rancid air, and many stores sold discreet nose plugs. Caden found himself just plugging his nose half the time.

In every crowd, on every street, and in every store was an ally of the King's United Society. The stark white uniforms were a blinding contrast against the dirty, unkempt city. Most weren't armed, but the Sentinels were. The Sovereign Lion watched all from the altered US flags fluttering from several buildings and flagpoles.

Whenever they drew near one, Caden looked over his shoulder, down another street, scratched his head, or something to hide his face more. He kept expecting Nathaniel to step from hiding, his white uniform still splattered with his brother's blood. Caden swallowed the hard lump of hatred in his throat and told himself to keep moving. If Nathaniel had sent word through the KUS radio coms, this would be the first real test of disguise Caden faced.

So far so good, he thought, passing a little girl and her mother, their white clothing nauseating. *I need a distraction,* Caden thought. *Just something to take my mind off-*

"You cannot fight."

Caden glanced at Elijah and frowned. "Yes I can! You've just never seen me in action!"

Elijah firmly shook his head. "When Asher marked your face. You, umm…" Elijah held up his fists and blocked his face.

"My defense?"

Elijah pointed at him and then scowled. "Very, very bad."

Caden crossed his arms and turned away. *I wasn't supposed to defend myself,* he thought. *That was the point!*

"I teach you."

Caden scoffed. "Oh, right. When?"

"In Israel."

"I'm going to Cairo. I'm not sticking around in Israel."

Elijah kept walking, his expression not changing the entire conversation. *Is he mad?* Caden wondered, seeing his pinched brown and set jaw. *No... He always looks like that.*

"It is not wise to go to a new place, where they speak languages you do not know, without money, food, or a real plan."

"I have a plan." Elijah arched a brow and glanced at him. Caden scratched the back of his head and sighed heavily. "So, what? I'll stay with you guys?" Elijah nodded.

Caden stared at him; he had been kidding. *I can't stay with you, I can't give you anything. Once this con is over with, you won't need me anymore.*

"You need friends." Elijah said.

"No, I don't."

I'm cursed, he thought, remembering Harrison's words. *I kill everyone who's close to me.* Elijah didn't answer. They walked another block, nearly getting run over by the red-helmet bikers, and kept going.

"I thought you were a Christian," Caden said. "Christians don't fight. Turn the other cheek. Love your enemy. Ring any bells?"

"Ring bells?"

"Ah, I mean, like, sound familiar?"

"We fight when Yahweh says to."

"Who's that?"

"God."

"Then just say God."

"It is Hebrew for God." Caden didn't answer as he suddenly glanced down at his leg. He was still limping, but he hadn't walked this long in a while. The pain was starting to get to him. "Sit?"

"No, I'm good." Elijah didn't listen and sat down on a bench. Caden joined and sighed as the weight came off his leg. "Will it be that dangerous there? In Israel?" He whispered. Elijah nodded. "Like, a war?"

"Wars."

"You mentioned genocide." Again, Elijah nodded. Caden cursed under his breath and looked away. What was he doing? Down the street, a Shade walked along the sidewalk. Caden's heart stopped. *Is it Scar?* He had given the Shade who attacked him a name. He figured he'd see it again. Seeing this Shade wasn't scarred, Caden turned away, pretending he couldn't see it. "Um..." he stammered. "Who told you all this future stuff?"

"The Bible. And Pastor Hakeem."

"Hakeem! Yeah! Where'd he go?"

"Went home." Caden stared at him a long moment and Elijah dipped his head. "He passed."

"Ah. So, he died, not he went home." Caden shook his head, biting back some low jabs about Christians.

"He showed me Yahweh," Elijah continued. "He showed me life." Caden's brows rose, but he held his tongue. "He was a good man. I'll see him again."

"Hum," Caden grunted. "What other crazy stuff did he teach you?"

"The antichrist will rule. He who everyone calls the king."

A chill ran down Caden's spine and he scooted further from Elijah. "Keep your voice down!" he hissed. "Can't you see the KUS everywhere?"

"I see all enemies."

"Then don't talk like-"

"The truth should be heard if enemies are close or not."

"Great, man, just not when I'm sitting next to you!" Caden cursed and ran fingers through his hair. "Are there more KUS in Israel?"

"I think much more."

"Great. You're gonna talk like this there too?" Elijah grinned and Caden stared at him. "It's not a joke. They'll kill you!"

"I speak what Yahweh wants."

Caden shook his head and turned away. "Religious nut."

"No, not religion."

"Yeah, yeah," Caden said and waved a hand. "A life-style. I've heard the sales pitch before."

Elijah fell quiet and Caden could feel him staring at him. "No matter what happens," he said quietly. "Yahweh will go before me and follow me. He places his hand of blessing on my head. I hear him say, 'this is way, walk in it'. So I walk. That is why we go back to Israel. My people, and everyone, must hear truth."

"And what is truth?" Caden snapped.

Elijah's head tilted to one side, as though amused. "You not the first to ask that. But I pray you are wiser than Pilate."

"Who?"

"The man who asked what is truth while face to face with Yeshua."

"English! That's all I speak-"

"Jesus. Pilate asked what truth was when Jesus was standing right there. Incredible. Jesus is truth. He was right there." Elijah shook his head and lay his huge hand on Caden's shoulder. Caden thought of pulling away but knew resisting a bear never ended well. "I pray you will not be as blind when Yeshua stands before you. He will not fail you."

Caden's jaw flexed as he turned away, biting back all the crude words building up inside him. "It would take a miracle for me to not punch Jesus in the face."

Elijah actually laughed. "Honesty is good. Really, now. What miracle do you need in life?"

"What do you care?"

"What do you need from God?"

I need Him to keep Ellie alive, Caden thought. *He should know where she is-*

Caden scowled. "Nothing. I've never needed Him."

"You paused too long."

He scooted away from Elijah again. *What is he trying to get me to do?*

"You need God to prove Himself," Elijah muttered. "He can. He will."

There's nothing He can do to change my mind, Caden thought darkly. *He is a lying, cosmic joke.*

"Make a deal with Him."

"What are you talking about?"

"If He takes you to Cairo and you find whatever you're looking for, you follow Him. Forever."

"I don't need Him," Caden grumbled.

"But you need that miracle." Caden closed his good eye, wishing he wasn't so readable. "You need Him. You know you do." Caden gritted his teeth and looked the other way, unwilling to admit it. "Think about it," Elijah said as he stood. "Wait here."

Caden didn't acknowledge him as Elijah stepped from the bench and flagged down a messenger bicyclist. Caden crossed his arms and sat back, his glare firm and unmoving. He glanced up beyond the skyscrapers to the blue sky. He shook his head and made fists.

With a sigh, a muscle in his jaw flexed. *Well, God, what do You say?* He thought. *Sounds like a good deal to me. Give me back Ellie. Alive! In one piece! You hear me? Not all twisted and crippled or a Puppet or mentally broken because of this messed up world. Healthy! Alive! Understand? And then... then we'll see if You're really as good as Mama Lo always said.* Caden waited for the lightning to leap from the clouds or an angel to slap him for praying an unholy prayer. Nothing happened.

Typical, Caden thought as he turned from the sky. *It's Your time to prove Yourself.* Again, nothing happened. Well, maybe something did. For some reason, Caden remembered an old Bible story Mama Lo used to tell. Something about a prophet proving God was real by sending fire down from heaven on Mt. Carmel. *Wasn't the prophet's name Elijah?* Caden's eyes narrowed and he glanced at Elijah as he handed something to the cyclist. *Coincidence,* he thought. His stomach twisted, remembering Mama Lo said God makes everything happen, there are no coincidences.

———

"IT'S TIME TO GO!" James called as Caden looked at himself in the mirror.

I have blond hair, Caden thought, gently touching the foreign tufts of yellowish strands again. He stroked his jaw, feeling the smooth skin and lack of scraggly beard.

"I think he's waiting, Caden."

Caden sighed and looked down. He had been dreading this moment. It was time to meet with Bobby Rut, the head of Whitney security. He would clear Caden and permit him to see Thomas and Amanda Whitney themselves. Apparently, since Thomas' promised reward money, there had been dozens of 'Alexes' to suddenly appear. The security detail at House Whitney cleared all such claims. When there were more claims than the security team could handle, they took a different approach to dealing with the liars. Those hopeful candidates would go to their interviews and, no surprise, would leave with a missing limb or, for some, never were heard from again. The claims greatly diminished.

I am big, Caden told himself. *I am bad.* He stopped and let out a sigh. *Raw Peace. That's all I need. Whatever that is... I need it now.*

He followed James from their luxurious room into a small meeting room on the ground floor. It had floor-to-ceiling windows showing Elliot Bay, and the welcoming furniture had been removed. Two chairs remained and they faced one another. One chair had very, very long legs, making the sitter about four feet above the ground. Small stairs leaned against the legs and led up to the seat. The other was unnaturally enormous.

Caden stopped short and stared at the two chairs. His nervousness vanished and panic overtook him. It grabbed his throat, making his knees weak and his hands clammy. He was sure his face was drained of color.

James walked past him and gave him an apologetic look. "I was instructed not to inform you of Mr. Bobby's, um... advantage."

Caden swallowed the hard lump in his throat. They were on the ground level, the front door wasn't far at all. *I could get away in this city. They couldn't find me. I can get to El another way.* He didn't move, knowing that was a stupid idea. He had to do this.

Caden took a deep breath and forced himself to approach the tall chair. He stared up at it and glanced at the massive one across. "James," he said as calmly as he could. "Warn me the next time I'm meeting with a Giant."

SIXTEEN
A GRINNING SNAKE

NO ONE KNEW where the Giants came from. There was no sign of them before the Day of Vanishing, but most people suspected they had been here all along. Some said they hid in caves, or deep in mountains, or hibernated like bears. Some conspiracy theorists said they were science experiments the government had been working on. Something about genetically altered human weapons; the next stage in evolution. The real crackpots suggested the people that vanished had turned into the Giants somehow because that made total sense. Or that the aliens who stole their loved ones sent down Giants to replace them.

Caden didn't believe any of it.

All Caden knew was there were no Giants in the world until after the Day of Vanishing. Then, Giants popped up all over. Not little baby Giants. Full grown, intelligent, healthy, humongous Giants. And everybody loved them. Even after they took over cities and stole all the resources in communities. What happened to the fairy tales of dumb, clumsy Giants that were always too slow to catch the hero? They were supposed to be disproportionate, sleepy all the time, with lots of weaknesses. Caden wished the stories were true. Wished all he needed was a golden harp to sing the Giant to sleep and he could escape.

Stop it! He scolded himself. *This is real! Not some fairy tale!* His hands were so cold and clammy, he didn't feel the smaller seat's wooden ladder when he grabbed it. With a deep breath, Caden rid his mind of all the things he wished Giants could be and clambered up into the highchair. He sat stiffly, his arms at his sides, his senses strained for any thumping footsteps or guttural words from a massive mouth.

"Comfortable, *Alex?*" James asked.

Caden glanced down at him. The Viper stared up at him with those pale green eyes. Its black tongue lashed out. *I'm going to die,* Caden thought, panic tightening his chest and knotting his insides. *I really just followed someone who's a Viper's pet. It'll laugh as the Giant eats both of us.*

"Alex?"

Caden cleared his throat and turned away. He had to pee. No, he was just terrified. A Giant? Talking to him? Now? No, this can't be happening-

I'm Alex Whitney, Caden thought, his eyes gently closing. *I am big.* He stopped his train of thought and thought of The Door again. That mysterious Door leading to a life he craved. *Raw Peace,* he thought. *Are you able to help me?* He hadn't asked The Door, or that odd Peace, to help him before. It was worth a shot.

Shalom, he thought, repeating the strange boy, Gideon's, greeting. *Peace.* Caden lifted his chin and opened his eyes, his shoulders square and gaze firm. *Ok... how would Alex act?* He slumped back into the chair and stared out the large window. Even when he heard heavy footsteps, he didn't turn. Even when the door opened, and someone grunted as they wedged themselves through, he didn't turn.

"Mr. Rut," James said from the ground. "Good to see

you again." Even when Caden felt his heart beating in his throat, he didn't stop idly watching a ship cross Elliot Bay. He still had to pee, and now he had to puke. He kept it in and sighed loudly as Bobby Rut sat in the chair across him.

"You're late," he snapped, and half expected to be thrown out the huge window. He finally turned and faced the newcomer. His stomach dropped and his nerves tingled with horror. *Don't scream,* he told himself. *It's only a Giant.*

Bobby Rut was enormous. The huge chair he sat in had looked big, but now seemed on the small side, for it barely contained him. If he had been standing, he would be ten feet tall, and Caden had no idea how he fit through the door. Did he turn sideways and crawl?

He wasn't fat or ugly at all, he looked like a very normal man, except his hands were big enough to wrap around Caden's body, his head alone was probably fifty pounds, and, if he stretched, he could touch opposite sides of the room at the same time. Bobby's skin was olive-hued, and his hair was dark and curly. He wore a crisp blue uniform, and a baton hung on a belt across from a massive knife. It was almost a sword, but Caden guessed in Bobby's hands, it was more like a dagger or pocketknife.

Don't scream, Caden thought again and tilted his chin.

"So?" He demanded. "When can I get to Uncle Tom's? I've been waiting in this place long enough."

"Don't like it here, boy?" That nearly did Caden in. Bobby's voice was so big and so deep, and his breath washed over Caden, moving his hair about and smelling strongly of hamburgers. Probably the entire restaurant plus a few waiters on the side.

"I've told you," Caden said, trying to sound irritated. "Don't breathe on me like that. It's disgusting!"

Please, don't kill me.

Bobby tilted his huge head to one side and sat back. The chair creaked; Caden was sure it would snap at any second. "You're costing Mr. Whitney a great deal of money staying here," Bobby said. He still looked down at Caden but angled his head in a way to not breathe over him.

"That's his job now," Caden retorted. "He's my last living relative. He cares for me? Ring any bells? And don't call me boy! You know me, Robby Butt."

Please, please don't kill me.

Bobby blinked and his huge fingers rapped on the chair's armrest. He grunted, sounding more like a bear's growl, and removed a thick notebook. In Bobby's hand, it looked like a pocket-sized notebook. The pen itself was more than two feet long. "I have questions-"

"This is ridiculous-"

"How many dogs have you owned?"

"Really? Not, how are you Alex? Are you wounded? Do you need anything? How big of a party do you want coming home?" Bobby's jaw, probably strong enough to gnaw off Caden's legs, flexed as he ground his teeth. Caden cursed under his breath and waved a hand. "Five! Five dogs! Next useless question!"

"This is to verify your identity."

"Sorry, lost my wallet and IDs. I was too busy getting kidnapped."

"What's your brother's name?"

"Frank." Bobby's brows rose and Caden laughed. "Sammy's dead. Died on the Day of Vanishing."

"How?"

"Bus ran him over."

"What did Mrs. Whitney wear to the funeral?"

"Duno, didn't go."

"Who was the butler when you were twelve?"

"This is dumb."

"Answer the-"

"Butler! That's all I called him." Caden scoffed, trying to hide his panic as he frantically thought through all the random details of Alex's life. "Teddy," he said. "I called him Teddy. Was that even his name?"

I think I'm tricking him, Caden thought, though his heart still beat a million miles an hour.

"Charlette died."Caden made himself frown the best he could and stared at Bobby, his split lip hindered it a bit. With a sniff, he turned away and shrugged. "Cool. I'll just get another stupid bird."

Bobby's questions continued. All were sporadic and left Caden feeling frantic for answers. For once, Caden was grateful for the time James and he had poured over Alex's life.

"Where'd you go to school?"

"How often did you get grounded?"

"What present did Mr. Whitney give you on your tenth birthday?"

Whenever Caden's panic overcame him, he started calling the Giant Robby Butt or declaring the test was boring or stupid. Internally, he'd yell at himself to calm down and that he would get to Ellie soon. It wasn't until halfway through that he remembered to focus on The Door of light and its warm love and security. *Raw Peace,* he thought. That kept him on track and his nerves in check.

After about an hour, Bobby nodded and scribbled more in his notebook. Caden fidgeted as he waited. He was trying to look irritated and impatient, but he was still fighting to stay calm. *We're doing it,* he thought, daring to hope just for a sec. *We're actually tricking him! Maybe I won't die!* Bobby quietly scanned over his notes again and Caden frowned.

"Are we there yet?" he asked. "Are we there yet? Are we there-?"

"Dye his hair again." Caden blinked, his back stiffening. "Alex's hair is a little more brown." Caden stiffly stared at the Giant, unsure of what to do.

James stepped forward and nodded deeply, more like a bow. "Thank you. Any other suggestions, Mr. Rut?"

"Are you serious?" Caden muttered and slouched back in the chair, his Alex posture gone. He hung his head and glared at James. "You knew this wasn't the real thing?"

"A few," Bobby said to James, ripping out a sheet of paper and handing it to him. "Slouch more. Talk less. Defiance is good. And, kid?" Caden glanced up at Bobby. "You play Alex pretty good. I nearly slugged you twice."

"Well…" Caden stammered. "Thanks for not."

Bobby chuckled, which chilled Caden's blood. "Wouldn't want to break you in half." Caden swallowed the hard lump in his throat.

"Mr. Rut," James said with a smile. "Does our arrangement still stand?" Bobby held out his huge hand and James gave him ten tams. The square coins looked like play money in the Giant's hands.

"And ten after," Bobby said, his voice a low growl. "Then I'll hand this kid back over."

Caden glanced up at the Giant, his hair standing on end. "Someone explain what's happening." He turned to James and steel entered his gaze.

"The Whitney's will see you as a fake in a matter of time," James said. "You cannot be their nephew perfectly. Mr. Rut will help you escape before they realize. Once the reward money is transferred, there will be a bomb threat on the Whitney House." Caden's brows rose and James shrugged. "It happens. Mr. Rut will usher you to safety, away from the house, and-"

"And take me to the airport." Caden turned to the Giant. "I'm going with the Mizrahi family to Israel."

Bobby's head tilted to one side as a huge smile

stretched across his wide mouth. "Where'd you find this level of crazy?"

"I'm not crazy."

"He jumped off a cliff," James said. "He isn't concerned about personal safety. Not like you and I."

"Obviously," Bobby sat with a grunt. "Israel, huh? You'll last a week."

Caden's jaw set as he lifted his chin. "That's my problem."

"There's more Giants there."

"You're not too bad."

"More Freaks."

"I've faced them before."

"And more Ghosts."

Is he talking about Spirits? Caden's stomach turned, unable to have a comeback for that one.

Bobby chuckled. "Maybe two weeks with that attitude. Regardless, you have to survive this first. And if you don't..." The Giant glanced between the two humans before reaching for Caden.

Caden couldn't help but shrink back as the Giant pinched his shoulder and thigh. "Hey!"

"Hum..." Bobby nodded and licked his lips. "I'll eat you first."

All color washed from Caden's face. *They don't really do that,* he thought desperately. *That's just in the stories!* But one look at Bobby's face told him otherwise. "But," Caden stammered. "But that's cannibalism."

Bobby's nose wrinkled as he stood. "Cannibalism is when the same species consume one another. Do you and I look remotely similar?"

"But," Caden said, then sat there with his mouth open. He turned away, feeling like he was going to puke.

Bobby laughed. It was just like a Giant laugh. Loud. Rumbling. Inhuman. Coldhearted. Caden nearly covered his ears. Bobby sighed heavily, laying his thick hand on his wide chest, as though that had been the best joke in the world. "I'll start the paperwork and get him cleared," the Giant said to James. "I'll see you boys in two days."

"Thank you, Mr. Rut," James said with a smile, and the Viper nudged his chin with a small, clawed hand, sending James into a small bow.

Caden cursed under his breath and rubbed his shoulder where Bobby had pinched him. *Raw Peace,* he thought, panic trying to press on his chest and make it difficult to breathe. *Raw Peace.* He cursed again and put his face in his hands. *Rut's right,* he thought. *I am crazy.*

———

CADEN NEVER THOUGHT his family was poor. Dad had been a car salesman, and before Mom got sick, she had been a nurse. There were a few rough times after Mom got sick, but Mama Lo and Papa always helped out. Caden and his brothers and sister were never without food. They always had clothes. They did pretty good.

Caden realized, standing inside the front door of House Whitney, his family was poor. No, they were *dirt* poor. They didn't have a butler or a helicopter on their roof or a fountain in their living room. *Is that a living room?* Caden wondered, trying to look around with his good eye. *Or is that other bunch of couches the living room? I guess there's more than one.* He was grateful Alex had never been to House Whitney and knew he could get lost for weeks trying to find the bathroom.

James gave him a sharp look and he stopped staring around. Alex wouldn't stare. This would be normal to Alex. James said Alex had lived in similar extravagance. Caden stared at the marble floor and put his hands in his pockets. He could feel his heart beating like a drum. He felt like he had to pee, but knew he already did before coming. He felt like puking too, but also got that out of the way before they left. Now, he needed to brush his teeth, or at least have a mint.

Keep it together! He internally yelled at himself. *You've faced Scar and people that wanted to make you a slave. You can take tribillionaires. Just be Alex. Take all their money. Don't get eaten by Giants. You can do this.* Caden cursed under his breath. *I'm so dead.* He took in a breath and lifted his chin. *Well, might as well go out with a bang.*

The butler had been talking, something about waiting in the foyer, but Caden hadn't heard him. *I'm Alex,* he thought. *What would Alex do?* He strolled past the butler, who sputtered in his speech and demanded Caden come back. Caden ignored him, walked to one of the couches, and threw himself onto it. He sighed, put his feet up on the armrest, and closed his eyes.

"Tell me when Aunty gets here," he called to the butler and refused to respond when the butler demanded him to return.

"Well," James muttered to the butler. "May we join him, George?" The butler grumbled something and Caden heard James, Elijah, and Asher walk from the entryway over to the couches.

"Sir," George said. "Take your feet off the couch. Please. You'll scuff the leather."

"It's leather," Caden mumbled. "It's tough." He didn't move. With a sigh, George walked away. Caden crossed his arms, willing his very rigid body to relax and look completely at ease. The huge room felt very quiet. Caden could hear a clock ticking from another room. No doubt it was the size of a dining table with diamonds instead of numbers.

Stupidly rich, Caden thought. *How do people live like this?*

"Why didn't Ophir come?" James whispered. "Mr. Whitney asked for all parties involved to come."

He's protecting his wife, doofus, Caden thought.

"She'll come," Elijah said calmly. Caden couldn't help but glance at him. The large Israeli sat in a cushioned, oak chair, his hands neatly folded in his lap, his face, as always, impassive and unreadable.

How can he be calm? Caden thought, suddenly mad at him. *Does he know Bobby's going to have us for dinner if we can't pull this off?*

Asher, on the other hand, hadn't sat. He stood, pacing back and forth, looking at a nude statue in the corner before pacing to a Grand Piano, and then a white fireplace that had never been used. "What are we waiting for?" he grumbled.

Caden didn't want to find out, but Alex wouldn't be so passive. Caden stood and strolled from their room, passed the front door and fountain, to a stairway that led up several flights. The banisters were solid oak and carved to look like ivy. A chandelier that probably cost more than the house Caden grew up in was suspended overhead.

"Sir!" George called. "Sir! You're not allowed up there!"

"I'm tired," Caden called. "I'm going to find somewhere quiet to crash."

"Sir!" Caden ignored him and continued up the stairs. "I'll call security!"

Caden's insides twisted. Instead, he channeled all his anxiousness and strained nerves into anger. "I'm tired!" His yell echoed in the vast room. He heard James' running after him.

Keep moving, he thought. *Alex wouldn't let a butler tell him what to do-*

"Al!" Caden stopped and glanced further up the stairs. An older woman stared down at him, her wrinkled face covered in makeup and her graying blonde hair styled perfectly. She gasped, laying a hand over her vivid red lips, and rushed down the stairs. She wore a slimming dress and her heels clicked across the marble steps.

Here we go, Caden thought as the woman nearly collided into him and tried to hug the life out of him.

Caden wrapped his arms around her and the two held one another. For a moment, just a little one, Caden pretended this stranger was Mom. He pulled her close and felt her tears on his shirt. At once, he knew this wasn't his mother in any way. His mother wouldn't smell like alcohol at ten in the morning.

"Hay, Aunty," Caden forced himself to say.

"My boy! Oh, my boy! I've found you!" Amanda Whitney pulled back and stared at Caden as tears smeared her makeup. "Oh, look at your face! What happened to you! It must've been the worst thing in your life! We'll find them. I swear to you, my boy. We'll find who did this to you. Bobby Rut will take care of them!" She nodded firmly. "You'll never have to worry about being taken again." Caden nodded and forced himself to half smile. His split lip still hurt.

"Oh, look at you," Amanda sighed and cupped his face in her hands. "But you're safe now. I found you."

"Well, Aunty, these guys saved me." Caden glanced back at Elijah, Asher, and James, who stood at the base of the stairway.

Amanda gasped again and faced them. "Well I... I know you," she said, pointing at James.

"Yes, Mrs. Whitney. I am James West. I was your nephew's tutor."

Caden gave him a sideways glance, trying to hide his surprise. *Why haven't you mentioned that before?*

"Oh, yes. You, let me see... you were the one Anthony let go?" Caden lifted his chin as unease tingled his nerves.

"Yes ma'am. I wanted to prove my loyalty to the House Whitney and find your nephew. And I have." Elijah glanced at James, his brow arched. "With the help of my friends here. May I introduce to you Elijah Mizrahi and his son, Asher Mizrahi."

Amanda nodded to them each. "Thank you!" She said loudly and clearly. "I'm so happy you found Alex!"

Elijah simply stared at her as Asher scoffed. "It is our pleasure, ma'am," Elijah said.

"Oh," Amanda sputtered and blushed. "You speak English. Good. Well… thank you."

We can't be tricking her already, Caden thought. *This is too easy.*

"Supper's ready, my boy," Amanda said, turning her full attention onto Caden. "Your favorite, duck hamburgers with onion rings, no fries, with ice cream sundaes. I remember from when we last saw you."

Caden's eyes narrowed. "I'm not six anymore."

"Well, it's good food. I'll smuggle in some of your favorite drinks if your uncle doesn't notice. What do you like? Anything!"

She looks so happy now, Caden thought. *Even giddy.* He almost felt bad for conning her. Almost.

"I'm tired," he said. "I'll eat later. I just wanna sleep."

"Oh, well… alright. As you'd like, my boy. You've gone through quite a bit, and we can eat together later."

She turned him up the stairway and they continued climbing. She kept talking and Caden tried to listen. His heart refused to slow. His strained nerves couldn't calm. *Too easy,* he thought. *James did say she was naive. Maybe that drinking problem is working in my favor.* Amanda leaned on him quite a bit, and though her words didn't slur, Caden wondered if she knew what she was saying. *We'll just get the money and leave,* Caden thought. *Easy. This will be easy.*

He looked ahead and saw a looming shape in the shadow of a hallway. Bobby Rut. An icy chill washed over Caden. Next to the Giant was a small man with a round, bald head. He was staring at Caden without moving. *He's not small,* Caden thought. *He just looks small next to Bobby. Who is he?*

He blinked as another ice bath came over him. He didn't look away from the stranger. Alex wouldn't. He continued walking until he reached the second floor, which acted as a balcony overlooking the foyer below. Amanda, unaware of who watched, started leading Caden away from them. *I'm going to turn my back on him,* Caden thought, knowing that never happened to him. *What would Alex do?* Without slaking his pace, Caden turned to the left and away from the man.

The stranger cursed and stormed across the balcony. Caden forced himself not to slow until Amanda noticed the new stranger. "Oh! Tom. Here's our boy! He's back! We were just going to his room. He's so very tired and-"

Thomas brushed Amanda from Caden's side and stood far too close to Caden. Caden had been right, Thomas was not small at all. He was nearly a head taller than Caden, and his thick, heavyset build made him look like a mini-Giant.

You're Alex! You're Alex! Caden thought, forcing himself to casually face his pretend uncle. He stared up at him and made a clumsy salute. "Hay-yah, Unk." Thomas' eye twitched, but he said nothing. *He's not falling for it,* Caden thought. His hands felt cold. He wondered what they would all do if he curled into a ball on the floor and pretended to hide.

"Amanda?" Thomas asked. For such a big guy, his voice was soft and quiet. It didn't fit him well. "Did you check?"

"Oh, darling. Look at him!" Amanda motioned to

Caden and beamed. "This is our boy! Once his bruises heal, we'll see that darling face we all love!"

"So, you didn't check."

Amanda's smile fell. "Tom, come now. He's our-"

"Open your mouth."

Caden blinked and stared at Thomas. *The gold tooth!* He realized with a jolt. He started to comply, happy to show Thomas the painful gums where his left molar should've been but stopped short. Alex wouldn't be so obedient. "You're paranoid," he muttered and turned to leave.

Thomas' grabbed right above his elbow and jerked him back. Caden nearly fell. "Thomas!" Amanda cried.

"Open your mouth," Thomas' soft voice whispered again as he withdrew a device from his pocket. It was a black rectangle with lights running up the side and a small knob sticking out one end.

"Uncle-" Caden's words fell short as heavy footsteps thumped behind him. A massive hand lay on the back of his neck. The thumb alone could wrap around his neck like a boa constrictor. *Rut,* Caden thought, feeling the eager power in the huge hand. He glanced at what Thomas was holding. It was a gold tester. He saw it before in a jewelry store Trace and he had raided. It would find no gold here.

"I had to pull the tooth," Caden said. "How else could I pay to get back home? You didn't send me anything!"

"Let's see," Thomas said.

Caden huffed but quickly obeyed as Rut's hand pressed on his back. Thomas leaned closer and withdrew a pen from his pocket. He stuck it in Caden's mouth and shoved his cheek to one side. His right cheek. Cold dread overcame Caden.

"Wrong side," he said with as much confidence as he could muster. He couldn't help but give James a quick, panicked look.

Thomas glanced at him. "Alex's gold tooth is the right molar."

"No," Caden said, unwilling to let his rising panic enter his voice. "The real Alex, *me*, knows very well where my gold tooth was!"

Thomas moved back and calmly wiped the pen on a handkerchief. "What did you call it?" Caden blinked. "What did you call it before I informed you it was a very stupid nickname?"

We're dead, Caden thought. *Why did I think we could survive this?*

It took a moment for Caden to realize the ground was thumping from heavy footsteps again. He blinked and saw more Giants stepping from rooms. James, Elijah, and Asher were surrounded. James was talking, explaining something, but everyone knew the truth. Thomas shook his head and threw Caden back, letting him fall into Bobby.

"No," Caden stammered, unable to believe what was happening. "Wait!" Bobby grabbed his arms and pinned them behind his back with one hand. "Uncle, I can explain!"

"Do not call me that." Thomas hissed. "Do not ever call me that!" Caden stared at Thomas, trying to think of something, anything! He looked at Amanda. She was staring at him, her eyes filled with tears again. Thomas sighed and turned away. "Take them downstairs. I'll deal with this mess after lunch."

"Mr. Whitney," Caden said. "Let me explain what we're-"

Thomas didn't look back as he walked from Caden. "Amanda!" He called over his shoulder. She jumped and gave Caden one last glance.

"Please," Caden whispered to her. "Please, Mrs. Whitney. I'm just trying to find my sister. Please!"

"Amanda!" She jumped again and scurried after Thomas.

"Please! Don't do this!" Caden didn't know what he was saying.

He knew it was no use. What had he been thinking? He was vaguely aware of Asher shouting as a Giant grabbed him. James was still talking, rambling bargains and pleas no one was listening to. In the midst of it all, Elijah calmly let a Giant grab him.

We're dead, Caden thought as Bobby drew him closer.

"Like I said," Bobby whispered high overhead. "You're first."

Caden's breath quickened as panic constricted his throat. He felt dizzy. Sick. His eyes fell on the Viper perched on James' shoulder. The little snake kept looking from one struggling, frantic face to another. Caden had never known snakes could smile, but that one was grinning like it had just won a prize.

SEVENTEEN

THREE CAPTIVES, TWO HEADS, AND ONE SHOE

CADEN COULDN'T SPEAK. He hardly felt anything either. It was like he was living another life and watching someone else get dragged through a mansion. His thoughts were funny too, slow and sluggish and not making that much sense. He would notice random pieces of furniture or art that caught his eye and he'd focus on it, taking in every detail.

That painting has a lot of sky in it. I wonder how much that statue cost. Don't panic. How many maids does it take to change all those light bulbs? Don't panic.

Caden grit his teeth as he tried to keep pace with Bobby's strides. He was nearly running with his arms still pinned behind him. He was going to fall on his face any second. *Bee's wax,* he thought, staring down at the quickly passing floor. *That's how they get the floor so shiny.* His eyes narrowed as he swallowed the hard lump in his throat. *I'm totally panicking.*

James was still talking. Did he just say something about offering more information? None of the Giants were listening. Asher randomly told them to stop yanking him around, which they ignored too. Elijah alone kept pace, his mouth sealed shut and dark eyes set ahead.

He's a robot, Caden concluded because, personally, he knew he was about to puke. Again. They were shoved into a massive elevator that quickly grew smaller the more Giants that entered.

"I swear," James was rambling. "I can get you the information. Go tell Mr. Whitney that! I can reveal the name of the true criminal!"

"That would be you, Mr. West," Bobby said from high above.

"What?" James sputtered. "I, I am here to serve the Whitney family! I've let bygones be bygones!"

"We all know your wife's dead because of Mr. Whitney." Caden glanced at James, his mouth slack.

"Oh, great," Asher groaned. "That's perfect!"

"This has nothing to do with Hannah," James said quietly. The Viper's black tongue flicked with a rasping, hissing sound.

Was that a laugh? Caden thought, his hair standing on end.

"I swear," James said, lifting his chin. Asher shook his head and one of the Giants laughed. Elijah didn't show any sign of surprise.

The elevator descended far longer than Caden thought possible. When the doors opened, the stark white walls of a hallway echoed the baritone barks of a Rottweiler. Caden flinched back, unable to hide a small shout. It took him a moment to realize there wasn't one dog, but two. Leaping against its chain, a two-headed Rottweiler bared its teeth, its mouth a frothy mess as claws scratched the floor. It had two extra front legs, and if he had time to look, he would have seen a second tail.

More Freaks, Caden thought, knowing one head could pin him down while the other ripped out his throat. At least the monster was given a short chain. Caden stared at the links as they led to a pulley and disappeared into the wall. It didn't look normal, like a mechanical leash.

Caden and the others were dragged down the hall, passed several doors, to one at the end. Inside, there were rings embedded into the concrete walls close to the ceiling every few feet. Caden stared at the rings and unknowingly started pushing against Bobby. *What are those for? Get them away!*

"Knock it off," Bobby grumbled and wrapped his thick arm around Caden's middle. Caden gulped as his feet left the ground. He dangled and watched the ground stream past with each Giant stride as Bobby held him under his arm. Bobby's hold loosened and Caden nearly fell, earning another shout. Instead, Bobby slammed him against the wall and knocked the wind out of him.

"Hands together."

Caden tried to breathe as he numbly obeyed. *Raw Peace,* he thought, *Raw Peace. Is that Heaven or something? Will I see you again soon?* Bobby withdrew string from his pocket. No, that wasn't string. It just looked like it in the Giant's hands. It was rope.

Caden watched as his wrists were tied. "Careful." he heard himself say. He could easily see Bobby sinching his hands clean off. "Sorry," he whispered and ducked his head as the ropes dug in.

"You were very close," Bobby muttered as he threaded the rope through the ring overhead. "Could've passed for Alex. That gold tooth gets most everyone."

Caden stared at the floor as Bobby pulled the rope, dragging his arms up over his head and sending him against the wall again. "Please don't eat me." He didn't know why he was begging. It was humiliating.

Bobby grinned down at him and shook his head.

"Once this door opens, it will trip the dogs' chains and turn them loose. They're also hungry."

"You'll be locked in with us?" Asher asked.

"The trip hasn't been set yet, so no." Bobby's walkie-talkie on his hip squawked and he grabbed it. It looked like a toy in his hands.

"Mr. Rut?" said the radio.

"What?"

"Mr. Whitney wants the big one upstairs. Northern Patio." Caden glanced at Elijah as Asher shook his head.

"Don't take him," Asher said as he strained against the ropes. "You hear me!"

"Asher," Elijah said quietly.

"He's going to watch you get eaten."

"You do not know-"

"Stop being so calm! You're going to die!"

"Son."

Asher stilled and faced his father. "Aba," he said. His voice cracked. Elijah gave a small nod as a Giant pulled the rope free from the ring. The Giant gave Elijah a tug and they walked out.

He didn't look back, Caden thought. *It's like... like he's not afraid at all.* Caden stared after Elijah. Would he see him again?

The Giants turned to leave one by one. Bobby gave Caden a mock salute before slamming the door shut. The room fell silent besides Bobby fiddling with the door outside. Probably setting the trip. No one spoke or moved as they listened to the thumping of Giant feet fading away. Caden continued to stare at the floor, his insides twisting harder and harder on themselves.

Just wait, he told himself. *Wait a little bit more. You're going to be alright. Don't panic!*

"What have you done?" Caden flinched at the steel in

Asher's voice. He was relieved Asher wasn't talking to him.

"My part of the deal," James answered, his eyes narrowing.

"You're running your mouth! Like a woman!"

"I'm trying to persuade them to-"

"No one respects you here! You said they trusted you!"

Caden shook his head as he looked up at his wrists. His hands were turning red. He wouldn't be surprised if they became purple within an hour. He stood on his tiptoes and strained one hand down. If only he could reach the other hand's sleeve.

"I said they *knew* me," James said. "I didn't say they trusted me."

Asher cursed and gritted his teeth. "You're lucky I'm tied up."

"Is that a threat?"

"Yes!"

"You should focus on not getting turned into dinner, not my history with the Whitney's!"

"Your *history* will turn me into dinner!"

Caden ground his teeth as his hand started to tingle painfully. *Come on, come on,* he thought.

"So," Asher snapped. "Hannah's your wife?"

"Keep her out of this!"

"And Thomas killed her?" Asher adjusted his hold of the ropes with a grunt. "How'd that happen?"

"None of your business."

"Did you run your mouth too? Turn her into a Giant sandwich or something?" James lurched toward Asher, his ropes straining. Asher laughed. "Coward. Couldn't protect your own wife."

"I can't do everything!"

"That's for sure-"

"I would've killed for the money we were going to get today!"

"I believe you-"

"My Hannah needed it! It wasn't much! The Whitney's could spare it and still live comfortably. It wouldn't destroy them to miss one trip to the Caribbean or whatever wine they import from Italie." Caden's eyes narrowed; his hand was really starting to throb.

"She was hurt?" Asher asked.

"Dying! And they just-" James gasped as he hung his head. "They couldn't stand to part with their precious money!"

Asher stared at James for a moment before turning away. "This is about revenge," he muttered. "Hey, answer me this? Do you know where the real Alex is? Like, did you take him in the first place?"

"No!"

Caden glanced at James. He looked like he had been strung up for days as he battled to calm down. The Viper clung to his clothes and hair, its little claws indenting his skin. *That thing's having the time of its life,* Caden realized. The Spirit turned and fixed its reptilian eyes on Caden. The two stared at one another until Caden ducked his head. *Focus,* he thought. *You almost got it! Just keep-*

"Are you interfering with my plan?" The question penetrated his thoughts. Caden sucked in a breath as he froze. *"I've heard of you, human,"* the voice hissed. *"You are trouble."*

Caden slowly looked at the Viper again. The snake's black tongue lashed out as it held his gaze. *Raw Peace.*

"That Door has no answers."

Raw Peace.

"Or hope for you. It was just a place."

Raw Peace! Caden cursed, took in a breath, and set all his focus on his right-hand sleeve. He strained against the ropes, feeling it dig into his wrist.

"What are you doing?" Asher asked. Caden didn't answer as he felt inside the sleeve. A small lip of fabric. He took in a breath and shoved one hand closer while the other strained to reach under the fabric. The ropes made his wrists raw. Caden's shoulders started to shake. *Come on!*

The hard, sleek surface of metal touched his fingertips. Caden growled through gritted teeth. He withdrew his hand and delicately held by fingertips was a shining razor blade. Caden gasped as he slumped against the wall. He glanced up, seeing his hand was purple. He was surprised it wasn't bleeding.

"Nice," Asher said. "Well, move it. Let's go!"

Caden scoffed and stood on his tiptoes again. He moved slowly, not wanting to drop the blade. How would he pick it up?

"Is that what happened to my razor?" James asked.

"You're welcome," Caden grunted as he strained against the ropes again and started sawing the blade. It was a very slow, very uncomfortable process. Asher kept staring at him, as though willing him to move faster with his eyes. It didn't help and Asher kept sighing and bouncing one leg.

James glared at him. "Your restlessness will get you killed."

"So will your mouth."

"I think you two should stay here."

"And I think you should shut up."

"I'm staying." Asher glanced at James. Caden was too focused on cutting the ropes to respond. "I have nothing to hide. They'll see that."

"They know this isn't Alex," Asher said.

"They know me."

"Yeah, they know you're a vengeful widower." James

didn't answer as he stared ahead, as though the two didn't matter.

Caden ground his teeth, his fingers bent awkwardly to reach the ropes. He had to hurry up, this was really hurting! The angle of his shoulders, which were still shaking, loosened. *Almost there!* The rope frayed. His fingers quickened, the blade sawing back and forth. All at once, the tension in the rope released and Caden lowered his arms. Blood rushed down into them, making them tingle as though they had been asleep for hours. Caden groaned and leaned against the wall as he hugged his arms. His shoulders throbbed. So did his fingers. He looked down and found blood seeping from a few small cuts from the razor.

"What're you doing?" Asher hissed. "Get over here!"

"Who says I'm untying you?" The look that shadowed Asher's eyes would've burned through led. "Kidding," Caden muttered and stood from the wall. Asher's ropes fell away much quicker. The two moved to the center of the room, throwing the ropes at their feet, and turned to James.

"You sure?" Asher asked. James didn't answer.

"He doesn't want the money," Caden said, slipping the razor blade back into its little pocket. "He wants revenge. He hasn't gotten it yet."

"You can't get revenge strung up like that."

James finally turned to them. "I have a message for Thomas Whitney. I can't tell him if I try to escape. You will get caught. Then you will be eaten. That's how House Whitney operates."

Caden's skin crawled. "Great. Thanks. Hey, you owe me a new tooth. How could you forget which side to pull!"

"How could you forget the tooth's nickname?"

"You didn't tell me-"

"I did! More than once!" Caden fell silent and tried to remember.

Asher glanced between them and crossed his arms. "So, you didn't intend to get the money?" he asked. James slowly shook his head. "You knew we'd get caught!" James didn't answer and Caden cursed. "What's wrong with you?"

It's that thing, Caden thought, his eyes darting to the Viper. *It's twisting him, tricking him into getting himself killed.*

"Let's go," Caden said quietly, and he turned to the door.

"Later, loser," Asher called and followed after Caden.

"There's a Freak out there!" James called.

"I know!" Asher snapped. The two stopped at the door and Asher leaned closer to Caden. "How are we getting past the Freak?"

"Any ideas?"

"I asked you!"

"I got us untied! You think of something now."

"Got anything else in those sleeves?" Caden shook his head and the two stared at the door. "Might be locked." Asher said.

"No. Bobby warned us what would happen if we opened the door, meaning we could do it."

"Ah. Okay. Then what?"

"That's *your* job."

"We could run real fast."

"We can't outrun a Rottweiler."

"Maybe it's heavier because it's a Freak."

"Or faster." The two fell silent. "We could use the ropes?" Caden offered.

"How?"

"I don't know... wrap it around its neck?"

"And what? Take it for a walk?" Caden frowned and

scratched the back of his neck. "Hum," Asher grunted. "There's a fire extinguisher."

"Where?"

"Saw one. Right after the hall bends. Those things are hard. They could knock someone out."

"Personal experience?"

"Hey, you gotta do what you gotta do these days."

"So, what? We run toward that?"

"And whoever gets it first takes a swing at the Freak." Caden continued to stare at the closed door.

"Gentleman," James called. "That is a very weak plan."

Asher turned, his nose wrinkled in disgust, but Caden grabbed his arm. "It is a bad plan. But. I don't see anything else to use."

Asher glared at James and turned to Caden again. "So, we're agreed?"

"This sucks."

"Got a better idea?"

"No!" Caden ran a quick hand over his face. "I'll open the door."

"No, I will. You run first."

"So, you can hang back here?"

"No, I'll run out too!"

"You better." The two continued staring at the door. Neither moved. Caden's hands felt sticky all of a sudden.

"Think you'll make it?" Asher whispered. Caden cursed and didn't answer, his heart beginning to pick up speed. "Alright then," Asher said. "Run fast."

"Yeah, yeah," Caden mumbled. He rolled his shoulders, just to make sure they were still working right, and grabbed the handle. "Ready?"

"Yep."

"One, two, three!"

The door opened. It wasn't even hard. Caden felt

whatever mechanism get tripped as the door swung. *Here we go,* he thought, his body's senses heightening as anxiety pressed on his chest. *About to die. Again.*

Asher raced through the door, Caden right behind. He heard distant chains rattling. Then barking. Loud, hysterical barking. Caden cursed again and refused to look back. Asher was already a few paces ahead of him. They sprinted toward the turn in the hall. Caden gasped as he propelled himself forward. His eyes fell on the red fire extinguisher. It was close. They were almost-

Something caught his pant leg. It wouldn't let go. Caden's glimmer of hope snuffed out as he found the floor swiftly getting closer. He fell fast and hard, the world spinning as he rolled. And there was something else. Something new. It was big and loud and on top of him. One dog's barks jarred Caden as the other firmly held his pants in its jaws.

Caden didn't think. Instinct took over. He drew his leg back and kicked, his heel landing a blow. He tried to kick again, but the dog leapt, moving from his legs and over his torso. He could see their fangs. They were huge! Drool flew as they advanced.

My throat, Caden realized. He protectively grabbed his neck as he raised a defensive arm. The dogs' duo heads lowered, growls filling Caden's ears.

Something red dropped on them. No, it swung. The dog stumbled, one dog head recoiling as the other turned, teeth bared. Caden gasped and scrambled back. Something moving fast drew over him. Caden realized Asher was standing over him, the fire extinguisher lifting high. The dog's body tensed, readying to pounce. Asher brought the extinguisher down with a loud, metallic clang. The dog dropped, one head slumping limply.

With a yell, Asher swung the extinguisher again, but missed. Caden dragged himself to his feet as the remaining dog barked wildly. He looked around, searching for something he could use. The hall was bare. In desperation, Caden had an idea. If he had time to think, he'd tell himself it was another stupid plan. He yanked his foot from his shoe, snatched it up, and threw it at the dog.

The dog turned, snarling, and the shoe bounced off with no effect. But the dog was distracted. Asher took his chance. With another metallic thud, the dog collapsed to the floor, blood staining the stark white hall. The two stood there panting and staring at the dog. Asher slowly turned and glanced at Caden. Drops of blood splattered his pale face. He grinned a wild smile. Caden found himself laughing as he retrieved his shoe.

"You hurt?" Asher asked.

Caden glanced down at his ripped pants. "Ah... nope."

"Wow, maybe Yahweh really is looking out for us."

"Whatever," Caden grumbled. "Let's go."

"Wrong way," Asher said, and he jerked his head to the elevator.

Caden frowned. "The Giants are up there."

"So is Aba."

Caden stared at Asher and shook his head. "They'll catch you."

"Suit yourself," Asher said as he turned and started running toward the elevator. Caden watched him go, his heart still pounding with force. He ran fingers through his hair and cursed himself. He started running after Asher.

———

CADEN COULDN'T HOLD back a scoff as he followed Asher through the huge house. There hadn't been a guard anywhere. *I guess no one tries to escape Giants. Idiots!* His smile fell as he thought about *why* no one tried to fight them. *They don't want to be lunch.* Caden sucked in a forceful breath, trying to keep himself calm as he followed Asher. They were heading north, by Asher's guidance. They assumed Elijah was at the Northern Patio with Thomas. They needed to find him and, and…

Caden had no idea. Take on armed Giants with a fire extinguisher and a shoe? *What am I doing?* Caden continued following Asher as they raced into a room with a piano and harp on display. *I could leave right now. Get out. But how could I get to Ellie? The Whitneys control all the airstrips this side of the country. I can't sail to Cairo! Hum… maybe I can.* Caden's eyes narrowed, and he lifted his chin. *I don't want to die of dysentery. I've got to fly. I've got to survive this. Somehow.* They entered another room, this one larger with a huge bookshelf, a taxidermied, full-body lion, and a floor-to-ceiling mirror. A suit of armor stood in the corner and clutched a long spear.

Is there something on the other side of The Door that could help me? Caden replayed the memory of the warm, real security he felt as that odd door opened. Could the people on the other side help him? Pop from wherever they were into this place and rescue him?

Caden's thoughts halted as he ran right into Asher. He bounced back, being smaller than Asher, and glared at him. Asher stood before the seven-foot-tall doorway they were going to go through. He wasn't moving. He slowly turned his head, dark eyes blinking rapidly.

"What-?"

Asher held up a hand. Caden shut his mouth. "Hide."

"What?"

"Hide!" Asher leapt from the door and charged deeper into the room.

Caden glanced around, suddenly wishing he was a kid so he could fit under the couch. *Maybe behind it?* He didn't have a choice. He raced to it and dove, landing on the hardwood floor. He looked under the couch and barely saw the door open. Massive feet, size thirty at least, tramped in. Another colossal set followed. A hard lump choked Caden for a moment as the Giants came in. He could feel their steps thudding against his chest.

They can't see me, I'm too small, he thought, promptly followed by, *they're not retarded!*

Where was Asher? If they saw one of them, they'd know others had escaped. Caden closed his eyes and held still, knowing he could do nothing but wait and pray. *I'm not praying,* he thought. *No one's listening.* He forced his breathing to slow. He couldn't make a sound. He had to be invisible. Not there. He wasn't there. But he was there. His foot was sticking out.

Massive fingers curled around his ankle like huge, thick snakes. The hand pulled. Caden couldn't hold back a cry as he felt the ground fall away and his head fill with blood. He swayed back and forth, a Giant holding him upside down by one foot. He gasped and twisted, trying to see who had captured him. Again.

Bobby's big head stared down at him, a smile stretching his wide mouth. Caden stared at him, too stunned to speak. He felt the Giant's fingers tighten around his ankle. He was about to yell at Bobby, begging him not to snap his leg off. He stopped himself; it didn't matter. The Giants already knew what they were going to do. So did Caden.

Grind my bones to make their bread, he thought, remembering the old nursery rhymes. Caden hung there, upside down, and waited.

EIGHTEEN

YOUR BOY

CADEN DIDN'T KNOW what to say as Bobby started to chuckle. It was a deep, vibrating sound that was too big to belong to a person. Caden glanced at the second Giant, and it took a moment to register the Giant was female. *A girl Giant*, Caden thought. *Don't hear about those.*

She was smaller than Bobby, not as muscular or tall, but still could squish Caden like a bug. Her red hair was pulled back in a tight bun, and her pasty, freckled face reminded him of Nordic folklore. She wore the same security uniform as Bobby, with a similar walkie-talkie, baton, and knife on her belt.

"You took the bait and escaped," Bobby said. Caden blinked as the Giant's hot breath washed over him. He coughed, wondering what was dead in his mouth.

The Giantess shifted her bulk as her eyes narrowed. "What happened to Pepper and Billy?"

Caden glanced at her. "Th-the Freak?"

"He's not a Freak!"

Caden flinched back. "Um…"

"Is he dead? He's not. Don't tell me you killed him."

Her green eyes darkened and Caden's stomach nearly emptied.

"No," Caden said honestly. "I didn't kill him."

"I swear, human!" She stepped closer and Caden whimpered despite himself.

"Tess, please," Bobby muttered. "You stress them out so much. All that cortisol makes the meat tough." Caden's breathing picked up.

"Right," Tess spat. "As if saying things like *that* helps!" Finally, Bobby's arm lowered and Caden lay on the ground.

He panted, trying to clear the panic from his thoughts. *I can't do anything,* he thought. *Totally helpless. Failure. Just like Dad always said-*

"Where's the other one?" Caden moved to stand, but something heavy and flat pressed on his back. The heavy thing pushed down, forcing out all Caden's breath in one loud cry. Panic consumed him as he felt his ribs bow.

"Don't squish him, Bob," Tess said passively. "I hate picking out the little bone pieces. Such a pain."

The weight eased up and Caden sucked in a breath. He coughed and lay there, suddenly knowing what a cockroach feels like. "Please." he wheezed. He glanced up and saw his reflection in the floor-to-ceiling mirror. Standing over him, amused, was Bobby, the Giant's massive foot planted on his back.

"Where's the other one?" Bobby repeated.

For the smallest moment, Caden wanted to tell him. "He's here! Look behind the curtains!" That's what he wanted to say. But that would get Asher caught.

He saved me from the Freak, Caden thought. *He also beat my face in! He should get roughed up too! But the Giants wouldn't rough him up. They eat people. Or worse. But he's a jerk and...*

All thoughts slowed as the memory of The Door flooded his mind. Those people, whoever they were, wouldn't have ratted out Asher. That's just not what people do when they are surrounded by such real, secure peace. They sacrifice. They fight for others. If Caden wanted to go there, wherever there was, he had to start acting like those people.

What would the Raw Peace want? Caden wondered. The answer hit him like a jolt of electricity. This thought process took a fraction of a second but knowing what should be done and deciding to do it took two whole seconds.

"He's not here," Caden said. He was stunned, his voice didn't shake. In the mirror, he saw Bobby's brows raise and Tess snicker.

"This'll be fun," Tess muttered.

"We heard two voices," Bobby said.

"I talk to myself," Caden shot back.

"Really?" Tess bent down, placing her thick hands on her knees. "Do you change your voice too when you answer your own questions?" Her laugh sickened Caden.

What've I done?

Caden wished he had someone's name to shout out, someone who'd come running to save him. All he kept thinking was Raw Peace. Whoever that was, whatever it was, Caden felt it was bigger and stronger than a Giant. But was it listening? All thoughts shattered as Bobby drew Caden's arm back and held it firm. The Giant slowly started pulling.

"Caden," Bobby said casually. "I need a snack."

"Mr. Rut!" Caden said through gritted teeth as his shoulder began to strain.

"Answer the question, and you'll keep the arm."

Caden gasped as he looked at his reflection, knowing his arm would pop off with ease in the Giant's hands. As he looked, something moved behind them. There was a shadow behind the taxidermized lion. It looked like a face.

Caden's heart leapt, realizing Asher was staring right at him. Their eyes met. The older boy's face was filled with horror.

He thinks I'll turn him in, Caden thought. *I should.* He could see The Door shutting on him, Gideon and the older woman who knew him never to be seen again. He couldn't bear the thought. He realized it was worse than losing Ellie.

"Mr. Rut," Caden said with as much control as he could muster. "Pain won't magically make me know something I don't!" Asher blinked, his mouth dropping open.

"Then we'll get an early snack."

Caden swallowed hard as his hands balled into tight fists. "Eat up." he whispered. Caden took in a breath, steeling himself. He closed his eyes, not wanting to see all the blood and gore. Bobby pulled slow and steady. Caden's muscles strained, like stiff taffy not wanting to stretch. He was suddenly aware of his shoulder joint. It wasn't happy. His head flew back as he yelled between gritted teeth. He wasn't thinking anymore. All he knew was pain.

Without warning, Bobby released him. Caden slumped to the carpet, his freed arm limp against him. He groaned as pain still overtook his shoulder. *It's still here!* He thought. He hadn't heard of someone loving their appendages, but in that moment, he adored his arm. *They didn't eat it! Does it work?* He rolled his shoulder, which was a bad move, and Caden buried his face in the carpet to hide the pain. He gasped again, clutching the throbbing shoulder. He rolled on his side and, in doing so, realized two things.

First, Bobby wasn't stepping on him. That was good. Second, someone was yelling. Someone angry. Someone big. That wasn't so good. Caden forced himself to move and faced the mirror. He froze. He couldn't believe what he saw. Bobby stood awkwardly, one hand drawing the huge knife from his belt as the other grabbed his butt cheek.

What's he doing? Caden thought, then saw blood between the Giant's fingers. Tess also had her knife ready. Both Giants' backs were to Caden. They were circling something small with a huge stick-

Caden's insides twisted with a sudden jerk. Asher stood with his back against the wall as he faced the Giants. He held out the suit of armor's spear. The tip was still red from sticking Bobby's backside. Bobby was yelling, either with pain or vengeance, Caden didn't know. Probably both. It filled the room and Caden felt the loud noise in his chest. Asher bared his teeth like a wild dog and yelled back. It sounded like a pathetic squeak compared to the Giant's. The Giants advanced, their knives, the size of swords, ready.

Help him! Caden's brain screamed.

He struggled to his feet and hugged his still throbbing arm. Something crashed and he ducked. Out of the corner of his eye, he saw Asher leap over the couch. Where he had been now had a big, clean line cut through the wall. Tess growled and stomped forward, kicking aside the couch and sending it against the wall. Caden looked around, trying to find some makeshift weapon. *There's nothing here!*

A dark shadow fell over him. Caden's skin crawled, and he slowly looked up. Bobby limped toward him. He wasn't amused anymore. Caden recoiled and slammed into the mirror. *I'm going to get ripped apart!* Asher yelled again, but this time it was shrill. Caden whirled, seeing Tess grabbing him around the waist with one hand. She lifted him off the ground with ease. Asher kicked to no avail. Tess opened her mouth wide.

"You're next," Bobby said. Caden faced him, seeing an unnaturally colossal hand descend.

"Excuse me!"

The two words seemed so out of place in the chaos that everyone stopped and turned. Standing in the opened doorway was George, the butler. He stiffly stood, hands behind his back and chin raised. He looked across the scene with indifference, as though this happened every day. "Do listen, Mr. Rut. That was the third time I called for your attention." Caden stared at the pathetically small human and knew he'd be the Giants' dessert.

"Little busy, George," Bobby grumbled.

"Are your walkie-talkies on?"

"Yes."

"Then listen to them too. We've been trying to get a hold of you."

Bobby growled like a dragon and stood upright, towering over Caden. "What do you want, little man?"

George didn't bat an eye. "Mr. Whitney requested our guests to be taken to the Northern Patio."

Bobby's head tilted to one side. "Guests?"

"Guests. The young Mr. Mizrahi and Mr. Deker."

My fake name. Caden thought with a start. *How does he know that? Elijah. What've they done to him?*

"I can escort them," George said. "You should go see the nurse, Mr. Rut. That looks... uncomfortable." Bobby grumbled again. Caden cowered despite himself.

He doesn't have to obey a human, he thought. *Why would he listen to that scrawny butler?*

To his complete shock, Bobby gave Caden one last horrifying glare and slowly limped away. He motioned to Tess and she reluctantly dropped Asher. The two stayed cowered until the Giants lumbered out of the room.

"Well?" George said.

Caden ignored him and raced to Asher's side. "You

alright?" He quickly looked Asher over, glad to find they both still had their arms and legs.

"Did you see that?" Asher asked as he eased himself to his feet. "A spear! He's got a second butthole now!" Caden stared at Asher in shock as the older boy started laughing. "Wish Aba saw that. Shoulder okay?"

Caden glanced at it. "I think... I don't know."

"Gentleman!" They jumped and faced George. "This way. Please!"

"Hey, we just almost died!" Asher snapped. "Give us a sec!" Caden and Asher looked at one another and Caden nodded. The two slowly joined George.

"Leave the spear here," the butler said.

"Not a chance."

"Mr. Mizrahi-"

"Take it from me!" George finally shut his lip and led the two from the room. Asher walked last of all, his spear held in both hands, poised for action.

I'm alive, Caden thought. *I have all my fingers and toes. Why do I keep surviving these crazy stunts? Is it something you're doing?* He glanced around him, as though another Door would appear out of nowhere. Could the Raw Peace hear him? Sounded absurd, but it wasn't just a feeling of peace. It was a living thing. Maybe even a person. Caden didn't understand it, but there was little he understood these days.

———

CADEN WAS sure he'd find Elijah tied to a chair, face a bloodied mess, as he tried to stay conscious. Instead, he found him lounging in a chair as he sipped tea and petted a golden retriever. This dog wasn't a Freak, which was relieving. The Seattle air was thick with approaching rain, yet sunshine still battled through the distant dark clouds.

A rock fire pit sat between outdoor couches. The patio was stone with a wooden shade cover over a sitting area. Thomas and Amanda Whitney sat across the table from Elijah as little sandwiches and tea sat between. The retriever perked up as George led Caden and Asher out into the open air.

"Ah," Thomas said as he glanced over his shoulder. "Sit. Eat." Caden's eyes narrowed. "Asher, put the spear down." Asher stiffened as Caden slowed. He considered standing behind Asher when Elijah lifted his chin and discreetly nodded.

I'm completely lost, Caden thought. *Again!* He hated not knowing what was happening. Asher didn't seem to mind. Seeing his father approved of Thomas' directions, he leaned the spear against the wall and sat down next to Elijah. Caden followed hesitantly, then stopped. There was another at the table he hadn't noticed; James. He was tied to the chair, gagged, and staring straight ahead. The Viper lounged across his shoulders, its triangular head leaning back and taking in the scene.

Great, Caden thought as he sat.

Thomas arched a brow at the spear, seeing the blood trickle down the shaft. He turned to Asher and the younger man gave a small, dark smile. "Anyone dead?" Thomas asked.

"Almost eaten, thanks to your Giant pets." Thomas grunted and sipped his tea.

Caden felt Amanda staring at him. Her eyes were red rimmed and she kept sniffing. She leaned closer to Thomas and took hold of his arm to lean on him. "Tom," she whispered. "Are you sure-"

"This is Oliver Deker. Alex is dead." Caden stiffened and glanced between the couple. Amanda pulled away from her husband and withered in her chair. She sat, shriveled back, her glossy eyes fixated on her untouched cup of tea.

Alex is dead, Caden thought, finding he wasn't surprised. He heard a hiss and his hair stood on end. What was that Viper doing? Laughing again? *We've gotta get out of here.*

"How do you know?" Amanda mumbled, her words a bit slurred.

What's in her tea?

"You have no proof-" Thomas slid a small paper across the table to her. She took it and quietly read. Caden watched as her saddened face flushed red and fresh tears filled her eyes. "What is this?"

"A report from our friends in the KUS," Thomas answered.

Caden stared at the table, the mention of the KUS making him want to be invisible. *They found me-*

"Officer Nathaniel in Camp Little Rock." Caden's heart skipped a beat as he closed his eyes.

Thomas sipped his tea as he casually watched a tear slip from his wife's eye. "He and his men found the address provided by Mr. Elijah here." Everyone turned to Elijah, who was enjoying his sandwich too much to notice.

He knows we're looking, Caden thought. *He's not as oblivious as he seems.*

"They found a body," Thomas continued. "In Nockville." Caden tried to hide his unease and shock.

"No," Amanda muttered.

"It was old. About six months old. You know, when we lost contact with Alex?"

I was in Nockville six months ago, Caden thought, his stomach turning. *This can't be a coincidence.*

"The doctor in Camp Little Rock had a minor in osteology. He could tell the bones were young, about twenty. And male." Amanda gasped, laying a hand over her trembling lips. Thomas didn't move to comfort her. Actually, her anguish seemed to please him.

"Did they find his sunglasses? The blue ones? He always had them."

"No."

"Then he wasn't-"

"But here's the real kicker," Thomas said as he leaned forward. "The body had a golden tooth." Amanda buried her face in her hands. Her shoulders were shaking. "Far right molar." Thomas watched his wife and sniffed indifferently before turning away. "Thank you, Mr. Elijah. It's nice to have closure." Elijah didn't answer as he stared at Amanda. He grabbed a napkin and held it out to her, but Thomas swatted his hand away. "Let her cry."

"You knew?" she turned to Thomas, makeup streaking down her face. "And you didn't tell me? I thought this," she motioned to Caden, "was Alex! I thought he was our nephew! Our boy!"

"You mean *your* boy."

Amanda's whimpering stilled as she stared at Thomas. "Now, what does that mean?"

"I know what you and Anthony did, Amanda." The look in Thomas' eyes darkened as Amanda leaned away.

"I-I don't understand-"

"Anthony and Cynthia had brown hair. You and Alex are blond." Amanda's mouth opened as she struggled for words that couldn't come. "That's why you took that self-reflection trip to the Philippines," Thomas whispered. Though he was quiet, steel entered his voice. "You were gone for several months. Left wearing baggy clothes and returned in your usual, slim wear. So strange how Anthony suddenly wanted to adopt during that time."

Amanda lay a hand over her stomach and turned away. She slowly stood and nearly stumbled from the patio. No one offered to help her as she made her way inside. No one spoke, and Thomas sipped his tea. His bald head was a bit flushed, and Caden knew he wasn't tasting his tea. Caden cursed under his breath and turned away.

"Mr. Whitney," Elijah said evenly. "Was that necessary?"

"Vengeance is always necessary. Isn't that right, James?" The tied man stared back at Thomas with a wild look in his eyes. "And what was your vengeance to me, sir? What dirt could you possibly have? Besides orchestrating the death of my wife's son."

Asher coughed on his tea and Caden couldn't suppress his gaping stare. *This just keeps getting better and better.* James leaned back in his chair as his breath quickened.

"Well?" Thomas grumbled and he yanked James' gag free.

"Yarrow," James gasped. "Yarrow's who killed him. I didn't! I swear!"

"Huhum," Thomas grunted, obviously uninterested.

"I can lead you to him. He's the one who-"

"You hired thugs to capture Alex. For money?"

"I-I just-" James turned to Elijah. The large man stared at him without moving. James hung his head and the Viper's tongue lashed. The Spirit's small, clawed feet dug into James' shoulder, making him gasp. "I wanted to take from you what you took from me!"

"I didn't kill your wife-"

"Yes you did!" Caden recoiled, the look in James' eyes could melt ice. "You did! All you Whitneys did! It was because of you! If only you gave me some money! She'd live! We wouldn't be here now!"

"Right, right," Thomas said, unfazed. "I see, it's all my fault." He waved a hand and the door swung as a Giant stepped out. The Giant approached, this one dark skinned with long, curled hair. Caden felt like he was punched in the guts as he froze.

Another one? His eyes darted to the spear, but he eased as the Giant grabbed James and the chair he was tied to. As though he was a doll, the Giant started walking James inside.

"I'll give you whatever you want!" James cried. "Yarrow? His men?" Thomas didn't answer as he added more sugar to his tea. "Curse you, Elijah! We are friends!

Friends!" Elijah didn't stir as he took another sandwich. "You betrayed me! How did you know any of this?"

"No," Elijah said calmly. "You betray yourself. You always say you talk too much when you drink."

James fell quiet. "No," he mumbled. "This isn't how it's supposed to happen." Caden gave him one last look before the Giant took him inside. His eyes fell on the Viper. Its black tongue flicked expectantly as its little hands clawed at James' with restless energy.

It's excited, Caden concluded. *What a horrible Spirit.*

"We will watch your death too, human."

Caden flinched back and raised a hand, as though that would help him. He cleared his throat and steadied himself. He had to stay calm when Spirits got into his head, especially around other people. Asher was staring at him. Caden crossed his arms and tried to ignore him.

"Well," Thomas said once James was gone. They could still hear him shouting. "Elijah. You still want three tickets to Israel?"

Caden faced Elijah and fidgeted in his chair. "Um," he muttered. *They forgot about me! I'm going to! I have to-*

"Four," Elijah said. "We're all going."

"Who's the fourth passenger?"

"My wife, Ophir."

"And why isn't she here?"

"Didn't want her to be Giant food."

"And yet you're going to Israel." Thomas shook his

head as he looked between them. "You understand Zone Apollo and Zone Ra are crawling with Giants?"

I think those zones are the Middle East, Caden thought, trying to remember the map from Camp Little Rock.

"There's Freaks," Thomas continued. "Monsters. And when I say monsters, I mean swimming, fire-breathing animals and titan-like land creatures from horror stories and folklore. Still interested?" Elijah nodded, answering for all three of them.

We're going? Caden thought, his heart quickening. *This crazy con is actually working! Sort of.*

Thomas sighed and held out his hands. "Very well." Caden fought the urge to fist pump the sky with a loud whoop. "Four tickets. One way?" Again, Elijah nodded, and Thomas chuckled. "You are all either very brave or very insane. I'll have my valet drive you to the airport tomorrow at six. Oh, and you're all flying economy. You owe me three grand for staying at the Four Seasons Hotel. Don't stay there tonight and don't be late for my valet."

"Where are we meeting?" Asher asked.

"Here. If you're late, no deal. To clarify, late means six o' one." All three nodded.

"We'll see you at five," Caden said as they stood.

For once, Thomas turned and regarded Caden. "You wouldn't happen to know Officer Nathaniel, would you?"

A cold thrill rushed up Caden's spine as he told himself to act calm. "Do I look like KUS material?"

"Over the radio, he mentioned someone who looks a great deal like you." Caden lifted his chin and stared down at Thomas. His feet were planted as he hugged his still throbbing shoulder. His unharmed arm's hand fisted. "Tall, slim, dark hair," Thomas muttered. "Your brows are brown. You should dye those too the next time you want to con someone out of thousands."

"Thanks for the tip."

"Officer Nathaniel said he was about your age too."

"You don't know my age."

"And last seen in northern Oregon. The kid's name is Caden Johnson." Asher's dark eyes hooked into Caden. Elijah's only response was a pause as he ate his sandwich.

So, Nathaniel did spread the word, Caden thought. His fisted hand became slick with sweat.

"Sound familiar?" Thomas asked.

"Apparently, I look like everyone important these days," Caden said as offhandedly as he could. "You're probably thinking of my twin. He's the evil one, you know."

Thomas' brows rose as he nodded slowly. "I see." Caden didn't turn away from Thomas and wondered if he could wield a spear with a hurt arm. Thomas finally turned from Caden and grabbed his cup of tea. "Have a safe flight, gentleman." Caden tried not to sigh with relief. "Mr. Elijah, thank you for sending your letter."

Caden glanced at the letter and suddenly remembered Elijah flagging down the messenger bicyclist before going to House Whitney. *Sly ol' man. Did he plan all this the entire time?* He wouldn't be surprised.

"Thank you for keeping your word," Elijah said with a bow. "May Yahweh be with you." Thomas glared at Elijah over the rim of his teacup as the three followed George from the patio.

Asher reached for the spear again, but Elijah shook his head and they continued into the mansion. Caden followed last of all as he tried to contain himself. The relief and thrill of finally going across the world with a chance to find his sister was snuffed out. Caden's heart couldn't slow as he felt his legs shake with each step.

Nathaniel's been telling people about me, he thought, panic pressing on his chest. *I don't want to be hunted anymore. I'm not an animal!*

He didn't respond as George introduced him to the Whitney's nurse who wanted to look at his arm. *Did Nathaniel tell the KUS in Israel about me?* Caden forced himself to breathe as he stared at his feet. He could imagine white uniforms waiting for him at the Israeli gate when he got off the plane. Would they execute him in the airport, or would they go on a drive first?

I'm not an animal, Caden thought again, as though already begging. *I just want to find my sister. Please. Just leave me alone!* Deep down, he knew his days of being hunted were far from over.

NINETEEN

LONG TIME NO SEE

CADEN KEPT his head down as he studied his shoes. He was in line with the Mizrahi family and a host of others to board the humming plane outside. The arm Bobby nearly ripped off was secured in a sling. The pain had subsided, but after sleeping in the car the night before, it was a little stiff.

Caden could see the US Flag fluttering close to the window, with it the Sovereign Lion. Its human-like eyes were fixated on him, as though it knew who he was. Knew the King's United Society was looking for him. Hunting him down. They were going to kill him, just like they killed Sophia, Harrison, and Simon. And Trace-

Caden sucked in a breath and glanced over his shoulder. His eyes darted over the unfamiliar faces of waiting passengers but didn't see Scar. Goosebumps still dotted Caden's arms as he forced himself to hold still.

He can't be here now, he thought. *He died or was wounded. Can Spirits even die?* He looked to Elijah, seeing the broad man's back as he waited before him. *Could he keep me safe?* Caden shook his head, knowing nothing could protect him from a vengeful Spirit.

Caden's thoughts stilled as uniformed members of the KUS strolled by. They had guns. And batons. Caden's heart quickened as he discreetly turned his head, inspecting the far wall. *Stay calm, stay calm,* he told himself. *We're almost on the plane.* And then what? Would there be safety for him in Israel? Caden's stomach twisted as doubts threatened to weaken his resolve. *I'll regret leaving,* he told himself. *There are Giants there. Monsters too. More Freaks. More KUS. More of everything I hate.*

Caden glanced at the plane outside and the little dots of people working beneath it. *Lil El,* he thought. *If there's anything to find. Probably long dead by now. A skeleton. I can't keep anyone alive. Everything I love perishes right before me. Harrison was right.* Caden glanced down, a pained expression on his face. *I am cursed. And a failure, just like Dad always said. GJ. Even if Ellie is alive, I'll kill her too-*

Caden hissed a curse and ran fingers through his hair. He shifted his weight and looked over his shoulder again, half expecting a white, mangled face to stare back at him from the shadows. *Raw Peace,* he thought, desperate for something real. Some truth. *Raw Peace.* He kept reciting that one phrase as the line moved. He handed over his ticket, noting the woman's pin. It was a Sovereign Lion. Caden was glad Thomas Whitney had let them bypass security. It was obvious he wanted them out of his way. Or dead. Did he think he'd survive Israel-?

"Stop it," Caden whispered through gritted teeth.

I'm not going crazy! These aren't my thoughts! He looked over his shoulder again.

Asher, who stood behind him, glared at him. "What?" Caden didn't answer as he continued onto the jet walk. "Seriously," Asher said, bumping his arm. "Looking for someone?"

Caden didn't answer a moment. *I can never tell them,* he

thought. *They won't understand Scar. They'll try to kill me like Nathaniel or use me like Grant.*

"I probably won't see America again," he said. Asher stared at him, his brow arched. Caden ignored his skepticism and continued to the plane.

It was an odd feeling stepping onto the plane. After such a long time of wanting to see Ellie again, he finally had a chance. He figured he would have to sail to her since the Day of Vanishing made air travel impossible for a time. Here he was, boarding a plane, headed to a country a few days walk from his little sister.

Well, he thought hesitantly. *Maybe the fates aren't as heartless as I thought.* He stilled, a coldness washing over him. *Or is this God?* He gritted his teeth and lowered his chin, unwilling to think of the madman in the clouds. *This has nothing to do with Him.* He stepped onto the plane and pointedly glanced away from the KUS Sentries already seated in first class.

He followed Elijah to the back of the plane and sat. He wanted to sit by the window, but Elijah claimed it first. Caden leaned back and continued to stare at the ground. Asher was watching him. *He knows something's up,* Caden thought. Ophir, who was struggling with her carry-on luggage, asked Elijah for help. He stood, squeezing past Caden, and came to her side.

We'll be alright, Caden thought hopefully. *We'll just fly for a few hours, land, the KUS won't stop me. They might. What if they do? They might've heard of me. I could be put in jail. What are their jails like? Rats and mud. Are they allowed to beat me and…*

Caden made a fist and squeezed until his knuckles became white. *What's wrong with me?* He looked around again, knowing the crowded plane could still hold a few Spirits. There were a handful of Vipers, one in a woman's purse and another walking along the ceiling. A Wither sat a few seats away. At least, Caden thought it was a Wither, the old man's face was a bit too bland with no defining characteristics.

A Shade could fit here, Caden thought, ignoring the Spirits as best he could. *I'm sure.*

His searching eyes fixed onto one of the boarding passengers. It was a large man, even a little bigger than Elijah. He wore a ball cap and a long trench coat. Caden's eyes narrowed; he had seen him before. *Who's that guy?* Caden's eyes widened as every muscle in his body tensed. It was Buck. Grant's henchmen. *If Buck's here,* Caden thought, his breath quickening. *Does that mean…? Grant is dead! No one can survive an ankle break today. He has to be dead.*

Caden couldn't bring himself to search as he ducked his head. Out of the corner of his eye, Buck came closer. *Find your seat! Get away from me!* Buck drew nearer. Caden's shoulder tingled as he remembered the large man's fingers digging in, holding him in place. Was Buck the vengeful type? He seemed loyal to Grant. He could finish what his leader started, making Caden a slave and using him to scavenge in Spirit-infected territory. To what end? Caden's guts twisted until they hurt.

I can't run, he thought, panic tightening his throat. *There's nowhere to hide!* Buck continued walking down the aisle. Caden could clearly see the bulge of a gun at his side. *He's going to find me.* Caden swallowed, unable to stay calm. *God? If You're really helping me, get rid of Buck! You can do that, can't You? Just-just do something! I don't want to be a slave…*

"Caden." Caden recoiled, finding Elijah standing over him. "Move over."

Caden quickly obeyed, his limbs working on autopilot. Caden faced the window, watching distant clouds and the Seattle landscape. His hair stood on end as he waited for Buck's beefy hand to seize his arms and drag him into the open. *Would anyone stop him? No one would fight for me. Why would they? I have no family, no alliances. The Mizrahi family only used me to get to this plane. Now, I had no further value. I am an unnecessary dead weight...*

"You okay?" Caden slowly turned and realized everyone had made it to their seats. The captain was speaking, something about buckling up for the long ride. Caden glanced at Elijah. He was staring at him with a pinched brow and narrowed eyes. "You are sweating."

Caden wiped his forehead and sat back, staring straight ahead. "I'm fine." Elijah continued watching him. *Buck must've walked by,* Caden thought. *He didn't see me. As long as I keep my head down, I'll be fine.* He breathed out a sigh as the plane began to move onto the runway. *I'm almost there,* he thought. *Just stay calm and don't mess this up!*

———

CADEN THOUGHT he'd watch the land he was born in fade into the distance, but he didn't. The country that was his, that was all he had ever known, could stay in the distance. Nearly his entire family was buried there. *Or rotting,* he thought. Dad was probably still slumped in his car on the highway, twisted in mangled metal and other less fortunates. And Trace. He was left alone. *Caden* had left him. Abandoned him. Just like Dad abandoned them. Caden was no better than his father.

Caden roughly scratched his head as he crossed his arms. *Raw Peace,* he thought with a curse. He fought the urge to search for Scar again. Even if the Shade was there, it wasn't letting Caden see it. Caden kept repeating Raw Peace as he closed his eyes and tried to sleep. His thoughts ping-ponged between finding Ellie's corpse and Buck and his gun seated behind him. When he did sleep, he dreamt of Scar smiling as Trace was shot to ribbons. He woke with a start, drenched in sweat. He hoped Elijah hadn't noticed, but he knew he did. Elijah seemed to notice everything.

But he's never afraid, Caden thought. He was like a boulder in the middle of a river; unmoving, steadfast, and forcing the current to move around it instead of being moved itself. *I want to be like that,* Caden thought as he tried to sleep again. He dreamt of Nate. Weak, frail, starving Nate. Needless to say, he didn't rest much. The shadows changed as the sun set and night took over. Caden found himself wide awake, staring into nothing, as everyone around him found peace.

Just ten more hours, he'd think. *Just nine... Eight... Seven.*

It felt like an eternity. The sun rose again, setting the sky on fire with golds and yellows. Caden looked out the window and saw something. A yellow sliver in the distance. Land. The other side of the world. His heart quickened and for once, he permitted himself a small, short-lived smile.

———

CADEN DIDN'T HAVE the slightest clue what to expect when landing. Did they wear turbans in Israel? Or was that India? Did everyone carry machine guns all the time? Would he be hated for being American?

Just get to Cairo, Caden thought. *Find Ellie. Maybe we can get home someday.* He doubted it. It was the last thing he was worried about; there was always a threat right in front of him to preoccupy his thoughts. This time, the threat was behind him. Buck hadn't walked past Caden once. It was like he wasn't even there. *He's behind me still. Maybe he's seen me. He definitely will when I get up.*

Caden stared at the floor as he felt the plane gradually descend from the clouds. If he got past Buck, the KUS

Sentinels might identify him. If he got past them, Tel-Aviv, where they were landing, might swallow him alive. If he survived the city, his trek to Cairo might kill him. Starvation. Dehydration. Scavenging gangs. Heartless terrorists. Someone mentioned a monster walking around out in the desert. A huge thing, able to crush humans with one step...

Caden put his head in his hands and squeezed his eyes shut tight. *What's wrong with me? Just focus on Buck! One thing at a time!* He didn't want to freak out. If he freaked, he couldn't think straight, thus putting a target on his back. A target Buck most definitely would pursue with the ferocity of any vengeful-

Scar! Caden's head snapped up and he looked around, his breath quickening. *Leave me alone! You can't touch me! You've already tired!*

"*I'm touching you now.*"

Caden stilled as all blood drained from his face. *No*, he thought. *You can't follow me here.*

"*What do you think could possibly prevent me?*"

Caden sat back and stared out the window, his thin hope for survival fraying. *That thing,* he finally answered. *The thing that scarred your face.*

"*What thing?*"

I... I don't know-

"*Let me educate you, human.*" Caden shrunk back in his seat, the Shade's words within his mind making him cold and numb. "*Nothing can deter me once prey has been sighted. Your flesh is mine. As was your brothers.*" Caden forgot to breathe. "*I agree with the Giants, your tender flesh is delectable.*"

Hot breath tickled the back of Caden's neck.

He lurched forward with a curse, the seatbelt biting into his middle, and raised defensive arms. Elijah leaned back as he regarded him with narrowed eyes. "Sit quietly. We almost landed." Caden didn't answer as his eyes darted all around, certain he'd see a white, shadowed figure grinning ear to ear. Elijah's head cocked at an angle and he looked over his shoulder.

"No, don't!" Caden gasped, suddenly remembering Buck. "Just-just sit down. Please!"

Elijah turned around and calmly folded his hands in his lap. "You have much explaining to do."

"I," Caden stammered. "I have nothing to say."

Elijah shook his head. "You will explain. Do not want dangers following you into Elezaro's home."

Caden shifted in his seat. "Who?"

"My cousin."

"I'm... I'm going to Cairo."

"After rest."

"I've troubled your family long enough."

"No. You come with us still. Elezaro wants to meet you."

"You've already told him about me?"

"Mr. Thomas had a radio so I sent a message ahead. Elezaro should be here soon."

"Did you tell him my name is Oliver or Caden?"

Elijah grimaced. "Stop this fake name. It's a waste of time."

Caden cursed under his breath, not wanting to tell Elijah the KUS wanted him dead. "Mr. Mizrahi, I can't stay with your cousin-"

"Want to sleep on the street? In the cold? What are your plans, Caden?"

Caden fell silent. He stared at his feet as the plane drew closer and closer to the ground. "I thought we'd go our separate ways." Elijah didn't answer. "I can't just go into your family's house and sleep on their couch. What do you want me to do? Eat from your fridge too?"

Elijah chuckled. "You Americans." Caden glared at him. "This is Israel. You stay. Three days at least."

Caden didn't answer, he didn't know what to say. What did these people want? "I can't pay you."

"Did I ask for payment?"

"I... I guess not."

"I asked for an explanation though."

Caden turned away as his eyes darkened. *I guess I could tell them about Buck and Grant. But not about why they want me. No one can know about me seeing Spirits. And them leaving me alone. Well... not killing me at least.*

"Yet."

Caden closed his eyes and felt himself leaning closer to Elijah. He realized with a jolt that the thought of leaving this family sickened him. Asher had almost died for him, and he had nearly been ripped in half for Asher. Elijah had orchestrated the entire con to end in the family's favor. *Caden's* favor. No, Caden didn't want to leave them. But he couldn't tell them the full truth.

"Alright," he muttered. "I'll explain. Now?"

"At my cousins." Caden nodded. "For now, that big man in the long coat is an enemy. Yes?" Caden nodded again. "Wants you dead?" Caden shook his head and then shrugged. Elijah casually glanced at Asher, seated nearby with Ophir, as the plane touched down. They made eye contact and Asher straightened in his seat, seeing his Aba's guarded posture.

"Walk in front of me," Elijah said calmly. Caden shot him a quick look; how was he always so steady as though nothing was wrong? "Just one enemy?"

"Yah." Caden waited in tense silence as the plane ran down the runway and eased to a stop. He watched Elijah out of the corner of his eye and slowly forced his bunched shoulders to relax. *Elijah's chill. If he is, I can be too.* He sighed a long breath and stared ahead, trying not to think of Sentinels or desert monsters or dead sisters.

———

CADEN HAD to tell himself to just walk three times as he slowly made his way off the plane. He wanted to shove the passengers and run for his life, but he made himself stay calm. He was shocked when they reached the gate. He was even more shocked to find that Israel, the far-off Middle East, didn't look all that different.

They also had clear floors and nice seats. There were restaurants and signs, mostly in Hebrew with English beneath, and bathrooms and all the things he'd seen in American airports. And there were people. Sure, their dress was more casual, less flashy, and a lot more old guys sporting long, long beards. But there were still families, still kids whining and pointing at the pinball machines, women clustered together in their little herds, and men trying to keep their little clan on track.

Caden tried not to gawk at the black cladded dress of some, and the men with two long curls while the rest of their hair was cut short. What baffled him the most was the bright, constant glow of lightbulbs in the ceiling above. The buzz of electricity was faint, yet he heard it. He had always heard America was one of the Dark Lands. Now, he understood why. Looking out the airport window, he saw streetlamps, telephone poles, and more working cars than he'd seen in years. He stared at an outdoor café, and its odd-sized tables and chairs. They were enormous. No one could possibly sit-

He gulped as three Giants walked past. He would've taken off running if Elijah hadn't gently, yet firmly grabbed his arm. There were more Giants outside, some seating themselves around the massive table. Trucks hauled trailers full of comfy seats with straps to be Giant taxis. Some of the doorways were two doors in one, a smaller-sized door for humans and a larger one for Giants.

Caden turned from the window, unable to see a Giant without thinking of Bobby pinching his shoulder, a hungry look in his eye.

He kept following the Mizrahis to a woman in a white, pleated uniform of the KUS' Sentinels. She held a scanner up to each passenger's forehead before directing them to the next station. Some declined the scan and she sent them in another direction.

"What is that?" Ophir whispered. "Are they looking for something in our heads?"

Caden blinked and lifted his chin. "NIIS," he said. "The king's neural implants." Asher and Ophir gave him a sharp look. "I heard about those; they're to unify people more, give us a way to communicate, and help each other. Something like that."

"Or control us," Asher muttered. "Wouldn't be surprised if these NIIS things take over, separating everyone."

Caden nodded. "The king's allies from the, um-"

"Yahweh's allies," Ophir whispered. "Will one go in the hand too?"

Caden glanced at her, surprised. "How'd you know?" She nodded slowly, her lips pressed together in a tight, thin line.

How do they know things? Caden wondered. *What's their trick?*

He glanced at the woman Sentinel and watched as she cleared another passenger. Caden rubbed his forehead, knowing no implant would be found there. What would happen next? He looked around, hoping there was some way to escape. He kept thinking of Nathaniel's dogs and the crack of gunfire. *They could've heard about me,* Caden thought. *They know I'm wanted. Is it dead or alive?*

Before he knew it, Elijah stepped before the Sentinel and handed her papers from Thomas Whitney. She read it over and quickly ushered them on with the group who had a NIIC. Caden slowly walked past, his nerves strained as his body tensed for action. The Sentinel turned her back on them and motioned for the next in line.

Did we just... how is this happening? Small hands latched onto the crook of his arm and Caden jerked away with a curse.

Ophir stared at him and grimaced. She spoke, her Hebrew irritated, as she grabbed his arm and pulled him back. She held him close and her words calmed and became gentle. "So jumpy. Scaredy cat. Stop that and walk with me." Caden scratched the back of his neck, realizing she was trying to reassure him.

They followed the NIIC group and other allies to customs. "They'll ask you questions," Asher said. "Don't lie, and don't act all nervous and awkward. They're not going to shoot you." Caden glared at Asher but was grateful for the heads up. Security did have questions for him, some more personal than he had expected.

"Where are you staying?"

"What's your business here?"

"Where are you going after this?"

Caden hardly knew the correct answers, but whatever he said, must have been enough for the guard. He tried not to look shocked when he was waved on. Caden walked through the sea of unfamiliar faces as his eyes stayed fixated on the floor. Sentinels were everywhere! The Sovereign Lion watched everyone from the Israeli flag overhead, the Star of David relocated to the far right to give the lion center stage.

They haven't caught me yet, Caden thought. *I guess Nathaniel's message didn't come here.* The tension in his shoulders started to loosen as he dared to lift his head. *But word can always come. At any time. They'll come for me. Again.* Caden cursed and ran fingers through his hair. *I can't live like this.*

He wasn't an animal. This running and hiding was wearing him out. When would he find rest?

Not in this life, he concluded. His mind suddenly flickered back to the cliff he hid on as Nathaniel hunted him down. He could've jumped. He could've ended all the pain with one small step into beautiful nothingness.

"But you chose to cling to life," hissed whispered words in his ear. White fur tickled Caden's cheek. He gasped, leaping away from Ophir with flailing arms. He struck a passerby and ran into another. They snapped at him, but he wasn't listening. His eyes darted all around as his heart quickened.

"Like a rat," Scar continued within Caden's mind. *"Clinging to a thread as the sewer water rises higher and higher."*

Caden hugged himself and stumbled through the crowd. Asher called to him, but he didn't acknowledge him. He had to get away. Had to escape the Shade that haunted him! Caden found himself leaning against a wall next to a door he guessed led to storage. No one was close to him and nothing dangerous seemed lurking behind the potted fern in the corner. Caden hugged himself, his chest heaving, and he tried to calm down.

I survived that stupid con and all those Giants, and now I've made it. I'm in Israel, just a few hours away from Cairo. Keep it together. Just keep it together! Caden took in a breath and straightened himself. *I can do this. I can-*

The door opened. Caden felt himself stumbling toward it. A hand. A hand had grabbed his shirt. It was pulling him through the door. Panic struck Caden as he turned to the passing people and sucked in a sharp breath. A forearm wrapped around his throat and cut off the airway. Caden's back arched as he gasped, but no air came. The terminal's lights and faces dimmed as he was dragged into darkness. The door led to a dimly lit hall, and if Caden had been paying attention, he'd have heard another door open before being pulled through.

Caden thrashed and kicked. He didn't notice the throbbing pain in his wounded shoulder. All his efforts were useless. Whoever had him couldn't be moved. His mouth gaped as he desperately tried to take in air. He had to call for help. He couldn't do this on his own! Why was he always alone?

"You simmer down now," a chipper voice said in his ear. There was no accent. It was a familiar voice too, spoken in a very familiar fashion. Deja vu confused Caden further. "The more you struggle, the more he'll like it."

Caden's blood turned to ice. *Buck! He did see me!* He stopped writhing, but he couldn't stop pulling against Buck's massive forearm. Caden's face felt tight, and he guessed it was turning from red to purple. Was he trying to make him pass out?

"Be quiet," Buck whispered and loosened his hold. Caden sucked in a breath, coughing and sputtering, as though drawn up out of water. Before he could fill his lungs entirely, Buck clamped a hand over his mouth. Caden reached to pull his hand away, but Buck was too fast. He grabbed Caden's arms and drew them back with a firm grip. Caden yelled, finally feeling his already strained shoulder's intensified pain. He fought to suck in air past Buck's beefy fingers.

This can't be happening! You can't take me like this! Through the thrill of panic and his pounding heartbeat, Caden realized what Buck had said. *Who will like me struggling?*

The door opened, revealing a shadowed figure. Caden watched as the stranger shuffled forward. One foot dragged across the floor and the stranger leaned heavily on a cane. He was tall and fit, his dark hair cut short, and blue-rimmed sunglasses hung from his shirt collar.

"Long time no see, Max!"

Caden couldn't withhold a groan as he pushed against Buck. Every muscle strained to pull away from the newcomer. He knew it was useless. He couldn't help it as Grant stopped before him, a wolfish smile plastered on his face.

TWENTY
CHALLAH IS BREAD

YOU'RE SUPPOSED *to be dead!* Caden's mind screamed as he stared at Grant. *I saw you! You can't survive a broken ankle anymore!* These thoughts were followed by a colorful array of curses. He saw this coming. Why hadn't he done anything to stop them? What could he have done?

"You know," Grant said. "I was just talking about you the other day. Someone mentioned Haunts are more prevalent in Jerusalem. They like it there. But now," Grant stepped closer. Caden knew, if Buck wasn't holding him in place, he'd be cowering in the corner. "Now, I have you." Caden tried to breathe but found it was near impossible again. "You still seeing Haunts? Are they still leaving you alone?"

Caden didn't answer as Grant's smile grew. Grant chuckled and lay a hand on Caden's shoulder. "I'm very pleased to see you again, Max. We're going to have fun." Caden didn't move as Grant's touch made his hair stand on end. "Do you like my cane? I knew a guy who owed me. Very talented man. Could turn a kitchen table into a shotgun."

Grant held up the cane, bringing it too close for

comfort. Caden tried to pull away. It was all instinctual. He wasn't completely thinking anymore, only reacting. The cane was solid oak and the handle was a metal ball. "Pretty little thing, isn't it?" Caden's insides coiled, knowing there was a catch. "But wait," Grant said. "There's more."

He grabbed the ball, turned it clockwise, and pulled up. It withdrew and revealed a thin, glinting blade jutting from the cane. Caden recoiled with a whimper. He was suddenly aware of his vulnerable belly. "It's it cute?" Caden didn't move, save for his exposed throat that bobbed as he swallowed. "And," Grant said, raising a finger. "When put back together," he reset the ball on the cane, "the ball is weighted. Perfect for breaking bones."

Oh God, no, Caden thought, too terrified to realize he was praying. *We have a deal! You want me? Come save me!*

"So, Max," Grant said evenly, drawing even closer. "Since our last deal ended so well, let's make another one." Caden didn't move as he felt Buck's hold tighten. "You be my slave, as I first intended, and you obey my every bidding."

Caden shook his head, and his hands became fists. *I am no one's property!* He knew that heartless treatment; his father taught him all too well.

"If you obey," Grant continued, "and never try to run or find someone to save you," he brought the weighted cane up before Caden's eyes again, "then I'll only break *half* the bones in your body." He rested the cane against Caden's chest. Caden felt the weight in the ball and his face drained of color. "Starting with your ankle," Grant muttered, that horrible smile never leaving his face. Caden closed his eyes tight as sweat trickled from his brow. "Wow," Grant muttered. "You really are scared, aren't you kid?" Caden could hear the amusement in his voice. "Good. Shows you've got a head on your shoulders."

I've got to get to Cairo! I can't be stuck with these two. They'll kill me!

"Mr. Yarrow," Buck said in a mild, even voice. "We should skedaddle." Caden blinked. He had heard that name before.

Grant glanced at Buck before returning his attention to Caden. "Buck here is going to take his hand off your mouth. You are not going to make a sound. Not even a sneeze, yes? Or I'll have to snap off your pinkies. Blink twice if you understand."

Caden blinked twice and Buck's firm hand slowly peeled from his face. Caden took in a breath of fresh air and fought the urge to scream. *I should risk it,* he thought. *Broken pinkies are better than half my bones broken…*

Something hard and cold pressed against the small of his back. It was small and circular. "And if you run," Grant continued. "Buck will fill you with lead." Caden's foggy brain finally registered the cold, circular thing as the muzzle of a gun. Grant grunted and began dragging his crippled leg to the door.

Yarrow, Caden thought, needing something else, something less horrible, to think of. *Someone was talking about you. Someone bad and slippery like a snake-*

Or a Viper.

Caden's eyes widened. He stared at Grant's high fashion, blue-rimmed sunglasses. The kind a spoiled, rich kid would've had. Someone like Alex Whitney. *That body,* Caden thought. *That body that was all ripped up and bleeding. Had that been Alex?*

Caden swallowed the hard lump in his throat as he followed Alex's kidnapper. He didn't feel anything but the hard ground beneath his feet and Buck's gun digging into his back. He was drifting through the moment, too terrified to feel it. The internal scream had become white noise again, and he was alone in the vastness of paralyzing anxiety.

Shouted Hebrew echoed in the hallway. Caden flinched and looked around, realizing they had left the storage room. Buck grabbed his shoulder as the gun bore into his back. Caden held his tongue and forced himself to be still. The hallway was still dark, yet they weren't alone. A man stood before the door, his arms crossed, and feet firmly planted. He frowned, drawing his thick mustache down further, and discreetly shook his head. Beside him stood a young man, his posture mimicking his companion.

Get help! Caden wanted to shout. *Get someone!*

Grant stepped forward and, to Caden's surprise, began speaking Hebrew. The man cut him off and waved a hand, his tone stern and irritable. Grant interrupted and Caden stiffened as he adjusted his hold on the lethal cane.

"He's my son!" The phrase echoed in the small space from behind. It was spoken with authority from someone who expected obedience.

Elijah, Caden thought, the tension in his shoulders slightly loosening.

Grant turned and scoffed. "Your son? That's the most pathetic excuse I've ever come across!"

"Let him go!" That was Asher. How many people were there? "You're outnumbered. Don't be stupid!"

Grant looked between Elijah and Asher and the two strangers. "He's mine. You thought you could hoard his abilities all to yourself?" Caden closed his eyes, wishing he hadn't said that. Elijah already knew Caden was lying about how many enemies he had. What would he think of him now? "And *I'm* not stupid," Grant snapped. He withdrew a gun from the inside of his jacket. "So, if you'll excuse us." No one moved.

"He is my son," Elijah said as before. "We will fight for him. There are four of us. You want the KUS here?"

"I can shoot very well," Grant said, a small smile dancing in his eyes. "No one will survive."

"Are you willing to die for him?"

"Are you?"

"Yes."

The single word shot through Caden. What was Elijah talking about? Dying for him? He's lying! *Why would he lie?* Caden wondered. *He has nothing to gain fighting for me.* The silence that followed filled the room with so much tension a knife could cut through it.

Grant's smile stretched his mouth as he shook his head. "Watch your back, boy." His voice was a near whisper. "You will see us again. Soon."

Buck's gun withdrew, and he released his shoulder. Caden shrunk back and raced behind Elijah and Asher. His heart was pounding and his hands shook. Sweat trickled down his brow and stung his good eye. Grant gave Elijah a mocking bow as he put his gun away. Buck returned his gun to the holster and the pair sauntered out the door without another word.

Caden stared at the shutting door, still not believing they were gone. He was alive and safe. For now. With a gasp, Caden backed against the wall and buried his face in his hands. He cursed and shook his head, the panic he felt, yet suppressed, welling up inside. *I've got to get a gun! They'll be back. I'm sure of it.*

A hand lay on his shoulder, and he recoiled. Asher stepped back. "Chill, man. We've gotta go."

You won't die for me, Caden thought. He was suddenly reminded of Bobby, wounded and bleeding, and Asher with a spear in his hand. *But you almost did. Why? What do you want?*

"Come on. Don't just stand there!"

Can I trust them? He felt his feet moving and Elijah drawing closer. He didn't realize it, but the tension throughout his body eased. *Just go with them. They've kept you alive this far.*

They left the airport with no more issues. Caden hardly noticed the hot, new air, the sandstone buildings, and the different faces. He numbly followed Elijah and the new strangers to a train station. He rubbed the small of his back and tried not to think of Buck's gun. It felt like it was still there, ready to fire. Ready to drop him.

Caden blinked, realizing they had boarded the train and Elijah was motioning to his seat. He obeyed, sitting close to the window, and Elijah sat next to him. Asher sat on the seat across them, beside the mustached stranger. The younger stranger sat with Ophir. Caden scarcely registered Ophir's soft voice, no doubt she was asking what happened. Elijah answered, his Hebrew words calm and quiet. Her eyes widened and she gave Caden a long, sorrowful stare. The train moved. They were on their way to... to...

Caden didn't know. He didn't care. He was still drowning in panic. He rubbed his brow as he sat hunched in the chair. "So," Elijah finally said. "I have questions." Caden didn't answer. "You answer yes or no. Yes?" Caden didn't move. If he could huddle into a tighter ball, he would.

"Hey," Asher said, nudging him with his foot. "That was a question."

Caden's stomach twisted. *Are they my enemies now too?*

"Yes," he mumbled.

"Are you hunted by the KUS?" Elijah asked.

Right for the jugular, Caden thought. "Yes."

"Do they want you alive?"

"No."

"Did you harm anyone?"

"No."

"Who we just met, are they KUS?"

"No."

"Different enemies."

"Yes."

"Do they want you dead?"

Caden blinked as he thought. "Eventually."

"What abilities do you have?" Caden fell silent. His shaking hands didn't stop their restless quiver. "Caden."

He faced the window as a muscle in his jaw flexed. *I can't tell them! Anyone who knows that either dies or tries to kill me.*

Asher sighed irritably and crossed his arms. "Caden, don't be difficult."

Caden closed his eyes and forced himself to breathe slowly. "I can't." No one spoke. He felt the weight of their stares. "I," he stammered, "I don't want... I-I just can't!"

Please don't hurt me. Please. Just let me go.

Out of the corner of his eye, Caden saw Asher lean forward, his mouth opening to speak, but stopped when Elijah held up a hand. "Why can't you tell us?" Elijah's voice was calm as before. "What are you afraid of?"

Caden shook his head. "You all will die." It felt funny to say. "Everyone who knows dies. Or tries to kill me. I... I can't have that again." He turned to them, looking each in the eye. "Whatever you do to me will be less painful than if I tell you. Believe me. Just," Caden's voice started to shake, and he steadied himself, "just let me off the train somewhere. You'll never see me again. I swear. Please."

He focused on Elijah, somehow willing him to agree. He knew he wouldn't. A man like Elijah was used to getting what he wanted. Caden knew from experience how hard he hit, his swollen, black eye reminded him every day. Caden wouldn't turn away from Elijah. He had to make him understand.

"Caden," Elijah said. "What do you think I will do to you?"

Caden squirmed, not wanting to give him any ideas. "I... I'm just not used to mercy. From anyone."

"Does risking my life for you mean nothing? I called you my son. Does that mean nothing?"

Caden struggled for words as the pain of his tormenting Dad got thrown into the mix. "A dad means nothing to me," he finally said. "Nothing but a threat."

"Well," Elijah said, sitting up straighter. "I'm not a dad. I'm an aba." Caden's eyes narrowed as he quietly tried to understand Elijah's meaning. Elijah let him think for a moment, and to Caden's surprise, he faintly smiled. "Any more enemies?"

Scar, Caden thought. *Definitely never telling him about that thing. I don't care if they are on my side.*

"The KUS," Elijah said. "Two bad guys. Any rich overlord you haven't mentioned yet?"

They did risk themselves for me, Caden thought. *Asher more than the others. Maybe I should tell them something. Not the truth! But, like, a half-truth?*

"There's one more."

Asher snorted a laugh and rubbed his eyes with a finger and thumb. "Of course."

"But it's, um, complicated."

Asher raised a hand and let it fall with a slap on his leg. "Complicated. Right. Why didn't I see this coming?"

Caden decided to ignore this and continued. "There's someone who wants me dead. I think. Or... to hurt me. I'm not sure. Someone's after me. He's, well, a monster and," he crossed his arms and took a breath, "he can't be stopped. At all. Not by us anyway."

"Monster, huh?" Caden glanced at the stranger. "We can't stop this monster?" His voice was heavily accented. "Who can then?"

Something that makes a lot of noise, Caden thought, remembering the attack on the cliff face. It felt like ages ago. He hadn't seen who wounded Scar, but the noise was overwhelming. He fumbled for words and didn't know what to say.

"I don't know. I didn't see his face."

"So, someone saved you?"

"Um, I think so."

"Why do you think so?" Asher asked. "He did, or he didn't?"

"I was just dragged off a cliff, okay?" Caden snapped. "All I could process was my leg was broken, and I wasn't dead yet!"

Asher snapped his mouth shut and tilted his head to one side. "You didn't try to commit suicide then?"

"No!"

"Hum. Yeah, that theory never made that much sense."

Caden scratched the back of his neck and waited for the next question. None came. "What now?" he asked.

Elijah's brow furrowed. "What do you mean? You still come with us. Nothing changed." Caden stared at him, waiting for the fine print that would wreck him. Instead, Elijah glanced outside and nodded to himself. "Sunset in a few hours. You will enjoy your first Shabbat. Very good way to end a good day."

Good day? Caden thought.

"Caden, this is Elezaro Mizrahi, my cousin." Caden found the stranger's hand extended toward him. He stared at it, wondering the last time he properly shook someone's hand. It felt like a silly thing to do for people who were nearly dying all the time. He took the hand and shook it. The man didn't smile. Come to think of it, most people here didn't smile. "*Shabbat shalom.*"

Caden stared at him. "Um, nice to meet you." Elezaro nodded and sat back.

The four fell silent and Caden found himself watching Elijah. Any moment, the huge man was going to grab him or remember that one little, horrible thing he wanted Caden to do. Elijah rested, his head leaned back, and he closed his eyes.

"Sleep," Elijah said, never bothering to open his eyes. "We travel for an hour."

He really means it, Caden realized, the thought striking him in the chest. *He wants me with his family.*

"Can I ask where we're going?"

Elijah cracked open an eye and studied him. "Jerusalem. Sleep. You're not my prisoner or hostage. You can leave at any time."

"And die alone in the streets," Asher added.

"Hili makes nice challah." Elijah said as he closed his eyes again. "You will like it. You will come."

Asher nodded as he pointed at Elijah. "Very good challah. Do you know challah?" Caden blankly stared at Asher. "Do you know anything about Israel?"

"Um, I know the Bible was written here."

"What?" Asher's face scrunched into a frown as Elijah smiled. "Not really. You know nothing else? It's bread. Challah is bread."

"And," Caden said slowly. "I know challah is a type of bread." Asher scoffed and grumbled something in Hebrew. The four quieted as the train continued on.

Caden ran fingers through his hair and noticed his hands weren't shaking anymore. *They could be telling the truth,* he thought. *Don't know why they're not making me talk. Maybe at Elezaro's house?* He doubted it. Who would harm someone after nearly dying for them?

Caden sat back and sighed. His eyes suddenly felt very heavy as exhaustion wrapped around him. He gave Elijah one last glance, he was already snoring, and permitted himself to relax. *I'm okay,* he thought. *I'm with friends, I guess.* It didn't feel right. No one was his friend. Everyone wanted to harm him. But not this family. Not these people.

I want something like this, Caden thought as he closed his eyes. *Something that's real and safe. It's kind of like the Raw Peace but... not as strong. I guess it's nice. I guess I'll stay.* It didn't take long for sleep to find him, and for once, Caden slept soundly.

————

THE NEXT SEVERAL hours were a blurred mess. After entering Jerusalem, Caden saw nearly ten Giants even before the train had stopped and decided his shoes were pretty cool to stare at for the rest of the time. He had had enough danger for one day and desperately needed a break. He stuck close to Elijah, closer than he thought he would, as they left the train and dove into the city.

Caden was bombarded by the foreign languages, some Hebrew, some Aramaic. People and buildings were everywhere. Everyone was talking. Horns were honking. Everyone quickly went about their day, constantly checking the sky.

"What're they looking for?" Caden asked Asher.

"The sun. Once it sets, it's Shabbat."

"So? Can't they be late?"

Asher glanced at Caden with an arched brow. "No."

"What is it exactly?"

"It's like a holiday."

"And it happens every Friday?"

"Friday sundown to Saturday sundown."

Caden blinked, stunned. "What's a holiday I know that's similar?"

Asher thought for a moment and then shook his head. "All your holidays don't focus on Yahweh or family. They're just so self-centered."

"Hey, I'm not insulting your culture."

"They are selfish!"

"Just answer my question, alright!"

"It's a dinner with family and friends while we recite traditional blessings. And talk about Yahweh, of course."

Caden's brows bunched as he turned away. "Of course." That didn't help him understand at all.

———

WHILE TAKING A BUS, Caden gained enough courage to look out the window and instantly spotted a Wither. It wasn't wearing anyone's skin yet and had the shriveled, boney build he was familiar with. He flinched back and studied his shoes again.

———

ELEZARO'S HOUSE looked like all the other ones around it, sand-colored bricks making a tall house that was tucked between more tall houses. They all seemed to be trying to climb over one another to get somewhere. Kind of like the people.

As they stepped from the taxi, Caden froze. Something was wrong. The bustling city was quiet. He glanced at Elijah, who gently smiled. "The sun," he said, pointing. "It is almost set. Everyone is home."

"I don't even hear a car."

"All transportation stops on Shabbat."

"Like... for the entire time?" Elijah nodded. "But, what if I need to get to the store or something?"

Elijah shrugged. "What's that thing you Americans say? Umm, snooze you lost?"

Caden smiled. "Snooze you lose."

"Plan ahead to rest for Shabbat. You Americans need to learn rest better."

"Thanks," Caden said dryly.

They approached the house and Caden felt like he was stepping into a new world far beyond anything he'd seen. Here was a family, a huge family, who wanted to be together. There were grandparents, a few uncles, some cousins, and Elezaro's own six kids. One of which, Ido, had come with his father and barred Grant's way from leaving with Caden. Hili, Elezaro's wife, shook Caden's hand and started talking to him in what he later learned was English. Her accent was so thick that he had no clue what she said. Whatever it was, her smile and excited tone made him feel welcome.

Shabbat turned out to feel like a family reunion that didn't suck. There was so much commotion, laughter, and Hebrew-English conversations. Caden never fully knew what was going on. At times, Elezaro and Hili would stand and say something in Hebrew. They would extend a hand toward candles, to the wine, or over the kids. Asher explained they were reciting blessings.

Challah bread turned out to be a real winner. Caden wanted to eat the entire loaf. If it was called a loaf. The dough had been braided, so maybe it was called a bread braid? Caden just ate it.

The food was delicious, but most importantly, the people were good. Caden felt it around them. It was something that he hadn't seen in his entire life. These people, these *strangers*, didn't mind him there. Actually, they seemed pleased he came. His presence brought them joy, and even though he didn't understand what they were saying most of the time, no one was bothered. He was accepted without doing something for them. He simply was, and that was enough for them.

Strange people, he thought.

Shabbat continued late into the night, and it wasn't until Caden nearly fell asleep in his chair did Elijah suggest he went to bed.

"Where?"

"Ophir will show you. *Neshama*?"

———

UPSTAIRS, in a small room doubling as a storage space, was a bed. Not some rug on the floor or even just a mattress. A real, blanketed bed with a pillow and everything. Caden stared at it as though it was a throne for a king. "I... I can stay here?"

"Yes, silly. Bathroom down the hall to the right." Caden didn't move from the doorway. He felt Ophir watching him. "Something wrong?"

Caden shuffled his feet and turned away. "Why are you all so nice to me?"

Ophir smiled and took his arm. "We know Yeshua. He changes everything."

"Who?"

"Jesus."

No, Caden thought. *It's not that simple.* But the look in Ophir's eyes told him otherwise.

Ophir rubbed his back and stepped away. "Try the light switch. There's power. Get some sleep. You look awful."

Caden smiled as she went to join the others. He stepped into the room, *his* room, and shut the door. There was a small window, which let in some of the full moon's light. The room was quiet and peaceful. Caden flipped the switch and a naked bulb blinked to life. He squinted up at the stark light, still in awe of the resurrected technology. With a sigh, he shut the light off. It was too bright. Too unnatural. He took off his shoes and jacket before easing into bed. He closed his eyes and sighed heavily.

Do the people behind The Door act like this? He wondered as he opened his eyes. *I hope they-*

All thoughts ended instantly. Every muscle tensed as Caden tried to understand what he was looking at. Or what was looking at him.

All over the place were eyes. They seemed to hover in the dark room, moving ever so slightly. None of them blinked. There were blue eyes, brown eyes, green and yellow. They were all staring right at him. They gathered together in a column at the foot of his bed, then branched out like the limbs of a tree, spreading across the ceiling.

Caden breathed out as he stared up, not knowing what to think. He forced himself to breathe again and realized, oddly enough, he felt surprised but not afraid. *Is this a Spirit?* He thought. *I haven't seen any with this many eyes. What does it want?*

Caden didn't understand much, but he did somehow know this: Scar and this new Spirit didn't live in the same camp. Sure, they were both Spirits, but this one was different. The eyes didn't seem to want anything from him or intended to do anything to him. They were just there. They didn't look at him like a piece of meat to devour, but something special, something valuable.

An eyeball Spirit, Caden thought. *Well... I need to sleep, so...*

The eyes didn't move. Caden rolled on his side and watched them for a few more minutes. He waited for them to move or attack him or do something. They did nothing but watch him.

Weird, Caden thought as he eased into his pillow. He closed his eyes and pulled the blankets close. "Goodnight." he mumbled to the Spirit. Caden drifted off to sleep as the eyes watched long into the night.

TWENTY-ONE

BROKEN SKY

CADEN STAYED with Elezaro and Elijah's family longer than he expected. There were days of eating strange, delicious food and trying to survive the culture shock. He quickly learned that he hated crowds, loud noises, and people with guns. So, he hated everything at first. Those first three days, he often retreated into his private room, too overwhelmed to face the vast city.

Elijah had to sit him down and explain that all the soldier-looking people with guns, who were absolutely everywhere, were good guys. "They're soldiers," Elijah said. "Everyone has to be."

"Everyone what?" Caden had asked.

"Every Israeli. When we turn eighteen. We all join the IDF for a time; the Israeli Defense Force. Asher just finished when we went to America."

Caden's brow scrunched as he looked out the window and eyed a young woman holding an automatic gun as people walked down the street as if she wasn't there. "So... you've all been soldiers? Even you?"

"Me. Ophir. Everyone."

"Why?"

"Our nation is always under attack. We all need to be ready."

Caden grunted with a nod. "That's a good idea actually."

"Relax around them," Elijah said. "I'll say when I see the KUS." Caden hadn't answered, but he ducked his head. The KUS were as numerous as the IDF. Their stark white uniforms made them stand out against the blacks and sandy browns of the land. They were given their space, but Caden couldn't help but feel them watching him. He still wasn't sure if they knew who he was.

Most people knew English, which was nice, but Ophir told him, on day four, he had to learn Hebrew. "Or Arabic or Russian. Something from here. You'll be miss handled if you don't speak them."

"Excuse me?"

"They'll think you're a naive tourist. You'll get over-charged everything. I mean, *everything*."

"Ah... okay." She started giving him simple Hebrew lessons, starting with the alphabet and small, childish words. It was horrible. Caden had flunked Spanish in high school. How on earth could he learn Hebrew? "It's all around you now," she pointed out. "You'll learn soon." He wasn't too sure.

Elijah also started teaching Caden. He was a man of his word. Every evening, the two would go to an alley close to Elezaro's house. There, Elijah would teach Caden defensive maneuvers. He said it was basic training for those in the Israeli Defense Force. Caden was grateful his broken leg had healed enough to withstand the workouts and steps. His right shoulder was still a bit stiff, but the exercise helped loosen it up.

The only problem was his face. He knew all too well how hard Elijah punched; he finally could see out of his bad eye. Elijah kept reminding him that he wouldn't hit him very hard, but Caden couldn't help but flinch back when Elijah got too close to his face.

"You hold still," Elijah said as the two squared up, fists raised.

"I can't!" Caden said, bouncing back on his toes as Elijah advanced. "Your fists are huge!"

"I won't hit hard. Just a little tickle."

"That's creepy, man. Don't say that." Caden kept losing his footing or simply running away when Elijah got too close.

"You let the storm inside you rule."

Caden sighed heavily. "What is it now?"

"You let all the chaos into your mind." Elijah shook his head. "Need peace in there."

Caden laughed. "I don't have peace."

Elijah stared at him thoughtfully and grunted. "I know."

"You know, huh? Where do I get peace? You seem to have it."

"Yahweh-"

"That is the stupidest, lamest answer! Is He the answer to everything!"

"Yes."

Caden threw his hands in the air. "Well, you're *wrong*."

Anger burned in his chest as he thought of his dead mom, how Mama Lo was stolen from him, and Trace's blood smeared against the tree. God wasn't the answer to peace. All the bad guys' blood on the ground was peace. He thought of his dad and Nathaniel. He thought of Scar, if that Spirit could die. No, God didn't bring peace. He probably didn't even know what that was! Caden rolled his shoulder and wiped the sweat from his brow, choosing to hold his tongue.

"Look at you and look at me," Elijah said calmly. "Who seems to be steady?"

You don't know what I've gone through! Caden thought, his eyes flashing. *Just shut up! All you God-nuts are the same! Judging us lowly sinners!*

"Who flinches at every sound? Who hides? Who is running from everything?" Curses flew through Caden's mind. Curses against God, Elijah, but mostly himself. "Come," Elijah said with a wave. "Let us go again."

They raised their fists and circled each other, but Caden wasn't paying attention. All he could hear was the roar of blood in his ears and the cry for vengeance in his heart. Caden's fists flew, whether they made impact or not, he didn't know. His blows kept going, each one faster than the one before. His knuckles started to hurt, but he didn't feel it. Someone was saying something. Elijah. What did he say? Stop or-?

Caden felt a firm hand shove him back and nearly send him to the ground. "I said stop!" Elijah bellowed as he backed away. Caden squared up again, ready. "Caden, we are done-"

"I'm not running!" Caden's yell echoed in the alley. "I'm not running from everything! I've seen things, survived things! You-you wouldn't understand!" Elijah fell silent as Caden coughed, his chest heaving. "I've lost everything I loved because of God! He killed my Mom! He let my brother starve! I watched my other brother get shot to bits! And my sister, I-I'm sure she's dead too. But I'm going to find her. I swear to anything *but* God, I will find her. With or without Him! I haven't needed Him so far, and I still don't need him."

Caden stared at Elijah with white-knuckled fists, waiting for a scoff or a degrading word. Elijah stared back, unphased and calm as ever. "I held my daughter as she bled to death."

Caden's eyes widened as his fists slowly loosened. "You had a daughter?"

"Chaya. My little girl. She wanted to be a dancer." A small smile lit Elijah's face. "She would turn on a song on her phone and dance in the kitchen. Hoppy, happy songs. One she did all the time." He paused, his brow pinching. "Can't remember... something about *'the skies are sunny and blue when I'm alone with you'*. She sang it very badly and too loud." Elijah looked down suddenly. "It was beautiful."

Caden stared at the man who couldn't be moved by anything or anyone. Elijah wiped his eyes with a finger and a thumb and looked away. *Is he crying?* With a sharp breath, Elijah straightened and coughed. "When she died, she was in so much pain, I-"

His words cut short and he looked down again. Caden took a step back and blinked. *He really is crying.*

"I wanted her pain," Elijah whispered. "I would take it all if... How could Yahweh take my little girl?" Caden turned away and crossed his arms, uncomfortable and relieved at the same time. He wasn't alone in his grief and demands to God. Elijah wiped his eyes again and cleared his throat. "She is safe with Him." Caden gave Elijah a sharp glance. "Yahweh can sing with her now."

How could he say that? God stole Chaya just like He stole Mama Lo! It wasn't right! But, staring at Elijah, his eyes a bit red and cheeks still damp, Caden knew Elijah still believed God was good. After so much pain, He was still good.

How can Elijah still be calm? Caden thought.

Elijah nodded gently and sniffed. "Your sister is in Cairo?"

Caden cursed and turned away; he hadn't wanted anyone to know. "I think," he said at last. "She went two weeks before the Day of Vanishing. I haven't heard from her since. I'll find her. I'll... I will do it." Elijah didn't answer. Caden hung his head and suddenly felt very tired. "I don't need peace," he mumbled. "It's useless anyway."

"The Spirits of this world bring chaos," Elijah said. "So Yahweh's weapon against chaos is peace. Peace is lethal."

Caden scoffed. "How?"

"How do you get peace?"

"I'm sure you're going to tell me."

"By going to war."

"That's not peace."

Elijah studied Caden for a long moment before lifting his chin. "You will see. Yahweh and Yeshua will come. They bring peace. So there will be war. And blood."

And that is why I don't follow a contradicting God, Caden thought.

Elijah sighed and walked to Caden. He lay both huge hands on Caden's shoulders and looked him in the eye. Caden blinked and told himself not to recoil. "I am sorry for all the pain in your life. Truly."

Before Caden knew what was happening, Elijah drew him into his arms and hugged him tightly. It was a big hug, one he couldn't escape from. Caden breathed out, realizing he didn't want to escape. He hugged Elijah back. *Is this what it's like having a good dad?* Tears filled his eyes. His grip on Elijah tightened as the tears fell. He buried his face in Elijah's shoulder. Elijah said nothing as Caden wept for his family, for the pain he had endured, and for the anger he held toward God.

———

CADEN FELT like he was wading through high school hallways again, with people passing on every side and everyone talking at once. Unlike high school, there were many different languages buzzing in his ears: Hebrew, Arabic, English, and oddly enough, Russian. And he wasn't in a hallway of lockers but a crammed, brick street in an old, old, old maze of streets that seemed stuck in time. Someone was really creative when they named it the Old City of Jerusalem.

Just follow Asher, Caden told himself. It was day five, he had finally convinced himself to leave Elezaro's house. Well, Ophir did most of the convincing by throwing his shoes at him and telling him to stop moping around. Something like that. She said a little Hebrew in there too, so he wasn't sure.

So far, he was glad he came. Sort of. There weren't many KUS allies or Sentinels, but there were more Spirits. It was like he had just stepped into their neighborhood. They were everywhere! Crawling up the walls, slinking through the crowd, staring down from windows, or riding on people's backs. Caden kept telling himself to ignore them, but it was like swimming through piranhas without acknowledging them. Kind of impossible. Caden sighed heavily, trying to relax, as they continued walking down the tight streets, passing vendors and delicious smelling foods.

Dogs barked behind them. *Nathaniel!* Caden instantly spun around, his heart skipping a beat. They had found him! His wide eyes darted through the sea of faces for any stark white Sentinels. How did they find him? He just wanted to get away-

An arm looped through his. Caden withdrew and made a fist, trying to remember Elijah's training. Ophir held up a hand and gently took his arm again. She drew him close and patted his hand as she dragged on. "Just dogs," she whispered. "It's okay."

Caden breathed out a long, held breath and tried to hide how much he was shaking. Asher glanced back at him, his brow arched as he studied him. Caden turned away. *I'm so pathetic,* he thought and fought to keep Trace's bloody body from his mind.

His quickened heart didn't slow as they turned a

corner and came face to face with a Wither. It had just donned a skin, looking like an old, hunched woman with a bandana tying back her hair. Caden watched as it adjusted the arm, skin, and belly, as though adjusting new clothes, before casually strolling through the throng.

Ignore it, ignore it! Caden told himself as he spotted a child, also adjusting its skin, pulling an ear and shifting a cheek, he suspected it also was a Wither. He cursed under his breath, not wanting to make a scene. *They won't hurt me,* he reminded himself. *For some reason, they won't ever-*

Ahead, from the middle of the crowd, a Shade straightened. It stood a head taller than everyone, its icy gray eyes scanning for more prey. Its face was intact, easing Caden's mind a little, but he realized he wasn't breathing. He let out a sigh and decided to focus on the ground. Until a Viper zipped between his legs, its little, clawed hands carrying it on. Caden closed his eyes and shook his head.

"You're okay." Ophir reassured him again.

Right, you keep thinking I'm afraid of dogs. This is crazy!

In America, he might've seen a Spirit every few days. Maybe two. Here, they were everywhere. Caden wanted to retreat to Elezaro's house, but what excuse could he make? He couldn't tell them what he saw. Not ever. *Just keep it together,* he thought. *If you ignore the Spirits, maybe they'll ignore you-*

Something like icy mist brushed his shoulder and side. He flinched back, not realizing he slammed into Ophir. It wasn't mist. It was like black, curling smoke that drifted through the throng. No, it didn't drift. It slithered. The curling blackness moved with purpose, intent on a direction. Caden watched it as a chill ran through his body.

There's more than Withers, Shades, and Vipers?

His knees felt weak as the realization struck his chest. The Spirit coiled in the air, soundless. The contrasting thick darkness and curling, smoke-like peaceful movements made Caden sick. The black mist finally glided to a high window and the room fell dark. Caden's hands became cold as he watched. From within glowed two red ember eyes. Caden felt the gaze stab through him like a hot iron. He looked down, his heart beating uncontrollably, as he fought the urge to run.

Why did I come here? His mind screamed. *They said there were dangers here! More Giants, more Freaks! More Spirits!* Ancient Spirits from an ancient world, and they were not going anywhere. Caden felt those burning eyes weighing on his shoulders until they rounded a corner. He let out a breath and glanced back.

"You're sweating." Ophir was watching him, her brows pinched with concern.

"Yeah, um..." Caden cleared his throat and wiped his brow. "I'm still acclimating to the climate." Ophir didn't answer and Caden shut his mouth, knowing if he continued speaking, he'd dig himself an even deeper hole. *How did no one see that? What was that!* As they continued walking, Caden saw more Spirits, mostly Vipers and Shades. *I can't keep watching them,* he thought. *I've got to do something else. Talk about something. Say something to Ophir!*

"Um," he stammered. "Where are we going?"

"The *Kotel.*" Caden glanced at her. "The Western Wall." His brows rose slightly. "The Wailing Wall?" Caden didn't answer and Ophir clicked her tongue. "You never heard-?"

"I never thought I'd come here. Like, ever."

"It is lovely here, isn't it?"

Caden breathed out slowly, his heart steadily returning to a normal rate. Then he saw another Wither and tried not to flinch. "It's... different. So, do we have to cry at this wall?"

Ophir smiled. "Many do. It is the closest we can come to the Temple Mount."

"Which is…?"

Ophir sighed and tilted her head to one side as she thought. Caden glanced at her. It looked like she was trying to take the best dessert in the world or the most breathtaking sunset and condense it into words. "It is where Yahweh kisses the earth. Let me explain."

Ophir shared the history of the Wailing Wall. After King Solomon's Temple was destroyed, King Herod rebuilt it on the Temple Mount. Because his design was larger than the plot allowed, he erected four support walls to hold the temple up. After the Romans destroyed the Second Temple, all that was left was one hundred and sixty feet of one of the supporting walls, called the Wailing Wall.

"Our wall is the closest we can get to the Temple Mount."

"Right, you said. Wait, you can't even go all the way in?"

She shook her head. "That is why *Kotel* is so precious. Yahweh's presence used to live in the Temple. The glory would fill it with golden smoke. If the unrighteous stepped into His presence, they would drop dead."

Caden turned away as his skin crawled. *So much for the God of loving and kindness.*

"It was powerful. It was beautiful."

"No thanks," he said, squeezing past a kid munching a melon. "I'll probably drop dead then."

Ophir laughed, much to Caden's surprise. "We all would if not for Yeshua. *He* is what makes us righteous, not us. We are horrible creatures without him." Caden didn't answer and Ophir sighed again. "It's nice."

"What is?"

"It's Yeshua's job to make me good, not mine. I can't do it anyways, so the pressure's off."

Caden could see her peaceful smile, it reminded him of

Elijah. *They're both peaceful,* he thought. *And they both buried their daughter. How can they not want to hate God for what He's done?*

"If Yahweh's presence is anywhere," Ophir said. "It'll be at Temple Mount. He'll be there."

"Don't you believe He's everywhere?"

Ophir was silent for a moment. "He is. But, after the Rapture-"

"The what?"

"Day of Vanishing. After that day, His Spirit stepped back. He's not here like He used to be. For those who believed in Yahweh, His Spirit would fill them."

Caden leaned back with widened eyes. "They're Puppets?"

"No, no! Yahweh doesn't control us! Silly boy. No, we are a team. Well, we were. His Spirit is still here, but won't enter us now."

Isn't that a good thing?

"We cannot hear from Him now. We cannot see Him. He is distant." She looked down with a hard frown. "I regret not coming to Him sooner. To hear His voice would be..." She trailed off and looked away. Ophir cleared her throat and patted Caden's hand again. "You'll see. At the Wall."

I hope I don't see, Caden thought but held his tongue. *If God's Spirit is there, will I see it too?* Caden's skin grew numb at the thought. He could imagine a massive creature shooting lightning from its mouth and rambling scripture. A dangerous, powerful thing that wanted him dead. Spirits always wanted him dead. Why would God be any different?

They continued walking until they finally came to an open space. Caden breathed the fresh air and was grateful to be away from the crowds. The opening was like a massive courtyard with stairs and walkways. A high wall in the distance was wedged between long buildings and an elevated, enclosed walkway. It was a small wall with green bushes growing sporadically from between the stones.

"Is that it?" Caden whispered. Ophir frowned and clicked her tongue. "Sorry! Just looks so… I don't know. Not very important."

"Ah, you're looking at it with your eyes. If only we could see with our spirits."

But I can. I see spirits. Luckily, God's monster-Spirit wasn't there. But there were others. More than before. Caden swallowed the hard lump in his throat and pressed on.

Beyond the wall, nearly hidden by other buildings, was a massive, golden-looking sphere. *No, that's the roof of some building.* He later learned it was the Dome of the Rock, an Islamic shrine Israelis weren't allowed to see.

"Isn't that where the Second Temple was?" Ophir gave a quick nod, her lips tightened to a thin line.

Close to the glinting dome was a crane beside the support structure of another building. He noticed Elijah had stopped walking and stared at it, his hands fisted. Asher shook his head and turned away with a curse. Caden glanced at him; he hadn't heard Asher curse before.

"Idiots," Asher hissed. "They really are doing it!"

"We knew they would," Ophir said quietly.

Caden glanced between them. *Is something wrong?* His question was answered by the increasing tension in Elijah's broad shoulders. "What is it?" Caden asked. Ophir didn't answer as she slowly let go of Caden and crossed her arms. He glanced at Asher and walked to Elijah. The closer he got, the more like an angry bear Elijah seemed. "Um… what's going on?"

"They are building another Temple."

"Oh." Caden glanced at the distant construction. "Is that bad?"

"It is a sign of the end."

"The end of what?"

"Yeah!" A stranger called. "The end of what?"

Caden turned and found a man quickly walking toward them, an odd device in his hand. It was a small, flat rectangle, and he positioned it so that the flat side faced Caden and Elijah. It took Caden a second to register it as a smartphone. *Why does he have one? They're useless now.* Apparently not, and the stranger was recording them. Recording Caden's face. A face he wanted to hide. With a gulp, Caden shrunk back and let Elijah have center stage.

"You said this is the end?" the man said, pointing the phone's camera at Elijah. "Why say that? We all want to know."

"We?" Elijah asked.

"I'm Lavi. I'm a journalist for *The King's Modern Times.*" Elijah's brow arched. "We're small, but we'll be roaring soon, like the Sovereign Lion. So, tell us about *the end.*"

Elijah stared at the stranger and his phone. Caden thought he'd scoff and stomp away in silence. Instead, Elijah shifted to face the camera and took a breath. "The end of the world."

Lavi chuckled. "And how do you think we'll die?"

"Yeshua is coming soon."

"He's been coming soon for a while now."

"The Day of Vanishing was raptured believers going home to heaven. Now is the time of destruction and wrath and fire." Lavi nodded slowly, a mocking smile twitching at his mouth. As they spoke, Caden noticed others had slowed to listen.

"Doesn't the Torah say Yahweh is slow to wrath, full of tender mercy? Why would He do such a thing?"

"This is Yahweh's mercy," Elijah answered. "When Gangrene rots a limb, the doctor amputates. Our sins have infected the entire earth. It is time to amputate."

"We are not an infected limb!"

"We all are. We have all turned our back on Yahweh."

"Isn't that judgmental?"

"If you are here on earth, you haven't chosen Yahweh."

Lavi shook his head as he motioned to the slowly growing audience. "So, you're saying I'm a wicked sinner who should die?"

"Yes."

Caden stared in shock at Elijah. How could he say such things to someone while keeping a straight face? Throughout the courtyard, Caden saw various Spirits stop what they were doing and face Elijah. *Oh no,* Caden thought. *What's happening?*

"All have sinned and not met His standards," Elijah continued. "That is why Yeshua came to die for our wrongs. Now, no punishment is due because Yeshua took it all." The distant Spirits dropped everything and started for Elijah. Caden's stomach twisted painfully.

"Why should we die then!" Someone from the gathering shouted.

"Sin is still here, and it is time to end it." Elijah lifted his chin and turned to those listening. "It is time for the end!" The crowd murmured as they looked at one another. They didn't look happy. Caden's eyes darted beyond the growing mass of people. The Spirits were getting closer. The Shades snarled, the Withers donned hulky skins, and the Vipers hissed.

"This is Yahweh's mercy," Elijah continued. "This is His love. He wants to end sin, but it is so deep into this world, into our own souls, so all must be removed first. A seed must die before new life can grow. All this," Elijah swept his arm in a wide arch, "will feel His fire. Whatever is weak and not built on Yahweh will burn to dust. Whoever stands on Him will survive and prosper in His fire." Someone shouted something in Hebrew, another in Aramaic, and Lavi recorded it all.

Caden was having trouble listening as the approaching Spirits drew closer and closer. *They're going to rip us apart,* he thought. He looked to Elijah, wanting to warn him somehow.

Elijah faced the crowd and lifted his chin. "The question isn't when is the end? It is already here!" Jeers and boos were his answer. "The question is will you last when Yahweh's fire falls?"

"Will you?" Lavi asked with a mocking smile.

"Um," Caden muttered, the Spirits surrounding them. He could hear the Shade's claws scrape the stone ground.

Elijah stared at Lavi and his recording phone. "I will. I stand on Yahweh's holy scriptures and will follow Him wherever He leads me."

"Elijah!" Caden called, seeing the bloodlust in the Spirits' eyes.

"Even to death," Elijah continued. "I am His servant. He is free to do to me as He wishes."

Then, the sky broke.

A loud, cracking sound echoed above, and something bright blasted down out of nowhere. Caden recoiled with a shout and shielded his eyes. Heat washed over him, feeling able to singe his clothes and hair. He could smell hot, burning stones and hear the crowd shouting. Something kicked him back and he flew to the ground. The crowd's shout rose to a shrill scream.

Caden felt pinned by something, by someone bigger and stronger than anything he's ever experienced. It was too big for this world to contain and too powerful to face. The white light vanished with the scorching heat, leaving everyone stunned and blinking.

Caden rubbed his chest and sat up, gasping. He blinked several times, his heart beating like a drum as he tried to catch his breath. Everyone was talking and shouting. He could only sit and stare at his feet, his hands shaking. He sucked in breath after breath, relieved he was still alive.

He should be dead. That *thing* should've killed him. He was so beneath it, so disgusting. He shouldn't even exist in the same world as it. Caden's eyes slowly filled with tears as his hands kept shaking. He had felt this might and power before. Then, it had been peaceful and protective, and he had wanted to feel it again so desperately.

Is this what lives behind The Door? Caden thought. *Is this the Raw Peace?*

Had The Door only been a small glimpse and this was the real, entire monster? No. Caden knew without a doubt this also was a small peek at the Raw Peace. Caden couldn't contain the tears as he shook his head. *Why am I still alive?* He looked to the sky where he imagined the light and fire had fallen from. *It didn't kill me,* he thought. He realized with a jolt he wanted it back again, even for a moment.

Slowly, Caden became aware of his surroundings. Everyone was on the ground, bewildered and shouting. No one had stood up as many sat limp and stared. *Where are all the Spirits?* Caden looked throughout the courtyard. They were gone, and he knew they weren't hiding from him. They had fled and weren't coming back anytime soon. *Does the Raw Peace scare them?*

The smell of singed stone still lingered in the air. Caden's gaze finally fell where Elijah had stood. He was lying on his back, his eyes were closed, and he was not moving. Surrounding him was a wide ring of singed, blackened stone. His shirt, over his chest, had been burned away, yet the skin beneath seemed untouched. Ophir screamed and scrambled to her feet. She raced to his side, shouting his name.

Dread stole the awe-filled wonder from Caden as he realized Elijah wasn't responding. Asher knelt beside Elijah and the two tried to wake him. He didn't move one muscle. *No,* Caden thought as he stood. *You can't die.* His insides coiled as Elijah continued to lay motionless.

TWENTY-TWO
YAHWEH'S FIRE

CADEN STOOD in the doorway to Elijah's room as his reddened eyes stared at the bed. Elijah lay, eyes closed, as still as he had been after the Raw Peace fell from the sky. Ophir and Elezaro bent over him and talked in low Hebrew. Caden closed his eyes and leaned his head against the door frame. His eyes squeezed tight and he quietly butted the frame with his forehead.

He can't die, we need him, he thought, hitting the frame again. *He's supposed to teach me how to fight. He hasn't done that yet. He needs to be a man of his word!* Caden gritted his teeth and rubbed his now red forehead. He cursed under his breath and restlessly shuffled his feet.

It had been two days since Elijah had fallen unconscious. He wasn't dead, much to everyone's relief, but he also wasn't responding. There were doctors in the city, and even a few hospitals were open, but Elijah didn't have a NIIC, which offered a huge discount. Everyone was short on money, so Ophir attended to him the best she could. Her tools were basic and unable to clearly diagnose what happened though.

"A coma," she finally concluded. "All his vitals seem normal, but he just won't wake."

Caden wanted to ask what happened, but he knew no one understood. Had fire fallen and burned Elijah's insides up? Why had the crowd all been thrown to the ground? What did the Raw Peace want? Caden questioned for a moment if the Raw Peace was evil and had deceived him, but he knew that couldn't be. Something so protective, so fully true couldn't deceive.

Caden tried to remind himself of that as he watched Ophir dab a damp cloth on Elijah's brow. With a sigh, she stood and grabbed an empty cup beside Elijah's bed. She walked past Caden and, in a moment, was followed by Elezaro. Caden lay a comforting hand on Elezaro's shoulder as he passed. The older man nodded soberly and continued.

Caden stared at Elijah and realized they were alone. With a gruff sniff, Caden walked in and waited. For what? Elijah to sit up and smile? Caden glanced at the door, making sure they were alone, and sat on the bed. "Hey," he whispered, doubting Elijah could hear him. "Um... I've been practicing my moves in the alley. Elezaro's shown me a few things. Um..."

Caden looked down and his guts twisted into knots. "You know, that fire, light, stuff that blasted into you was crazy. I fell over too. But, um... I've felt that before. Whatever it was. Like, a force? A life? But not human. Maybe alien? No, that's stupid. I dunno. Something big. Something beautiful. Don't tell anyone, alright? I saw it before meeting you guys. It was like a Door or something."

Caden leaned closer to Elijah, suddenly eager to tell someone about what he'd seen. "It opened, and I could feel safety and protection. Like, a mom's hug, but bigger. I didn't know what to call it, so I just named it Raw Peace.

Is that stupid?" Caden smiled as Elijah continued to lay there. "I dunno. But the other day, it was the same feeling. Stronger and dangerous though." He slowly shook his head. "I don't know what it is. I like it. The Door and Raw Peace have helped me survive a lot. I keep thinking of it, like it's the only real thing in the world anymore. But I I'm rambling now. I should let you rest."

Caden patted Elijah's limp shoulder and stood. He didn't move for the door. He hadn't said what he wanted to say. What if Elijah died tonight? Caden would regret never telling him, but it was so hard to say. He sniffed and rubbed his eyes as tears filled them. *Why do I keep crying these days? I'm such a wimp!*

With a growl, Caden straightened and faced Elijah. "You've gotta wake up, man. We need you. Everyone looks to you and-and you're just not allowed to die!" Elijah didn't stir. Caden hadn't known what he was expecting. "I," Caden turned away, "I've never liked my Dad. He never liked me either. So I..." Caden swallowed the hard lump in his throat. "I don't want my *good* Dad to die. Please. Just wake up." Caden watched Elijah and swatted a stray tear from his cheek.

"Please," he whispered. "I need you, Dad. Don't go. Don't..."

Caden hung his head, knowing he was rambling again. He ran a hand over his face and forced himself to stand tall. He turned to the door and stopped short. Asher stood in the doorway. Caden cursed as he crossed his arms. "How long were you standing there?"

Asher shrugged as he slowly drew closer. "He's a good dad, isn't he?"

Caden turned away and rubbed the back of his neck. The two stood side by side as they stared down at Elijah. Caden shoved his hands in his pockets as Asher slowly shook his head.

"How did your dad die?" Asher whispered.

Caden blinked and glanced at him. "Your dad's not dead." Asher didn't respond as he continued staring at Elijah. "Highway accident. Day of Vanishing. There was a huge pile-up and, when he never made it home, we just figured he died in that." Asher nodded slowly and sniffed. He turned away and cleared his throat. "What'd you do?"

"Ah, we," Caden shook his head, "we had a party." He remembered Nate, Trace, and he went to a convenience store down the road to get beer and pizza. It had already been looted. Nate had shrugged, glanced around, and nudged open the door. It was the first time Caden had looted anything. Trace had tasted his first beer that night, and they all ate way too much pizza.

"It's not the same," Caden said. "I had a bad dad. Like, really bad." Asher said nothing. He continued staring without hardly moving. An empty, vague look washed his face of expressions. Caden looked down and lay a hand on his shoulder. He was about to say something normal and fuzzy, like Elijah was going to make it and everything will be alright.

Instead, Caden lifted his chin. "He might die," he whispered. "I'll be here." Asher answered by withdrawing a bus ticket from his pocket. Caden cursed. "They're for tomorrow."

Caden cursed again. "I can't leave now!"

Asher held out the ticket. "They weren't cheap."

"They'll do refunds."

"Not anymore." Caden grimaced and cursed. "Stop that."

"I-"

"Go find that sister of yours." Caden fell quiet. "She needs you. She's your family."

"*This* is family too." Asher arched a brow as he held the ticket out further. With a sigh, Caden grabbed it.

Asher fell silent again, his attention on Elijah. "Sorry, man." Caden whispered. Asher gave a small nod. With a final glance at Elijah, Caden turned and walked out the door.

Elijah, wake up soon, he thought as he walked to his room. *I'm leaving. I want to know you won't die.* Caden glanced at the ceiling and, for once, considered God. *Just... don't steal him yet. I know he's Yours, but come on. I need him more than You do.* Caden went to his room and started packing his sparse belongings.

———

CADEN HARDLY TOUCHED his food that evening. Everyone was talking about the latest reports from beyond Jerusalem. It was said Russia was coming with a huge army. There was talk of war and more IDF, both serving and in reserve, were being summoned.

Caden didn't hear any of them. All he could think of was Elijah's unresponsive state. Caden's bag was packed and Elezaro let him borrow a map and a compass. He first had to teach Caden how to read both items, which he said was ridiculous, and Caden had to remind him that youth weren't made to join the military in America.

"You should!" Elezaro declared. "Makes you capable and tough!" Caden couldn't object. Elezaro laid out the series of buses he'd have to take between Israel and Egypt. It was complicated, so Caden took notes. To save money, Caden suggested walking a portion of the journey. "Why not through here?" He pointed to an empty, sandy-colored section. "I've heard there are monsters there. And Giants. Freaks too, but I've seen that before. America isn't totally safe either."

"Terrorists there too," Elezaro had said. "Even before

World's Crash, nobody went through the Sinai Desert alone. Avoid most danger and go around."

"Most?"

Elezaro shrugged. "Sometimes things just happen."

He tried to recite all the Hebrew phrases Ophir had taught him, "Where's the water?", "I don't have a gun", and "Don't shoot, I'm a tourist." Very comforting. If only Elijah was going with him. That Raw Peace he had in his pocket would really help Caden-

Someone gasped and dropped a dish that shattered. Caden flinched as everyone turned, women gasping and children squealing. Caden spun and froze. Coming nimbly down the stairs was Elijah. The entire table erupted with excitement and commotion as chairs were shoved back and people leapt to their feet. Caden sat without moving, his mouth shamelessly hanging open.

Elijah spread his arm as Ophir fell into his embrace. She was crying with a huge smile on her face. Asher followed close behind. Elezaro and Hili followed, hugging them both, and the entire family surrounded Elijah, each hugging the person closest to them. From the middle, Caden saw Elijah's face smiling and laughing. Their eyes met and Elijah nodded for Caden to join them. Hesitantly, Caden drew closer, hugged Asher and Elezaro's younger son and kept looking at Elijah.

I'm not part of this family, he thought. *But you sure think I am.* Elijah's smile widened and Caden found himself smiling too. *You really care about this guy, don't You?* Caden thought to God. He doubted God was listening, but it didn't hurt to try. Caden's smile widened as he watched the Mizrahi family hug and cry and praise Yahweh. Finally, everyone pulled themselves away from Elijah and ordered him to sit.

"Aren't you eating?" Ophir asked, and he shook his head. "You must! You've been in a coma for three days-"

"I was not in a coma. I, um, I was busy." Ophir blinked as everyone quieted. Elezaro chuckled and said something in Hebrew.

"Sit," Elijah said, raising his voice. "Everyone sit! I have much to tell you." Everyone obeyed and the women hushed the children. Caden quietly sat and studied Elijah. He was standing differently, straighter with his shoulders drawn back. There was something about his eyes too. They were hard with determination. Elijah waited for everyone to still and he took in a breath.

"I'll speak English so Caden can understand." Caden nodded his appreciation. "What happened at the Wailing Wall was Yahweh coming down." Anxious commission buzzed throughout the room.

Caden's brows pinched together as he crossed his arms. *That wasn't God,* he told himself. *That was the Raw Peace! I know the difference!*

"The Spirit of Yahweh has filled me," Elijah continued. "And now lives inside me."

Caden's head tilted to one side as his eyes narrowed. *He doesn't look like a Puppet.* He blinked slowly, remembering his conversation with Ophir. Yahweh didn't make people into Puppets, they were a team. *But how could a human mortal be on the same team with a god? That would make a lopsided, ineffective team.*

"I have not been in a coma," Elijah said. "Yahweh's Spirit and my spirit have been talking and working together. Yahweh has a plan for me. For all of us." Ophir lay a hand over her mouth and drew to Elijah's side. She seemed to realize something the others hadn't grasped yet.

"I have a job now," Elijah said, taking her hand. "A job from Yahweh. You are all able to help, but I will do this job, with or without you."

The family stirred again and Elezaro frowned. "Why wouldn't we come? Lead, Elijah, we follow." The chorus of agreement caused Elijah to dip his head in a silent thanks.

"So," Asher said over the noise, which quieted them. "What is this job?" Elijah straightened even more and paused as though choosing his words carefully. Caden leaned closer, yet his crossed arms tightened as though a defensive wall. If this really was from God, Caden was sure he wouldn't like it.

"I am to tell all the world Yeshua is coming soon." Elijah's voice had tightened with excitement as he looked at each family member in turn. "I am to prophecy and tell everyone how to find and follow Yeshua. I will bring Yahweh's Spirit to relight his church, as olive oil relights a lamp. The light will spread and His Spirit will find any whose hearts are not hard and who is willing to kneel to Yeshua and deny the antichrist."

The entire room was silent.

"I must warn all who will listen that the end is here," Elijah said. "There will be war. There will be death unlike the world has seen, both in Spirit and natural life. There will be false prophets and thousands martyred. I must warn the nations. For those who choose Yahweh, He will spare their souls. We are His final remnant." Again, the room was silent. Elijah turned and looked at Ophir. She lifted her chin and smiled as her hold of his hand tightened. He smiled back, grateful for her unquestioning support.

"Umm," Elezaro stammered. "You really will need us. Can't do this alone."

"There will be another like me," Elijah said.

"And what are you?" Caden heard himself ask. He couldn't hide the skepticism in his voice. This all sounded like Bible mumbo-jumbo. How hard had Elijah hit his head when he fell? Caden felt everyone turn and stare at him. *That's right,* Caden thought, *I'm the only non-Christian here. Do they believe everything so blindly?*

"I am one of two Witnesses," Elijah said.

"A witness of what?"

"Of Yahweh's Spirit."

Caden nodded slowly as he thought. "So, you're just going to start preaching at everybody, telling them to repent or Jesus is going to, I don't know, send them to Hell?" Elijah nodded and Caden couldn't hold back a grin. "People will hate that. They'll hate you."

"Sin usually hates truth."

"They'll try to hurt you. Kill you even." Elijah continued staring at Caden, as though he already knew. *He's okay with that,* Caden realized. *How can he be okay?*

"Let them come," Elijah said at last. "Yahweh will protect me."

Caden rubbed the back of his neck as he looked away. "Hum, well, prayers don't really protect people from bullets." Elijah's brows drew low. Caden stared back up at him, unmoving. "You're going to let Yahweh kill you just because He blasted you with some light and told you cool stuff?"

Asher glared at him. "Don't talk to him like-"

Elijah held up a hand. "He has good questions." Caden sat back, surprised. "Yahweh will keep me safe. He has armed me with His fire."

"His fire?" Caden asked. "What does that mean?"

Elijah didn't answer for a moment. Calmly, he strolled to the light switch and turned it off. The room fell into darkness, save the few candles flickering down the table. Elijah returned before them and looked at Caden. He opened his mouth to speak, but no words came.

What's he doing? Caden thought.

From the back of Elijah's mouth, something began to glow. It was an orange, hot light that steadily intensified.

Caden's eyes widened as embers drifted from Elijah's lips. Something bright and flickering lashed about in Elijah's mouth. It took Caden too long to recognize fire. The flames slipped from Elijah's mouth and danced about, illuminating Elijah's face. The family gasped, recoiling, and Elijah shut his mouth, extinguishing the fire. He calmly walked to the light switch and turned the lights back on.

Caden stiffly sat in his chair, his chest heaving. What had he just seen? That was impossible! No one could have fire in their mouths! *But it came out of his mouth. Out of it! Like it was from inside him!*

Elijah silently stood as the family's uproar slowly calmed again. He looked at each member. "Our King Yeshua is coming," he said at last. "Are you ready?" Heads nodded as hands were raised in praise to Yahweh. Some were laughing while others were crying. Elijah's intense gaze fell on Caden.

Caden wanted to shrink back under such a stare as Elijah's question screamed in his mind. *Am I ready? Am I ready for Jesus' return?* He scratched the back of his neck, unable to answer.

TWENTY-THREE
DOEG

CADEN DUCKED his head as Elijah's family continued praising Yahweh. He stood from the dinner table, uncomfortable and isolated. He didn't follow this weird God of theirs. He didn't belong here. *I've got to sleep,* he thought. *I'm leaving tomorrow.* He left the table and didn't make eye contact with Elijah. *Just leave me alone. I'm not part of this.*

Elijah's hand fell on his shoulder. "Where are you going?"

"To bed. I'm leaving tomorrow."

"Tomorrow? But I have things to say."

"Wait for tomorrow."

"But you're leaving."

"I can't," Caden sighed, "I can't be here. All this isn't me. I'm not-"

"Not what?"

Caden pulled free from Elijah's grasp and glared at him. "Ophir can sum up what you're going to tell everyone. I've gotta go."

"Alright. Go on to your room. I'll be up soon."

"I don't need you to tuck me into bed."

"Yahweh has a message for you." Caden tried not to

step further away as his guts knotted. "I will tell you tonight."

"Save it."

"I cannot."

"Elijah-"

"Why would I obey you over my Yahweh?"

Caden fell silent and knew Elijah would do anything Yahweh said, no matter how drastic or dangerous. "Fine." Caden hissed as he turned and marched to his room. *This is crazy! First, there are the Freaks, then Giants, now a fire-breathing prophet? What messed up story am I in?* He shook his head and gritted his teeth. *God's story. He's sure having fun messing with us. And now He has a message for me. He better not call me GJ! He will though.*

Caden's steps slowed as a nervous thrill washed over him. *He'll blame me for getting Trace killed. And not saving Nate. He knows I ran. I should've stayed. Why did I run off? I didn't find any food and he died without me!* Caden ran his fingers through his hair. He felt sick. *God'll want me punished.*

A thought struck Caden like a blow to the face. *Would Elijah do anything to me?* He opened his bedroom door and stared into the sparse room. *He wouldn't hurt me, would he? But... if Yahweh told him to.* Caden shut the door and slowly came to his bed. He stared at the bat he stashed under the pillow. It had been in Harel's room, and Caden had played dumb when the little kid spent a day looking for it.

I could hit him first. I shouldn't be jostled around by anyone again. I refuse to be a hunted creature, never able to rest or live. The tyranny of God and his useless promises will end. Caden sat and grabbed the bat, feeling it in his hands. *Elijah will inflict God's wrath. I will not give either of them the pleasure of my demise.* A muscle in Caden's jaw flexed as he stood, taking the bat in both hands. *It's only a ball,* he heard. *His head is simply a ball ready for a home run. The cheering audience will be the spray of blood on the walls, a banner of triumph and success!*

Caden's eyes darkened as he took the batter's stance and stared at the shut door. *This so-called Witness won't foresee such an attack, and no one will suffer under his heavy truths! Without him, the second Witness will be easy to slay. Then the king and his Sovereign Lion can rule without obstacles of Yahweh and his disgusting anointed few-*

Caden took in a sharp breath, blinking hard. He faced the bat, seeing his knuckles were white as he held it ready. *What am I doing? I can't kill Elijah!* Caden stumbled back and plopped down on the bed. He gasped, sweat dampening his brow as he tried to calm down. *What's wrong with me? Why would I want to kill Elijah!*

As he sat, something drifted from the ceiling. He watched its slow descent, waving back and forth. It was a single, long hair, like the fur of a dog. It was as white as a ghost. Caden gulped and looked up.

Scar stood on the ceiling, its icy pale eyes boring into him. The Shade's surviving ear turned back like an angry cat's. From its cheek to the corner of its mouth was bare skin, the fur unable to grow over the scar tissue. The flesh was meaty and a grayish red. The scar latched onto the Shade's lips and turned it up on one side, like a constant, mangled smile. The rows and rows of long teeth gleamed in the light as Scar licked its lips, its long tail lashing.

The two stared at one another until Caden remembered to breathe with a loud gulp. He leapt to his feet and jumped to the door. Scar dropped, landing on all fours, and blocked Caden's way. Caden stumbled back and raised the bat. A low, guttural growl rumbled from the Shade as it laughed.

"More pathetic attempts to harm me, human?" Caden flinched, hating when Scar spoke directly into his mind. *"You're mine tonight. Your little watchdog has abandoned you."* Scar crept on all fours, its bold, bird-like legs scratching

up the floor with each step. Caden leapt over his bed and glanced at the window. Could he escape through it?

"I can pass through solid matter, foolish human," Scar said in Caden's mind. *"But please do try. I will enjoy watching you drop twenty feet. Again."*

Caden stiffened and faced Scar, knowing running would only please the Shade. He raised the bat. *What are you waiting for?*

Scar grinned and crouched. "As you wish." It hooked the bed with one clawed hand and launched it across the room at Caden. Caden lurched back, stepping to flee, but the bed crashed into him, slamming him against the wall. He heard his head bounce off the wall and he slid to the floor, blinking back the lights flashing in his vision. He held his head and moaned.

A quiet caterwaul drew him from his dazed state and Caden turned, recoiling without thinking. Scar stalked along the wall parallel to the floor as though gravity was having an off day. Caden blinked, trying to understand. He scrambled to his feet as Scar's cat-like wail morphed into a yowl.

The Shade leapt and Caden swung the bat. The bat made impact, slamming with a loud crash. Caden gasped and tried to back away, but the bat didn't move. He turned and found the bat embedded in the wall. It didn't budge. With a curse, Caden released it and backed into the corner. He looked all around, his heart beating loudly in his ears as panic tightened his throat. *Where is he?*

"You cannot see me." Caden felt nothing. Like the vast emptiness terror brings. He had forgotten what that cold emptiness felt like. *"I will appear moments before turning you inside out."*

Fur brushed Caden's ear. He yelled and raced away, leaping beyond the bed. He heard the bed slam against the wall and claws scraping the floor. Caden flung himself at the door. If only he could get to the others. They would know what to do. Wouldn't they? They never seemed afraid of Spirits and-

Claws hooked Caden's clothes, lurching him back With the shirt collar digging into his throat, he gagged and fell backwards. He slammed into the floor hard, his head bouncing again. He blinked through the pain and tried to drag himself back. *Where is he? Where is he!*

"Peekaboo!" Scar stood over him, tattered bits of Caden's shirt dangling from its claws. "I find you guilty of maiming my face."

"No!" Caden cried, raising a defensive hand. "I didn't do that!"

"I find you guilty-"

"I don't even know how that happened to you!"

"And I resolve to reduce you down to nothing but scar tissue and blood." Caden shivered as he battled the urge to lay still and let Scar finish him off. The Shade's smile stretched, twisting his scar further. "No, little human. Like a cat and mouse, I am not yet satisfied with your attempts to survive. Besides, I will annihilate your soul before your flesh."

Someone, Caden thought desperately. *Someone, please.* He crawled back, but he knew running was useless.

"No one is here," Scar answered with its inner voice. *"You are again abandoned, unvalued, and rejected-"*

The door opened with a creek. Both Caden and Scar turned. Elijah calmly entered and stopped short as he stared directly at the Shade. A hissing yowl ripped from Scar's throat as it spun, fur bristling and lips drawn back.

"No!" Caden cried, reaching for the Shade. Scar's body coiled to leap onto Elijah.

Without batting an eye, Elijah raised a hand. "Be gone, in the name of Yeshua." Scar's yowl shrilled. The Shade's body shuddered as its head flew to one side, as though struck. Scar stumbled, yipping, and faded through the floor. In moments, the Spirit was gone.

Caden gasped as he stared where Scar had been. He waited for Scar to resurface with fangs ready to taste their blood. *He's tricking us! Hiding to attack when we aren't-*

A hand lay on his shoulder. Caden fell back with a curse and curled into a ball. "Caden." It was Elijah. The voice was peaceful, yet firm. Caden couldn't withhold a moan as he tried to loosen his tense body. Everything was shaking. Everything hurt. His head spun as Elijah helped him stand. He tried to support Caden to the door, but Caden guessed it didn't go well because the next thing he knew, they were sitting against the wall.

Caden put his head in his hands and tried to breathe. It was like inhaling jello. Elijah quietly sat beside him. After several minutes, Caden sat up straighter with a curse. "How did you do that? You just," Caden waved his hand as though swatting a fly, "Just that! Teach me!"

"It is Yahweh inside me."

Caden cursed again. "Yahweh this and Yahweh that. If He's so good, why is my whole family dead?"

"You don't know about Ellie."

Caden frowned and glared at Elijah. "I didn't tell you her name."

"*He* did."

The two sat in silence until Caden closed his eyes and lay his head against the wall. *God is evil. God likes to hurt me. He can't be my only defense. He just can't!*

"Is there another thing that scares Spirits away?" Elijah shook his head, and Caden slumped. "I won't follow your God."

Elijah smiled softly. "What are you talking about? You've been following Him a long time now."

"No," Caden said sharply.

"Who do you think your Raw Peace is?"

Caden didn't answer as his stomach twisted. "You heard what I said when you were in that coma?" Elijah nodded and Caden's hands became fists. "What hit you the other day was too dangerous and wild to be the Raw Peace. They are different. They are!"

Elijah smiled as he shook his head. "You said the Raw Peace was protective and safe. How can something bring total safety without the power and aggression to defend properly? The safest place is resting in the paws of a lion."

"Don't talk about the Sovereign Lion."

"The Lion of Judah. Yeshua. Our true King."

No, Caden thought defiantly. *The Raw Peace isn't the same as, as whatever that was. Can't be. They're similar, but the Raw Peace can't be God!*

"You have been following Yahweh," Elijah continued. "Looking to Him. Asking Him for help."

"God isn't the Raw Peace!"

"Who lives in me?"

"What?"

"What Spirit is in me now?"

Caden frowned and leaned back; he hated the idea of Elijah being God's Puppet. *But Ophir said they're not Puppets. They're teammates.*

"God's Spirit," he answered, and Elijah nodded.

"He is in me. When I speak with His name, I speak His authority. Nothing evil can fight against that. Didn't you see?"

Caden didn't answer as he turned away. *The Raw Peace and God are totally different. I don't know what Elijah keeps going on about. This isn't-it's just not right!*

"What are you afraid of?" Caden's answer was gritting his teeth and not moving. "Why are you so determined to make God the bad guy?"

He is the bad guy! Look at my life!

"Have you ever wondered if your deepest sorrows are actually Yahweh being merciful?"

Caden ran a rough hand over his face and turned away. A vein was starting to stick out on his temple as rage pumped through him. *Mom's death wasn't mercy. Nate wasting away wasn't mercy either!*

"Yahweh being loving-"

"If that is Yahweh's love, I hope He hates me forever!"

Elijah gave a soft chuckle and nodded. "It is loving for an Ima to help up her child after a fall. She kisses him and cleans the scrapes. It is the same love if an Aba kills the one raping his daughter." Caden gave Elijah a sharp look. "Love is not always gentle, but it is good. Yahweh is love. He is good. Even in deep pain."

Caden stared at the floor again, unable to speak. He thought of his entire life, the pain of his dad's constant ridicule and rejection, his mom's death, Mama Lo being raptured, and watching his siblings die. How could that be love? He hung his head and wished he could shove off all his pain like a heavy backpack. *I'm sure Elijah'll say Yahweh can carry it for me.* Would He? A God carrying the woes of a little, insignificant human? Caden inhaled sharply, not wanting to think about that.

"A message," he said. "You mentioned Yahweh said something. To me?"

"He said to come back here when you are done. He said to bring everyone with you."

Caden leaned back with narrowed eyes. "What does that mean? Will I find Ellie?" Hope burst in his chest like the sudden light of a firework.

Elijah simply stared at him. "He also said to teach you there are good and bad Spirits. They're not all Demons, like that one we just saw."

"Will I find Ellie?"

"Some are good Spirits, here to help you, like Angels."

"Elijah-"

"Yahweh said to tell you no more about your walk through the desert."

Caden's eyes narrowed further. "Why not? And I'm not walking through the desert. Asher just got me a bus ticket."

Again, Elijah fell quiet. "Well… umm…"

What isn't he telling me?

"Lastly, Yahweh said to stop hiding. He sees who wants to hurt you. The KUS, Grant Yarrow, and Doeg. He knows. He has been protecting you and will keep protecting you."

Caden didn't answer as he raised a brow. *God hasn't been looking out for me. I take care of myself!* Even as he thought that, Scar's mangled face came to mind. He hadn't done that. Something, or someone, else had stepped in and saved him. *Was that Yahweh?* The thought gave him a chill.

"Wait?" he muttered. "Doeg? Who's that?"

"The Demon we just saw."

"How do you know his name?"

"Yahweh told me."

"Right. Demon?"

Elijah nodded. "Not all Spirits are bad ones."

"Show me a good one and I'll believe you."

"You have seen one. Twice. The Door and the Consuming Fire."

Caden put his face in his hands as he tried to grapple with this new information. *Scar's real name is Doeg. Apparently, I'm walking through the Sinai Desert, not taking a bus. God loves me so much he kills everyone around me. And, one more message? Oh yeah, to come back. And drag everyone else who's with me, whoever they are. What if they don't come? Do I have to make them?*

"Is that what you wouldn't tell me?" Elijah asked. "That you see Spirits. And live."

Caden's stomach tensed as he shifted and rubbed the back of his neck. "That's why Grant wants me too," he mumbled. "He wants to make me a slave."

"He can't. Yahweh's got you."

Caden grunted. "We'll see."

"Well, now I see them too."

"Why didn't Scar-er, I mean Doeg, freak you out? He's horrible!"

"When you see Yahweh's Consuming Fire, you see nothing can snuff Him out."

"It's not that simple."

"It is. But that doesn't mean it's that easy." Elijah stood and held out a hand to Caden. Caden stood, steadying himself against Elijah, and then checked his balance. Seeing he was well enough, the two righted the bed and yanked the bat from the wall.

"Sleep," Elijah said. "Doeg will not return. This is Yahweh's house. And you make sure not to let Doeg in."

"Are you crazy! I wouldn't do that!"

"You can by listening to its lies."

Great, Caden thought as he removed his ripped shirt.

"Goodnight," Elijah said as he turned to the door.

"Hay, um..." Elijah stopped. "Thanks. I think Doeg was going to kill me. Or worse."

"Thank Yahweh. I'm just the weapon in His hands."

Caden sighed. "Whatever, dude. Thanks Yahweh! There! You happy?"

Elijah grinned. "Caden."

"Hum?"

"You called me Dad when I was still not awake."

Caden ducked his head and stepped back. "Sorry. I know I'm not family. I'll stop-"

"Call me Aba," Elijah said. "That's more fitting."

Caden stared at Elijah, his mouth slack. "Ah," he stammered. "I'm not your son."

"Yes, you are."

Caden blinked, taken back. "Um... okay." A small smile spread across his mouth. "I've never liked the word 'dad' anyways."

Elijah nodded and stepped toward the door. "Goodnight, son."

"Goodnight. Aba."

When the door shut, Caden sat on his bed and realized, for once, he didn't feel alone. *The Raw Peace is Yahweh,* he thought, as though trying out the idea. He frowned but didn't fight it. *The Raw Peace is Yahweh.* He lay down and stared at the ceiling. Doeg's claw marks left long lines overhead. Caden's stomach turned as dread washed over him. Doeg could come back. Elijah might not get back in time. He couldn't win against a Demon-

Elijah's a weapon in Yahweh's hands. Yahweh's the fighter. And He's fighting for... for me. Caden frowned again, but once more, didn't curse the idea. Instead, he let it rest in his mind as he rolled onto his side. *Yahweh is fighting for me. I'm worth fighting for. God finds value in me.* Sleep found him easily, and if Doeg whispered anything in the night, Caden didn't hear a word.

TWENTY-FOUR
PLANS CHANGE

CADEN WOKE to someone prodding his side. "Stop snoring," Asher hissed. "You'll wake everyone up! Stop drooling too!" Caden swatted his hand away and rolled over. "Come on," Asher said a little louder. "You don't want to miss your bus." Caden mumbled something and snuggled deeper into the blankets. "Get up or I'll eat your share of breakfast," Asher said before walking out the door.

With a groan, Caden forced his eyes open and rolled on his back. Scar's claw marks across the ceiling turned the room into a horror movie. But Scar wasn't his real name. What was it? *Doeg*, Caden thought, a chill washing over him. *Wonder if it eats breakfast. Maybe some dog or lost kid-*

He gave his head a quick shake, not wanting to think of the Shade and whatever it was doing. He stood and rubbed the sleep from his eyes. Downstairs, he could smell the fish cooking before he saw it. Even though the sun had yet to rise, Ophir and Hili were already busy in the kitchen, chatting and cooking for the family. Caden smiled at both as he got himself some water.

"*Boker tov*," Ophir said with a smile.

Caden stared at her and blinked slowly. "*Boker or*," he stammered. Ophir beamed and Hili encouraged him in Hebrew. He assumed it was encouragement.

"Good, getting good," Ophir said with a smile. "You'll be bilingual yet!"

"We'll see," Caden said. "I'm still confused when I try to read. Everything's written backwards."

"*You* write backwards!"

Caden shook his head as she offered him a plate. There was steamed fish, melon slices, a bit of cheese, and poached eggs in tomato sauce. "Thank you-"

"Ah! No! Come now. Say it right."

Caden thought for a moment. "*Toda raba*."

"Oh, very good!"

"Can I eat now?" Hili laughed as Ophir scowled. "Ungrateful! Just like my son!" She nudged Caden toward the kitchen table and he smiled seeing the twinkle in her eyes. She watched him sit, a distant look in her eyes.

Caden grabbed his fork but stopped and stared at Ophir. "What?"

"Do you have to go today?"

"I," Caden sighed, "Yeah. I've got to go." *I've rested long enough.*

Ophir frowned and nodded. "Well, do what you got in mind," she said. "Then come back and we'll have a party. Alright?" Caden smiled as she went back into the kitchen.

Heavy steps came behind him and Elijah walked past with a simple nod. He went into the kitchen and wrapped his arms around Ophir as she started cooking more poached eggs. She smiled as he kissed her. Caden could barely hear their whispered words. He saw how she relaxed in his embrace and how his constantly impassive stare was broken by a small smile.

I'm stalling, Caden realized. *I want to stay here. I want to be safe with these people. This family. My family.* Caden turned away and kept eating, suddenly homesick. Everyone else was at peace here. *It's the Raw Peace,* Caden realized. *I think a little bit of it is here. Or... Yahweh's Peace. Is He here?* Caden glanced around, as though he could see the One who ruined his life. It didn't feel so ruined anymore.

Caden's thoughts halted as Elijah came to join him. They sat side by side in silence, enjoying each other's company and the food. "You're up early," Caden mumbled.

"Wanted to bless your journey."

Caden shifted uncomfortably but didn't answer. They fell silent again and Caden finished his breakfast. He sat, quietly drumming his fingers on the table, not wanting to consider the countless possibilities he could die in the Sinai Desert. *I'm taking a bus around it,* Caden thought. *I can't go through it. There are Freaks out there. Monsters too. But Elijah said-*

Caden sighed and ran his fingers through his hair. "Thousands of years ago," Elijah said suddenly. "My ancestors were slaves in Egypt."

Caden grunted. "You're telling me it's a bad place?"

"Hush," Elijah said. "Listen more, speak less." Caden frowned and crossed his arms. "My ancestors had no hope for a good life as their masters crushed them. Yahweh sent Moses to the pharaoh and asked for our freedom."

I've heard this story, Caden thought. *Mama Lo told it one or two million times.*

"Pharaoh did not listen," Elijah continued. "He would not let us go free. God let bad thing after bad thing come, sorrow after sorrow, until the pharaoh said yes. We left Egypt and entered a desert. There, Yahweh taught us how to stop living and thinking like slaves and how to be free men. A free nation with Yahweh as our King. Only after

He taught us a new way could we enter the land He promised and make a new home. Do you know what desert we were in?" Caden shook his head. "Sinai Desert."

Caden's crossed arms stiffened like a defensive wall. He could feel a sermon brewing. "You are a slave to your own sin." Caden turned away and suddenly found his fork interesting. "You are being crushed by sin, and there is no hope when you are ruled by it. Yahweh wants to set you free. He wants to call you from your old master, into something new. You don't have to stay a slave. Caden."

Elijah's hand lay on his shoulder. Caden didn't move. "Listen when Yahweh calls you. He wants you free more than you do." A muscle in Caden's jaw flexed and he looked in the opposite direction. "He wants you free so deeply He will let bad thing after bad thing, sorrow after sorrow, come. Don't be stubborn like pharaoh and have a hard heart. Hold onto the heart of flesh He has for you, a sensitive, listening heart. Follow Yahweh. Go into the desert. Let Him teach you how to stop living and thinking a sinful life. Be changed. Be free."

Get your hand off me, Caden wanted to say, but held his tongue. He stared at his plate, the pictures on the wall, a fly that kept buzzing around the light, anything but Elijah.

"Go into the desert," Elijah whispered and scooted back. Caden didn't answer as he brushed the shoulder Elijah touched.

I don't like God's version of love, Caden thought. *It's not... nice.* He shifted in his chair, Elijah's words echoing in his mind. *Don't have a heart of stone but a heart of flesh. What's with all these religious riddles?* Caden rubbed the back of his neck and glanced at Elijah. *How can he encourage me to follow Yahweh when his daughter's dead?*

He cleared his throat. "Do you really believe Yahweh loves you, even after burying your daughter?"

The deep hurt that flashed across Elijah's eyes startled

Caden. Chaya's death, though years ago, was still fresh. How could it not be? Elijah ducked his head and calmly folded his hands on the table. "I've forgiven Yahweh. And, umm, I know Chaya is a soft, sweet girl." Elijah's frown deepened as he stared at his plate. "This cruel, new world would crush her." He took in a deep breath and lifted his chin. "It is Yahweh's mercy and *love* that took her so soon. Her soul would not have lasted long."

Caden stared irritably at Elijah. Couldn't he say one bad thing against Yahweh? Just once! Would that be so hard? It would make Caden feel much better about his own feelings toward God.

"Call me before you go," Elijah said as he stood and gathered their plates before walking to the kitchen.

Elijah just wasn't being honest and was trying to make Caden look bad. How selfish! Caden sniffed and turned away, knowing his thoughts were a pathetic tantrum. *He doesn't hate God*, he thought. He continued staring at the empty table as Asher came through the door and sat at the far end of the table. *Thought he already ate.* Caden watched him out of the corner of his eye.

Why is he even up? Caden thought. *He's never awake this early.* Caden shifted to face Asher. "Why aren't you asleep?"

"I got up." Caden's gaze darkened, and he held his tongue until Asher set down his fork. "I'm seeing you to the border."

Caden's brows rose. "Why?"

"You don't have a NIIS."

"Neither do you."

"There's been a change of plans."

Caden blinked, his stomach twisting. "What're you talking about?"

"Done eating?"

Caden's brows furrowed. "I'm taking the bus. I don't need whatever you've come up with-"

"I'll tell you on the drive. Let's go." Caden didn't answer as Asher kept shoving food into his mouth. With a sigh, he took his dirty plate to the kitchen.

———

WITHIN THE HOUR, a taxi had arrived for Caden and Asher. Elezaro clapped Caden on the back and said he was glad to see him go, that Caden stank up the place, and there'd now be more food to pass around. Caden had smiled and shook his hand. Hili gave hugs and a satchel of extra food. Ophir was trying not to cry, but she wasn't doing a good job hiding it. She grilled Caden on all the safety measures he should take, how to protect his still recovering leg, even though he felt just fine, and reminded him how to say 'don't shoot' in Hebrew and Aramaic. Caden had to hold up a hand with a gentle smile and pull her into an embrace.

"I'll be fine," he whispered. "You worry too much." Ophir nodded with a sniff. Caden stared at Elijah and the large man slowly smiled. They hugged, long and heartfelt.

"See you soon," Elijah said.

"Does that mean I'll find her?"

"See you soon."

Caden cursed under his breath. "You're so frustrating." Elijah grinned. "See yah. Aba." Elijah nodded.

Caden turned to load up his bag and found it was stuffed more so than he had left it. He glanced at Elijah, who shrugged. "You are going into the desert." The taxi driver gapped at Caden, frowned, and then shook his head.

"No, I'm not!" Caden cried.

"Elezaro and I have supplies. A sleeping bag, a little shovel-"

"Not going."

"Rope, some lighters, warm blanket-"

"Elijah!"

"He says you'll go into the desert."

"Well, *He* isn't my boss."

"Yet."

Caden grumbled under his breath as he lugged the backpack onto his shoulder and threw it into the back of the taxi. He shut the trunk and found himself standing, as though waiting. For what? *The urge to leave,* he thought with a sign.

"Move it," Asher said as he got into the taxi.

He waved to the Mizrahi family and wondered if he'd see them again. Elijah sure thought so. Maybe he would. They waved and shouted their goodbyes. Caden leaned closer to the taxi driver to tell him which bus station, but Asher beat him to it. Caden cocked an eyebrow as the taxi started up and they drove from the house that had become Caden's home.

"That's not a bus station," Caden said.

"Just follow my lead," Asher said, handing him a tembel hat, a shemagh, and dark-tinted sunglasses.Caden crossed his arms and glared at the offered accessories. "The bus station is crawling with, am... with your *friends.*" Asher shifted and cast a quick look at the driver.

Caden's eyes narrowed. *Is he talking about Sentinels?*

"You said there weren't any friends there."

"Well," Asher whispered, "things change."

Caden stared ahead, his mind spinning. *Why are Sentinels suddenly around bus stations? They haven't been there all week!*

"Maybe that station we passed the other day to the market-"

"They're everywhere," Asher said quietly so the driver couldn't hear. He extended the hat, wrap, and sunglasses again. "I guess that Nathaniel *friend* of yours caught up to you."

A lump formed in Caden's throat as he took the hat and glasses. *I can't deal with the KUS right now. I'm so close!* His pulse quickened and he lifted his chin, feeling himself slipping down into cold blackness. The cold, deep emptiness of overwhelming fear. *Raw Peace,* he told himself, making a fist.

"So, what's the plan?" He asked, donning the hat.

"We fly."

"Good," Caden said. "We'll be in Cairo in no time."

"If Jerusalem knows you're here, so will Cairo."

"That's where I need to go." Asher shook his head. "I'm not walking through that desert!"

"There's no Sentinels."

"Yeah, there are terrorists! Monsters! Freaks! Giants! And other crazy things I haven't thought of yet!"

"Want to avoid Sentinels? Then go through the desert."

"I'll die."

Asher shrugged. "Then be smarter and quicker than you usually are."

Caden cursed under his breath. "Isn't there another way?"

"Sure," Asher said. "If we had more time and six or seven thousand shekels."

Caden cursed again. "This isn't happening," he moaned, his head in his hands.

"I know it's bad, but face it," Asher said. "Stop whining. Whining will kill you. Accept what's happening. Adjust." Caden gave Asher a look that made it clear he should stop talking. Asher held up a hand and sat back. "Just trying to help." Caden shook his head and blinked, trying to grapple with the quickly changing circumstances.

"Fly," he muttered. "Okay. How? There'll be Sentinels there too. Do you even have tickets?" Asher nodded. "And we'll land…"

"In the Sinai Desert."

Caden ran a hand over his face. "That's in Egypt. We'll have to be cleared to cross the border."

Asher shook his head while keeping a close eye on the driver. "Hey," he said to the driver, holding out a few shekels. He said something in Hebrew and the driver nodded, took the shekels, and turned the radio on loud. "I got a hold of Thomas Whitney."

"How?"

"Phones. Remember them? He wants you dead."

Caden scoffed and adjusted his hat. "Get in line. What for?"

"Because you're coming back to America to stir up trouble. You like how you look like Alex. You're planning on using that to con your way to the top."

Caden rubbed his eyes with his finger and thumb. "And he fell for that? That seems a bit… dumb of him."

Asher shrugged. "Yahweh lets crazy stuff happen. And, you know, Thomas seems to hate all of us."

"Great."

"I offered to get rid of you by getting you on a plane to the Sinai Desert."

"We're taking Whitney Wings. Again?"

"Put on that Alex charm you did so well in America."

A muscle in Caden's jaw flexed. "A little warning would've been nice."

"This is a warning. Adjust!"

"I am adjusting!"

"Don't talk to anyone on the plane too."

"Wasn't planning on it."

"Anyone going to that desert is either a trafficker, terrorist, madman, or blood-enthusiast. Or all the above." Caden cursed again. "Stop swearing. That's awful."

"Stop messing up my plans! I was supposed to get on a bus! Just sit back and drive!"

"Be my guest! The KUS will have you in an hour and do whatever it is they want with you."

Kill me, Caden thought, the baritone barks of dogs echoing in his memories. *Like an animal.* Caden fell silent as he felt his world steadily tilting, as though ready to fall. *No!* He thought, lifting his chin. *I've fought too hard for this! I've come too far! I'll make it!* Uneasiness weighed on his shoulders.

The drive was quiet and tense. They rode in silence and Caden fought to keep his thoughts on finding his sister. *Where are you Lil El?* Cairo wasn't a small place. The radio had talked about terrorists in the Sinai Desert that attacked surrounding cities. People were dying. Refugees were fleeing into Europe. She could be in Russia for all he knew. Bad move though, Russia sounded ready to attack at any time.

Caden ran his fingers through his hair and took in a breath. *Remember our deal?* He thought, glancing out the window, past the tall buildings, to the cloudy sky. *You give me back my sister. Alive! And healthy and I'll,* Caden looked down as a muscle in his jaw flexed. *I'll think about following You.*

After praying, he always expected thunder to roll or the ground to break open and swallow him whole. Hadn't that happened to sinners in the Bible? Caden sat back and forced his eyes closed. He had a long way to go and getting himself all worked up about Yahweh wouldn't help. *He's probably not even listening anyways.* Caden's hair stood on end; he wasn't too sure about God ignoring him anymore.

TWENTY-FIVE

THE END OF ALL THINGS

CADEN AND ASHER drove in the taxi for a long time. Caden was too busy searching for Sentinels without looking suspicious that he didn't know how much time had passed. When the taxi slowed, he looked around and found they were at an airport. Caden glanced at Asher as they stepped out of the cab.

"Put on your best Alex Whitney face," Asher muttered as they grabbed their bags.

Caden stopped short. "Now?" Asher gave a small nod. Out of the corner of his eye, Caden saw a man in a suit approaching. *Here we go again,* Caden thought as he leaned against the car. "Hurry up! I want to see the surprise!" Asher bit his tongue and heaved Caden's huge pack from the trunk.

The suited man stopped beside Caden and nodded. "Mr. Whitney."

Caden didn't answer as he stretched his legs and yawned. "Where's my flight?"

The man's mouth twitched, and he stepped back, containing himself. "Right this way, Mr. Whitney." Caden didn't acknowledge him and tried to hide his amusement of Asher struggling with his bag as they entered the airport.

They bypassed security and customs, heading through back hallways and passages. Caden's skin crawled; he was expecting Bobby's huge fingers to seize his arm again and rip it free. Nothing happened. Caden kept his indifferent, bored air going as Asher struggled to keep up. They stepped outside and were escorted to a private hanger. A few people were loading luggage into the smaller-sized airplane. *Whitney's Wings* written along the plane's side.

"Sir," the suit-man said as he motioned to the stairs leading to the plane's door. Someone took their huge bag before boarding.

This can't be a private jet! Caden thought as he climbed the steps. *This could be a trap. Some sick joke from Thomas Whitney. I should ask more questions!*

Inside, gruff faces glanced their way as they quietly found their seat. Russians were at the back and stared at everyone as though deciding if they were worms for bait or fish to fry. A handful of Israelis huddled around an old guy who looked able to watch torture and death without flinching. A man in nice clothes loudly laughed with three women who leaned close to him, wide smiles on their faces. Caden nearly shivered as he sat; it reminded him of Grant and his gang of wolves. Asher and Caden gave each other quick glances but didn't speak as they waited.

The KUS can still get to me, Caden thought. *Someone must've seen me. They'd say something. Get a Sentinel or two over here. Would they ship me back to Nathaniel, or would they make me kneel in the hanger and shoot me there? More efficient to shoot me here.*

It wasn't until they were in the air did the anxiety twisting his guts ease. He glanced down at the ground hundreds of feet below. The Dome of the Rock shone in the far distance, the sun glinting off the gold-like roof. Somewhere down there was home.

I'll be back, Caden thought. *If I survive.* He leaned back and tried to rest. He couldn't relax with the thought of Russian cut-throats sitting a few feet away. Weren't the Russians going to invade soon? *I've got to get used to this.*

It was like being back in the States, but here, everyone had been raised with a gun. Everyone knew how to survive, and more importantly, everyone seemed to know how to kill. Caden had seen plenty of bodies, but only a handful of deaths. Caden looked down at his hands, a lump forming in his throat, realizing he was not strong enough to take a life. Sure, he might have the physical ability, but could he respect himself after killing another? Could the Raw Peace?

We'll find out, Caden thought as he watched the clouds zoom past.

———

THE SINAI DESERT WAS ROCKY, hot, and yellow. Caden hadn't seen ground of such an odd color. The hot wind kicked up the yellowed dust, making the air smell dirty. Hardly any plants could be seen as rocky mountains jutted along the horizon. The airport they landed in was just a runway with armored hummers parked around and a few camels. *I've done it,* Caden thought. *I've finally lost my mind. This is suicide.*

Caden's thoughts of hiding in the plane were squished by the armed muscle walking behind the passengers to the plane's door. He acted like he was escorting them out, but everyone knew they were being kicked off. Caden wrapped his shemagh around his face and followed Asher into the sun. They went to the back of the plane and waited for the luggage. Everyone ignored each other, as if they didn't exist. Some took off in the hummers. The others took camels. The Russians started on foot.

The attendant retrieving the luggage handed Caden his bag and gave him a long, hard stare. "You go there?" He pointed into the desert. "You mean to?" Caden took the bag. "Alone?"

"You know not to ask questions!" The man frowned and continued his work without another word.

Asher stuck by Caden's side as they walked to the edge of the runway. They stood silently and Caden slid on the backpack and adjusted the straps. Asher shuffled from foot to foot. He kept looking around, sliding his hands in his pockets, and yanking them out again.

"Well," Caden said. "Um…" *I hate goodbyes.*

"I should go with you."

Caden frowned. "There's not enough supplies."

"You'll get lost."

"I've got a compass." Asher shook his head and crossed his arms. "I'll avoid the terrorists, I bet I can smell the monsters before I see them, and we already know how well I handle Giants."

Asher glared at Caden. "This is serious."

"I know. It's too serious." Asher didn't answer. "You're gonna get back on the plane?"

Asher sniffed and held out the small pack he had brought. Caden took it and unzipped the side. Within it was a pocket book, a box of ammo, and a gun. "Shoot to kill." Caden looked up at Asher. "They will too."

Caden's pulse quickened as his chest tightened with dread. "What's the book?"

"It's the Bible."

Caden's shoulders sagged. "The Bible? I need to conserve weight! I can't take *that*!"

Asher held the bag out further. "It's your bag of weapons."

Caden scowled. "A book is not a weapon."

"It's not just a book."

"Whatever."

"Try it. I dare you. The gun will protect your body and the Bible will protect your spirit."

Caden sighed and secured the little bag around his waist. It fit well, added some weight, but he could manage. *Maybe Doeg will leave me alone now,* he thought. Deep down, he suspected just having a Bible close was not enough to stop Demons. He actually would have to crack it open and read the words.

"Thanks," he muttered.

"Asher nodded. "You know He's who you're really looking for."

Caden blinked. "I'm looking for my sister."

"No, you're searching for Yahweh and if He'll come through for you or not." Caden didn't answer as Asher slowly nodded. "You know I'm right." Caden glanced away. "You'll find Him." Caden could hear the smile in Asher's voice. "Just look for Him with all you've got."

Ellie, that's all I'm after, Caden thought. He felt the weight of the Bible as he shifted from foot to foot and slowly lifted his chin. What if he did find Yahweh out here? *The Raw Peace is Yahweh,* Caden reminded himself. If he could feel the Raw Peace again, see its power and fire, this all would be worth it.

Behind them, the roar of the plane kicked on, sending up dust. The two looked at one another and Caden stepped back. *I wish you could come with me,* he thought.

Asher opened his mouth to speak but stopped. Instead, he stepped forward and gave Caden a bear hug. "We will fight side by side again," Asher said. "Come back home when you're done out here, *achi.*"

"I will," Caden said. "What's *achi*?" Asher withdrew and stepped towards the plane. "Hey! What's *achi*!"

"Brother!" Caden blinked with a start as Asher grinned. "You still have a brother! Don't die out here! I can't stab Giants up the butt for you anymore!"

Caden smiled. "Watch out for Russians!"

Asher waved and raced to the plane, shielding his face from the dusty wind. Caden held his shemagh close as he watched Asher board the plane. He wanted to watch him fly away, but had to turn his back as the plane moved, kicking up more dust until Caden could hardly breathe or see. The roar of the engine intensified as the plane picked up speed down the runway. Caden blinked the dirt from his eyes as the plane soared away, the sound fading with it. Caden watched until the plane was a dot in the sky and looked around. He was alone. He sniffed gruffly and kicked at a rock before turning around. He kept walking until the plane's hum faded to nothingness. The wind was his companion, the rocks and the vast sky. Caden stopped and stared at the emptiness and realized it felt just like the void inside him. The nothingness where his internal scream heightened to white noise.

I'm going to die alone, he thought, looking down. There were monsters and Freaks out here. Looting terrorists would dismember him if they caught him. Where was Grant traveling? This sounded like his paradise. Would they cross paths? Demons love chaos too, so Caden prepared himself to see more. Maybe the smoke-one was out here, or even the eyeball-one who watched him as he slept. There was no sign of Doeg, but that Demon knew how to bide its time. And if all these threats happen not to bother Caden, he could die from starvation, get lost, or simply cut his foot and die from an infection. The list went on and on. Including the end of the world.

If Elijah was right, they were living in the End Times. Very creative title. The Rapture had happened and this was the Tribulation? Something like that. There was supposed to be mega death, lots of chaos, an antichrist, who Elijah said was the king. That confused Caden because the king only brought peace and prosperity wherever he went. That is, until you cross him and his Sentinels shoot you to bits. Caden still didn't understand why the Demons ordered Nathaniel to do that. Trace's body flashed through Caden's mind and he squeezed his eyes shut tight.

There was talk of a war with Russia as the great nation descended closer to Israel every day. Elijah could breathe fire like a dragon, which apparently was part of the End Times too. And there was another Jesus freak who could breathe fire and know the future too? It just sounded too crazy to be real. But it was real. It was happening, whether Caden liked it or not. This was the end.

Caden cursed and ran fingers through his hair. He thought of Elijah and Ophir, hugging in the kitchen, Elezaro and Hili laughing as their children chased one another. Of his own room, his own place, just like a normal person had. And Asher. The one who challenged two Giants with only a spear to save Caden's life. Why had Caden left that? He had finally found home and left it far behind.

Beyond the welcome he felt with the Mizrahis, there was one thing he missed most of all. The Raw Peace lived with them. Inside Elijah now too. He wanted to go back and, somehow, take a bit of that Peace with him.

I could do with some Peace right now, he thought, his backpack already feeling heavy. He glanced up, thinking the Raw Peace was Yahweh. Caden sniffed and turned away, a muscle in his jaw flexing.

"Well," he said. "If You really are the Raw Peace and that crazy fire that fell, I um... I need help." Caden cleared his throat and scratched the back of his neck. "So, time to prove Yourself. Help me find my sister, and I'll try to stop hating You. So much. We'll see. Ah, what am I doing? I don't know how to talk to You!" Caden cursed and grabbed the backpack straps.

Maybe Asher's right, he thought. *Maybe I'm really looking for God. He showed Himself to the Israelites out here all those generations ago. He can do that to me too.*

With a deep breath, Caden straightened his back and fixed his eyes ahead. "Prove Yourself," he whispered.

Caden started walking deeper into the Sinai Desert. The wind buffeted him, he narrowed his eyes and pressed on. He had to keep moving, no matter the odds. How else could he find Ellie? More importantly, how else could God prove Himself? He tried to contain the overwhelming fears of the future, of God's coming wrath, and the end of all things.

Raw Peace, Caden thought, *Raw Peace. The Raw Peace is Yahweh. It's always been Yahweh.* Caden's jaw flexed, still unsure how he felt about that. Regardless, he kept reciting the phrase as he walked into the wasteland and its hidden evils.

A LOOK AT BOOK TWO: DEN OF LIONS

The longer Caden Johnson lives in a world full of giants and demons, the more terrified he becomes. He's sick of it—sick of fearing God, too.

But in the Sinai Desert, Caden finally finds what he's looking for. With his little sister and the knowledge of God's undisputed presence in tow, he returns to Jerusalem accompanied by Russians who begin attacking with deadly missiles and bombs. Separated from his family once again and struggling to survive, he finds refuge with the worst guy in the End Times and is given his first mission from God—spy on his mysterious new host.

As Caden goes along with God's outlandish ideas, the more fatal his situation becomes. Walking into a den of lions, Caden must choose which God he really serves. His is own fears…or King Yeshua.

A unique blend of genres, Den of Lions is teen fantasy and apocalyptic Christian fiction at its best.

AVAILABLE DECEMBER 2022

ABOUT TERRY JAMES

Terry James is an author, general editor, and co-author of more than 40 books on Bible prophecy and geopolitics—hundreds of thousands of which have been sold worldwide. He has also written fiction and nonfiction books on a number of other topics. His most recent releases are *The Disappearing: Future Events That Will Rock the World* and *Lawless: End Times War Against the Spirit of Antichrist,* a compilation by top authors, speakers, and broadcasters on issues facing this generation. His most recently released novel, *Michael: Last Days Lightning,* achieved number one in Christian fiction on Amazon.

Terry is a frequent lecturer on the study of end-time phenomena and interviews often with national and international media on topics involving world issues and events as they might relate to Bible prophecy. He is partner with website founder Todd Strandberg and general editor of www.raptureready.com—rated the number one Bible prophecy website with more than 250,000 unique visitors and 3 million hits per month.

Terry speaks often at prophecy conferences and has appeared on national secular programs such as *The Nostradamus Effect*. He is a member of the Pre-Trib Research Center, founded by Dr. Tim LaHaye. Currently, he lives with his wife Margaret near Little Rock, Arkansas.

ABOUT HEATHER RENAE

Heather Renae's ministry is writing sci-fi and fantasy for Jesus. She's inspired by her walk with the Master and her mountainous home in Eastern Oregon. When she's not writing, she's hiking, enjoying friends and family, and chasing after her two kiddos—lovingly nicknamed her scallywags. To see what she's up to, follow her on Facebook at Heather Renae.